Amy McLellan

Remember Me

ORION

An Orion paperback

First published in Great Britain in 2019
by Orion Fiction,
This paperback edition published in 2020
by Orion Fiction,
an imprint of The Orion Publishing Group Ltd.,
Carmelite House, 50 Victoria Embankment
London EC4Y 0DZ

An Hachette UK Company

1 3 5 7 9 10 8 6 4 2

Copyright © Amy McLellan 2019

A CIP catalogue record for this book
is available from the British Library.

ISBN (Paperback) 978 1 4091 8514 7

Typeset by Deltatype Ltd, Birkenhead, Merseyside

Printed in Great Britain by Clays Ltd, Elcograf S.p.A.

www.orionbooks.co.uk

To Adam
For everything. Always.

Chapter One

Everyone looks the same. That's the problem with these TV series set in indeterminate olden times. The beards, the straggly hair and the dirty tunics mean it's hard to tell one earnest plotter from the next. Even the rich ones – easily identifiable because their robes are trimmed with fur and they have more lines – look like they need a good wash.

I share this observation and Joanna sighs dramatically. She hates me talking during her shows but I can't help myself, particularly when it comes to plot holes. When you've actually read the books the series is based on, you become very proprietorial. As someone who's in a book club and describes herself as an avid reader on Match.com, I'm surprised Joanna isn't more understanding.

I pour myself another glass of wine and Joanna gives me the side-eye. I'm not supposed to drink but sometimes I must, just to feel part of the human race again. Besides, *she's* drinking. She can be very insensitive sometimes.

Another mud-smeared soldier walks in and whispers in a lady's ear.

'Who's he?'

'I thought you were reading.'

I raise my eyebrows at her but go back to my book and

re-read a paragraph. It's a froth of a love story and isn't taking. I look back at the screen, waiting for dragons to appear, but it's still soldier types whispering in darkened rooms. I can't help myself.

'Who's that?'

'Jesus, Sarah. Really?'

It's not my fault if I can't keep up with the television. I'm just trying to pay an interest but she gets so irritated, as if I'm butting into real-life conversations. I know she'd prefer it if I went upstairs and left her to watch her shows in peace but that's not really fair on me, is it? I wonder which of them she's got a crush on. The warrior? The earnest one? Maybe it's the woman. It's hard to tell with Joanna. She's my sister but sometimes she's a closed book.

I am just reaching for the last of the Rioja when there's a crunch of feet on gravel and a shadow slides past the window. Joanna shakes her head with irritation. 'What's he doing here?' she mutters. She blows out a heavy sigh as she extracts herself from the sofa. 'I suppose I'll get it, then?'

I shrug. We both know I can't answer the door, particularly not the back door: that means it's someone we know. I'm better with strangers but that's not saying much. I'm not really a people person any more.

She huffs and puffs from the room and I seize my opportunity. Goodbye Westeros, hello Classic FM. Triumphant, I settle back onto the sofa, Debussy washing over me and the last of the Rioja in my glass. I lift my glass in a silent salute to the unexpected visitor. Snooze you lose, sis. But the triumph fades when she doesn't return to chide and tut at me. I wonder what she's up to. I strain to catch a voice. They must be whispering. Is it a date? Has she got a secret lover? I wonder if she's been Internet dating again; she'd sworn off after the humiliation of the philandering pensioner. But she's always so secretive. Is that why she lets me drink wine, so she can have her secret assignations behind my back? It's not like I can tell anyone anyway.

I'm about to drain my glass when there's a sudden crash and Joanna cries out. There's the low rumble of a man's voice and the scrape of chair legs against the floor. Then silence. I pause as I run through all the justifications to do nothing, imagining the embarrassment of walking in on my sister in the throes of passion with her mystery man. It wouldn't be the first time I've read a situation all wrong.

I stand up carefully and kick off my slippers so I can pad quietly across the carpet in my socks. The radio is still playing, and the bright jangle of the adverts provides cover as I inch open the creaking door and step, silent as a sleuth, into the hall. There, in the sudden bright light, with our gaudy coats hanging on pegs and that awful oil painting Joanna bought at the WI on the wall, my fears seem silly. I get a sudden urge to laugh as a memory bubbles to the surface: a television advert from our childhood, a grown man tiptoeing into the kitchen in his striped pyjamas to steal lemonade. Such an absurd image for my brain to hold on to when so much else has been lost.

I'm about to turn back and leave Joanna and her secret lover when she moans again. This time it's followed by a violent crash, and she cries out, not in rapture but in fear.

I shove open the door, my temper up and as ready for a fight as I can be. I lose valuable moments surveying the horror before me. There's broken glass on the floor, wreckage from some kind of violent struggle, and the loser, a woman in a yellow cardigan, is slumped and bound in a kitchen chair. My sister. There is blood oozing from a deep gash on her forehead and her skin is ghostly white, beaded with sweat. She looks at me with wide, terrified eyes and tries to speak but her mouth is gagged with a jay cloth. There's a sudden footstep behind me and strong arms seize me. I scream but at once there's an arm clamped round my neck, pressing against my windpipe. I claw uselessly at the arm as I'm propelled across the kitchen floor towards Joanna. I try to resist but he is so strong. Joanna's eyes are wide with terror and she bucks in her chair, trying to get free. The pressure on my throat tightens and my world compresses to a vital urgent fight for breath. My eyes swim with tears, my feet thrashing as I try to land a kick, while my hands scrabble desperately to try and loosen the relentless pressure on my neck. The panic starts to swell as it dawns on me that this pathetic scrabbling, this useless flailing, could be how I use my last moments on earth. I try to muster all my strength but the life force is leeching away from me. I am going to die. There's a momentary release as he adjusts his position, grabbing my right wrist in a vice-like grip. I suck in a whisper of air just before he increases the pressure on my neck and with his other hand lifts my wrist so that my hand scrapes against Joanna's cheek. My nails scratch her wet skin and her eyes meet mine. She's trying to tell me something but her mouth is clagged with that awful rag and I can barely see now, through the tears and the darkness fogging the edges of my vision. Everything is distant, like I'm looking up at the world from the bottom of a lake. My whole being shrinks to a focal point, to an arm across my airway, to a crushed centimetre of cartilage and tissue, to a single breath. I see my death mirrored in Joanna's horror-stricken, dilated pupils.

Just as the blackness closes in, the pressure on my throat is released and I fall to my knees, air rasping into my greedy lungs as tears stream down my face. I am alive. I put my head down, my forehead on the floor, and suck in lungfuls of air before raising my head fearfully to see who has done this to us. A tall man in a black hoody looms over me, the lower part of his face

4

covered with one of those black fleeces that bikers wear. It's imprinted with a realistic image of a skeleton's jawbone, like an x-ray image of bones and teeth, adding to his menace. My insides feel like liquid; this man, I know, brings death to our house and I am the only one who can stop him. I grab a shard of broken glass, the only weapon to come to hand, and leap up to lunge at his face. But he's quick, turning effortlessly to dodge my attack. I lunge again, my hand slick and warm with blood as the shard digs into my palm, and almost connect, dislodging the skull face mask. He laughs, a twisted hollow sound, as he swiftly grabs my wrist and turns my arm painfully behind my back. Every muscle and sinew screams, and my body buckles to try and release the pressure on my contorted arm. He jerks a knee into my gut, knocking the air from my body and I collapse to the floor.

He stands over Joanna, a knife in his gloved hand. I know that knife: it's the pink one Joanna ordered from the shopping channel to cut meat. I scrabble desperately across the floor to stop him but I'm too late: his hands are so quick and the knife is so sharp. Joanna makes a low surprised gasp as blood, her blood, drips from the knife, pooling darkly on the kitchen floor. He steps back as if to admire his handiwork and I rush forward to help her. There is so much blood. It pulses through my hands, the air thick with its coppery sweetness, as I desperately try to stem the flood and piece her back together. But hands grab me and pull me backwards, away from my dying sister. My legs flail, trying to find purchase on the floor but he's so strong that it takes just seconds to propel me out of the kitchen and into the hall. He pushes me towards the stairs and I stumble, a bloody handprint smearing the paintwork. Joanna will be mad with me, I think, but the thought is fleeting. His boot lands in the small of my back and my legs fold beneath me like a comedy drunk. My head bounces off the bottom stair onto the parquet of the hall. He laughs as my skull lights up with an explosion of pain, then all light and sound is extinguished and I fall into the deepest black.

Chapter Two

A hammer, or is it a drill, maybe a vice, ratcheting up the pain, screw by screw. I can't identify the tool. I can't see anything yet. There is just pain, blinding, deafening pain. It blocks out the world, like white noise. I wish it would stop. I force open a sticky eyelid, and feel my world tilt. Dizzy and nauseous, I close my eye again. The pain is so intense I can even hear it. Definitely a hammer, it's like a pile-driver inside my skull. It even hurts to breathe; my throat burns with every inhalation.

I try to move and the pain flares white inside my head, down my spine. The noise has stopped and I open my eyes again and wait for the world to stop spinning. I am on the floor, my body twisted uncomfortably, one arm numb, my hips screaming in protest. I scrape my fingers against the floor. Wood, not carpet. I am on the hall floor by the bottom of the stairs. Did I fall downstairs? Does Joanna know, or has she already left for work? I roll onto my side, releasing the trapped arm, which flops rubbery and useless. What has happened, why am I on the floor? Why hasn't Joanna come to help me? Adrenalin flushes through me, a surge of icy dread floods my veins: have we had another fight? I moan, crumbling into myself with guilt. I know I'll get the blame again.

I close my eyes and try to breathe through the pain and

nausea but the hammer blows start up again, echoing round my skull. I open my eyes, blinking against the light, but the noise is relentless. It's not just inside my head, it's outside. Outside. I am suddenly frozen with fear, my heart thundering in my chest. Outside. I remember now, I know why I'm on the floor, I know why everything hurts. Outside is thundering at the door. He's back.

I push myself into a sitting position, a thunderous headache pounding behind my eyes, my breath burning in my throat. He's here, pounding at the front door. I desperately crawl towards the kitchen. I have to find Joanna, she was hurt last night. This time it's my turn to protect her.

There's a phone on the kitchen wall, I swipe at the long twisty cord and pull down the handset. I need to call the police but my rubbery arm is hot and uncooperative as blood finds its way back to my hand. Hot tears burn my eyes as I fumble the numbers, and then I see Joanna. She's lying on the floor in a dark puddle, her back to me.

Broken glass cuts my hands and knees as I pick my way across to her, a prayer whispering through my veins. Please, God, please let her be OK, please, God. The puddle is sticky under my knees and she is so very still. I touch her shoulder, then press my fingertips to her face. She is cold. I jab at the telephone again, and hear a dial tone, then a distant voice. I rasp into the handset. 'Police. Hurry, please.'

The noise outside is louder now, the house under siege. I want to lift Joanna's head off this sticky hard floor, where her blonde curls are stiffening in the dried blood, but it's too heavy. My fingers connect with something cold and hard and I instinctively close my fingers around it; I won't let him hurt us again. I press myself into her, willing my life force into her cold still body, and then the front door crashes open.

Footsteps crunch over broken glass. There are voices, men,

a woman too. I hold Joanna close, whimpering with fear. It's selfish when she is already gone but I don't want to die, I have barely lived.

'In here.' It's a man's voice.

I flinch, every sense heightened. Footsteps scuff over the parquet and my fingers tighten on the metal. I won't let him hurt us again.

Someone gasps. 'Oh my god.' A voice I think I know.

'Get him out of here.' I don't recognise this one.

More footsteps, the crackle of a radio.

'Sarah? It is Sarah, isn't it?' The voice is gentle. A woman.

I lift my head from Joanna's hair and squint up at the voice. It's a woman in a police uniform. Oh, thank god.

'Is there anyone else in the house, Sarah?'

I run my tongue over my cracked lips. 'A man attacked us.' It hurts to talk. 'Last night.'

The woman turns and looks behind her. There's another police officer, a man, shoulders like a battering ram. He nods, and leaves the kitchen. I can hear him opening and closing doors, his heavy tread on the stairs, the sound of him pulling back the difficult sliding door on Joanna's wardrobe which you have to jerk and lift off the runners to open fully.

'Clear,' comes a voice.

I can hear sirens in the distance. More voices outside. My head pounds and the room swims, and I vomit on the floor by my feet, the retching sending shockwaves of pain through my body.

'OK, Sarah, we're going to get you some help,' says the woman, lifting her radio to her mouth. She's young, not a line on her face, even with no make-up. She's blond, with her roots showing through, her figure hidden under her bulky uniform, a small tattoo of angel wings just visible on the inside of her wrist. Someone retrieves the phone handset, finishes the call for me: *It's OK, we got this*.

There are footsteps in the room again now. The big policeman is back, surveying the room, before his eyes come to rest on me again. 'Come on, Sarah,' he says, his voice gentle and coaxing, his hands spread, as if approaching a cornered animal. 'Put the knife down.'

The woman takes a step back. She hadn't noticed the pink knife in my hand, still half hidden by Joanna's hair. I pull the knife out from under Joanna's hair and release it, noticing how the wide blade is crusted with black blood. Joanna's blood. I retch again, but nothing comes up.

'That's it, good girl,' says the man, talking to me as if I'm a small child.

The sirens have stopped. There are more footsteps now, more voices. People in uniforms, some of them police, some of them paramedics, stand in the doorway and look down at me and Joanna. Their faces are impassive but I know what they're thinking: they think I killed my sister.

Chapter Three

We never use the dining room, not since James left home. It's become a dumping ground: two suitcases in the corner, Joanna's exercise bike gathering dust and a pile of clothes destined for the charity shop. James used to do his revision in here, books sprawled across the dining table, his laptop glowing blue late into the night. He marked this room as his territory: his compass scored his initials into the table top, cans of Fanta bleaching the wood white. After he left, Joanna and I had stared fondly at the damage, evidence that once this house was a home where we raised a child and how different it was from our own childhoods, when a broken glass or ink-stained skirt prompted slaps, pinches and the silent treatment. I am glad the years didn't turn us into our mother, at least not in that respect. Perhaps it's because we have both lost so much over the years that it's hard to be upset over little things like scratches on a table. And besides, we never used the table: we are kitchen snackers and tray eaters, the radio and television our dining companions. Once James left home, Joanna gave up worthy family dinners, or maybe it was just my company she couldn't stand?

It's cold in here now. We probably haven't had the radiators on since James finished his exams. Already there's a bloom of damp under the windowsill. I remind myself to tell Joanna, and then reality rushes in like a sucker punch to the gut that leaves me gasping for air.

A hand touches my shoulder and I flinch. It's another person in a white suit. They are all over the house, grounded astronauts, padding around, murmuring in corners.

'You OK?' says the white suit. It's a woman with short-cropped black hair and elfin face. She looks about twelve. A child playing dress-up: today, Mummy, I shall be a forensic crime scene examiner.

I nod. It's instinctive. *Don't make a fuss, Sarah, no one wants to know your dramas.* Mother's voice. But of course, I'm not OK. Nothing will ever be OK again. There's an ambulance parked outside, ready to take Joanna away. No blue lights. They don't need to rush to where she's going. There are so many people outside. A lot of police, most of them just standing around. A large white tent has been erected by the front door. It looks like the preparations for a macabre garden party, with police tape for bunting.

I look away and hug myself. It's so cold in here. I just want to go and lie in my bed with the duvet over my head and never wake up again. An image keeps replaying in mind, my sister's blood, slick and hot, pulsing through my useless hands, and I think I may never sleep again.

'Sarah. Is it Sarah?'

I realise the twelve-year-old is talking to me. I nod again but I can't recall the question. She glances away, over my shoulder and she mouths something. Now, there's someone else with me, another woman, with blond hair this time. Have I seen her before? I'm usually good at noticing little details but I can't seem to focus. I can hear people tramping in and out, occasionally saying things I don't understand or opening big black carry cases with a snap that makes me jump every time.

She starts talking to me but I can't seem to concentrate on her words: the image of Joanna's body, her blood on my hands, replays again and again.

'Your full name?'

'What? Oh, Sarah Wallis.'

The woman nods at me. 'And you live here with your sister, Joanna Bailey?'

I nod.

'Does anyone else live here?'

'James.' Then I shake my head. 'But he left last year.'

'Who's James?'

'My nephew. Joanna's son.' My voice breaks, a hard ball blocks my throat. What will I tell James? He's only twenty and this is the second parent to be killed. Hot tears burn my eyes. What can I say?

'And it was just you and your sister in the house last night?' asks the policewoman again.

I nod. 'But then the man came to the back door.'

'What time was that?'

I try to think. Joanna was watching her show. And I was being a bloody cow about it. I always made life so difficult for her. I couldn't even answer the door so she could watch her show in peace. It should have been me, my blood. And it swims before my eyes again, Joanna's blood spilling through my fingers, my fumbling hands unable to hold her together or make it stop.

The policewoman is talking again. I raise my eyes to her face and try to concentrate.

'Is that OK with you, Sarah? We're going to get you checked out.'

I realise they want to take me somewhere. 'What?' I croak, my mouth dry, my throat closing as the familiar panic starts to swell.

'We need you to see a doctor, to make sure you're all right.'

A doctor. I know doctors, I can do doctors. I have spent so much time in hospitals they are almost a safe place for me. Almost. My body shivers violently with cold and what I suppose is shock. They let me get a coat and my handbag and then I'm shepherded out through the battered front door, blinking in the white light. The cold air tastes of wet grass and diesel fumes. Cars have churned up the gravel and there are deep tyre treads across our scrap of front lawn.

I shiver in the cold spring air. The ambulance has gone; where have they taken Joanna? But before I can ask, I am guided into the back of a police car which quickly pulls out onto the street. The trees are in bud and there's a confetti of pink blossom on the grass in front of the church. The rush of colour takes me by surprise: it's the first time I've left the house in six weeks.

Chapter Four

When I dream, I am whole again. I am the person I think I used to be, the person I want to be again. I dance in my dreams. Music plays, and I kick off my high heels and feel the beat pulse through my body. People turn to watch and I smile to myself: I am good at this, being the centre of attention, all eyes on me. I only feel this way in my dreams now.

But then, like a chord change from major to minor, the mood darkens. Elbows jostle me, a drink splashes on my dress, and someone treads on my bare foot. Bodies press in on me, a swell of heat and muscle taking up all the air in the room. I feel small and delicate, in my bare feet and my flimsy dress. I am not safe here. Someone pushes me, and I stumble. I look up and see a blank face, a white featureless mask from which eyes as black and calculating as a shark's glitter menacingly at me. I shiver with fear and the mask laughs in my face.

I wake with a gasp. A face looms over me. Dark skin. A long nose. Square-framed glasses, Armani. Long, black hair falling over a white coat. The face smiles.

'Good,' says the face. 'I know you want to sleep but we just need to observe you for a bit longer. That was a nasty bang.'

A torch flashes in my eyes. Fingers press to my wrist. Am I

still feeling sick? No. Can I read a printed card? I can, though my voice rasps painfully through my bruised throat.

The doctor gives me a warm smile. 'That all looks positive. Feeling a bit better?'

I nod. It's instinctive. *Don't make a fuss, Sarah.* I am clean and my wounds dressed, but I am not better. They have taken phials of blood, scraped swabs from under my fingernails and the inside of my cheek, and photographed the bruises on my abdomen and round my throat. My hands are swaddled in thick bandages like a boxer and a cut on my forehead has been taped together. Everything hurts but somehow I am alive. Why didn't he just stab me, like Joanna? Why her, not me?

I drift in this quiet room, listening to the hum and beep of the building, the squeak of rubber shoes on the floor. The police are outside waiting to talk to me but the doctor insists I have to rest. They don't let me rest though, a procession of people come to check on me, updating their statistics, monitoring me. There are hushed conversations in corners, paperwork is checked and cups of tepid tea dispatched.

Every time I ask about Joanna or James, I'm told not to worry, just get some rest, the police will see you soon. I sink back in my pillows and keep my eyes shut, hoping the next time I open them I'll be back at home, staring out of my bedroom window at the squirrels doing their gymnastics in the rowan tree and listening to Joanna bustling in the kitchen. But when I open my eyes, a stranger leans in and tells me I can go. Immediately, there are more strangers. One of them is a woman in a police uniform. She gives me a white T-shirt and grey tracksuit, which is too big so I have to double over the waistband. I try to focus on her voice – had she been at the house earlier? – but I can't tell. She's stocky, a little taller than me, her blond hair scraped back in a ponytail and she has a large mole on her right cheek.

Unfortunate, I think to myself, but I hear my mother's nasty voice in that thought and chide myself.

Outside the leaden skies are darkening and clouds bloom like bruises on the horizon. It feels like rain is brewing. We get into the car and I lean my face against the window, blankly watching the world go by. My stomach hurts and I casually wonder if I could have internal bleeding. I don't much care.

The police station looks like a regular office block. I have passed it lots of times and never even noticed.

'Sarah, are you all right?'

The voice cuts across the car park. A big man, bearing down on me, his belly straining against his shirt. A familiar voice but out of context and my brain fumbles for the name.

'Excuse me, sir.' The male police officer shoulders past the man and I'm propelled up the steps into the station.

'Sarah! It's me. Alan. Get a lawyer, love. Make sure you get a lawyer.'

I look back. Alan, of course. Our neighbour. Was he at the house this morning with the police? Why does he think I need a lawyer, does he think I did it? The station door swings shut behind us and panic catches in my throat, snatching away my air as heat flushes through my body. There are too many people for this small reception area, they are sucking up all the air.

Two women, one with a black eye, sit in plastic chairs bolted to the floor, swiping furiously at their phones with gaudy nails. Next to them, an old man snores and I catch the smell of urine wafting from his stained trousers.

The police officer punches a number into a keypad to open a locked door.

The woman with the black eye looks up from her phone. 'Why she getting seen to? We've been here for hours.'

I shrink back from the attention, struggling to get air past the hard lump in my throat. Can't they see I'm sick? My hands instinctively reach for my throat but the woman just eyeballs me, hard as nails. Suddenly, I'm pulled away and guided into a little side room. I sink into a chair and put my head between my knees, cover my ears with my hands and focus on breathing deeply, waiting for the panic to subside. Nobody says anything. Perhaps this is normal here. After a while, someone brings me a mug of milky tea and a cheese sandwich.

I am alone at last. I need this, these moments with my thoughts in this bare room. I hadn't realised quite how much I've come to live inside my own head. I have become unused to people and today there have been so many people. My head is ringing with the noise of them and the effort of making sense of it all: the little looks, the glances, the pursed lips, the quizzical frowns, the different accents and little speech impediments only someone like me would need to notice. But it all takes so much effort. I am so tired I am numb. I can't even cry.

I stare at the wall, it's a sickly green, scuffed and pocked with pinholes. The colour reminds me of the peppermint creams my mother used to dole out on long car journeys. There's a small table, two chairs, no window.

The wall swims in front of my eyes. I lean forward and rest my pounding head on the table. It smells faintly of bleach. I don't know what time it is but I guess it must be dark outside now. People will be heading home, making dinner, watching TV, blissfully unaware of the horror that at any moment could burst in through their door. Once that had been me. I thought our house was safe. It was my refuge from the world but still the horror had reached in and found me.

I close my eyes but at once the night swims before me. Bursting into the kitchen. Our pink meat knife, from the shopping channel. The man. All in black. The way he moved. Poised. That was the word that came to mind. And then the blood. Hot and sticky, and the smell, that tang of iron, the surprising sweetness of it. For a moment I want to gag, the taste of the milky tea rising biliously in my throat. My head reels as the horror spools before me, looping again and again. The man. The red knife. The blood. The skull mask. But why?

The door opens behind me and I start. I must have drifted off. I wipe my mouth clumsily with my bandaged hand as two women sit down opposite me. One is the policewoman with the mole, who introduces herself as PC Casey Crown, a superhero name, and the other is smaller, with dark skin, cropped black hair with a long fringe and bright watchful eyes. She's wearing high heels and a trouser suit and although she's tiny, it's clear she's the boss. I nod a wary greeting and it hurts my brain. I can't take more people, more talk.

'Good to see you again, Sarah. I'm DS Samira Noor, I'm the deputy senior investigating officer.'

I recognise her voice. It's the twelve-year-old from the house, all dressed up in grown-up office clothes now. There's something about the way she introduces herself, a hint of pride, that makes me think this is a new role for her. She's young but she's on the up, and she wants me to know it and respect her. I would do the same if people kept mistaking me for a child.

'Sarah, we're going to get someone to come and sit with you while we talk to you. Is there anyone you'd like us to call?' She speaks slowly, like I'm a little kid.

'James.' Oh god, James still doesn't know. He needs to be told about his mum. He's doing an ultra-race in Snowdonia this weekend; what a homecoming this will be. Will I have to tell him? How do you break that kind of news? My eyes prick with hot tears.

Noor shakes her head. 'We're still trying to reach him. The number you gave us is wrong. Did he change his number recently?'

I'm not sure. I don't really have much contact with James, not since he moved out. 'Joanna would know,' I say, pointlessly.

Noor smiles patiently. Clearly, Joanna isn't going to be telling us. 'Is there anyone else you'd like us to call?'

I shake my head. No, there isn't anyone. Not now. There's Dr Lucas, but you can't call your psychiatrist to come and sit with you in a police station, can you? Joanna was my person.

'OK then, Sarah. This is what we'll do. We're going to interview you under caution. We'll find an appropriate adult to come in and sit with you and the duty solicitor here too.' She must have seen the look on my face because she deftly continues, trying to reassure me, still talking like I'm a child on the verge of a meltdown. 'We understand you're a vulnerable adult and we need to make sure you understand what's happening.'

Alan. Of course. He'll have told them everything. Alan has no filter. All my secrets, everything I try to hide from the world, will have been laid out. And now they think I'm a freak. A vulnerable adult. They have no idea.

Chapter Five

In other circumstances I would laugh. My appropriate adult, a baby-faced law student doing pro bono work for CV points, arrives in denim dungarees, sporting large feathered earrings and a stud in her nose. She's wearing thick square-rimmed glasses that would make me look ancient but somehow only magnify her youth.

'Sorry,' she says, introducing herself as Cassie and sliding into the seat next to me, smelling of coconut and smoke. 'I was at a barbeque in Much Wenlock when I got the call. I didn't have time to change.' She smiles apologetically, flashing braces at me.

Nice enough girl I'm sure but I feel like I'm the appropriate adult in the room, not her.

The duty solicitor isn't much better. He's younger than me though the dark circles under his eyes and the five o'clock shadow grazing his chin age him. He stifles a yawn and his hands tremble as he shuffles his paperwork. He barely looks at me as he reads the file, firing the odd question, scribbling notes with a chewed biro. You would think a solicitor could afford a better pen.

In comparison to these two, the child-sized DS Noor is a model of professionalism in her dark trouser suit and neatly manicured nails. I know her day has been as long as mine but she looks fresh and sharp, and she wastes little time getting proceedings underway. She reads me a caution but stresses I'm not under arrest, they just need to ask questions to ascertain the facts. She checks I understand. I nod. I am not under arrest – yet.

But nodding won't work – I am being taped. I clear my throat and confirm I understand but I give DS Noor a cold stare: I know her game. She speaks softly, she reassures, but she's out to trap me. She gives me a fleeting, knowing smile, like she can read my mind. Good luck with that, I think: if she can read minds, I'd love to know what mine has to say for itself.

'Do you understand what DS Noor is saying?' repeats my appropriate adult.

'Yes,' I say. I lean towards the tape recorder and enunciate my words clearly. 'I understand.'

And so, it begins. DS Noor picks over the night like a crow stripping carrion, every phrase excavated, turned over and examined until the bones of the night lay bare and white.

'You told Sergeant Bower that your sister recognised the visitor?' says Noor, consulting her notes.

'Yes. She saw him walk past the window and said "What's he doing here?".'

'But you didn't recognise him?'

I took a deep breath. How much to share? How much can I bear to tell in this stark room, to these people?

'Sarah,' prompts DS Noor. 'Did you know him?'

'I don't know.'

'You don't know?'

'It's complicated.'

'I understand there are issues, but I am going to need you to explain.' DS Noor is quiet but firm.

'Sarah,' prompts my babysitter. 'Do you need a break?'

DS Noor flashes her a look, clearly irritated at the interruption. I don't need a break. I need to get this over with. 'I didn't recognise the man but it doesn't mean I didn't know him.' It's a chilling thought, that someone we know hated us enough to attack us so violently, so coldly. 'I was in a car accident twenty years ago. My brother-in-law was killed and I was in a coma for almost a year. It left me with a neurological condition. Prosopagnosia.'

Blank looks. 'It's sometimes called face blindness but that's not really accurate.'

I have their interest now, even the weary solicitor is paying attention.

'I can see faces, I just can't recognise them. It's like there's something missing in my brain, a sort of rolodex you all have that allows you to remember faces and match them to names.'

'So your mum could walk in now and you wouldn't know her?' asks my babysitter.

'With people close to me' – so that would rule out Mother – 'I work out a system, the other things I can recognise about them, like their hair or voice. When I used to go out with Joanna, she'd wear a really bright cardigan, hideous really, but it helped me to pick her out in a crowd if we got separated.'

My voice breaks, remembering Joanna in that bloody Per Una waterfall cardie, mustard yellow with frills and pom poms. Who puts pom poms on a cardigan! She hated it but it did stand out and helped me navigate many a trip into town until my other issues put a stop to all that. God, Joanna, how am I going to live without you?

'Wow,' breathes Cassie. 'I never heard of that before.'

I shrug. There are many things that can go wrong with the brain. Compared to some of the cases in Hillwood House, the rehabilitation centre I was sent to, I was one of the lucky ones.

'You can't remember faces but you can other features,' muses DS Noor. 'Did the man have any features you recognise?'

I shake my head. 'He was all in black. I never even saw his hair. He was tall, athletic. Strong.'

'Age?'

I hesitate. I saw so little of his face. He was mainly behind me, had that been on purpose? Even when I saw his face, my eyes had been blurred with tears. 'Not old-old,' I say firmly. 'Not ancient. He was strong. Fast.'

'Perhaps his voice?'

I shake my head. 'Just a laugh when he kicked me.'

'Anything else? Anything you can think of, Sarah.'

I am desperate to remember something that will make sense of all of this. I feel sick with panic, but I replay the scene again, putting myself back into that kitchen. So much blood, the sticky heat of it pulsing through my useless hands. The pink knife.

'I think he'd been in our kitchen before. He used our meat knife. He must have known ...' My voice trails off. I can't bear to think someone we know well enough to have spent time in our kitchen, to know our utensils, would do something like this.

But DS Noor doesn't look impressed. 'It could just have been opportunist. All kitchens have sharp knives.'

I grudgingly accept she's right. It just seemed so personal somehow. Joanna loved her colourful knives. We also had a green paring knife, for vegetables. Joanna liked little touches like that. I choke back another sob. I can't believe she's gone.

'Anything else, Sarah? Come on, even the smallest—'

Cassie cuts in. 'Do you need a break, Sarah? You look tired.'

DS Noor swallows her irritation and checks with me. 'Sarah?'

'I'm fine,' I lie. I feel sick and clammy, and the bruising round my throat means every breath hurts. I want to climb into bed but how can I ever go home after this?

24

'Do many people know about your condition?' The police-woman checks her notes. 'The pro-so-pag-nosia?'

I'm impressed: few people ever bother to remember the proper name and even fewer get close to pronouncing it correctly.

'I don't know. James, obviously. Some of the neighbours, like Alan. Our GP. Joanna's friends. I mean, I don't know who else she might have told.'

'What about you, who have you told?'

'It's not the kind of thing you talk about.' They don't need to know I don't talk much to anyone any more.

'Really?' says Cassie. 'But don't you tell people when you first meet them that you've got it? Wouldn't that help, if people knew, so they can introduce themselves?'

I feel a flush of irritation. My babysitter didn't even know the condition existed until a moment ago and she's trying to tell me, someone who lives with this day in, day out, how to manage my life. I notice *she* hasn't bothered to try and pronounce prosopagnosia.

'I may have prosopagnosia but I'm not a fucking idiot. You try buying a paper and casually dropping it into the conversation. Besides, people can take advantage. It makes you vulnerable.'

It comes out sharper than I intended and I see the solicitor glance up quizzically. I catch myself. They don't need to see that side of me. I take a deep breath and look at Cassie, who's flushed red at the rebuke. 'Maybe I do need that break.'

DS Noor nods briskly, ends the recording and leaves us alone. I'm allowed to use the toilet, and sit in the cubicle forlornly, resting my elbows on my knees, my head in my hands. I am so tired I could fall asleep right here, but every time I shut my eyes the horror fills them. Who would do this? Someone that Joanna knows. Someone who knew about my condition. But we don't know that many men and the ones we do, well, I am pretty sure they just don't have it in them. There's Alan next door and yes, he's an oddball, but he's a gentle giant. There are Joanna's work colleagues; I know there's someone called Alex on the senior management team she said was an 'utter knob', could it be him? There are a couple of ex-boyfriends but she's been single for ages now. Or has she? I remember, with sudden clarity, that funny little smile on her face the other week, singing in the kitchen in a new dress and she'd been to that fancy lingerie shop on the High Street. I'd seen the packaging and the receipt: one hundred and twenty-three pounds on a bra and two pairs of knickers instead of the usual three-for-a-tenner deal at M&S. And she's been distracted lately, letting me drift through my days, not nagging and getting at me all the time. It had been a relief, really, so I'd never questioned why. Why was she so distant? Was there someone new on the scene, and if so, why would she keep it a secret from me?

There's a discreet cough outside. I get to my feet, flush the loo and find Cassie lingering by the sinks. I know it's her because who else would be wearing dungarees and feathered earrings in a police station. Wacky dressers are my friend.

She smiles at me tentatively. 'How you holding up, Sarah?'

I study my face in the mirror over the hand basins. I look pale, the unforgiving strip lighting picks out every strand of grey in my blond locks and there's a smear of dried blood near my hairline. I glance at Cassie's reflection in the mirror next to me, the dewy freshness of her skin, her shiny hair, the luminescence of youth that even braces and square glasses can't dull.

'I'm OK,' I say blankly.

'It's me, Cassie,' she offers.

'I know.' Our eyes catch in the mirror and I nod at the earrings. 'Feathers, not many people wear those in a police station.'

She grins, a flash of white enamel and braces. 'I know, right? I can't believe I get my first AA call and I'm dressed like this.

Not quite the first impression I was hoping for.'

'Don't worry. First impressions don't really count with me.' That's not true, of course. I have a memory but this is what counts for humour in the prosopagnosia world.

'I think we should, you know, go back in.'

I nod, brace myself. Everything feels so unreal. Is my brain up to its old tricks, is this just some dark delusion and Joanna will walk in soon, bossing me downstairs to go and see Dr Lucas to get my meds tweaked until the horror melts away? I follow Cassie out into the corridor to find a dynamo in a trouser suit cruising towards me.

'Ah good, Sarah. You OK to carry on.' It's a statement not a question so I don't bother to answer. For someone so small, DS Noor is something of a steamroller. We're back in the peppermint cream room, the crumpled solicitor has another cup of coffee and DS Noor is checking her paperwork, keeping us all waiting. I know this isn't an accident. Already I can tell she is the sort of person who never goes into a meeting without knowing exactly what she wants to say. The silence grows oppressive. Cassie shuffles nervously in her seat, bangles jangling. Panic stirs again, that tightening across the chest. I close my eyes and focus on breathing, talking myself down. See, that constriction in your airway is in your mind, you can breathe. Let it all go, just breathe.

'Sarah.'

Noor's voice makes me jump. I open my eyes, focus on her face, searching for clues as to what she's thinking. I know I'm not going to like it. I swallow and press my palms together, the pain in my cut hand forcing my brain to stop its silly introversion and pay attention.

'Sarah,' repeats Noor. 'I want to ask you about the last time you had a fight with your sister.'

Ah, that.

27

Chapter Six

Eighteen years ago

I open my eyes and already I can hear distant crying. The room is light. I must have forgotten to close the curtains last night. I wonder how long I've been asleep. An aeroplane steams a diagonal path across the pane and I watch the plane's vapour trail slowly disintegrate. Soon another plane will cross the window to mark out a cloudy white cross in the sky. Sometimes I play a little game and make myself lie completely still until every patch of vapour has gone from my square of sky. It's surprising how long it takes, our skies are criss-crossed like giant hopscotch grids, people endlessly coming and going. Not me, though.

The crying rises in crescendo. I am sick of everyone being sad all the time. This constant sadness and tears is not me. I was never like this before. Ah, before. Before the accident. My life has been dissected into two parts, before, and after. Before is the better part. If you want to watch the film of my life, catch the prequel. The sequel is a bummer.

I can hear whispering too. There are so many secrets now. I know Joanna wants to protect me but I don't know from what. What could be worse than this? I am a stranger to myself, and everyone is a stranger to me.

I struggle upright and wait for the vertigo to pass. No wonder I dream of dancing: it now takes concentration to walk ten simple steps across the room. I am old before my time and it makes me furious. I have been robbed of my youth. I feel such a rage all the time. Dr Lucas says it will pass. She says I need to focus on coping strategies and that as I recover and find my way back into life the rage will pass. I know she's right. I know I need to work at this but everything is so hard now. Some days I just lie in bed all day, watching the vapour trails. On cloudy days, I don't even do that.

I stand on the landing, listening. I start when I see a stranger looking at me and then remind myself it's my reflection in the mirror. I am still pretty, you can hardly see the scar now my hair's grown back. But I need a cut and colour and some shimmer on my cheekbones, a flick of eyeliner, anything to add life to the pale blankness of the face staring back at me. Growing up, everyone always said Joanna was the brains and I was the beauty. I suppose that wasn't very nice to either of us but secretly I always thought it was better to be the beauty even though you're never meant to admit things like that. I wonder what Joanna thought about it. I suppose if you're clever, you think that's better and don't mind so much. And after all, some people don't have brains or beauty.

I step past the mirror and make it to the top of the stairs. Slowly I crouch down so I can just see through the top of the bannister. A woman is taking off her coat, putting away her shoes. There's a small child standing there, still in his coat and wellies, crying.

'Come on, sweetheart.' It's Joanna's voice, though she never used to say things like 'sweetheart'. It's a trick she's developed, to soften the constant irritation that creeps into her voice when she speaks to me. And now this boy. 'Let's get those wellies off, sweetie.'

He cries all through this operation. Joanna crouches at his socked feet, helping with the poppers on his coat. He stops crying as she whispers secrets to him. 'Remember, you're Mummy's brave boy. You're a little soldier and this will make everything better, just you see. Trust me.'

He's nodding now, and sniffing he examines something small in his hand. It has all his attention and soothes his distress. That's how I am with my vapour trails.

I shift my weight and the creaky floorboard gives me away. Joanna, shrugging on her big yellow cardigan, turns and paints a bright smile on her face.

'Hello there, sleepy head.'

I stare down at her. The child looks up at me. My mind is a blank. I should know him because clearly Joanna knows him, and he knows me: I can tell from the wary look on his face.

I have to get to the bottom of this. I start the journey downstairs. It's tricky: hand on the bannister, right leg, left leg, adjust hand, repeat. I pause and look at the child again. He's putting his wellies on the shoe rack. He lives here, I realise with a shock. I should know this, shouldn't I?

'Sarah? Everything all right? We're just going to make some tea and toast.'

Joanna's prattling brightly but I can tell she's bracing herself. The boy, too.

'Who is this? What's going on here?' I can hear the panic in my voice. I am so scared at the sudden blankness. Why can't I remember?

Joanna steps forward and holds out her hand to help me down the last two steps. 'This is James, Sarah. My son. He lives with us. He's just a bit upset about something that happened at nursery but nothing some tea and toast can't cure, eh, buddy?' She smiles brightly at James and ruffles his hair. There are tears streaking his face and a bubble of snot forms at his nose. I have never seen this kid before, I am sure, but Joanna wouldn't lie to me. Every time I think I'm getting better I find I'm back at square one.

'Have we had this conversation before?'

Joanna glances at James but he's fixated on his toy, a little wooden fire engine. Joanna weighs her words. 'Sometimes there's confusion,' she soothes. 'But come with me, I think I've got the solution.'

She bustles me into the kitchen as if I'm a little kid too. I'm shaking my head. I don't want tea and toast. I am exhausted. I just want to go back to bed, to watch the planes and drift off to sleep.

But she settles me at the kitchen table and busies herself with the kettle and teabags. I stare at the child, James, as he plays with a plastic kitchen set. Just like mama, I think bitterly. How did I forget Joanna had a child? Perhaps I am getting worse, not better. I must ask Dr Lucas.

Joanna comes over with mugs of milky tea and, ta da, some crumpets dripping in butter.

'I forgot we had these,' she says happily.

I think about making an amnesia-related joke but it's too much effort. Joanna never had much of a sense of humour anyway and the kid's too young. Tough audience. He sits in his high chair with a tumbler of milk and a crumpet, which he sucks and chews, butter running down his chin, bits spewing all over the table. He still has snot encrusted round his nose. I have to look away.

Joanna rummages in a drawer and sits down next to me with something wrapped in a John Lewis bag. She looks at me expectantly, and I can tell she's hoping to build me up to something like excitement. Clearly the crumpets weren't a happy oversight but part of the warm-up act. I may be neurologically impaired but I'm not totally oblivious. I know my sister too well.

She pulls a big book out of the plastic bag. It's a high-end scrapbook, with a pretty fabric cover and thick, embossed pages. 'This,' says Joanna triumphantly, 'is your book of very important people. Look, Sarah.' And she turns the pages, showing me what she's already written down: my name, date of birth. A photograph of her, of the boy James, with their names and their relationship to me written in capital letters and then details to look out for: height, weight, age, accent. On the next page there's a picture of a bald man with a round face and spectacles. Dr Shah, our GP, apparently. According to Joanna's loopy handwriting, this Dr Shah is about five foot six, plump and has a strong accent. He favours a jaunty bowtie although Joanna has added in brackets *not guaranteed*.

'What about Doctor Lucas?' I ask flatly.

'Well, we don't live near Hillwood House any more, Sarah.' Joanna is speaking very slowly, her words chosen carefully. I think of eggshells for some reason. 'Do you remember, Sarah? We talked about this. I had to move for my job. So you won't see Doctor Lucas any more.'

I feel panic wash over me, a great hot wave that floods my system. I push back from the table and tears blur my eyes. This is too cruel. I was making so much progress with Dr Lucas.

'Sarah ...' warns Joanna, nodding at the child. He's watching me with fearful eyes, his bottom lip quivering.

I glance down at the scrapbook, my eye caught by a photograph of a woman in a green dress, sitting in a garden chair and squinting into the sun. She has short hair, flecked with grey. She isn't smiling. This, I read, is Mum. *5'4", size 12, short hair, wears a crucifix*.

Something like grief hits me. I feel so lost. How can I not remember my own mother's face? I pick up the album — it's what Dr Lucas would call a coping strategy but now I'll never get to tell her about it — and hurl it across the kitchen. It knocks a cup off the worktop and coffee dregs leak down the cabinet front.

'Sarah!'

The child starts to cry. My rage is building. I can't believe this is my life.

'I don't care about your fucking job, Joanna. I need to see Doctor Lucas, I need to get my life back.'

'My job is what pays for all this, Sarah.'

I laugh wildly, almost hysterical now. I can feel it. I swipe the plate of crumpets from the table.

'Fuck your job!' I scream, competing with the wails of the child. 'I'll find Doctor Lucas and then I'll get my own job.'

'Jesus, Sarah,' hisses Joanna, hurrying to the distressed boy.

The crying is like a physical assault, drilling into my brain, and I cover my ears with my hands as I lurch from the room. As the anger recedes, I am hit by an overwhelming tiredness. The stairs loom like a mountain, and I'm weeping with the effort by the time I get to the top. I crawl into bed and pull the duvet over my head, waiting for the pounding, pulsing headache to recede, and pray that the next time I fall asleep I don't wake up.

Chapter Seven

I have lost all track of time. The questions stopped because Cassie – and I have to give her credit here – insisted I have medical attention. The pain radiating from my throat had started to pulse through my body with every breath until I broke out in a clammy sweat. If DS Noor was annoyed, she hid it well.

Cassie came with me in the car to the medical centre, thumbs swiping over her phone at astonishing speed. She's lucked out really, her first appropriate adult gig and she's babysitting a crazy woman who, it's becoming clear, is in the frame for very messily murdering her sister. I am probably already reduced to a hashtag in her timeline.

I must have slept in the car on the way back from the medical centre, one of those instant shutdowns, black and dreamless. I wake with a start, confused to find myself in the back of a strange car, my hand bandaged, the driver dressed in a police uniform. For a moment I float, untethered to this world, and in that moment, I have a sister. Then, cruelly, I crash back down to earth, the police uniform and the bandages suddenly make sense, and my sister is gone for ever.

'You all right, Sarah?' The driver has turned around to check on me. She's blond, with tired eyes and a prominent mole on her right cheek. It's superhero cop Casey Crown. I struggle upright in my seat and run a bandaged hand through my greasy hair, a movement that, thanks to the pain pills the doctor gave me, I can now perform without breaking into a cold sweat.

I look around and try to get my bearings. We're in the car park outside the police station and the dawn sky beyond the roof tops is stained with pink. *Red sky in the morning, shepherd's warning.* I hope it isn't an omen of what the day will bring, although really, what could be worse than what's already happened?

'Sarah?' Cassie touches my arm gently. 'You OK?'

'OK,' I confirm, my voice scratchy.

PC Crown nods. She is a woman of few words, which has come to be a trait I admire. I am pretty sure I used to be a gabbler, a gossiper, a last-word-haver but I don't have much to crow about these days. Joanna is the queen bee now, while I have sunk in on myself, like a deflated soufflé. Besides, I find too many words chafe my damaged brain. I flinch from talkers, their babble grates like salt rubbing at a wound, forcing me to retreat to the quiet of my bed where all I can hear is the rhythmic thump of my heart and the distant hum of lorries on the bypass. According to my new GP Dr Monks, this physical reaction to noise is just another symptom of my social anxiety disorder. It's called misophonia, and he prescribed more antidepressants and put me on a waiting list for CBT, again – I promised to go this time.

Joanna was less tolerant. According to her, my misophonia is selective. 'It's not all about you,' she'd hissed after that incident at the school fete when I'd had to flee in tears midway through the deputy head's meandering monologue about a kitchen refit. Joanna soothed it over with a box of chocolates. She always knew how to handle my episodes. How will I function without her? I may never leave the house again. I look out at the police station and think perhaps prison would suit me. But it would have to be solitary confinement. Being locked in a cell with a talker would finish me off.

PC Crown gets out of the car and opens the door for me. I ease myself out, grunting like an old woman, clutching paracetamol for the pain and diazepam for shock. I nod my thanks and she nods back. Yes, she's my kind of person.

Unlike PC Crown, my babysitter is a talker. We are back in the peppermint cream room, and I'm presented with a milky tea and a Mars Bar. Breakfast. I don't have any appetite but I sip the tea. They've told me I'm free to go at any time but I wouldn't know where to go or what to do. I wonder where they've taken Joanna. I can't bear to think of her on her own. Is James with her? Does he know?

The door opens and a small neat woman in a navy trouser suit enters. Dark hair, big black eyes, the proportions of a tall child. I deduce it's DS Noor. She looks around, nods to me and Cassie and exits again. I raise a quizzical eye at Cassie.

'I think we're waiting for the duty solicitor,' she explains.

I absorb the news. They must think I'm guilty if they want me to have the crumpled solicitor present. We sit and wait. I run my finger over the pitted edges of the table and think about all the people who have sat here before me. Misery seems to hang in the air like a poisonous gas, seeping into my skin. I close my eyes, focus on breathing, trying to calm myself. I can't afford to panic. I must be very careful what I say. They already suspect the worst of me.

The door opens again and two people enter, the small figure that must be DS Noor and a man in a dark suit and blue tie, clean shaven and emitting a strong chemical smell of shower gel and aftershave.

'Right,' says DS Noor, beginning her legal preamble. She names everyone present and I learn the man's name is Carl

Snell, and he's today's duty solicitor. He looks up and nods a brief greeting at the mention of his name.

'At least you've showed up awake unlike the fellow who was here last night,' I joke.

I feel Cassie wince next to me and the air seems to rush out of the room.

'That was me at the end of a sixteen-hour day,' says Carl Snell quietly.

I flush, and stammer my apologies. I am so annoyed at myself, what a rookie mistake.

'Don't worry about it,' he says, and looks back down at his notes.

I'm aware of DS Noor gazing at me like I'm a specimen in a lab. 'Let's crack on, shall we,' she says. 'Now that everyone's here.'

Snell frowns down at the desk. Noor's barb is clearly directed at him.

'OK, Sarah, just before you were taken to the medical centre we were about to discuss what happened in December, when my colleagues were called out to your house to investigate an incident of domestic violence.'

'It was a misunderstanding. Really.'

'Your sister told officers you'd attacked her.'

'Yes, but she later admitted she over-reacted,' I protest. 'She was just mad with me and wanted to teach me a lesson. Give me a little scare.'

'Why did she feel the need to do that?'

I sigh. I know how awful this looks. 'I suppose I can be, um, difficult to live with. Since the accident, I sometimes suffer with mood swings, I get depressed and anxious. I'm much better now but it's still not easy being like this. I'm not myself, and I never will be again.' Hot tears of self-pity prick my eyes. 'It's

37

hard to accept how much my life has changed and I suppose we take it out on those we love.'

'You loved your sister?'

'Yes, of course. She's my – she was my sister. And my rock.' The tears are falling again now. 'She looks – looked after me.'

'But you hit her. In statements taken at the time, it says you hit Joanna and threw a cup of hot tea over her.'

'It was an accident. I was angry and I went to throw the cup against the wall but she got in the way.'

'And the hit?'

'I don't remember that.' It's the almost-truth. Sometimes the anger is like a pulsing white beam of energy that I can't resist. I don't remember deliberately hitting her but at some point my hands had connected with her head. I remember being shocked, and instantly backing down, full of remorse. God, she made me pay for that. I would have preferred it if she had hit me, I could have coped with that better than her martyrdom. But I can't explain all these nuances, these swings of the pendulum, without making it sound like a confession. 'I admit I get angry but I don't remember hitting her.'

'Were you drinking?'

'I may have had a few. I'm not really supposed to drink. Joanna knows that.'

'What happens when you drink, Sarah?'

I don't know what she means. When I drink, I feel normal for a glass or two. The headaches and the gritty dirty feelings of shame come later.

'I'm not Jekyll and Hyde,' I say. 'I don't turn into a monster, if that's what you're getting at.'

'I'm not getting at anything. A lot of people find drinking changes their personality in ways they don't like or don't have any control over.'

'I'm not an alcoholic. Joanna would never let me drink too much.'

She nods, makes a note. 'And drugs, Sarah. What are you taking?' She doesn't look up from her notetaking.

'I'm on medication for my moods and anxiety,' I say.

'Prescription drugs?'

'Yes, anxiety meds and anti-depressants from my GP and sometimes painkillers for my headaches from my private psychiatrist, Doctor Hannah Lucas.'

She writes this down and then, still not looking up from her notes, she asks: 'Sarah, was your sister scared of you?'

I laugh. 'Scared of me? It was more like the other way. It was her house. Her money. I knew I had to behave. She was the boss.'

It was our little joke. When the window cleaner came, he always asked 'Is the governor in?' Everyone knew she was in charge.

'Did you resent her for that? That she was in control of you like that? I mean, you're a grown-up woman and your big sister is still telling you what to do. I think a lot of people would have sympathy if that sometimes became overbearing.'

Noor picks her words carefully. I can see where she's leading me with this. Overbearing; she wants to use it as a euphemism for bossy and controlling, to draw out little resentments and bitterness like thorns from a wound, to bleed my anger and then use it against me. I press my hands together, making the shredded skin sting, using the pain to centre myself.

'Joanna was a wonderful sister. She looked after me. And sometimes we argued, yes, sisters do that. But I loved her and I would never, never hurt her.'

DS Noor looks through her file again, her head bowed. Her hair is cut in a short modern crop, the locks so silkily black they are almost blue, like the sheen on a raven's feather. Her

39

nails are cut short, neatly manicured, painted in pale pink. She looks up, catches me staring and smiles. She pulls a photograph from her file and puts it on the table between us and spins it so I can see it clearly. Cassie and Snell lean in to look.

I sit back and feel the blood rush to my feet. I know what the photograph shows. I'd meant to remove it years ago but it was just another of those little jobs that gets forgotten. And now it's staring me in the face as I sit in a police cell being questioned about my violent rages. And it looks very bad.

It's a photograph of a bolt on a door. On the outside of my bedroom door.

'Who put this bolt there?' asks Noor, softly.

I swallow, gulping down my fear. 'Joanna.'

'Why did she put a bolt like that on your door?'

Cassie and Snell stare at me and I can almost hear the cogs in their brains whirring.

'She was worried I might attack her.'

Chapter Eight

Sixteen years ago

I thought libraries were supposed to be quiet places. Instead there's a bunch of raucous pre-schoolers beating the hell out of some tambourines. I sink down on a faux-leather pouffe in the furthest corner from the cacophony, my legs a little shaky after the walk. Posters on the noticeboard advertise dementia-friendly walking groups and dog-free cafes, or is it the other way around? Sometimes words still get jumbled up. I get stuck in verbal culs-de-sac or take circuitous detours to find the right word. I know Joanna gets exasperated. I can't blame her. I drive myself mad.

The pre-schoolers are now mauling the harmonies of 'Row, row, row your boat'. I don't know how Joanna can stand it but she's crazy for all these groups. Drinking insipid tea in village halls while James hammers at wooden train tracks. Gooing and clapping her way through Baby Bounce and Rhyme. Gossiping with other mums at Tiger Tots, a cruelly loud session in an echoing gymnasium that mainly seems to involve James sobbing his way round some kind of toddler assault course.

'I have to get out and have adult conversation,' Joanna likes to say of these outings.

I try not to take offence at the implication that me, the person she actually lives with, is incapable of grown-up discourse.

'And it's good for James. He needs to spend time with other kids.'

The words linger in the air like poison gas. Because of course James has no siblings: that avenue of his life has been cut off. Joanna never talks about Robert. Sometimes I'll catch her staring at their wedding photograph but she quickly puts it down when she realises I've noticed. Is it healthy, this silence?

She won't talk about the accident either. So I'm left with these blanks in my memory: I can't remember the years leading up to the accident and nothing of the accident itself. Even the months in hospital are gone. I remember Hillwood House, and Dr Lucas, and slowly my short-term memory has returned. But my mid-twenties are gone, although it's a different kind of blankness from the accident itself. The accident is a black hole, no memories escape from that void. But the years before, they're more of a murky brown, like a dirty fog or silted-up pond, through which I occasionally glimpse shadows, outlines and snatches of memory.

Dr Lucas was very interested in my descriptions of the lost memories and believes two different types of amnesia might be at play: one related to the obliterating trauma of the accident, and the other some subconscious suppression of distressing memories. Yet when I try to replay the years before the memory loss, there's a rush of colour and joy and life, and no hint of trauma or upset. After all, I was well and truly free of Mother by then.

Who was I in those lost years? Did I have a job? Lovers? Friends? I try to recall my last memories and there's a flurry of images, like flipping through a photo album: a beach in Bali, long tan legs crusted in sand, a jewel-bright bikini, a cocktail glass, cheap silver trinkets from the market. Another snapshot, me in a steamy bathroom, sweeping moisturiser over my cheeks, glitter on my eyelids, my housemate – Kitty, or was it Caz – griping at me for taking too long in the bathroom, hammering at the door. *The taxi's waiting.* Me, again, clutching my high heels as I run for a bus in bare feet, my skirt hitched up and hair tumbling from its topknot. I just make it, and everyone on the bus cheers. The bus driver winks and lets me on for free and I think, *That makes up for being late on my first day.*

I am like a detective, trying to piece myself back together to the person I was before the accident, to somehow start again where I left off. I worked to party, to travel, to glam it up with glitter and high heels. I was not a reliable employee. I was a gossiper, a drinker, a person who took the bus and took the piss. I like to think I was fun. I was not a library kind of person. I was not a Market Leyton kind of person. I was London and festivals and Bali. I had friends. Where are my friends? Joanna says they came to visit at first, laden with flowers and teddies and tears, but I was in a coma for so long that gradually they faded away. And family, it seems there's just Mother left and she's lost to dementia, in a home down south. Joanna visits sometimes but she leaves me behind: she says it's too upsetting for Mother to see different faces and besides I still find travelling exhausting and stressful.

Dr Lucas told me to be patient: it takes a long time to recover from head trauma and I need to be kind to myself. I wonder if my recovery is still on track; I wish we still lived near Hillwood House so I could see Dr Lucas. Joanna works in HR, she could have got a job anywhere, I don't understand how we ended up in this nowhere town that feels like it's clinging to the very edges of life.

I pick up a book from one of the nearest shelves. It's a guide to brewing your own beer, wedged between *Beekeeping For Beginners* and *World of Crochet*. That sounds like a nice place to live, soft and homely. If only there was a DIY guide to rebuilding your life after serious head trauma.

'There you are!' It's a woman in an offensively bright cardie, a snotty kid trailing behind her. It must be my sister. 'We're all done. Have you picked anything to read?' She peers at the book in my hands. 'Home brew? I'm not sure that's wise.' She plucks another book off the shelf. 'Crochet. It would be good for your dexterity.'

She's speaking in that loud, high voice, the same one she uses when she's trying to coax James onto the potty. I hand her the book, and she smiles brightly, like I've just presented a wonderful turd. Is this what motherhood does to you? Thank God I've been spared that.

I wait by the entrance while she picks out her books. I'm supposed to be keeping an eye on James but I can't tell him apart from the other kids milling round the wooden boxes of picture books. A woman with a tattooed arm makes eye contact and mutters something about kids and half term. I suppose she thinks one of the kids is mine. I shrug. She raises her eyebrows and gives me a vicious look. 'Stuck-up cow.'

I'm shaken by the sudden hostility. I am not equipped to respond. Joanna joins me, glancing round, and I tell her about the woman.

'But that's Meredith, from Tiger Tots. You see her every week. Oh, Sarah.'

I can tell she's annoyed. I have already noticed it is very important to her that other parents like her. She's desperate for approval from these people, yet who cares what they think? You can only do the best you can. Perhaps it's because our own childhood was so strange that Joanna's now on a mission to be the Best Mother Ever. I've tried to tell her there are no prizes handed out but she looks at me strangely and says I wouldn't understand.

'Where's James?' Her eyes flit anxiously round the children's section, where a handful of rug rats are still mauling books or mewling for snacks. I nod at the box of books where I think James is but, bloody typical, he's not one of them.

'For Christ sakes,' says Joanna breathily and she shoots off, calling his name, a high note of panic in her voice. Other parents, and the pregnant librarian in her hippy clogs, join in. One mum goes outside, looking up and down the High Street, calling his name. I just stand there, too many cooks and all that.

'I got him,' says a voice. It's a woman with a tattooed arm. It would be, of course. 'He was at the photocopier, little tyke.'

She leads him over to Joanna, who's got her hand on her heart, blinking back tears.

'Think he needed a little private time, he's had a little accident,' says Tattoo, her voice carrying over the cooing and sympathy of the other mums.

Joanna flushes red. I can tell she's mortified. She lost James and now he's pooed his pants in the library. This is not Best Mum Ever territory.

I take the brunt of it, of course. She hisses and tuts and grimaces the whole way home.

'He was the only kid in a Batman T-shirt. I thought you could remember that. I can't be everywhere all the time, Sarah.'

Yeah, yeah, I know.

'I need you to try and stick to the system. I'm not wearing this bloody cardie for fun. It's for you. And with James you just need to pay attention.'

I'm sick of this now. I'm not the bad guy. I've got brain damage and that woman was rude to me. I'm the one who should be upset. I didn't even want to go to the library.

The rage is like a living physical thing: I can feel it, it has an energy of its own that I can't resist. In fact, it's almost a relief to give in and let the anger have its way. I kick a hole in the kitchen door, smash two cups and a glass and cast a box of cereal across the floor. I storm from the kitchen and almost fall over James' bloody booster chair. I kick it, hard, and it smashes into the hall radiator. The impact reverberates loudly, and the little shelf above the radiator rains down keys, loose change and uncollected charity envelopes.

James is screaming in the living room, his mouth a perfect round circle as Joanna tries to comfort him, white-faced, a scratch down one cheek where blood beads against her pale skin – did I do that? It's enough to bring me to a standstill. The rage leaves, slinking away as quickly as it rushed in, and I'm a spent husk, sobbing in the hall.

This is the worst I have been, I am sure. And then I doubt myself: there have been other rages. I drove the car into the garage wall when she wouldn't take me back to Hillwood House. I remember screaming at her as she lay cowering in bed one night: I don't know why. Now my knuckles are bloody and bruised from where I punched the wall, and my throat is raw with screaming and crying. I don't even know what I said. I have to see Dr Lucas. I need help. I flounder upstairs, and sink into my bed and weep, ashamed and scared.

Downstairs Joanna starts to clear up. James has been placated with some loud television and I hear the sound of the hoover, Joanna talking on the phone, her voice too quiet for me to catch. Perhaps she is arranging for them to come and take me away. I'm not sure I would blame her. At some point I fall asleep, a deep sleep distorted with strange images that fade away like ships lost to fog as soon as I wake. I stumble to the bathroom with a full bladder and it's then I find out the extent of Joanna's housekeeping. She has fixed bolts to all the bedroom doors with one difference – mine is on the outside.

Chapter Nine

There's a knock on the door, a police officer intervenes and whispers in Noor's ear. They confer and Noor makes her excuses, taking Snell with her. Cassie and I look at one another blankly; we are both in the dark. But I'm prepared for the worst. I know how bad it looks, I was covered in Joanna's blood, my fingers were on the knife and no one else saw the man in the skull mask. But to my surprise, when Noor and Snell return it's with news that I'm free to go. It appears the initial forensics report and the extent of my injuries provide enough evidence to lend some credence to my story that this was more than a drunken spat between warring sisters.

I should feel relief but instead my hands flutter with anxiety and my stomach churns uneasily. There is safety of sorts in the small peppermint cream room, where other people are in control and no one can get to me. Suddenly I am cast adrift, with no one to anchor me, and somewhere a dark shadow, a predator in a black hood and leather gloves, circles in the depths. What if he comes for me again, how will I protect myself?

Noor grimaces as she packs away her notes, questions still unasked, suspicions unanswered. She cautions me not to leave town and I'm left feeling that the police assigned to the house are as much to observe me as to protect me from the killer.

'Have you found James yet? Does he know?'

'Our victim support specialist is on her way to him,' Noor says. 'The race organisers told us that his route was being tracked in real time via Beacon. We're just getting the co-ordinates so we can reach him.'

None of this makes sense to me so Noor patiently explains how an app on his phone is linked to one of his friends. It's some kind of safety feature which means his location can be tracked in real time as he navigates his way through this hundred-mile three-day trek. He'd been so excited about this charity expedition, he'd trained hard all winter and a good time would have been a real boost for his confidence given work has been so hit and miss lately.

I rack my brains to try and think of James' friend. He shares a small house in Shrewsbury with a motley assortment of rudderless youth, drifting from job to job. I can remember vague mentions of festivals and films they've been to, and their run-ins with the landlord. One of his housemates is called Blue, it's the kind of name that sticks in your head. I wonder if Blue will be there to comfort him when the police arrive. I can't bear to think of him in distress. What on earth am I going to say to him? Will he want to come back home to live now? We are not close, but he is all I have left.

'And Joanna?' My voice cracks to a dry whisper. 'Where is she? Can I see her?'

'Joanna's body will be at the mortuary now. It will need to be formally identified before the post mortem. This can be done via video link.'

'I'd like to see her.' I never got to say goodbye to Mother. I was having a lot of panic attacks then and Joanna said the mother we knew had really died years ago. But I need to say goodbye to Joanna. There is so much we never said when we had the chance. I should have told her every day how much I loved her, how much I appreciated her.

'I think you should rest, Sarah. You must be exhausted,' says Noor, getting to her feet.

I am being dismissed. Just like that. I don't get up. I am so tired it takes all my effort to stay upright on this chair, never mind get up and start to rebuild a life without Joanna. I stay in my seat, two pathetic tears rolling down my cheeks. 'I need to see her.'

Noor glances at me. 'All in due course, Sarah. You must understand the circumstances of her death means it takes a little longer than normal to arrange things.'

The circumstances of her death. Such a civilised phrase to hide the brutality of that man, the pink meat knife held so casually in his gloved hand, Joanna's little gasp and the warm blood pulsing through my fingers.

'You OK, Sarah?' Cassie notices my rising distress. She places a hand gently on my arm. It's so long since anyone was tender towards me. Joanna was brisk and business-like, and though I knew she cared for me, no one could ever describe her as tender. I suppose she got that from Mother.

Cassie guides me to my feet, her hand at my elbow. 'Come on, Sarah. Let's get you out of here.'

I am like a leaf on the tide. I have no agency of my own but am shunted from one place to the next, I am handed leaflets and given instructions my exhausted brain just can't take in. They give me back my handbag and it slowly dawns on me that I have nowhere to go; my house is a crime scene. One of the leaflets includes information about organising a professional deep clean once forensic services have finished in your home. I don't know why it upsets me so much but suddenly tears are running down my cheeks: the thought of strangers going into my house and cleaning up Joanna's blood. It seems like another violation. It should be me, I should be the one to salvage the broken crockery and clean her blood from the kitchen she was so proud of, not strangers on a minimum wage, just working through their job sheet. Cassie puts her arms round me and I collapse into her, her feathery earring tickling my cheek. She smells of coconut and chewing gum, and I cry until her T-shirt is wet with my tears. Should I ever happen to see her again out in the world, I wouldn't even recognise her. Without Joanna and our cardigan code, everyone is a stranger to me now.

It is Cassie who sorts out accommodation for me. Her thumbs swipe over her phone and I'm booked into a Premier Inn, TripAdvisor rating four, and a taxi is on its way. This is kind of her, she didn't have to do this. She uses the credit card Joanna gave me for emergencies; I have no idea what the limit is, I've never had to use it before. My room is down a dreary corridor but is comfortable and clean, with a large bed and net curtains obscuring the view of a car park and the canal beyond. I have never liked canals; there was one where we used to live that Mother said attracted low life and we were warned never to venture there after dusk. Even in daylight, I find the glint of the dark water unsettling and I pull the drapes and slump onto the large bed.

I feel numb with tiredness. I wonder how long it would take to die if I just stayed in bed and never came out. And now Joanna's gone, would anyone even notice? I think about James, my only living relative. He's a young man with his whole life ahead of him. He doesn't want the burden of a mad old aunt to look after.

I wince at the face in the mirror: the bruising across my throat is purple and my face is pale and strained. Who would do this? I keep replaying what Joanna said — *'What's he doing here?'* — and trying to match that weary irritation to the men we know, or rather, *she* knew. So much of her life took place outside the house, there could be a whole cast of possible candidates I don't even know exist. I think about work, that man she hated, could it be him?

I remember a while ago, we had a funny conversation where she asked me what I would do if I found out someone had done something wrong. Would I report them, or give them a chance to make amends?

'It depends what it was,' I'd said. 'Some things you can do over, some things you can't. And you'd have to be sure you had all the facts.'

'Yeah,' she'd said, considering my words, 'you can't wreck someone's life on hearsay.'

She looked thoughtful, but then shook herself. 'Forget it. I'm just hypothesising.'

And I had forgotten it, but now it swims to the surface of my memory, as clear and bright as sunlight on water, ringing with significance. Had she found something out about someone, and had that someone come back to silence her for ever? I shiver, and double check the bedroom door is locked. You're safe, I tell myself, no one can reach you here.

But I thought I was safe in our house and look what happened there.

Chapter Ten

Joanna is everywhere. I lived with her so long and relied on her so heavily that I find there is no aspect of my daily life that doesn't carry an echo of her. I stand in the darkened room, eating complimentary shortbread biscuits and a cup of tea with four sugars, thinking how Joanna would mutter warnings about diabetes and cholesterol if she were here. My damp towel on the floor. The unmade bed. The extra diazepam I took for breakfast. She would say I'm 'letting myself go'. She never had much patience when people fell apart at times of crisis; I suppose she was widowed young, with a baby, a seriously ill sister and a dementia-ridden mother to care for and she just got on with it. She had no choice. Even so, I, more than anyone, knew she wasn't as strong as she liked to pretend, I knew her soft underbelly, her vulnerabilities. She tried to hide them from the world but you can't hide from your sister. Perhaps that's why I got on her nerves so much; I knew the real Joanna, not the Facebook version.

The phone trills in the room. At once my heart thuds desperately, panic flushing my body. Who would be ringing me here? No one knows I'm here, do they? I let it ring out but after a few seconds it starts to ring again. I pick it up, hands shaking.

I can hear sounds in the background, a roar, the sound of a car indicator.

'Aunty Sarah?'

'James!'

I can hardly hear what he's saying. Is it the connection, or is he crying? I'm crying; it makes it more real now that he knows too. He says something but the line keeps cutting out. I catch the words 'identify the body'. Another voice comes on the line, a police officer, I think, talking about taking time to grieve and supporting James at this difficult time and then the line goes dead. I stand, holding the phone in shaking hands, wondering if he'll call back. Does James want me to identify the body? How will I do that? Would they expect me to travel there on my own? My heart rate accelerates and my mind starts to churn obsessively at the thought. I never travel far from home without Joanna. I don't even know how to begin. Would I take a taxi? How would I do that? My breathing tightens into shallow ragged gasps. I do not know how to live without Joanna.

Even the thought of leaving the hotel room makes me want to rock in the corner. How can I support James when I cannot even support myself? Joanna was our support. She was the pit prop holding us both up and already, without her, I can tell we're crumbling. I have a panic attack just going to the Co-op. James has barely held down a job since he left home and seems completely unequipped for the world of work. Joanna and I failed him there. He can find rare moths and identify a bird by its call and hike thirty miles in a day but I doubt he could tell you who the prime minister is or how to get a TV licence.

But who am I to judge? Joanna did everything. She was not only my conduit to the outside world, she was my buffer against it. Without her, I feel raw and exposed, vulnerable. It sounds ridiculous – after all I am forty-six and live in a wealthy country with a functioning social support system – yet I feel as if I've been abandoned, a new born left on a mountainside to die. I start crying but it's not for Joanna, it's for myself.

I cannot settle. Fretful, I sit on the bed, twisting the covers between my hands, watching the door. Every noise, the distant slam of a door, a child's excited shriek, the rattle of the housekeeping trolley, is like the twist of a knife in my gut. I position the desk chair in front of the door but I am under no illusions that it offers any protection against the man who attacked us.

I pace the room to distract myself. From the chair by the door to the window is nine paces. From the desk to the bedside table is four. These are the dimensions of my life now. I read the hotel directory from cover to cover, wondering how long I will be staying here. I can get extra pillows and extra toiletries if I call housekeeping. If I could get myself to the restaurant I could bring food up to my room. But I can't bear the thought of leaving this room. I don't feel safe here, but outside is an unknown. Do the people who work here know why I'm here? The thought of them staring at me, asking questions, pointing . . .

A door slams down the corridor, voices and footsteps approach. I freeze, terrified they are coming for me. A woman says something I can't quite hear and a man laughs, so close it sounds like he's in the room with me. They pass by but I can't relax for now I hear the clink and rattle of the housekeeping trolley down the corridor. I can't bear the thought of people coming in here, seeing me, judging me, but somehow I can't bring myself to open the door and hang the Do Not Disturb card on the outside. I hover by the door, staring at the corridor through the warped lens of the spyhole. There's no one out there but the strange fish-eye view lends the corridor a menacing slant and I'm convinced the moment I open the door someone will appear, a cleaner, a guest, the killer. I dig my fingers into my wounded palm, full of self-loathing. How did it ever come to this?

I turn on the television, drifting through channels like a phantom wandering through different dimensions, snatches of life where people are helping injured animals, renovating old houses and cooking elaborate meals in steamy kitchens. Suddenly I hit the local afternoon news and our house is on television, with police standing out front and a pile of flowers and candles at the gate.

I kneel in front of the television, my hands on my face, my heart thundering in my chest.

A woman talks to the camera about her shock. 'I just don't know what to tell the kids. You never think it will happen so close to home.'

Now another lady is being interviewed, claiming to be good friends of the family. 'She was a lovely lady, always well turned out. But we didn't see much of the other two, kept themselves to themselves. I think the sister was a bit of a recluse. The lad's grown up and moved away now, so you do wonder if they were targeted because it was just two women on their own.'

She drones on and on. I don't know why they give so much airtime to this woman. *I think the sister was a bit of a recluse.* How dare she talk about me like that? She doesn't know us, or at least I don't think she does. Maybe she was a friend of Joanna's. But she's no expert, she shouldn't be speaking on television and speculating about what happened. Who is she? She's no one. Just a parasite feeding off the drama.

The news has moved on now, some other hard-luck story about cancer misdiagnosis, some other person's tragedy. Soon, we will be old news too. People will say, 'Speldhurst Road, wasn't someone murdered there?' And one day it will fade altogether. Like hot breath on a cold window, given enough time none of us leave a trace.

Chapter Eleven

Between the tears and the sedatives, I somehow fall asleep. I drift in and out of strange dreams, traces of memories flicker before my subconscious then die, like a match struck in the darkness. I see myself dancing in bare feet in an empty house, sharing a secret smile with a man in the mirror; a car driving too fast down country roads, laughter trailing from the open windows like a chiffon scarf streaming in the wind. And then the laughter distorts, until it's the sound of a baby crying. Suddenly, a voice speaks in my ear, so close I can feel warm breath on my neck. *For the wages of sin are death.* It's Joanna's voice, she's here!

I sit bolt upright, wide awake. The room is dark and still, there is no one here, but still I hear the voice, ringing through my head. I savour it, try to hold on to it: the last trace of Joanna and it is slipping away, now just a distant echo, a ripple fading back to nothing. I don't believe in the afterlife – any faith I had seeped out of me years ago, air from a slowly deflating balloon – and I know it's just my subconscious trying to deal with the trauma, but I allow myself to take some comfort from the dream, from the illusion that Joanna, just for moment, was by my side, speaking to me again.

For the wages of sin are death. I was always the naughty

one, always pushing back against Mother's rules and bringing punishment down on both of us. I couldn't wait to escape, cashing in the premium bonds Nan left me for a month's rent on a house share in London, working a series of temp jobs to pay for parties and travel and festivals. I was young and gorgeous and making up for lost time.

I smile to myself even now. They were good times, even if so many of them are now just a drunken haze. Why should I feel guilty, just because Joanna chose to stay behind and suck up to Mother? I try to imagine what it must have been like in that house, just the two of them, the seeds of dementia starting to germinate, the religious mania deepening. I saw it myself when I went home at Christmas or when I was broke and between jobs. And then Joanna left too. Got a good job, bought a nice flat, met Robert, got married and had a kid.

I don't remember much of that: even her wedding day is a blur. Did I get drunk then too? I remember Mother in the church, looking like a bank teller in her formal blue suit. *Looks don't last for ever, Sarah, and no one wants damaged goods.* That's the wedding spirit, Mother.

Joanna wore a long white dress with a sweetheart neckline, her dimples on full beam, her skin glowing. I don't really remember Rob. He was a pilot and was away a lot. He was a looker, definitely a nine to her seven, and he knew it, too. I used to tease her, warn her she'd better watch out or the stewardesses would be hitting on him on all those lonely long-haul trips to exotic locations. Looking back, it probably wasn't very kind of me but she used to laugh, and say she was only in it for the free air miles anyway. Beyond that, my memory fades to a dirty fog. There's something there, snatches of conversation, snippets of places and people, but nothing I can make any sense of. If Dr Lucas is right and I'm suppressing these memories, then I've done a good job of it. I suppose I just carried on as I had in my early twenties, working, drinking, travelling, until one day, for some reason, I got into a car with Rob and baby James and everything changed for ever. It is the moment my life pivots around and I can't remember anything about it. And now I'm facing another pivot: before Joanna was killed, and after. And this time I'm on my own.

I cry until I fall back to sleep, then wake to the sound of a door slamming, and the smell of bacon. My stomach growls, a cavernous rumble. It's after nine, no wonder I'm hungry. My flesh has been stripped away over the last forty-eight hours and my collar and hip bones protrude. When I was younger I would have celebrated such a dramatic weight drop but now that I'm the wrong side of forty-five, it just makes me look ill.

How long will I stay here? And how would I get home from here? And home ... The anxiety builds again, my heart hammering so fast I am sure I am about to go into cardiac arrest. I could die here and nobody would know. This is where Joanna would usually intervene, talk me down and hand me another diazepam. But I'm on my own now, trapped in this room, with my pulse rioting under my fingertips.

A knock on the door jolts me out of an obsessive count of my pulse.

'Aunty Sarah, are you there?'

James! We are not a family of natural huggers but I pull him into a clumsy embrace, a collision of elbows and shoulders.

'They told me you were here,' he says, disengaging himself and holding up a keycard that matches mine. 'I'm down there in 223. I hope you don't mind, I booked in and put it on your card.'

Of course I don't mind! For the first time since it happened, I feel I can breathe again, a deep inhalation and a shaky ragged sigh of relief. He's about four doors down on the other side, closer than we've been for a year, but it still seems too much distance in a world so full of horror. I want us to hunker down, batten the hatches and hold each other tight. Could we request neighbouring rooms, or would that be strange? After all, I tell myself, he's a grown man now, he needs his space and I mustn't scare him off by being too demanding.

'Can I?' he questions, nodding over my shoulder.

'Yes, yes, come in.' I lead him into the room, and he's so tall and young and vibrating with pain, he seems to fill the space. His cheekbones slice the air and purple shadows trace his eyes. It feels strangely intimate to be here together, with my unmade bed, the sheets strewn with biscuit crumbs, soggy teabags by the kettle, damp towels on the floor. Joanna would despair of me but James doesn't notice. He shuffles to the window and peers out through the net curtains at the car park below, his thin shoulders hunched. I want to fold him into an embrace and make the pain go away, to be the mother to him that I yearn for myself, but how can I ever replace Joanna? Besides, I don't have the words, I don't know how to do it. And what words could ever explain what happened?

'Your mum ...' I stumble, no words seem adequate.

He turns to me, his face stricken, and slumps into the chair, his head in his hands. 'I identified ... her. I had to do it by video link. I couldn't face it.'

He runs his fingers through his dark hair. 'Now I feel like a failure, like I've let her down. She should have someone with her, you know.'

I let out a long shaky breath, relieved that one huge task has been done without me having to leave this room, and sink onto the corner of the bed near him and reach for his hands. His fingers are long and tapered, but strong, like a piano player. 'Oh James, I am sure they'll let you see her again. And your mum would understand, you know she would.'

He looks up, and tries a wobbly smile. 'It doesn't sit right, that's all. I'd like a do-over, you know.' He gently retrieves his hands and shoves them deep into his hoody pockets as if to make sure I can't take them again. I wonder what the police have said to him, does he think I might have hurt Joanna?

'What about you, Aunty Sarah? The police said he attacked you too. Your neck ...'

I instinctively put a hand to my throat, encouraged that the police are telling people I was attacked. It must mean they believe me. 'I'm OK. Cuts and bruises. It's just my head. I can't get it out of my head. And it doesn't make any sense. Everyone loved your mum, who would do this to her?'

James sniffs loudly and rubs his hands through his hair again. 'The police think it was someone she knew.'

'Yes, she recognised him when he came to the door.'

'Was she seeing anyone again, Aunty Sarah? I warned her about Internet dating. People are never what they seem.'

'No, not that I knew, not after the philandering pensioner.'

James's brow wrinkles. 'Who?'

'No one, don't worry. Just some guy she had a date with who it turned out was fifteen years older than his profile and was dating women in three different counties. Don't worry, she saw through him quickly. We had a laugh about it.'

Eventually, we'd laughed. I don't tell him how for months she'd enjoyed her flirty email exchanges and expensive dinners with the philanderer at a time when her confidence had been low. The eventual revelations about his real age and intentions had been a bitter blow.

James looks furious. 'Who was he? Have you told the police? Someone like that, you never know what he might be up to, preying on the vulnerable. Mum had some money tucked away. It attracts the wrong sort of people.'

'She was too trusting,' I agree. 'She thought everyone was

like her, James, decent and honest, but there are some shits out there.'

'The police should definitely look into him. What about other men?'

I shrug. 'I don't know. She was off men, really. I did think maybe someone at work. She said she'd found something out about someone.'

He looks up, sharply. 'Who?'

'I don't know. She never said. She said she wasn't sure what to do. It was a while ago though so maybe it all got sorted out. There was a man she didn't like there, Alex someone, but I don't know if it was him.'

I wished I'd paid more attention when she talked about work. There were so many names, people I'd never met and was probably never going to meet, so I just used to zone out. Why did she think I needed to know about someone's sick cat or the new coffee machine? I would give anything now to hear her prattling on about work.

'Did she say anything to you?'

James looks blank. 'I never really listened when she talked about work.' He sighs heavily, probably feeling as guilty as me. We should have listened when we had the chance.

'I'm sure if it was something to do with work, the police will find him,' I say, trying to reassure him. Joanna was bound to have kept records of what she found out; she was meticulous in her administration. I can't think of any other reason why anyone would want to hurt Joanna. She was as straight as a die. He balls his hands into fists and thrusts them back into his pockets. He looks so thin and tired. I bet he hasn't eaten either. Perhaps we could go out together and get some food.

There's a noise out in the corridor and I stiffen, suddenly on high alert. I put my fingers to my lips as I strain to hear what's happening out there.

James looks at me, puzzled. 'It's OK, Aunty Sarah, it's just housekeeping.' He doesn't realise – or perhaps he does – that this doesn't bring someone like me any comfort. I can't bear the thought of people coming in here. He sighs heavily, and unfolds himself from the chair and walks across the room. 'If you don't want them to come in, you just put the Do Not Disturb sign on the door handle.' He does this in one easy fluid movement and then shuts and locks the door again. 'Ta da!' he says, smiling, and in that moment, I see Joanna; he has her dimples.

I choke back some tears, a hard lump in my throat. I see him register this, and he walks over and picks up the TV remote. 'Shall we have a brew and watch some TV, Aunty Sarah? I know you don't like it but I just need to veg out for a while, you know, try not to think. And I think Mum would want us to be together. You know.'

I smile, nodding through my tears, thinking, oh, Joanna, you would be so proud of your boy right now. We settle down to watch some cooking show, drinking tea side by side on the king size bed. At some point, I fall asleep, and when I wake up, still fully clothed in the blue light of the muted television, there's just a warm dent in the bed where my nephew has been.

Chapter Twelve

15 years ago

I can hear thunder in the distance. I wait for it to pass but it rumbles on and on, and I realise the noise is just outside the house. I hoist myself out of bed and wander through to Joanna's room at the front of the house to peer down into the street. There's another lorry outside number 24, the third one today, and a large man in an old T-shirt, sweat patches under both arms, is hauling out an old leather armchair. They really should switch the engine off when making deliveries. It's a good job Joanna isn't here. She hates that kind of thoughtless pollution.

The man has the armchair on the back of a little trolley now and is pushing it towards his house. He sees me in the window and waves cheerily. He mouths something but I don't catch it through the double-glazing and I shrink back, alarmed. Who is he, is he the new neighbour? Joanna has been watching the comings and goings with interest, reporting back that she thinks he's late forties, maybe early fifties, no sign of a wife or kids yet and she thinks he does something with cars. I suppose she's hoping he might be a romantic prospect but he doesn't really look her type. From up here, I've already seen his thinning hair and too much of his backside when he bent down.

But she's desperate to meet somebody. She's thirty-four and this is a window of opportunity to net a new man, start again, maybe have more kids. I know she worries about being alone. She doesn't talk much about Rob but I suppose she's done her mourning and it's time to move on while she can. She went out for drinks with some mums she met at the school gate, and came home flushed and shiny, her eyes glassy with the pinot grigio and laughing about the sole dishy dad who does the school run while his wife manages a buy-to-let property empire. 'Look at me,' she said, tip-toeing back into the house in case she woke up James. 'A merry widow!'

I felt jealous, then, of course I did. I used to love going out, getting off my face and waking up the next day with a banging headache and stories to cringe over with the girls. Will it ever get better? Will it ever happen for me again? Not the boozing, it's not really recommended for people with neurological impairment, but the friendships and the laughter and the tingle of a new romance. I'm still young, I have my best years ahead of me, and I'm not totally repugnant, but I suppose nobody's going to come knocking on my door. I need to get back out there.

There's a knock on the door. I tiptoe to the top of the stairs and see a figure outlined in the glass. Oh fuck. I hate unexpected visitors but ever since that parcel got redirected, Joanna has told me I must answer the door. When I do, I'm face to face with a middle-aged man in a sweaty T-shirt, low slung jeans and workman's boots. He's got a friendly smile and awful hair, too long and curly at the front but balding on top, which he's trying to disguise with an ill-judged comb over. I guess this is the man I saw from upstairs, our new neighbour.

'Hi there.' He beams, and holds out a large hand. 'I'm Alan, number twenty-four.'

I shake hands warily. His palm is calloused, and there's tape around one fingernail. 'Sarah,' I say.

'Nice to meet you, neighbour. Lovely little area, isn't it? Don't worry, I'm not planning on lowering the tone.' He laughs. 'Yes, lovely street, big gardens. That's important. They don't build them like that any more.'

There's an uncomfortable silence. I realise he's waiting for me to say something. I am out of practice at social chit-chat.

'Where have you moved from?'

'Bit further north, Lancashire. More civilised down here, eh? Shropshire people, bit more la di dah, eh?'

I'm not sure what to say about this. Shropshire has never struck me as la di dah, but then I don't know Lancashire. 'What brings you here?' I ask, pleased at my sudden conversational ease. 'Do you have family here?'

He hesitates, a cloud crosses his face. 'No, no family, never been lucky like that.'

'Work?'

He frowns and I check myself; I shouldn't pry. He will have me marked down as the neighbourhood busybody, which would be somewhat ironic. 'Semi-retired, actually,' he says, looking uncomfortable now. 'No, I just like it here, lovely town.'

This is a conversational dead end for me. Market Leyton is many things but it is not the kind of place you'd come to without good reason. We're only here because Joanna struck lucky on the job front, dragging us north and now, as she likes to say, we're priced out of going back. She always brings this up to shut down any hint from me that it would be worth relocating to be closer to Hillwood House. I remain convinced that I would have made a better recovery if I was still under Dr Lucas.

'So, it's just you two ladies, is it?' he asks. 'Don't worry, I'm harmless. No dead bodies under the patio.' He laughs manically.

I'm not sure what to say to this. 'My sister, Joanna, will be back soon.'

'That's it, Joanna!' His face brightens. 'I bumped into her

last night and then couldn't remember her name. Shocking confession, eh, don't tell her! She looked smart, a professional lady, is she?'

'She works in HR. A big legal services group.'

'Beauty and brains,' he says. 'You work ... Sarah, is it?'

I'm unwilling to go into my whole life story so I use my standard line. 'I'm on a career break.'

It's something I heard one of the dads say at a kids' party once and I filed it away for future use. Joanna always laughs when she hears me trot it out. 'Break from what? Do you think they've noticed you've left yet?'

She finds this fantastically funny but we can't all be corporate high flyers. Still, Alan accepts this; perhaps 'semi-retirement' is his version of my career break. It seems we're both hiding something.

I clear my throat. 'Would you like to come in? A cup of tea or something?'

He beams. 'I won't this time, Sarah, I've got a lot to do. Still unpacking, at sixes and sevens, where does all this stuff come from I'd like to know. It needs a woman's touch, that's what it needs.'

I tuck this fact away to tell Joanna later – he's single.

'I saw a swing set,' he says. 'You got a little one?'

'James, my nephew. Joanna's son.' I hope it doesn't put him off. Maybe I shouldn't have said anything; Joanna will be cross if I dash his interest before he's even really moved in.

But Alan beams some more. 'I love children,' he says. 'Nothing better than hearing kids playing outside. It's the sound of summer, eh? You got a treehouse? I'll make you one. They're my speciality.'

He rattles on, something about water meters and very soon he's on his knees on our driveway removing a metal cover I've never even noticed before, up to his elbows in water.

'Yeah, thought so,' he says, with some relish. 'Noticed it with my meter readings. There's a leak down here. I'll get onto the water board but you really should go back through your bills. You could have been overpaying for years.'

'Really? Right. Thanks.' I must remember to tell Joanna. She deals with all that sort of stuff. I didn't even know we were on a water meter. Is that why she's so sniffy about my long baths?

Alan's back on his feet now, wiping his hands on his dirty jeans. He looks down, and shakes his head. 'Look at the state of me,' he laughs. 'You must wonder what's moved in next to you! I promise I do scrub up good. You won't recognise me next time you see me.'

I wince at that; there's no way he could know about my condition but it slices close to the bone. Even so, I am already getting a feel for him, details to jot down in my VIP book, little mental reminders by which to recognise him: his height and that awful hairstyle, not to mention a barely perceptible northern flattening to his voice from his years in Lancashire.

He chatters on for a while and I find my smile becoming fixed and vacant. This is too much social for me. Perhaps he notices my fading interest, for he stops short, clapping his hands together as if to signal the end of the conversation. Maybe I should introduce a clap when I've had enough of people.

'Great to meet you, Sarah. Give my best wishes to your lovely sister, Joanna! See!' He taps the side of his head with a grubby, taped-up finger. 'I remembered her name. Maybe next time you see me I'll be looking more presentable.'

He chortles to himself and heads onto the pavement to cross onto his property. 'And don't forget about the water company. Leaks cost money!'

I close the door and retreat into the house, suddenly exhausted. I wonder what Joanna will make of Alan. He's a single man so she'll pump me for information. I replay the conversation in my head, trying to tuck away interesting facts, but I'm left with the impression that he ended up knowing a lot about us but I still know nothing of substance about him.

Chapter Thirteen

We are on our third day in the Premier Inn. It's a strange time, cut off from the world, eating supermarket sandwiches and packets of biscuits that James picks up from the Tesco Express. A victim support officer called Sam Nowak, blonde with angel wings tattooed on her wrist, comes to speak to James. I can't help worrying that I'm not getting the victim treatment, even though I'm the one with concussion and severe bruising. She can't tell us much, just that enquiries are still ongoing. James tells her about the philandering pensioner and she says they've already spoken to him; he was in Coventry with his girlfriend on the night of the murder. James looks unconvinced but I'm just amazed the guy is still getting dates.

'We're still trying to contact some of the men,' she says.

'How many men were there?' asks James, stricken.

Nowak laughs nervously. 'A handful over the years. Your mum spent all those years raising you, it was her time now.'

I nod, blinking back tears. It should have been her time but someone stole that from her. But who, some random bloke from Match.com? It just doesn't make any sense. Nowak can't give us any answers, it's just platitudes and soothing noises. But there is some news: we can go back to the house. She advises

us to hire a specialist cleaning company. 'It's a job for profes-
sionals,' she says. 'You don't need to see that.'

Around lunchtime, James forces me out of the room so the
chamber maid can freshen up. We sit in the small restaurant
downstairs, and order some hot food and a couple of lemonades.
I'd love a proper drink but James has always been tee-total and
it seems disrespectful to drink on my own.

We don't talk much. James spends a lot of time hunched over
his screen analysing his statistics from the ultra-race. He shows
me the app, which logged his route, his pace, his altitude.

'Got slower here,' he says, showing me some numbers. 'Look,
I really start to drop off the pace from about mile twenty-eight.'

'I'm not surprised. It is mile twenty-eight, after all.'

He frowns. 'No, you don't get it,' he says, scrolling through
more numbers. 'I trained hard for this. No, look at the time.
It was the night Mum, you know ... It's like part of me knew
something was wrong.'

I shrug. I hate any kind of mystical talk. 'It was also night-
time, James, your body would be naturally slower.'

He looks hurt and I kick myself. Of course, he wants to think
he had some magical connection with his dying mum. He's
looking for comfort and reassurance from me and I can't even
do that right. 'But you're right,' I say, trying to make it better.
'It does seem strange. I'm sure your mum would have been
thinking of you, maybe you picked up on that.'

He brightens, nodding, his eyes still fixed on his screen. I
don't mind, it's just nice to have him around. I'd like to check
my emails on his phone but I don't like to ask. I want to keep
my tread light, not impose myself in any way, give him no
excuses to fear staying with me. He's already mentioned work
a couple of times and how he needs to get back.

'I'm sure they won't mind, James,' I soothe, thinking the

petrol station where he works can manage without him for a few more days. 'Not given the circumstances.'

His face darkens briefly. 'I can't afford to lose another job.'

I put a hand on his arm. 'James, you're in no state,' I say, trying to keep the note of pleading out of my voice. 'And I'll help you out. You're not on your own. We've got to stick together. We're family.'

He doesn't say anything. He shuffles his arm free and picks at the gammon and chips he's ordered. He's never been a big eater. I thought I couldn't face anything but I've virtually licked the plate clean of my bland chicken curry and rice.

'Just think about it,' I say, not wanting to press him on the matter. 'Don't make any decisions today. Sleep on it.'

'I can't just sit around doing nothing, Aunty Sarah. I think I'll be better at work, keeping busy.'

The comment hangs in the air like a bad smell. I'm sure he didn't mean anything by it but I can't help wincing; after all, it's been years, decades even, since I've done anything meaningful with my life. His face reddens and I can tell he's worried he's upset me.

'What are you going to do, Aunty Sarah?' he asks softly. 'I mean now, without Mum. Will you be all right on your own?'

I dig my fingers into my thighs, gouging them into my hateful, useless flesh. I must be brave. I can't impose my failings onto this beautiful soul with his whole life to live.

'I'll take some time, take stock,' I say, as if that's in some way any different from the preceding twenty years. 'I'm sure at first I'll be very busy with plenty of things to sort out, you know, the house, the funeral.'

The F word. I wish I hadn't mentioned it. James visibly blanches, and seems to retreat even further into himself. Grief has hollowed out his features, his jaw tightly angled, his eyes sunken into his head. I long to hold him, for us to cry together, but we're both being brave for one another, holding on by our fingertips. I wonder if he cries himself to sleep at night as well.

'Will you stay in the house, you know, after?'

For some reason, I have just assumed I will. Where would I go, if I'm not there? *Prison*, whispers a little voice in my head but I push it down. I have to believe the police are making progress tracking down the killer; after all, they're clearly going through Joanna's phone and emails and have already questioned the philandering pensioner. Perhaps they're now working their way through the people she works with, finding out any dirty secrets. Joanna worked in HR, she might have known all sorts of things that people would be desperate to keep quiet. I am sure it will only be a matter of time before they find him. But even if they catch the killer, will I ever feel safe in that house again, won't it always be a place of death and violence now?

'I don't know,' I say, hesitantly, my mind spooling through the images of the night again, a cold sweat pricking down my back.

'I'm sure Mum will have made arrangements, like, you know, for the mortgage and stuff,' says James, his head bowed over his phone again. 'She wouldn't leave you homeless.'

I look up sharply. Is that what he meant by staying in the house, that I might not be able to afford to carry on living there? I hadn't even thought of that possibility but of course, it *is* a possibility. I have some savings but how long would they last? I have no idea what the mortgage is on the house, or what the monthly outgoings might be. Did Joanna have savings? I suppose they would all go to James. Ice water seeps through my veins. Could I end up homeless? This is a new horror and I realise, once again, what a naïve fool I am, how ill equipped I am for life without Joanna.

James is talking again, his voice reaching me across icy

wastelands. 'So if you could do that, Aunty Sarah, it would be great. I can't face going there, not yet.' I realise he's still talking about the house.

I clear my throat. 'Of course, James, don't worry about a thing. I'll take care of it.'

His face relaxes, softens, and I realise how much tension he's been carrying around with him. He's so young to be dealing with this. 'Thanks, Aunty Sarah. I know I'm being a wimp but I just can't face it. And don't worry, I know Mum will have made sure you're taken care of. She'll have been insured up the eyeballs, you know what she was like. Hope for the best ...'

'... prepare for the worst,' we finish together, sharing a smile. Joanna was a list-maker, a planner, a packer of spare clothes and snacks and baby wipes, a checker of weather forecasts and a buyer of road cover. She planned for contingencies but I bet she never planned for this. Who could ever have foreseen this? Her sister and her son sitting in a cheap hotel while her murder scene is forensically scraped and photographed for evidence. No, Joanna, you tried to manage every risk out of life but somewhere along the way you met the wrong person and they circumvented every safety net you put in place.

In the evening, Alan comes to visit. He and James are regularly in touch, and it's nice to see James has kept up this strange friendship. Compared to the shifting bunch of oddballs he lives with – Blue! – Alan seems a good friend, a steadying influence, a much-needed father figure. And at least I get a proper drink now Alan's here, a pint for him, a glass of Rioja for me and a lemonade for James.

Alan has come with a plan. He thinks we should launch our own appeal for witnesses because he's convinced the police investigation is flawed. How he's now an expert on forensics and police procedure I don't know but James is lapping it up.

'I know they've asked around our road and down to Elm

Avenue,' Alan is saying, 'but I know, because Polish Bob from Broadoaks, you know, off Clairemount Drive, says they haven't been down that end at all. But if you think about it, if you were making a getaway you'd head that way because you can go down the snicket—'

'The what?'

'Snicket, you know a little alleyway between gardens. It's an old northern word. Much underused in my opinion, but anyway, I digress. The point is the police clearly haven't been thorough in their approach to this. They should be up and down every street this end of town and speak to every householder. Someone must have seen this man. There could be footprints in the gardens, and once you get into that snicket between Broadoaks and the houses on Station Road then you could have a vehicle waiting, hop in and you're off up the A41 and gone.'

He sits back, slightly flushed, and looks at us expectantly. I'm not sure what to say and shift in my seat uncomfortably. I think this is a terrible idea but I don't want to tread on James' toes. This is his mum, after all.

'And I know this isn't politically correct or whatever' – I brace myself, for I know Alan has a deep loathing of what he calls *political correctness gone mad* and can speak at length on the subject – 'but it doesn't hurt that you're such a pretty thing, Sarah. I know, I know, I don't want to embarrass you, but it doesn't hurt. Get you in front of the cameras, particularly with that bruising round your neck, and it will get people's attention, get them involved, pull some heart strings because the truth is, Sarah, someone out there knows this man. He's probably done it before and someone will be having doubts, covering up for him. We need to flush him out.'

'I can't go in front of cameras, Alan.' My heart is already pounding at the thought and I wipe my suddenly sweaty palms on my trousers to try and calm myself. I clear my throat and attempt to reason with him. 'Sorry, I don't think it's wise. He attacked me too, you know. I don't want to rile him and have him come back to finish the job.'

Alan looks deflated but then his eyes fall on James. 'Of course, you're not the only looker in the family, Sarah,' he muses.

James sucks on his bottom lip. 'Whoa, Alan, I'm not sure. I mean, I wouldn't know what to say. I'm not really into public speaking.'

'We could film it ourselves,' says Alan, thinking it through. 'No audience, no need for any public speeches or the like. Just you, me and Polish Bob on the cameras. Seriously, I know you two are shell-shocked but the clock is ticking on finding this killer. The longer it goes on, the harder it will be to find him.'

James nods, thoughtfully. 'Alan's right,' he says at last. 'I mean, someone must have seen something, right? Noticed something strange, had a few doubts, seen something odd about this person. I mean, you can't do that to someone and just carry on living your life like ...' His voice breaks off, fat tears swelling at the rim of his eyes. He sniffs loudly, embarrassed.

'There, there, lad,' says Alan, patting him on the back. 'Don't you fret. We'll find this, well, I can't call him what I'd like to with ladies present, but we'll find him, don't you worry.'

James nods, and runs a hand surreptitiously across his eyes. I feel like my heart could break. But I still think the video appeal is a bad idea.

Chapter Fourteen

Fourteen years ago

Today is a good day. I have been into town, successfully navigated the horrors of the Post Office, which is always busy on a Monday with the small-town chatter of people who have rubbed shoulders alongside each other for years. Joanna is already one of them: people know her through the playgroups she attended with James and now he's started school there's a twice-a-day pop of school-gate pleasantries. I have only picked James up a few times, and each time I have found it a social minefield, aware of some mums giving me the side eye and unsure whether it's because I'm unwittingly ignoring people I should know or whether they're just the school-gate mean girls. It feels very tribal. I try not to show I care but it's an ordeal that leaves me damp with sweat, my hands trembling. Even the teachers look at me warily. I can't recognise James when they're all wearing the same white polo shirts and burgundy jumpers so I'm dependent on him recognising me. Sometimes I have to confirm my identity and I feel everyone staring, wondering if I'm some weird child-snatcher. Once James came out and said he didn't recognise me. I don't know why. Perhaps I'd changed my hair, or had a new coat. The teachers wouldn't let him leave with me and I got so flustered I couldn't remember the codeword to show I was an approved contact so they had to call Joanna out of work. I only pick up in emergencies now, with James booked into after school clubs on the days Joanna works. I suppose that was the start of the retreat; children are like the entry card to making friends in a new town and I am locked out.

Today I have pushed myself. I have done some nonsense chore at the Post Office for Joanna and then treated myself to a browse round the shops. I have been on my feet longer than normal and by the time I get to the church I can feel a tremor down my bad leg and at once little germs of anxiety begin to multiply. *What if you can't do this, what if the pain comes on, what if you fall, what if you need to ask for help?*

By the time I turn into Colclough Road, I am damp with sweat and my foot drags slightly. I am level with the house with the skip full of ripped out kitchen units, when there's a voice at my shoulder.

'I knew it wouldn't be long before they renovated. They put old Jack in a home and now they're gutting the place, getting it ready to sell is my bet.'

I turn startled, and the movement off balances me so that I stumble over my lazy foot. A man reaches out and puts a steadying arm under my elbow. He's tall, wearing a flat cap and one of those waxed jackets.

'Sorry, didn't mean to scare you.' His voice has a slight northern burr. He tips a finger to his cap, pushing it back slightly as if a glimpse of his receding hairline might help me recognise him. 'It's me, Alan, from number twenty-four.'

Alan. We've met a few times now. He lives alone and seems desperate for company. He regularly pops round with toys from boot sales for James, a box of eggs from his hens, the parish magazine and flyers for local events.

'He's getting to be a pain in the neck,' grouses Joanna, who had quickly written him off as a potential mate. He doesn't bother me so much. I spend so much of my time in my room that she takes the brunt of his interest. At some point she must have told him about my condition. I haven't discussed it with him but I've noticed he's always careful to introduce himself whenever he sees me, and he does that thing of talking slightly slower and louder as if I'm simple.

'You all right? You look a bit peaky. Here, take my arm.'

He doesn't wait for me to respond but links his arm round mine and insists on walking me to the back door, where Joanna greets us, her concern quickly souring as Alan follows me into the kitchen. I sink gratefully into a kitchen chair, my legs trembling and pain radiating from my right hip. Joanna passes me a glass of water and some painkillers, which I swiftly down before allowing my head to sink on to the table.

'What happened?' she barks, as if Alan is in some way to blame.

'I found her on Colclough,' says Alan. 'Looked a bit peaky.'

'Pushed myself a bit too hard,' I say, raising my head.

Joanna sighs heavily but before she can embark on a lecture, Alan interjects with his own diagnosis.

'What you need is to come out walking with me. All this walking in towns, it's hard on your joints. You need country walking, softer underfoot and hills to regain muscle strength.'

Joanna raises her eyebrows and looks like she's about to rebuff him but I find myself agreeing with Alan. I want to get better. I want to be strong again. I want my life back, and if it means putting up with Alan's babble, I'm willing to do it. And I'll be less anxious walking in the hills where I don't have to fret about social encounters.

Joanna is sceptical. 'You're just encouraging him,' she grumbles later when we're alone. 'He'll be round all the time now.'

'You're always telling me to get out and about. Well, now I am. I thought you'd be happy.'

She shrugs. 'Just don't drag me into it,' she mutters.

But when Alan comes to pick me up in his battered estate, I can tell she's pleased to see me heading out. I've refused Alan's offer of a pair of second-hand walking boots and I'm instead wearing my nice bright trainers, black leggings, matching hoody and a red Pac-a-mac. He looks at me dubiously.

'Just be careful of your ankles in those,' he says, eyeing my turquoise trainers warily. 'They might get muddy. It's not a catwalk, you know.'

'Life is a catwalk,' I say.

'Vanity thy name is woman,' says Alan, but I think he rather likes what he refers to as my 'feminine ways'.

It's one of those days when the sky is paper white, and there's a strange haze on the horizon where the hills undulate, like the purple-grey outline of a slumbering giant. I dose in the car and wake to find us twisting down narrow lanes into a deep tree-lined valley. I have to crane my neck to see the hills above, their great grassy flanks stretching skywards. Alan changes through the gears and the old car grinds its way up a narrow track until we emerge onto open moors where the heather stretches away like a purple sea all the way to the horizon. We pull up in a small parking area next to a school minibus belonging to a prestigious boarding school.

'Duke of Edinburgh awards,' says Alan. 'The poshos love it up here.'

I can see why. There's something invigorating about being this high. The horizon stretches out and I can see the rolls and folds and crevasses of the land, where the glaciers once pushed through and melt water carved out valleys. This is a place marked by forces that took place over millennia and my troubles seem petty by comparison. I suck in the heather-sweet air. I can breathe properly up here.

I turn and catch Alan watching me. He smiles.

'Beautiful, isn't it? Medicine for the soul.'

He's right. I can relax here. There's no one around. Even the boarders with their backpacks and Ordnance Survey maps are nowhere to be seen. Just some sheep calling to their lambs to stay close as they maraud among the heather.

'There's no one about up here, not in the week, so you don't have to fret about meeting people,' says Alan, reading my mind. He laughs to himself. 'There's no one to hear you scream.'

I give him a sharp look. I know it's a clumsy attempt at a joke but surely even he knows no woman wants to be in the middle of nowhere with a man she doesn't know that well making jokes about murder.

It's funny how much easier it is to walk here. Everyone says the brain is a muscle, well, if so, it's like mine has been clenched into a tight fist since I woke up from the coma and I can almost feel it relaxing, strand by strand, the knots yielding and unwinding as I breathe in the sky, the wind, the lonely call of the circling kite.

Alan talks, a lot. But I seem to be able to handle it better out here in the open, where his voice is half lost on the wind. We pass a couple of walkers, but there's no social expectation: we shout our hellos and nod our greetings but nobody's here to talk. As we muster up a grassy track back towards the car, I find I'm panting hard, not with a panic attack but effort, and my legs shake like a new born lamb's when we finally stop. But it's a good tired and I begin to see a way back to me.

Our walks become a regular feature. Not every week, but at least once a month and I soon build up to seven or eight miles. My muscle tone improves and my leg is much better, as if the connection between foot and brain has somehow managed to rewire. Sometimes we bring James with us, smiling as he splashes through muddy puddles or tries to catch fish in an empty yoghurt pot. Alan's good at voices and keeps James entertained when his little legs tire by acting out skits from his favourite CBeebies show, getting all the voices and silly dances spot on until even I'm laughing.

It's an education too. Alan teaches us how to spot the difference between the tail feathers of a kite and a buzzard, the tell-tale screech of a jay as it bolts through the trees, where to pick wild bilberries. He coaches James in how to skim a stone across a lake as still and shiny as a mirror, and we all holler with delight when James finally gets a stone to skip across the water.

I learn a bit more about Alan, too. His parents worked at a boarding school up north, it's unclear in what capacity. 'I'm used to the ways of the great and the good,' he likes to say 'But we're all the same when it comes down to it. As my old mum used to say, there's no airs and graces when it comes to childbirth, the lavatory or the deathbed.'

Alan worked for an engineering company in Lancashire, making widgets or something for car engines, but was pensioned off early for disability. I've noticed he has a slight limp in his right leg, like me, but he's coy about the details.

'Not all disabilities are visible, you should know that,' he chides when I try to pry.

It's still not clear to me why he left and moved to Shropshire, to a town where he didn't know anyone. Perhaps he has told me but I missed it; his stories are like tangled knots, somewhere there's an end, you pull it and it all comes clear. He's also reticent about his love life – 'Never met the right woman, Sarah. We can't all be as lucky as Joanna' – a comment that feels a little off given Joanna's luck involved her husband dying in a car crash less than two years after they married.

A couple of times he brings his shotgun and teaches me how to use it. I can't bear to shoot any animals but rather enjoy blasting some makeshift targets, my brain waking from some deep slumber as it focuses on the new skill.

'You've got good hand-eye coordination,' says Alan, after I successfully pelt the little wooden skittles he's hidden among the scrub and I positively glow with pride.

Why did nobody else notice that when I was growing up? I remember a PE teacher trying to get me onto the netball team as a shooter but Mother had disapproved. *You don't have time for that, Sarah.* I don't know why we didn't have time; we didn't do anything other than Bible class or handing out leaflets in the local shopping centre to warn the heathens against Sunday opening hours. I wonder what else I might have been good at if I'd ever had the slightest chance to try.

Alan's talking about building up our distance. There's a twenty-mile trail he knows out into the Berwyn Mountains.

'We can work up to that,' he says. 'Do some longer walks. When you're a bit stronger I'll take you up to my bothy. Sometimes I sleep up there if I'm doing a long hike. There are waterfalls, caves and abandoned mine shafts. The system actually runs under my bothy. I'm sure it was a smuggler route once.'

'Smugglers, up here. We're so far from the sea.'

'There used to be smuggling on the River Severn,' he says defensively.

I defer to his knowledge. I am never sure of myself when it comes to learning. I was never a good scholar and my concentration is shot to pieces following the accident. But perhaps I could work on that, like I have the walking, perhaps start on some short books and work my way up.

'Do you think there's buried treasure?' pipes up James, who's been studying a ladybird climbing up his arm.

'Could be, could be,' says Alan. 'People were always bury-ing things in the old days. There were no banks to keep your money safe and there were always armies coming through, plundering your home. It was their right, you see, in the name of the king.'

'Or queen,' says James, loyal to his all-woman household.

'Mainly kings,' says Alan.

That evening as we drop James with Joanna, who's looking pleased with herself after a day alone, Alan asks me to the pub for dinner.

'Come on, it's the early bird at The Chetwynd Arms, and we've earned it after all those hills.'

I hesitate. I don't want to give him the wrong idea. But then he's been so kind taking me walking and entertaining James, it would be churlish to refuse and leave him to another dinner at home alone. But it's an awkward evening. I don't like going out at the best of times and I feel a scruff in my jeans and trainers when the other women in the pub have made a bit of an effort. I don't even have any eyeliner or lipstick with me.

People in here know Alan, and seem delighted he's got com-pany. A couple of people remark on it, friendly enough, but I don't know them – or do I, I can't be sure so I get flustered and hot before we've even sat down.

'Don't mind them,' he says. 'They think we're on a date. They don't realise you're way out of my league.'

He gives a little laugh but I can tell he's waiting for me to correct him, to make some signal that we are, indeed, heading towards date territory. But I am so far from date territory it's like I'm on another planet. I order a glass of wine, to keep him company really, and only mean to have a sip or two but in my anxiety, I drink it too quickly.

I start to talk too much, trying to shut down any oppor-tunity for him to return to the subject of dates. When my food comes – a Moby Dick of a fish with railway sleeper chips and a huge tureen of mushy peas – I wolf it down, desperate to soak up some alcohol and bring the evening to a swift end. But now Alan's so busy talking, stories that seem to drift and collide into one another, that his food goes cold, so I'm sat there with an empty plate willing him to shut up and eat. The waitress collects my plate and tries to take his, not realising he's still eating because it's been so long since he last lifted a bloody fork to his mouth. When he does finally start to eat, the silence is unbearable.

He tries to press me into having a pudding – 'Go on, Sarah, it's not often I get to eat dinner with such a pretty face' – but I have to plead illness. And it's not really a lie. By now, I am hot and panicky and it feels like my heart is skipping a beat – could it be the wine, or maybe all the grease from the fish and chips? I'm sure I will actually be sick or have a heart attack if I don't get out of here soon. Alan's face falls, it's clearly not how he wanted the evening to end, but he's always very solicitous and he quickly settles the bill – refuses all offers of mine to pay – and bundles me into the car. We keep the windows open in case I'm sick, and I virtually run from the car into the house.

Joanna switches off the TV, takes one look at me and gives me the 'told you so' look.

'I did warn you you'd be leading him up the garden path. Alan's vulnerable, Sarah, he's not just some fellow from a bar you can pick up and put down. This is our next-door neighbour, a lonely man, you can't mess around like you did before because we have to live next to him. What did you think he'd start thinking?'

My mouth falls open. Alan, vulnerable! I'm the vulnerable one, clawing my way back to life. And her moral tone. So what if I messed around when I was young? I was free and single and hot. Sometimes she really does sound like Mother.

84

After that I start to dodge Alan. We do a few more walks, always with James, our little chaperone, but I start to make excuses, first it's my leg, then it's a bad bout of flu – and that's no lie, I am properly ill for three weeks and wiped out for almost two months – and after that we sort of lose our routine. But he still takes James sometimes. They come back with ladybirds in jars, a collection of pheasant feathers, once a sheep's skull bleached white by the sun. Joanna accepts these treasures with good grace. After all, Alan's nature walks buy her spare time at the weekend for shopping or reading the paper over a long lunch. And none of us think it's strange that James' closest friend is a man in his fifties.

Chapter Fifteen

It is PC Crown who arrives to take me home. James left early this morning, saying he needs to be back at work. I tried to dissuade him, I'm sure the drivers of Shropshire can manage without his talents for another week or so, but he's adamant he needs to stay busy.

He's given me a list of things to do – call the solicitor, the bank, the life insurance company and the Department of Work and Pensions. 'You have to think practically, Aunty Sarah,' he'd said, reading the rising panic on my face as I read through the list. 'There will be bills to pay and you don't want to miss out on anything you're due.'

'When did you get to be so grown up?' I asked, looking up at him through a screen of tears, heavy with guilt. It should be me in charge, making lists and thinking about the practicalities. I mustn't be a burden on him. It was bad enough that I dragged Joanna down.

'It's a hard knock life on the mean streets of Shrewsbury,' he said, a wry smile on his face.

'Never change, James,' I said, holding my palm against his cheek. 'You're a good boy and your mum adored you.'

We couldn't say much after that. We both started crying, even though I'd promised myself I'd hold it together and wouldn't burden him with my distress. He tried to hide his tears, and shuffled off, embarrassed, hoisting his backpack over his shoulder, just a casual wave goodbye. I wanted to say so much more to him. I should have told him how much I love him, how he's my nephew and I'll look after him. He can stay in Market Leyton with me, get back on his feet, re-sit those exams. He's a bright boy, he shouldn't be wasting his talents working in a petrol station. He just needs a little direction, a little time to find himself.

Outside, it's a cold day, white clouds scudding quickly across a blue sky. The stiff breeze and the bright daylight are an assault on my senses after so many days cooped up in the air-conditioned, mood-lit cocoon of the hotel room. My teeth clatter together violently but I'm not sure whether it's the cold spring day or my fear.

'We'll soon warm this baby up,' says my police escort, PC Casey Crown, fiddling with the controls on her car.

I manage a weak smile but inside I'm in torment. With every mile we travel, it feels like the house is winding us in on an invisible thread, dragging us back not only across town to the scene of the murder but across time, to that moment when a man almost choked the life out of me and then stood over my sister and stabbed her to death.

Fear twists my bowels, spikes my heart rate. What if he is watching the house, waiting for me? What if he is lying in wait to finish the job? Would PC Casey Crown be able to hold him off? But as the car slides down the High Street, past the charity shops, Boots and the kids loitering outside Greggs, it is the sense of loss I dread most, that moment when I confront the inescapable reality that I will never again walk in to find Joanna singing along to Radio 2, never again get to grumble as she watches her shows or share a laugh over pictures of the latest catwalk creations in the Sunday papers: what we liked to call the 'Prosopagnosia Collection' for their eye-catching monstrosity. I don't think anybody else will ever understand me. Joanna and I learned together how to manage my condition, how to make it work so I could function. It was all my other issues we couldn't cope with.

We turn onto Cheshire Row, past the library and up towards the Co-op. We are only about a minute from home now, and I fight a desperate urge to fling open the car door and run. We're not going fast, how much harm could it do? It couldn't feel any worse than this rising panic, for I am sure I'm about to enter cardiac arrest.

I'm distracted by the opening of the car window.

'Breathe,' instructs Crown. 'And for Christ sakes, if you're going to be sick do it out of the window.'

She is remarkably perceptive for someone who should be 100 per cent focused on the road. I have often noticed that people who don't jabber on do tend to be more sensitive. I suppose your brain can focus on other things if it's not constantly having to generate a stream of verbal consciousness.

And here we are. Speldhurst Road, an anonymous row of 1970s houses. Brown boxes with big windows, comfortable-sized rooms and long back gardens, but undeniably drab. A bit like Joanna, I used to think. Now I feel nothing but a rush of love for the place she worked so hard to make a home.

'This is where we became our own little family,' she used to say, enjoying a glass of wine in the back garden on the bench under her climbing pink rose, catching the last of the evening sun. Gertrude Jekyll, that was the name of the rose. She'd planted it so she could see its blousy blooms from the kitchen window as she did the washing up. She was always trying to make the best of everything. Even me.

'Got you house trained at last,' she used to joke when I took out the bins or emptied the dishwasher.

'But can a dog change a fuse?' I would laugh back, proud that I was always better at the handy tasks than her.

'I was thinking you're more like a husband,' she'd said, 'but better because you don't leave the toilet seat up.'

'And we'll never get divorced either,' I'd said, trying to keep the joke running. But somehow it fell flat. I don't suppose either of us wanted to think we were yoked to one another for ever, that things might never change for the better.

Well, now they've changed but we didn't divorce. It was 'til death us do part. Oh Joanna, why did it have to be you? Tears run down my cheeks again. I try to wipe them away surreptitiously, but it's like I've sprung a leak and can't stop.

'Tissues in the glove box,' says Crown.

A wad of aloe vera infused tissues soon turn into a sodden ball as I mop up my tears. Crown pulls up outside the house and gives me a moment to collect myself. There's a snowdrift of floral tributes against the wall, cellophane-wrapped bouquets and posies, a couple of teddies and some candles.

We get out of the car and I stop to look at them. I never knew Joanna had so many friends. I read some of the cards, furtively: it feels like I'm reading someone else's mail, but really, Joanna will never see these so who are they addressed to but me? *Rest in peace, beautiful lady*, says the childish scrawl on a bunch of petrol station carnations. *God bless you, angel in heaven*. A small teddy holds a red heart that reads, *Remember Me*.

I don't know why strangers would feel compelled to do this – some people have a very strange response to tragedy. I personally would steer as far away as possible. I wonder if there was a shrine of flowers at the scene of the accident when Robert died.

One bouquet stands out, beautiful big yellow roses – Joanna's favourite – hand-tied in brown paper and twine, very arty and a cut above the rest. I stoop to check the creamy white card. *Joanna, RIP. I will always remember you. Simon.*

My heart lurches and I instinctively look over my shoulder, as if he might be lurking down the street.

'Everything all right?' asks Crown, following my glance and squinting down the street. 'Come on, I think we should get you inside.'

I nod, and follow her over the churned-up gravel to the front door, my mind whirling. How would Simon know what had happened to Joanna? We thought he'd left the country years ago. How long has he been back? And did Joanna know?

'The tributes are something, aren't they?' says Crown. She's noticed how it's shaken me and gives me a reassuring smile.

'There was one from her old boyfriend.' It seems the right thing to do to tell her. It could be important, him suddenly turning up like this.

'Any reason to think he'd want to hurt Joanna?'

My mind spins. There was a time I thought Simon was harmless, boring even. But then he went and surprised us all.

Chapter Sixteen

Eight years ago

I love it when Joanna has a first date. She gets so nervous she likes to have a cheeky G&T and she pulls me in for giggles and reassurance, almost as if we're friends. I can tell she has high hopes for this one though she worries he's too far way, in the Cotswolds, the very outer limits of her search radius. 'It's not that far,' I say. 'You could meet halfway.'

Not today, though. For their first date he's making the trip. He likes to drive, apparently. She's picked the venue, a fancy restaurant with decking and fairy lights that look out onto the River Severn. She'd shown me the emails, fizzing with excitement.

You pick where you feel safe. It's a big deal meeting an ~~axe-wielding psychopath~~ lovely guy you've met off the Internet.

He signed himself just as an S, which I thought was a bit of an affectation. It's not like Simon is a long name. Looking at the menu online, I note that starters are eight pounds, mains at least twenty-five. The cheapest bottle of wine is thirty pounds.

'It hasn't put him off,' she says, her eyes gleaming.

'Maybe he's expecting you to pay,' I point out. 'This is the twenty-first century.'

'I always pay my share,' she says. 'And I'd happily pay it all for a nice evening out and some decent grub. I can't face The Swan again.'

There's a honk outside; her taxi is here. She kisses James on the top of his head, and he draws his eyes away from *Doctor Who*. 'What's that smell?' he asks.

'Chanel, darling. Very expensive.'

He nods, and drifts back to his programme. He's at that funny age now, on the threshold of those difficult teenage years, but right now, in his pyjamas and his fluffy slippers, his hair still wet from his bath, he still looks like a young kid. I feel a pang of something, a sort of funny yearning that this is what I've missed out on, a kid of my own. Maybe I should get myself on Match.com. I've still got time.

'He'll be fine,' I reassure Joanna. 'We'll just watch this, then another chapter of *Harry Potter*.'

I follow her out into the hall, where she's hovering, fussing with the belt on her wrap around dress. 'You look lovely,' I say. 'Bring me a doggy bag.'

She flashes me a grin. 'I'm not sure places like this do doggy bags.'

'Places like that do whatever you want as long as you're paying,' I say, like I would know. The last place I ate out was a Little Chef on the way to some retail park near Manchester.

The house always deflates a little after she leaves. One day, I think, pouring myself another gin, she'll go on a date and it will be the beginning of the end of our life here. She will meet someone and want to start again, which means I will have to start again. The enormity of it makes me feel dizzy, or perhaps it's just too much gin on an empty stomach.

We end up watching two *Doctor Who*s and then some other trash about cars, and then it's too late for Hogwarts, which doesn't seem to bother James but I'm itching to read. He climbs into bed, lying straight and neat under his star-print duvet like a little toy soldier.

'Is she coming back?' He always asks this if she goes out in the evening. I suppose it's natural for a child who has already lost one parent.

'Of course,' I say. 'She's just having a nice meal with a friend and then she'll be home. But you'll be fast asleep by then.'

'I won't,' he says, earnestly. 'I am going to stay awake.'

'OK, you do that,' I smile. I can tell by the drowsy heaviness of his eyes that he's ready for sleep. I am an expert when it comes to sleep. 'Sweet dreams.'

She comes back at midnight, a proper Cinderella. I'm asleep on the sofa but I wake up at the sound of tyres on gravel, the thwump of a car door. I peer out through the front curtains and catch a glimpse of a Bentley and a tall, heavily-built man in a suit, murmuring to Joanna in the glow of the dipped headlights. I pull back, and wait in the kitchen, the kettle on ready for the debrief. The key turns in the door, there's a murmur of voices, a low laugh, and then the sound of a car reversing. I can tell straight away from the glow in her cheeks and the little secret smile that it's been a successful date.

'You like?' I ask.

She smiles, raises her eyebrows. 'Tolerable,' she says, but the little smile on her lips betrays her true feelings. She peels off her high heels and loosens the belt on her dress. 'That's better.'

'Should I make space in my VIP book?' I probe.

She smiles that little smile again. 'There's potential.'

'Impressive wheels.'

She doesn't comment, her eyes on her phone. Texting already, she must be keen.

'The bill?'

She lets out a low whistle. 'But he wouldn't let me touch it. Very old school. But it will be my treat next time.'

'There's going to be a next time?'

She warms her hands round her mug of peppermint tea. 'I really, really hope so.' Her face is radiant, an inner light bringing a glow to her skin, a sparkle to her eyes. I know that look; it's not just the giddy flush of hormones through her system, it's hope. I feel a stab of jealousy. Will I ever feel like that again?

There's a movement in the doorway. 'What are you doing up?' cries Joanna.

James stares at us, his face pale and pinched and his hair mussed from the pillow. 'I told you I would still be awake.'

'He was worried you wouldn't come home,' I explain to Joanna.

'Oh, James.' She moves towards him and gives him a cuddle. 'Don't be silly. Of course I was coming home.'

He doesn't say anything but I can guess what he's thinking: Dad didn't come back.

Chapter Seventeen

The first thing that hits me is the smell, a strange chemical undertone, and then the air, cold and damp, like the house already knows the heart of it has gone. The door has been fixed and new locks fitted, though the paint is scuffed and chipped where the police forced entry. There's the faintest smear at the bottom of the stairs where my bloodied hand touched the wall just before he kicked me to the floor. The horror of that night fizzes before me and I bend over and retch violently, vomit splattering the floor and skirting boards.

'Oh God, sorry, sorry,' I mumble, hastily wiping tears from my eyes.

Crown looks at me with sympathy. 'It's OK, Sarah. Are you all right? We don't have to do this now.'

I shake my head. Despite the terrible memories, this is still my home. I function better here than anywhere else and to leave now wouldn't solve anything. I would still have to walk into the kitchen at some point.

I point towards the kitchen door. 'Come on,' I say, my voice scratchy from the vomit. I cough, tasting bile, and force myself to take a long deep breath as we step into the ground zero of my life. The kitchen smells of bleach and lemon and polish. At once my eyes are drawn to the floor, the spot where I found

Joanna. The wood has been scoured and scrubbed but I can still see the outline, like the tidemark on a beach, where her blood pooled.

The night flashes before me again. The speed of the pink knife, that little gasping noise she made. Did she know she was dying then? Did it hurt? I have to think it was painless, I have to, or I don't think I could bear to go on.

'I did try to stop him, you know,' I say, my eyes still mesmerised by the rust-red blood stain. 'I tried, but he was so strong.'

I am choked by tears again but they are angry tears, angry at him, and at myself, for being so fucking impotent. 'I tried but I just couldn't stop him. I don't want you to think I didn't try.'

Crown is a blur through my tears. I wish I knew what she was thinking. I am desperate for her to believe me.

'Who would do this to us? Who?'

'That's what we're working on,' she says. 'We'll get there, don't worry.'

I notice she doesn't say, 'We'll find him, don't worry.' Does she suspect me? I picture myself curled up on the floor next to my sister's dead body, the pink knife in my hand. Of course she suspects me. They all do.

I cannot settle. I have a shower and dress in clean clothes, examining my cuts and bruises. Already the deep cut on my hand is knitting together. The human body's ability to heal is amazing and I can't help stewing over whether Joanna could have been saved. What if I'd been able to apply more pressure to the wounds or if I had been able to disarm the man and call an ambulance? Was she still alive when he knocked me out? If I'd been able to get away, perhaps she could have been saved. All those hours I sat and stared at the planes out of my bedroom window or sulked around the kitchen, I should have been making better use of my time, I should have learned karate or boxing or first aid, anything, anything that might have made a difference.

I keep the curtains drawn and the lights on. Being back here, I feel her presence everywhere. I keep turning to say something to Joanna, keep expecting to hear her key in the door or to see her sitting outside with a coffee, and every time another wave of grief washes through me.

I wander into the living room, thinking back to that night. *What's he doing here?* She knew him, and she didn't seem scared of him. Could it have been Simon? Wouldn't she have expressed some surprise to see him back here, after all this time, after everything that happened? Unless he was the mystery man? But why wouldn't she tell me, how could she keep something like that to herself?

It strikes me there was so much of Joanna's life that was invisible to me. My whole life was laid out for her, like an exhibit in a display case for her to approve and tweak and control. Her life, however, was more like an iceberg and I only saw the bit bobbing along on top; where she kept house, watched her shows, fussed over me and James, and grumbled about not having enough time to read the books for her book club. But under the surface, she had a whole hidden life going on: her work, her colleagues, her Internet-dating misadventures, her crafters class – all that bloody bunting! – and her time on Facebook and Mumsnet. She went to spa weekends now and then – she took me once, and it's the kind of idle anonymous time wasting that I can get behind, but I was never invited again. Perhaps she didn't like my company, we didn't speak much all weekend but I thought that was the point. So, who did she go with the other times? Names would float by in conversation, Carmen from work, Jilly from crafters and the book club crew. But were there other people? Did she take men with her? And if so why did she keep them secret? It's not like I would tell anyone.

I drift upstairs into Joanna's room, her pretty bedding pulled tight and the cushions arranged just so. There's a framed artwork, James' handprint aged four, and a wicker heart ornament with a chalkboard slogan: *Home is where the heart is*. She was a sucker for shabby chic tat.

On her dressing table there are favourite photos in gilt frames. Joanna and Rob on their wedding day, my sister radiant in her big dress, Rob's hand skimming her waist. Another of the wedding party, I am apparently the one in the green dress and Mother is the older lady in the severe blue suit. My favourite photo is one of me, Joanna and James eating ice-creams on the seafront at Aberdovey. I know the photographs are of us because who else would they be, here in our house, but I can't recognise them. Joanna could have stuck in pictures from magazines and told me it was us and it would be all the same to me.

I catch a face in the mirror and there's that usual nano-second of shock – who's that woman? – before I accept it must be me. My skin is so pale you can see blue veins, my throat is mottled purple, black and green, and there's a visible twitch in one cheek. I need sleep but I'm too agitated to lie down.

James' old room looks cold and bare, his empty single bed forlorn, the mattress bare and the hangers in the wardrobe naked. The emptiness is like a reproach. He should be home with me. We need each other. It's silly for him to be at work at a time like this. I will call him in the morning, make his bed and air his room. And that's when I notice: the computer in his room has gone. There's a square outlined in dust where it's been removed. I head downstairs, and check the living room. Joanna's laptop has gone too.

Then I remember something the police said ... I find the

leaflets the police gave me and rummage through until I find the paperwork that tells me they have taken the computers and our mobile phones as evidence. Oh shit. The computer in James' room was my lifeline to the outside world. How will I shop or bank or log in to my chatroom?

I think about my online friends from the head trauma support forum, where I post as BettyBoo72. We have never met, we don't even know each other's real names, yet sometimes it is only a motivational cat meme or jokey emoji from fellow survivors that gets me through the day. I like to think I was a support to them too. If I anonymised some of the details, would I dare tell my online friends about what's happened? No, I think not. It would be too identifying, given the murder has been on the news and I certainly wouldn't want to be publicly linked to some of BettyBoo72's comments. It's better people don't see the real me right now.

Chapter Eighteen

I can hear the church bells, golden notes tumbling through the sky, a peal of joy, again and again. It must be a wedding, because I'm wearing a beautiful dress that froths and swirls round my legs as I dance. Is it my wedding? The dress is white, and all eyes are on me. Their attention is better than champagne, and I laugh and sway giddily, drunk on love. A hand touches my flat belly, and a strong arm, black hairs coiled under white cuffs, snakes round my waist. I turn in delight and lift my face for a kiss but before our lips touch, my eyes open and I pull back as if burnt.

I wake up with a gasp, my heart racing. The man in my dream, the man I was about to kiss, it was Rob, I know it was. It's the strangest feeling to recognise someone again, even just in a dream. I can barely remember Robert and I can't recognise faces, yet there, in my dream, I knew that man was my sister's dead husband. Why am I dreaming about Rob? It must be from looking at the photographs earlier. Somehow those wedding day images have stuck in my brain and merged into my usual dreamscape.

I wander back into Joanna's room and pick up the wedding photo, picturing myself in the white dress, Rob's arm round my waist, everyone toasting us. Rob was handsome, and he had a sort of reckless confidence that appeals to me, based on my hazy recollections of my torrid teenage passions, the ill-advised assignations with unsuitable men that marked my twenties, and the fantasies that are the closest I now get to romance. Not at all Joanna's type but then they do say opposites attract. By that reasoning, what I probably need is a sensible man, an accountant or lawyer, who likes books about military history and spends every Sunday washing the car while I take the kids to ballet or football. It's the kind of future I would once have sneered at. Now it just makes me want to cry with longing.

There's a knock on the door and I almost drop the photograph. I set it down carefully, as if someone outside might be able to hear me, and tiptoe to the top of the stairs. I glimpse a shadowy figure through the glass and there's another firm knock as a woman's voice calls out.

'Sarah, you in, love?'

I try to place the voice but it's beyond me. It's not PC Casey Crown, I'm sure, nor DS Noor; neither of them is a 'love' kind of person. Could it be Sam Nowak from victim support? Her voice escapes me, and she is the kind of person to 'love' or 'sweetheart' me. Do I ignore the caller – my preference – or risk the potential consequences of avoiding police questioning? I decide to let fate decide by walking very slowly down the stairs; if the woman gives up and goes away before I get there, then the decision is taken out of my hands. I will have tried my best.

But the woman waits patiently. She sees my figure approach, and says, with relief, 'There you are, love.' I open the door cautiously to see a young woman, shoulder-length brown hair and a sprinkle of freckles. She gives me a sympathetic head tilt. 'Hello, Sarah, love, how are you?'

She says it like I should know who she is. She hands me a shop-bought cake in a big cardboard and cellophane box. It's carrot cake with thick icing, one of my favourites. Do I know her, or is the cake a lucky guess? I can't place her voice.

'Couldn't believe it, I mean, you don't expect it round here, do you? I'm so sorry for your loss. Your sister was a lovely lady, one of the good ones, wasn't she?'

I nod. I suppose she was. I look down at the cake. It's a big one. How will I eat all this? Perhaps the woman sees my confusion, because she's talking at me again.

'I'm so daft, aren't I? A cake. I just didn't know what to say or what would be appropriate. Here, let me take that through for you, those cuts look sore.'

And before I can say anything, she's taken the box from my hands and has edged past me into the hall.

'Through here, is it, love?' she says, nodding down the hall.

She must see the faint outline where the bloody handprint has been scrubbed away but she doesn't say anything and walks through to the kitchen, setting the box onto the worktop. The smell of bleach is overpowering.

'Lovely view from here over the garden,' says the woman, looking out at Joanna's roses and the big trees at the bottom of the garden, where a swing sways forlornly in the breeze. 'They built these houses with families in mind, didn't they? Lots of space. Not like these new builds on the new estate near Morrisons. No space to swing a cat, never mind room for kids to run about. You any idea how he got in?'

I'm shocked by the sudden change in direction. The woman has turned to face me again and I notice her eyes stray to the floor and the faint outline that marks the spot where Joanna died.

'Is that where it happened? Oh love, how are you coping?'

I clear my throat. 'I'm sorry, I don't know you, I'm sorry, my head is all—'

She cuts over me. 'Of course, darling, don't apologise. It's me, Lisa, your neighbour from down at number thirty-two. Just down the road. We're just all in shock. When it's so close to home. Here, let me make you a cuppa, love, you look done in.'

She busies herself with the kettle, opening and shutting cabinet doors while I wonder if she's one of the neighbours who was interviewed on the TV news. I'm amazed at how confident she is, quickly finding her bearings in this strange kitchen, finding milk, teabags, teaspoons, but then I remind myself she might have been here before when she was visiting Joanna. She's rattling on, cutting me a slab of cake. It's very good, moist and with thick icing, which is always the best bit.

We settle down in the living room, me careful to make sure she doesn't sit in Joanna's spot. She hides a lot of questions amid her chatter and I try to answer; it seems churlish not to when she's been so kind and I do feel a bit better with the tea and cake inside me.

'Have the police got any leads?' she asks. 'I hate to think of this fella out there. We've got kids to think of.'

I shake my head. 'I don't know what they're thinking.'

'They took you off for a while . . .' Lisa lets it hang, while she cuts me another slice of cake. 'Just tidying the edges, love.'

'Mm.' I don't really know what to say.

'Mind if I make use of your facilities, love? Pelvic floor shot to pieces after kids. No, you stay there. I'll pop these in the kitchen and then nip up. I know where it is.'

She picks up the coffee mugs and bustles out. I eat my second slice of cake and wonder what Mother would say about two servings of cake for breakfast. It's exactly the kind of decadence that she always warned would lead straight to hell. Carrot cake as a gateway drug. The thought almost makes me snort with laughter but I catch myself as the door opens and Lisa comes back in. She shoots me a strange look, and I think how it must look: bereaved sister, laughing as she eats cake in the house where her sister was brutally murdered just days ago.

'Good cake, isn't it? It's from Irwin's, the little bakery in Salters Court. You should try their coffee cake, to die for.' There's an awkward pause.

'It was delicious, thank you. It was very thoughtful of you.'

She beams. 'You're welcome love. Look, I'd better go. I'll pop round another time. It's times like this you need friends and neighbours. We need to pull together, stand up for our community.' She steps towards me, and enfolds me in an awkward embrace. She's small and light and highly fragranced, notes of Oil of Olay and Elnett hairspray: the scents of my teenage rebellion.

'You stay there, love, I'll let myself out.'

But I follow her doggedly through the hall; I want to make sure the front door is properly locked. I go into the front room, and peer out through the curtains and watch Lisa turn through the gate, where there are more people gathered. She has a quick word with them, and they look up and stare towards the house. I shrink back, suddenly scared.

I go back to the kitchen, and look at the cake, and the neatly washed mugs now drying on the side. I replay the conversation in my head, all those questions, my stumbling answers. I wonder how many more neighbours will be round, bringing cake and sympathy to sate their curiosity? I crouch down and put my hand to the blood stain, as if some trace of DNA could connect me to Joanna. But there's nothing, just the slightly gritty feel of the floor, a powdery trace of cleaning product on my fingers.

I sit there on the kitchen floor, stewing over my visitor. I hear the phone ring and it goes to voicemail: it's Dr Monks, calling to let me know he's left a repeat prescription for all my meds at the dispensary and pleading with me to get in touch if

I need anything at this difficult time. I breathe a little lighter, knowing my meds are waiting for me. My anxiety is ramped so high I feel like my jaw could snap and my brain is stuck in a rut, brooding obsessively about Lisa's visit.

She was friendly enough to come around with cake, so why can't I remember Joanna ever talking about her? I know I wasn't much for neighbourly relations but surely even I'd remember someone who knew us well enough to know her way about our house. The thought is like an itch. My mind scratches at it obsessively. Lisa, from number 32. I get out my VIP book and look through the neighbours, reading Joanna's neat captions carefully. There's Alan. There's Mary across the road with her poodle, Pickins. I remember she was very particular when we took the photo that Joanna spelt Pickins' name right. There's no photo for Number 28 – it's let out to students and has a never-ending array of young faces and cheap cars parked outside. They're pretty studious though, and don't make much noise. Number 30 is the Shahs, who tend to keep to themselves, though they're unfailingly polite and the kids haul huge school bags from that grammar school. There's a gap where the photo for Number 32 should be and just a brief caption – *Dennis and Elsie* – in Joanna's stylish hand. My breath catches in my throat. Has Lisa somehow removed the photo for Number 32? Did I get the name wrong? Lisa, Elsie, they use a lot of the same letters, after all. Did my brain jumble them around, or did Joanna write the wrong name in the first place? Or maybe Dennis is divorced and Lisa is his new woman? I can't rest, scratching away at this.

I wander the house restlessly and spray on some White Musk, taking comfort in Joanna's scent. I am used to my own company and it's not like Joanna and I lived in one another's pockets but the weight of the emptiness presses down on me.

Minutes drag. Even my breath sounds loud in the ringing emptiness of the house.

I begin to feel the familiar panic build and know I need to do something to avoid a full-blown attack. I scour the house for some meds and find some expired Valium at the back of my knicker drawer. I crunch down a couple, and then open a bottle of red. Just half a glass, enough to take the edge off. Pacing restlessly, I find myself in the hall again. Number 32. It's just five houses down. I could run it in under a minute and at least it would put these obsessive thoughts to bed. I pull on my denim jacket and trainers and then don't give myself time to think, out of the door before my anxiety has time to paralyse me.

It's raining now, spitting like muted gunfire on the cellophane wrappers of the shrine; drowning the little tea lights. I run down the road, and it's good to feel the raindrops in my eyes, the slap of the breeze in my face. I'm panting by the time I reach number 32. It's a neat house with a Honda Jazz parked in the drive, the lawn lined with hydrangeas. I hesitate, trying to calm my breathing and work out what I'm going to say. The cake, I'll thank her again for the cake. It was very kind of her.

But it's an old man who comes to the door. He's a little gaunt and stooped at the shoulders, with white hairs sprouting from his eyebrows and a tuffet of blood-stained tissue paper on his chin where he's nicked himself shaving. He looks a little infirm, his hands have that old-man shake, and he eyes me warily. At first I think it's because he's on guard for scammers but it quickly becomes clear he's confused. And my visit only makes thing worse.

'Lisa, Lisa? There's no Lisa here. Who are you?'

'I'm Sarah from number twenty-two. A lady called Lisa visited me, she said she lived here.'

'Lived here? There's no one here.'

'What about Elsie?' I ask desperately, though I already know Elsie won't be the young, Elnett-fan who visited me earlier.

'Elsie? What do you want with Elsie?' He starts to get agitated, he's shaking his head and his rheumy eyes brim with tears. 'Have you seen her? Is she coming home?'

He steps outside and starts looking up and down the street. 'Is she coming? Where did you see her?'

'No, no,' I say, getting worried. 'Please, Dennis, let's get you back inside. There's been a mistake. Come on, let's get you inside.'

I grab hold of his arm, but he flaps me aside like a fly. He's surprisingly strong now he's all worked up.

'Elsie! Elsie!' He's shouting loudly, looking around wildly. 'Come in, love. I'll get us a bit of tea. Elsie!'

He turns to me, big tears streaking down his face. 'I know she's been looking for me. She's gets lost, you see. Elsie!'

The commotion attracts attention and a dark-skinned man in a suit comes over from next door.

'Dennis, Dennis, what's the matter, mate?' He turns to me, and whispers. 'What's happened, who are you?'

'I'm looking for someone called Lisa. She told me she lived here but it got him all upset,' I say, wiping my face. 'I didn't mean ... she told me she lived here...'

'Don't you live down the road?' asks the man, who now has Dennis by the wrist and is stroking his hand gently. 'Where that poor lady—'

'Yes, my sister.' I start crying again. This has been a terrible mistake. The old man is still babbling about Elsie, calling for her, like animals do when they're separated.

'I'm so sorry for your loss,' says the man, and it's not clear who he's speaking to, me or Dennis. 'Help me, can you? He'll calm down in a bit, when we get him in.'

Dennis' hand is soft and dry, like old paper. His nails are too long, I notice, and I guess he's only just managing to keep up appearances. Now that I'm close to him I can see there's a stain on his pullover, and there's that old-man smell, like he doesn't wash enough. I know what that's like; it's so easy to let things slide when you realise no one will notice if you wash or not, eat or not, live or not. Inside, the house is still neat and tidy, though the air is stale. It's a house where the business of living is slowly being suffocated by the business of dying.

The neighbour introduces himself as Mo Shah. He's clearly dealt with Dennis before, and with great tact and consideration settles the old man in the front room. Dennis sits in a well-worn high-backed armchair, the arms a little shiny with use and an embroidered cushion moulded to the shape of his back. Next to him there's a little table topped with a lace cover, where all his essentials are at hand: the remote, some pills, a box of tissues, the local paper, a pair of spectacles. I wonder how much time he spends in this chair all by himself. Mo goes into the kitchen while I sit with Dennis, perched self-consciously on the edge of the sofa, aware I'm probably defiling Elsie's spot. And I can't help thinking I'm looking at my future, slowly going mad with loneliness and grief, locked in my house, staring across at Joanna's empty spot.

Mo comes in with a cup of tea for Dennis and then walks me to the door.

'Where's Elsie?' I ask.

'She passed two years ago. It hit Dennis very hard. They'd been married fifty-one years. He's deteriorated a lot in the last year. I'm not sure how long he'll be able to keep on living alone. Who was it you were looking for?'

'Lisa. A young woman. She visited me earlier today, said she lived at number thirty-two.'

Mo thinks, sucking on his teeth. He has very smooth skin, like a polished horse chestnut, but I see now the flecks of grey in his hair, the laughter lines at his eyes. 'I can't think of any Lisas. You're sure it was this road?'

I nod, sadly. 'I didn't mean to upset Dennis. I'm not very good with people.'

'You're having a rough time,' he said. 'I'm so sorry. You've got a son, haven't you?'

'Nephew.'

'Will he be coming back now?'

I blush. It feels like a dirty secret that he's away at a time like this. 'We're not sure yet. We're both in shock.'

Mo nods. 'Well, if you need anything, you know where I am. I'd better get back in now, make sure Dennis is OK.'

'Thank you, you're very kind.'

I wander home, unable to shake the feeling that the houses are watching me, unseen people peering out, judging me. I wonder if Lisa is behind any of these doors, watching me, laughing at my mistake.

I make some tea and fetch the VIP book and that's when I notice it. A couple of pictures have come unstuck and have drifted down the side of the sofa. One is of a young woman – the name is Charlene Walker, who I think used to run the playgroup in the church hall, she was pally with Joanna for a few years – and the other is of an elderly couple, leaning on their garden gate. I check the back. *Dennis and Elsie, number 32.* Dennis looks stronger in this photo, a casual confidence in the way he stands at his gate, his arm resting on his wife's shoulders, her smile a little frozen. Did they know then, were the first signs already evident of Elsie's illness, of his creeping dementia, of the great sadness that would soon crash down on them?

I flick through the pictures in the book. One of these people could have killed my sister. Here's Carmen, Joanna's friend from work, with her olive skin and that stripe of silver in her dark hair. There are so many people that have drifted in and out of our lives, mainly out: it seems like the years have shrunk our world to a small core of people. There are names in this book I haven't heard for years. Simona, the mobile hairdresser. I liked her. Why did we lose touch with her? Barry and Jean who lived opposite. They moved to Abersoch on the Welsh coast. We had postcards for a couple of years and then nothing.

On another page I come across Simon Carmichael. I'm surprised to see his photo still in here. The other men Joanna had dated for any material period of time – a Brummie called Paul who liked to take her horse-racing but dropped her when his ex-wife clicked her fingers, and then there was the charmer in the Paul Smith suit who we dubbed the philandering pensioner after it emerged he had two other women on the go at the same time – had both had their photos unceremoniously binned. Yet Simon Carmichael has survived. I stare at his photo: he was a plain-looking fellow but he had an openness about his face, a smile that reached his eyes, that made you feel he was comfortable in his skin. He was easy if not scintillating company, nothing to dislike. I suppose you could say he was a good match for Joanna until the end when he'd disappeared without a trace. Gone abroad, we'd heard from his landlord. We suspected an unknown wife had finally put her foot down. That had been three or four years ago now, and yet she'd kept his photo. I chew on my thumbnail, peering again at the photograph. Was he back, and if so, had Joanna found something out about him, something he'd be prepared to kill for?

Chapter Nineteen

I have been expecting the police but even so it's a shock to have two detectives flashing their ID on the doorstep. For some reason their very presence makes me feel guilty and I'm sure they pick up on it, which makes me overcompensate by actively trying to act innocent – and I *am* innocent – but that just means I'm stiff, unnatural and look guilty as hell.

They make an odd pairing: a petite dark-haired lady in a grey trouser suit with a pixie cut that only emphasises her youth, and a large man, carrying too much weight around his belly and a sheen of sweat on his upper lip. There's a strange expectant pause when I open the door. I am almost certain the lady is DS Noor but I don't want to risk getting it wrong. I also sense this is a test: she's waiting to see if this prosopagnosia is real, or if it's some elaborate ploy to somehow conceal my role in Joanna's murder, and I'm determined not to fall into her trap.

The woman smiles at me, a strange little nod of recognition: she knows I know her game. She flashes her ID badge – it *is* DS Noor – and introduces her tubby sidekick as DC Rawlinson. He's older than her – though that's not hard – and I wonder how that dynamic plays out.

I take them into the living room, where we're confronted

by unwashed mugs, a sad mound of used tissues, the blanket and pillow on the sofa where I sleep. I kick yesterday's worn knickers under the sofa but not quickly enough to escape Rawlinson's sneer, and clear a space on the sofa, where DS Noor perches neatly, her legs crossed, showing off a beautiful pair of black high heels. I notice how delicate her ankles are, her wrists as thin as a child's. Don't police have to do a fitness and strength test? I'm not sure how either Noor or Rawlinson would have passed.

Noor dispatches Rawlinson into the kitchen to make teas. I wonder how he feels at being bossed about by someone who doesn't look old enough to buy alcohol never mind lead a murder investigation. I can hear him crashing about and am itching to go in and supervise. I wonder whether he's tempted by the remains of the giant carrot cake and realise I must stop making judgments based on people's size. It's a legacy from Mother, who was zero tolerance on what she called 'gluttony'. What would Mother make of me now: eighty per cent carrot cake and twenty per cent diazepam.

Noor wants to talk to me about my medications. She has a sheaf of paper in her hands but it's angled so I can't read what it says. There have been so many over the years: tramadol for pain, sertraline for depression, Xanax for anxiety and countless others. There were ones we called the fizzy blues, that made me giddy, and one anti-depressant we called the blob because I put on so much weight. It's a mark of my recovery that I'm now on a pared-back regime, just pregabalin for anxiety and panic attacks from Dr Monks and sometimes painkillers from Dr Lucas.

'You're on medication, Sarah?' asks Noor, reading from her notes.

'Yes, for anxiety.' I'm aware I'm anxiously wringing my hands like a supplicant before the king and force my hands between my knees to keep them still. 'TBIs, traumatic brain injuries, can make it hard to function sometimes.'

Noor nods as she reads through her notes again. Rawlinson comes back in with mugs of tea, and gives a knowing glance to Noor. I bet he's been snooping. I don't know what they expect to find. I have nothing to hide.

'And what's the advice on drinking alcohol when you take these drugs?'

'It's frowned on but I don't drink very much. Joanna wouldn't let me.'

'Did you argue about that?'

Did we? Not really, it was a campaign of sighs and eye-rolls and barbed comments. I just seethed quietly and took what I could get. It was the tone for our whole relationship, really.

Noor has already moved on. 'We need to talk about your social media use, Sarah. We've looked at your Facebook page.'

I snort with laughter then. 'Facebook, what use is that to me?'

'It's not just pictures of faces,' says Rawlinson, like I'm an idiot. 'People use it to post messages. You can read and write, can't you?'

I don't like his tone, and neither does Noor, who fires him a blistering look. He rolls his eyes and walks to the window, shaking his head. He's clearly rippling to have a go at me, or Noor, or perhaps both of us.

'We've printed off some of your Facebook posts,' explains Noor, peeling off more pages from her folder.

I look at them in astonishment. There's my name, the name of our town and a picture of a woman with a double chin and blond hair scraped back in a messy ponytail.

'Is that me?' I ask.

Noor nods. 'Yes, but it looks like an old picture.' I nod. It was when I was on those awful pills.

I stare at the print outs with interest. Apparently, I've been a member of Facebook for two years but only started posting in the last couple of months, making lewd comments about that S&M film all the mums went mad for and I have also liked some rather unsavoury far right material.

I look up, blushing and red-faced, at DS Noor. 'Honest to God, this isn't me. I wouldn't post stuff like this. I'm not a racist. I honestly have never seen this before.'

Noor hands me another sheet. On December 10 I declared my status as 'upset', with matching emoji and then wrote: *When people who should know better try to control you. Don't judge until you've walked in my shoes.*

Another update on December 29. Status: Angry. *Can't choose your family. So much for blood being thicker than water.*

I shrug. I have never seen these messages before.

'I didn't write these. I have never been on Facebook before.'

Noor is inscrutable as she peels off another print out. Status: Angry. This is accompanied with a gif of a cartoon character with steam coming out of its ears and below I've written: *Sisters. Can't live with them. Can't live with them. Grrrrrr.*

One person has liked this. It's a woman I've never heard of yet apparently we are 'friends'. Her name is Moira Brown and she has bright pink hair. She has asked me, 'What's up hun?' and I have apparently replied that 'Joanna is doing my nut in'. *She won't give me any ££££ and keeps on and on at me about getting a job. Nag nag nag. No wonder she's single. It's making me feel a bit stabby and I'm her sister!!!*

Moira tells me to, 'Chillax honey', followed by a stream of love heart emojis.

I gape at what I'm seeing. 'I have never seen this before. You have to believe me. This isn't me. I have never ever seen this.'

'You've told us before that you sometimes have mood swings, anger issues. You've suffered from memory blackouts in the past. You drink alcohol even when taking some serious medication. Our officers have been called to this address before for a claim of domestic violence. I look at these messages and I see siblings fighting, resentment and anger building over the months to create a tinder box.'

I swallow. 'I can see that's how it looks but, honestly, I have never seen this before. I'm not on Facebook. I don't have an account or a password.' I'm shouting now. I'm desperate for them to believe me.

'You do have an online presence though, don't you?' says Noor quietly.

I realise there's no point bluffing. She already knows the answers. 'Yes, I belong to an online forum for sufferers from TBI, traumatic brain injury. It's called Headliners.'

A cold chill runs through my veins. They have James' old computer, they'll have seen my postings. Headliners is my only real social connection to the world. It's the only place left where I can be myself and that isn't always a nice person. I know I've moaned about Joanna on there. A lot of people do about their carers: you depend on them so much, they have so much power over you it becomes demeaning and you resent them for it. But you're allowed an anonymous rant, aren't you? It's a safety valve to let off some steam so that in real life you can be pleasant and appreciative of everything they do for you.

I flush suddenly, remembering that the forum also has some adult boards, where BettyBoo72 has been known to contribute to pass the long empty days, safe in the knowledge nobody will ever know it's me. A little online flirting and role playing among adults who will never meet – let's face it, among my community, I'm one of the lucky ones and even I can't leave the house – doesn't hurt. But even so, I'm hot with shame to think Noor and Rawlinson will have read those messages.

'You probably think you have me all figured out,' I say, on

the defensive. 'But Headliners is my support group. We support one another. And sometimes we all moan about our carers. Everyone does, don't they? Even husbands and wives aren't kissing and cuddling twenty-four seven. You have no right to judge me. You don't know what it's like.'

Noor nods. 'You understand we have to look into this, Sarah. We have to examine every angle.'

'But you just seem to be looking at me. And I would never hurt Joanna, and meanwhile some mad man is running around. Have you talked to this Alex at her work, yet? She never liked him and she said she'd found something out.'

Noor smiles patiently. 'We're looking at all angles,' she soothes.

Rawlinson makes a little impatient movement. 'Come on,' he says. 'Let's have another gander at the crime scene.'

It seems they want me to walk them through it step by step. Again. Snell had told me the blood patterns appeared to back my claim that I'd spent the night lying unconscious in the hall and that Joanna's body had been knocked to the floor, and a chair moved after she'd bled out. There were also slight marks on her wrists and mouth that might support the fact she'd been tied up, but there's no sign of the binds or the gag. This, plus my injuries, is what stands between me and an arrest. 'It creates reasonable doubt,' Snell had said, 'but they could come back with an alternative and equally viable scenario.' That, I gather, is what they want me to help them with now.

I lead them through to the kitchen, and scan it, trying to see it through their eyes. The first things I spot is the wine bottle, down to the dregs, a stack of unwashed mugs and the remains of the carrot cake. My anxiety levels build again, my guts churning uncomfortably at the thought of transporting myself back to that night. It's always there, like a twitch in my eye, a flicker at the corner of my vision, a never-ending newsreel of horror that spools again and again. I dig my fingernails into my palms and hope I have the strength for this.

Noor looks around the room, checks something against her notes. 'This isn't going to be easy, Sarah, but we do need to understand what happened.' She doesn't look up from her notes. Rawlinson leans his bulk against the worktop, arms folded, exuding a barely contained menace. Is it me he hates, or Noor?

'I want you to think back to that night, really visualise it, see and hear it again. Sometimes it's the smallest thing that gives us a lead. If you're ready?' I nod, my throat feels tight as if my airway is closing up and I instinctively raise a hand to my throat. The coppers seem oblivious to the looming medical emergency. Are my lips going blue? Surely they have first aid training. I try to calm myself – nothing bad is happening, this has happened before and I didn't die – but instead I find myself obsessing about how quickly Noor could perform an emergency tracheostomy if needed. Rawlinson's watching me and I continue to massage my throat, focusing on drawing in whatever air I can and all the while that little inner voice is ratcheting up the fear. *Oh God, it's really happening this time, you're going into asphyxia, this time it's real ...*

'So, Sarah, you hear a disturbance and you come downstairs,' says Noor, reading from her notes.

And just like that I snap out of my mental torture chamber.

'No, no. I was in the living room.' It seems my airways are open and I can talk after all. I feel a flush of relief, quickly followed by anger as Noor and Rawlinson share a quick look and I realise they were trying to trip me up. I can't afford a panic attack now, I have to concentrate.

'Ah, of course,' says Noor, flicking a quick smile my way. 'Shall we start there?'

We troop back into the living room. I show them where I

was sitting, Joanna's usual seat, and the window where she saw the man go by.

'She knew who it was, you're sure?'

'Yes. She said, "What's he doing here?"'

'And how did she sound when she said that? Surprised, happy, scared?'

'Just a bit irritated. She was trying to watch her programme.'

Noor checks her notes again. 'And you saw the man too?'

'No. Maybe a shadow. I heard it rather than anything else.'

'You were reading?'

'Yes.' We have been over this so many times. And I suppose that's when they catch you, when you're complacent, not really focusing, and you sleepwalk into a trap.

'So, Joanna gets up and goes to the door.'

'The back door.'

'And while Joanna's in the kitchen, what do you do?'

'I put the radio on. Read my book.' I don't mention the guzzling of the wine. 'And then I realise she's been gone a while.'

'How long?'

I don't know. I wasn't really watching the clock. Time has become a peripheral concept to my life. She asks me what I heard, and I struggle not to cry. This is one of the most painful bits of the memory for me. When I first heard the noises, if I'd rushed in then or called the police, perhaps I'd have been able to stop him. Instead I hung back, getting angry that Joanna was having some secret assignation when instead she was fighting for her life, probably wondering where I was, why I wasn't coming to help. Tears start rolling down my face at the thought that once again I'd let her down.

'If I'd gone straight away, I could have stopped him.'

'There's no way of knowing that,' says Noor. 'You could both have been dead instead.'

118

Do I catch Rawlinson rolling his eyes at this? I'm not quick enough to be sure.

We walk through how I crossed the hall towards the kitchen, at what point I heard Joanna's cry of pain, and how quickly I threw open the door. Noor makes me explain what I saw and gets me to position the table and chairs as they were that night.

'And where was Joanna?'

I point to the chair at the far end of the table, nearest the kitchen sink.

'DC Rawlinson, would you do the honours?'

He peels his bulk from the counter top and lumbers slowly across to the chair. He sits down, vast thighs spread, arms folded across his chest. It's a gorilla power move but is it directed at me, or Noor? I glance at Noor but she seems completely unperturbed. She's so calm and collected, nothing distracting her from the task in hand. She gets out a tape measure and measures Rawlinson, checking something against her notes. 'Eight centimetres lower,' she says to him.

'And in inches?' The contempt in his voice makes it clear it's her he's got the problem with.

'About three inches,' she says calmly.

He rolls his eyes, and wriggles his bulk a little lower in the chair, his legs spreading even wider. I feel a great urge to kick him in the balls but clearly that wouldn't help my case.

Now she gets me to show her where I was standing when he came at me from behind, then where he made me stand when he forced my fingers down the soft wetness of her face. Everything is so very still and quiet suddenly, as if I'm straddling the fragile space between two separate dimensions, one where I'm re-enacting my sister's murder and the one from a week ago, where the man pressed his forearm across my throat and I looked into Joanna's terrified face through eyes hot and blurred with tears. Strangely, it is the dimension where my sister is still alive, where I'm fighting for air, that seems more real. Noor taps my arm and gives me something to hold. I take it and look down at it as if from a great distance. It's an old school wooden ruler she's been holding along with her paperwork, and for a second, I'm confused. And then my stomach plunges. I am to re-enact the killing using the ruler. I have to show her how he was standing over Joanna, the knife held casually down by his side.

'I know it's hard, Sarah.' She reaches out hesitantly and touches my forearm, very quickly, very softly. I get that's a big deal for her. She's not a toucher or hugger, and this little moment of humanity prompts more crying from me. I wipe my eyes with hands, and get some paper towels to try and deal with my nose. 'We're almost done.'

She gets me to stand over Rawlinson, and I feel my skin prickle at the proximity to him. She's at my right shoulder and slips the ruler into my hand again. 'Can you show us what you saw him do next?' I close my eyes and the image of the black-clad man standing over Joanna, the pink knife in his hand, flashes before me. I switch the ruler to my left hand and make a swift jabbing motion up into Rawlinson's abdomen.

Noor watches dispassionately and writes something into her notes. 'You're sure it was the left hand, Sarah?'

'Yes.' And in a moment, I suddenly realise what's going on. I'm left-handed. The killer was left-handed. I turn and look at her, sniffing wildly. 'But it wasn't me. I didn't do it.' I pull down the neck of my top, exposing the bruising across my throat. 'I didn't do this to myself! Look at me. I was attacked.'

Rawlinson looks at me, nodding at my neck. 'No finger marks round your throat so we can't tell if it was a man's hand or a woman's hand.'

'It wasn't his hand, it was his arm. He was standing behind me.'

120

'Or she,' he says pointedly.

They both look at me, watching my reaction.

I swallow. Surely they can't think Joanna did this to me? 'Joanna would never hurt me.' My voice is very small.

'A struggle, a fight, she's choking you. You panic, you pick up a knife. It was an accident. Self-defence. People will understand that. You have to do what you have to do.'

'No! It wasn't like that. There was a man here, he attacked us. You know Joanna found out something about someone, she didn't know what to do.' I'm gabbling, my words coming out too fast. My mouth is dry and it hurts to swallow, and my brain starts to throb with the effort of concentrating for this long.

'What did she find out, Sarah?'

'I don't know. She didn't say. But there was a man at her work, one of the big bosses. I told you, his name was Alex something. She hated him, said he was a knob.'

Noor smiles wryly. 'Every work place has got one of those, Sarah.'

Rawlinson scowls. He clearly thinks this barb is directed at him.

'And then there's Simon. He left her in very suspicious circumstances and I know he's back in the area because there are flowers at the gate.'

Noor frowns. 'Yes, we're trying to contact him, although the flowers were delivered by the local florists, actually. Our officers saw them arrive.'

'Oh.' So maybe it isn't Simon. Maybe he just saw the news report on the Internet and ordered the flowers from wherever he is in the world. He always had money to throw at a problem.

'Sarah,' says Noor, pulling my attention back to her. 'We've had the preliminary reports back from the pathologist. Obviously, we have the murder weapon and we've now had more detail about the nature of the stab wounds that killed Joanna.'

I swallow. I think I know what's coming, I can feel it, like when you see rain clouds moving in and their shadow races over the land towards you.

'The scratch marks down her face are a match with the swabs from your fingernails. The wounds were consistent with a left-handed attack, and our pathologist believes the direction, and the force involved, means it could well have been the work of a woman of your build.'

'I know what you're getting at,' I say. 'You're trying to say it was me.'

Noor doesn't say anything. She wants me to talk, to explain all of this. I wonder if this is legal, if I should have a lawyer. But how do you get a lawyer, and if you ask for one isn't it almost as good as a confession of guilt?

'Someone is trying to frame me. There was a man here. He must have known I was left handed. And that I can't recognise faces. He set me up with the Facebook account and wrote all those posts to make it look like another domestic.'

It sounds wild and desperate, even to my ears.

'Another domestic?' asks Noor quietly.

'You know what I mean. He must have known we've had a stormy relationship over the years. But that doesn't mean I killed her!'

I shout this last bit, and then collapse into a kitchen chair, wringing the piece of kitchen towel in my hands. God, if I'd known every little row I'd ever had with Joanna would be brought back to hound me then I'd have kept my bloody trap shut. If you can't say anything nice ... Mother's voice again.

'I know it sounds crazy, but it's the truth. Someone is framing me for Joanna's murder.'

'Who would do that, Sarah?'

'I don't know, I just don't know.' I'm crying again. I feel so piteous. Who would hate me so much? I barely know anyone.

122

Is it someone I've unintentionally blanked and they've got a grudge against me?

Noor pulls up a chair and sits opposite me, our knees almost touching. Her voice is soft, low and compelling.

'Sarah, what you're suggesting is a highly sophisticated, daring and calculated crime, with all the tell-tale theatrics of a psychopath. Someone capable of extensive planning and rehearsal. Someone who knows about your condition and your family dynamic. Someone who knows it was just two women on their own. Someone who decides to kill your sister to teach you a lesson. Think about that. Then tell me if you know anybody who fits that description?'

I shake my head slowly. It's true, when you put it like that it sounds crazy. Completely unbelievable and over the top. Perhaps it is confabulation. Perhaps my brain really is deteriorating again. Perhaps I really did do it.

'Occam's razor,' says Rawlinson suddenly. 'The simplest solution tends to be the right one. Listen to what you're saying and then think about why we're asking these questions. And then you might want to get yourself a lawyer.'

It's clear he doesn't believe me. Is this it then, are they going to arrest me?

'I didn't do it,' I plead, looking at Noor. 'Please, you have to believe me. Look at me. I didn't do this to myself.'

It seems the doubt thrown up by the blood splatters and my injuries is the only thing keeping me from a formal charge for my sister's murder. Noor again advises me not to leave town. They're going to continue their investigation and they're not ruling anything out. On the doorstep she turns and gives me a searching look.

'One last thing, Sarah. It's your decision but my advice would be to avoid any more press interviews.'

Any more press interviews? I watch them climb into a

shiny Toyota, Rawlinson reversing a little too fast, the wheels spitting gravel as my mind spins. I haven't given any press interviews, have I? Am I losing my mind? Did I kill my sister? Am I blacking out and doing things my conscious brain can't remember? I shut the door, my hands shaking so much that I struggle with the chain. I sink to the floor, my back to the door and my head in my hands, utterly exhausted. I take a long deep breath, and lift my head to stare at the faint outline of my bloodied handprint on the wall, remembering with horrifying clarity the moment my cut hand touched the wall, the help-lessness as he dragged my fingers over Joanna's face, the terror of his arm crushing my windpipe. I can't believe my brain has made all of that up. I can't believe I could have stabbed Joanna. But I know now that if I don't find the killer, I'm going to be going to prison for her murder.

Chapter Twenty

Eleven years ago

I can hear someone crying. The noise is relentless, it rises and falls like waves. I fumble about for the light, my bed clothes kicked aside, tutting as I hear the creak of a door and a woman's voice, muffled through the wall. I shrug on my blue dressing gown, swearing quietly as my fumbling fingers fail to knot the belt. I try again and my shoulder collides with the doorframe, a bruising reminder to tackle just one task at a time, walking or knot-tying. Out on the landing, the lights are on and I can smell the distinctive punch of urine rising from a tangle of wet sheets at the top of the stairs. My nose wrinkles in disgust. A boy, naked from the waist down, is bawling just inside the bathroom door.

This is James, I presume, Joanna's boy. I want to help him but the noise he's making cuts through me like a power drill.

'James, come on, get your pants on,' I say. I'm trying to speak calmly but it comes out a bit shouty to be heard over his bawling.

'Come on, James, you're a big boy now. Don't be making this racket.'

The boy howls louder at my intervention, which seems

completely unreasonable when I'm being so calm and he's the one waking the neighbourhood with his noise. Then it strikes me, what if this isn't James, what if it's one of his pals on a sleepover? I can't remember another boy being here last night but then I checked out early with a sleeping pill and a glass of white wine.

'James, is it you? Boy, come on, boy, stop this racket.'

I can feel the heat rising inside me. The noise is like a physical pain, grating the membranes of my wounded brain until all I can see or hear or feel is a white ball of pulsating pain.

There's a sound behind me, a tread on the stairs. Half blind with the noise, I turn and see a woman, her arms full of clean linen from the dryer. It must be Joanna, she seems to be in a constant cycle of washing and drying these days. She pushes past me roughly, and nudges the crying boy further into the bathroom.

'It's James, Sarah, you know that, who else do you think it would be?' she says briskly. 'He's upset. Go back to your bed, you're just making it worse.'

I don't see how she expects me to sleep with this racket going on so I head downstairs to make some hot milk. The oven clock tells me it's ten past one. It's dark outside, the blackness impenetrable here, and when I switch on the light I jump to see a face suddenly reflected in the window. It's just your own reflection, I tell myself, but it's a dispiriting thought: I look old, and I've put on weight since I've been taking these new anti-depressants. Joanna says it's worth putting on a few pounds if it means I'm stable but I think I'd rather be mad than fat. I pull the dressing gown tighter, almost in tears that I've lost my looks as well as my mind. I've always been the pretty one. Now I'm nothing.

The milk sizzles against the side of the pan and I switch off the gas. Joanna hates me using the hob after that time I let the pan boil dry but I refuse to let her infantilise me. She's had James in night nappies so long it's no wonder he's wetting the bed. She's over-mothered him so much that he hasn't developed properly. She hasn't welcomed my advice, however.

'Keep your mouth shut if you've nothing constructive to say,' she snapped, adding that I was 'sounding more and more like Mother'.

In my book, that's one of the worst insults you can throw so I had clearly touched a nerve.

There's a noise outside. Is it a fox poking round the bins again? I lean forward, trying to see beyond the yellow glow of the kitchen light into the darkness beyond, when suddenly a man looms up at the window.

'All right, Sarah? It's me, Alan. I heard a lot of noise and wanted to check you ladies are all right.'

I open my VIP book with trembling hands. The man has moved away from the window but I can see his shape looming outside the back door. Here he is, Alan, fifties, with a tweed cap, a little jowly, no beard. Underneath Joanna has written *Alan, number 24, tall, cap, slight stiffness in R leg, clean shaven. A talker.*

I open the door a crack and peer at the man. He isn't wearing a cap but he does look like the photo, albeit with the pallor of night time and a stubble of white bristle across his cheeks and chin.

'It's Alan, love,' he says and he takes a step forward, into my comfort zone, so that I'm forced to take a step back and the door falls open.

'I was up for a pee, you know how it is at a certain age, and heard a commotion through the bathroom window. Not double-glazed in there, you see. Thought I'd better do the neighbourly thing and check you ladies are all right.'

He's in the kitchen properly now. He's in his dressing gown

and pyjamas too, and it feels strangely intimate to be standing here together like this. Things have always been a bit awkward since I stopped walking with him.

'James got a bit upset. He wet the bed again.'

'Oh, poor lad.' Alan looks genuinely upset. 'Would it help if I popped up? I get on well with the boy and I was a bedwetter myself. I know how it feels. Maybe he needs a man rather than his mum fussing over him now he's getting bigger.'

I shrug. I can't see Joanna accepting his help – she's particularly sensitive to accusations he needs a male role model in his life – but perhaps she needs to hear what Alan has to say. After all, this problem has been going on for months now. I've told her the boy needs professional help but she buries her head in the sand. She has a pathological fear of people judging her parenting. I tell her it's not like anyone's going to take him away because he wets the bed but she always mutters darkly about checklists and labels.

Alan clumps upstairs while I sip my milk, flicking through one of Joanna's celebrity magazines. I don't recognise anybody apart from the Queen, she has a very distinctive style.

Minutes later, they're both in the kitchen, Joanna holding a bundle of urine-soaked bedding, which she dumps by the washing machine. She opens the back door and guides Alan out. 'Yes, thanks again, we'll take it from here.' She shuts and bolts the door before he's even finished saying his goodnights. She turns to me, her face white with anger.

'Never let him upstairs again,' she hisses fiercely, the muscles in her jaw taut. 'We can't trust him with James.'

Chapter Twenty-One

The phone rings and I stumble across the room, my heart racing, a cold dread in my veins. I just want to be left alone in the gloomy cocoon of the house but I can sense the outside pressing in. I no longer have Joanna to protect me.

'Sarah! I've been so worried.'

'Doctor Lucas!' Relief floods my body.

'I couldn't believe it when I saw it on the news. Who would do such a thing? How are you, how are you holding up?'

'I just miss her so much.' Huge ugly sobs rise like bubbles from a mud pool, choking my voice, convulsing my body. I don't need to put on a brave face for Dr Lucas; she has seen me at my worst.

'There, there, darling girl. You let it all out. I can't imagine what an ordeal you've been through. And when I couldn't get hold of you, I thought something awful had happened to you too.'

'He. Attacked. Me. Hit my. Head,' I manage to blurt out. 'Concussion.'

'You've been checked out properly, did they know your medical history?'

Did they? I can't remember. The last few days have been a blur. 'I'm fine, really. Just cuts and bruises. But Joanna ...' I can't talk any more, the sobs bubble up, choking me in tears and snot, expelling pain into the air. Dr Lucas always encourages me to let my pain go; no matter how much I cry in our sessions — it is a little running joke that at Christmas she always gives me a gift-wrapped box of tissues — I always feel better afterwards, lighter and cleaner somehow. I'm desperate for that feeling now but somehow I don't think however much I cry I will ever wash away this pain, it feels imprinted in my soul, tattooed on my skin.

'Let it out, darling,' says Dr Lucas soothingly. 'This is going to be the start of a long journey for you. I'm so so sorry.'

I don't know how long I cry down the phone for but eventually, and very gently, she brings the call to an end. I suppose she has other patients to see. 'We've obviously missed our session this month,' says Dr Lucas, 'but I hope I'll be able to see you next month. But we can stay in touch by phone if you need more support.'

'You know they think I killed her?'

'That's ridiculous.' Do I hear a note of doubt creep in Dr Lucas' voice? Does she think I might be capable of hurting Joanna? 'Of course you wouldn't hurt her, dear. Why would they think something like that?'

'They seem to think I'm a mad woman with a history of violence towards my sister,' I say, with a funny strangled laugh. 'I don't think they even believe in the prosopagnosia. As if anyone would make that up!'

There's another pause on the other end of the line. I wonder if there's someone else there, listening in. 'Sarah, darling, I have to go. My case list is very heavy today. I am so very sorry for your loss, so so sorry. We'll speak very soon, my darling. Remember your breathing exercises.'

We say goodbye. I always feel better after talking to Dr Lucas. She knows me better than anyone. I can tell her things and know I won't be judged, know that it's all part of a process, part of my recovery. She likes to say 'there is no such thing as normal' and it makes me feel better that I'm not such an outlier on the fringes of life. There are others like me, and many a lot worse. I just hope there will be enough money for me to keep seeing her.

I pull on one of Joanna's Prosopagnosia Collection cardigans, drinking in her smell: Fairy washing powder and White Musk perfume from the Body Shop, which she wore all the time after an alpha mum at the school gate said she smelt of teenage romance. Apparently, that was a compliment. I can't think of anything worse, it conjures up sweaty bodies, acne face wash and oozing hormones. But now, sniffing the collar of the cardigan, I find it a pleasant smell, sweet jasmine, summer nights and Joanna.

If I close my eyes I can almost hear her voice in my ear again, as she pulls on her best Boden frock and M&S sandals for a date at The Swan, which seemed to be the destination for all the hopeful mid-life Internet daters. 'Wish me luck, Sarah, I've got a good feeling about this one.'

There's a knock at the door. The back door. I jump, my heart at once racing, my mouth dry. Is the killer back? Surely not in broad daylight, with a police car still parked outside. I creep slowly out of Joanna's room to the top of the stairs, and peer cautiously down. The door rattles again, and a voice calls out: 'Sarah, Sarah, you in there? It's me, Alan from next door.'

Alan, of course, he often comes around the back. It used to drive Joanna mad because he could push through a gap in the hedge between the two gardens where the old pear tree died. She used to speculate he'd poisoned the tree on purpose just so he could have easy access, but even I thought that was crazy talk: Alan loves nature.

I go into the living room and pick up my scrapbook of very

131

important people, or vippers for short. It became a bit of a joke. Sometimes when we were out, Joanna and I would catch one another's eye and whisper our verdict on whether someone had vipper potential: Very vipper. Almost a vipper. No vipping way. The book is well-thumbed now, the fabric cover faded and worn. I know Alan's page, he's near the beginning, we have known him a long time. Could he have done it? He's an oddball, but a murderer, after all these years?

I edge towards the kitchen, my heart thundering. There's a man peering in through the kitchen window. He spots me and his face lights up. I check his appearance against the description in my book: tall, receding hair, more grey than brown now, a little jowly round the jawline. He's wearing a white shirt, a little tight round the belly and rolled up at the sleeves, cords and a quilted bodywarmer with lots of pockets. He's one of those people: he always has a pen, phone, charger, string, rubber bands, dog poo bags (he hasn't got a dog) and sweets on his person at all times. Once I got locked out of the house and he didn't have to go home to get any tools: he had a torch-screwdriver-penknife-combo in his pocket. We always thought it was one of his eccentricities but is it normal to be walking around tooled up like that? Is it wise to let him in?

But he's already talking at me through the closed door, and it seems rude not to open up. Is that how it happened to Joanna, I wonder? She was so programmed to be polite she opened the door to her killer? And now I'm doing the same thing, the programming to be compliant runs so deep. Suddenly he's in the kitchen with me, his presence filling the space, so many words that my brain is already struggling to keep up. He has always been a talker, I suppose it comes of living alone. Perhaps I will become a talker too, now.

'I guessed you wouldn't have been to the shops,' he says, emptying the contents of a plastic bag on to the kitchen table.

'I know what you're like but you have to keep your strength up. Look, only £1.25 for these sausages. It's because of the dates but you can freeze them if you can't eat them all today.'

I sigh inwardly. All of Alan's shopping comes with special instructions because it's never just off-the-shelf. It always has to be a bargain. It is perhaps the one thing Mother and I agreed on: *you get what you pay for*.

'Two for one on the biscuits, Sarah. I know you like a biscuit with your tea. Hey, hey, as well I came round.' He's in my fridge now. 'You're out of milk.'

He rabbits on like an old woman and my headache pounds behind my eyes as I drift in and out of the conversation. There are so many names and they all seem to have been talking about Joanna but I keep losing track of who said what. Do I even know Bob who does computers and says the police are messing up the investigation? And Svetlana, I know the name, he's mentioned her before, is she from the library, but why is he telling me about her Vauxhall Astra? What's that got to do with Joanna?

Alan eyes me carefully, then stands up, gets a glass of water and pops a couple of paracetamols out of a blister pack and hands them to me.

'Nineteen pence in Superdrug, Sarah. Never buy the brands, you're only paying for the packaging. Get those down you, you look a little peaky.'

He watches me take them, then joins me back at the table. He's a big man, particularly in his padded jacket with its bulging pockets. I feel a little shiver of fear. How well do I really know Alan? I've always written him off as harmless but Joanna was always wary of him. Did she have a reason for that? I think I should mention it to the police.

'I just can't think who would want to hurt you or Jojo,' he says, draining his tea. 'I mean, this is what worries me. There's a golden hour to catch a killer you know and they've blown that. They've had you in for questioning, they've been on at me, and James' – this is news to me – 'but all the time there's a madman out there on the loose.'

'What are they talking to you and James about?' I ask.

Alan looks uncomfortable. 'Well, love, they wanted to know about you and Joanna, what your relationship was like. And about your little problem, you know.'

Oh right.

'And then what I saw when I came round that morning,' he says. His brow wrinkles. 'I can't say I liked their tone.'

So, Alan was the one who found us and alerted the police. Is that suspicious, or not? I'm not sure. 'Why were you here?' I ask.

'I saw Joanna's car in the drive. Well, you can set your watch by Joanna leaving for work so I thought maybe she was poorly or having car trouble. Thought I'd offer to help.'

I look at him sharply. He's always watching us. I bet he knows more about Joanna's comings and goings than I do.

'I knew straight away something was wrong. Kitchen looked a state and when I went round the front I could just see a shape on the hall floor through the glass. So 999.' He shudders. 'Never like having to make one of those calls. Police were very quick though, give them their due.'

I nod. If only I'd called 999 the moment I heard a noise in the kitchen.

'Police battered their way in and I can't say I think much of your security, love, two women on their own you should have had a better door. And by then you must have come around, because we walk in and there you are, in here with her, covered in blood. Well' – he looks away, shifty – 'you know the rest.'

I picture them bursting in and finding me in the kitchen, cradling Joanna, the knife in my hand, covered in her blood.

I don't know why they haven't charged me already. I was caught literally red-handed, with the murder weapon in my hand. I wouldn't cope in prison, I know that. So many people, all trapped together, living together, eating together. I just couldn't handle it. But how to prove I'm innocent? Could Alan help me? He's still talking, rattling on about someone in the Co-op who has told him there was an unsolved murder in the town about twelve years ago. He's going to try and find out more details but I don't see how something that far back can be linked to Joanna.

'No stone unturned, Sarah, no stone unturned. What if we have a serial killer in our midst, eh, what then?'

He seems almost excited at the prospect, and I feel another prickling of unease. Why was Alan spying on us, why was he round so early? I look at him as he chunters on and remind myself I can't trust anyone.

Chapter Twenty-Two

I am going to do this. I take a diazepam and a glass of red wine — the shiraz, one of the good ones Joanna never lets me drink — as I attempt to walk a pharmaceutical tightrope to make sure I numb my anxiety enough to get out of the house, but without completely fogging my brain. I need to be able to think. I need to protect myself from whoever is trying to frame me.

A stiff breeze spits pellets of rain against the windows. The shrine rustles in the wind, and the little tea lights have all gone out. The street is deserted. No sign of Lisa, or Dennis or Mo. In one day I met more of my neighbours than I did in all of the preceding year.

I hurry through the rain slick streets. Someone's recycling bag has spewed cardboard over the grass verge and blossom blows in eddies in the middle of the street. I hug Joanna's Joules raincoat around me, my head low against the rain.

The Co-op looms ahead, a dog tied to the railing outside. This place is catnip for old people, they can't get enough. Joanna said you could never be alone in the world when you've got a Co-op down the road. She found this comforting, but to me it became a place to be avoided. However, I can't continue to live on carrot cake and biscuits and I need to see the papers. I wish I'd asked Noor when they'll give me my phone and computer back if only so I can avoid any more trips to the Co-op. I am so glad to live in the time of Internet shopping. Even my friends are virtual.

It strikes me then that the Facebook page that Noor showed me with all those awful postings will have been visible to everyone I know. What must people think? That I'm a racist slutty bitch. And I always thought people round here blanked me because my condition made me uncomfortable company. Instead, it's because they hate me. How am I ever going to put this right?

I scurry into the shop, keeping my head low. I buy all the papers, noticing with a quickening of my heart that our house is the front page of the local news. *Cops Hunt Market Leyton Killer*. I fold it up, hiding the headline, and put it in my basket. I buy tins of soup, some apples, a small loaf and milk, using the self-service till to dodge the queue: bring on the robots, I say. Next stop, the surgery, where I dodge the nosy receptionist and go straight to the dispensary. The woman in there is always overrun and barely looks up as she repeats her advisories and hands over the pills.

It feels like I've pulled off a bank robbery and I take my meds on the move, confident I now have the pharmaceutical cushion to complete my mission. I'm aware, of course, how ludicrous this all is; most people can run a few errands without building it up into a military campaign but I have to take my wins where I can find them.

The library feels like safer territory. It's big enough for me to lose myself among the shelves and the new automated machines, where you can check books in and out yourself, the subject of heated discussion in the town when they were introduced last year, mean I can dodge the librarians. The doors slide open at my approach, and I shake the raindrops off my hood. There are a couple of pensioners at the machine, stabbing at the touch screen and getting flustered. It distracts the librarian – I can't tell if it's the bossy one or the one who's always over friendly – and allows me to slip in undetected. On the new fiction shelves, a couple of books jump out at me – one of them has had great reviews in the paper and the other is on Joanna's book club list – but I'm not here for the fiction today. Instead I slope round the back, towards the reference and self-help books.

I find an empty spot by the travel section and settle down to read the local paper. Our case is the front-page story and takes up another full page inside. This is big news for the town. I scan for my name but I haven't been named, instead I am 'another woman living at the house, believed to be the victim's sister.' I am relieved to see there's no mention of me being under suspicion, although it does say 'a forty-six-year-old woman was taken to the Rodham Road Police Station but no charges were brought'. DS Noor is quoted, saying 'We're investigating all lines of enquiry at this time', and Alan pops up too, appealing for witnesses to 'a cowardly attack on two vulnerable women'. I feel a rush of warmth towards him. At least he's on my side.

The story on the inside pages is an exclusive written by a young female reporter, Anita Gannon. I peer at the thumbnail byline photo: she's young, with short brown hair and a smug smile. I don't recognise her but I know this must be Lisa. Her piece boasts of her 'exclusive access' to the 'house of horrors'. Suddenly it's clear to me why DS Noor told me not to do any more press interviews. I cringe at the thought of Noor believing I would willingly invite the press into my house to discuss Joanna's murder; what must people think of me? I wonder what the circulation of the Gazette is, and how many people have read this and think I'm guilty. Hell, I would think the same. But at least I'm not losing my mind. Or not about this, at least. I read on, with a fascinated horror.

Sarah, the victim's sister, is visibly shaken, with extensive bruising and cuts to her hands. There has clearly been a violent struggle here yet Sarah says she wants to stay, despite the memories of the attack. Police sources suggest it is not the first time they have been called out to the Speldhurst Road address but Sarah insists she and her sister had a good relationship. 'She's been there for me through thick and thin. I don't know what I'll do without her,' said Sarah, adding she intends to stay in the £240,000 house in the leafy Broom End part of town. 'Joanna wouldn't want me to give up.'

My pulse accelerates, a shot of anger, like poison, speeding through my veins. There are photos, snapped no doubt on her little trip to the 'facilities' of the faint smear in the hall, a photo of the kitchen, with a red ring highlighting the faint stain on the kitchen floor. The caption reads 'Evidence of the horror that unfolded that night'. I am just grateful she wasn't brazen enough to take a photo of me. I suppose that would have blown her cover. I wonder if this breaks journalistic rules and if I could complain to someone but I know it would be foolish to take action. The last thing I need is to draw the ire of the press.

I fold the paper as small as I can and shove it back in the bag, wishing I could pack away my feelings as easily. I feel contaminated by the article, even though I know I'll read it again later, like picking at a festering wound.

'Help you with anything?' A librarian bustles around the corner, her enormous bosom like the prow of a great ship. I think it's the bossy one – my preference really over the matey friendly one – but it's hard to tell; they're both plump, favour long flowing garments (I suspect Per Una again, it seems to be the go-to collection for women of a certain age) and have a jolly hockey sticks briskness about them.

'I'm good, just browsing.'

'Good, you know where I am,' says the librarian, speaking over her shoulder as she passes by and round the stack, an ocean liner cruising on by. Definitely, the bossy one. The friendly one never lets it lie.

I find what I need between the self-diagnosis medical books – a section I long ago discovered should carry trigger warnings for anyone prone to anxiety – and the car manuals. The psychology section is just one shelf but I'm delighted to see there's a whole sub-genre on psychopaths, including books by Robert D Hare, the man who designed the test to diagnose psychopathy, and the famous FBI profiler John Douglas. Based on this snapshot, it's clear there are more books on psychopaths than building assertiveness or understanding emotion. I wonder what that says about our society. Determined to know my enemy, I check out all the books on psychopaths and yet again, I am glad of the anonymity of the robo-librarian. No awkward conversations about my taste in reading matter.

I hesitate then, lingering in the doorway. There are computers at the library, in fact it's the busiest section, but I would need to set up an account and password to use them. Could I do that without calling down the attention of Bossy or Matey? I would really like to check my account at Headliners, and I could do an online grocery shop. But today's trip out has gone so well I don't want to spoil it by over-extending myself. I can always come back. Build myself up to it.

My reading matter does not help my sleep issues. It's estimated one per cent of the global population are psychopaths but they are found in much higher concentrations in prisons and boardrooms. They don't feel fear, or love, or shame or happiness but they're always chasing those feelings, which leads them to reckless behaviours: crime, violence, sex. Many are charming, intelligent and master manipulators. They learn to mimic what they don't have, so they can blend in with the rest of the population, wolves in sheep's clothing. Some are high achievers, their vast egos and ruthless wiles propelling them to the boardroom or top office. Others underachieve – they're smart but lazy, believe the rules don't apply to them, and so fall into a life of disappointment and villainy.

It's unsettling reading, particularly as it's impossible not to see myself in some of the behaviours. I hear the whisper of Mother's judgments. *You're a brazen hussy. Addicted to your cheap thrills. The darkness will devour you and then you'll be sorry.* Her words had only spurred me on and I had been determined to prove her wrong by being the wildest, happiest, most desired person in the world, always chasing the pleasure of the new dress, the coolest party and the hottest guy, but the highs were so transient that my hunger for more burnt ever fiercer. And I was a serial under-achiever – I could have done so much better at school, I know that now, yet despite my awful school reports and flunked exams, I'd always believed I was better than everyone else. Had Mother seen something in me, had she seen the warning signs, was that why she kept me on such a short leash? Yet surely if I was a psychopath, I wouldn't recognise any of this. Surely the fact I find this reading so unsettling is proof I'm not one of them, surely my grief for Joanna is proof that I can love.

And as I read on, flinching from the case studies of casual violence and calculated cruelty, I no longer see myself. These men – and they almost all are men – walk anonymously among us, studying us and exploiting our humanity without remorse. The crimes they commit are horrific, marked by brutal and sadistic violence, usually with a sexual element, and completely devoid of compassion. Many take on jobs that allow them to travel, facilitating some predatory need to hunt for fresh prey and conceal their tracks. Yet they also crave recognition and want to be acknowledged for their brilliance and intelligence – and it is this arrogance that often leads to their capture as they seek to insert themselves into narratives about the crime, lingering at the scene of their arson or creating elaborate trails for the police to follow. This is not me. I go out of my way to hide away and shun the limelight.

What I don't understand is why a psychopath would target us. Noor's right. This was a cold and calculated crime. Over the top in its drama but never out of control: it was carefully choreographed to frame me. But why? I can't think of anyone we could ever have caused so much harm that they would want to ...

Of course, the accident. The moment everything changed for me, for Joanna, for James. And for other people too. Because someone died in that accident. Robert Bailey. For Rob everything stopped then. And I suppose he must have had other family members, people who've been grieving all these years, perhaps warped by their loss, who have been biding their time, waiting for revenge. I know so little of Rob, other than he was a pilot. Joanna said he had no surviving family, which was why he'd been so devoted to her and James. He'd recreated what he'd lost so young. But perhaps she was wrong. Perhaps there had been someone. I pick up the photo of the wedding party. There's another man standing there, next to the one I think is Rob. The best man, I suppose. I peer at him, studying the two men in their morning suits, white roses pinned to their lapels, like it's a spot-the-difference puzzle. This other man is taller than Robert, broader in the shoulder and his hair is darker. He's good-looking too, they have the same cock-sure gleam in their eye, the same full lips. Could this be a brother, or cousin? Who would know? I pull the photograph out of the frame but there are no names, no clues as to the man's identity.

I go into the old box room that became Joanna's study and open her filing cabinet. Everything is very organised, classic Joanna, and I am flooded with longing to see her again. I find what I'm looking for in a folder labelled Important Documents: a creamy envelope marked wedding certificate. I open it up with trembling fingers and read the witness names: Mother and someone called Gary Brown. So not a brother then, maybe a half-brother? But why would Rob's best man want to kill his widow twenty years later? It makes no sense.

I wish I knew more about the accident. Perhaps someone else had been injured or killed. I believed it had just been our car that had lost control on a bend and hit a tree. But what if I'd got that wrong? What if there had been another car, other victims? What if someone out there has been biding their time, waiting to exact revenge for injury to themselves or a loved one? It's been twenty years, is that how long it takes for a mind to be warped by grief? Is that what I can look forward to?

I pace the house, rubbing my skin with anxiety. There's a noise outside and I freeze until I hear the yakking of the jackdaws on the roof. The psychopath books have unnerved me and I go around the house checking all the windows and doors are locked.

Somehow I need to find out more about the accident. Joanna was always so reluctant to talk about it. We all tiptoed around trying not to upset the grieving widow but she didn't seem to understand the impact this silence had on her son. She lost a husband but he lost a father. She once told me it was worse for her because she remembered Rob, whereas James had no memories to grieve. I'd replied that it wasn't the grief Olympics and to get over herself for the sake of her son, which probably wasn't the most tactful way to handle it but she knew better than most what it's like to grow up without a father that no one talks about. Mother never talked about our father. We have no knowledge of his personality, his likes or dislikes, and we filled in the gaps with our own lurid imaginings until he became a larger-than-life fictional character that no real man could ever match.

James used to ask me about Rob but my memories were sketchy at best.

'Do you remember him, Aunty Sarah? Mum never talks about him, it's like he never existed.'

I heard the pain in his voice, the hunger for any crumb of information and promised to talk to Joanna about it. 'It's not healthy keeping all these secrets,' I told her. 'He needs to talk about this.'

I don't think she ever did give him the answers he needed. Instead, it seemed to me, she spent much of his childhood looking for someone to replace the husband and father who had been so cruelly ripped away. Rather than facing up to the past, she was busy racing towards a new future. But your past is like a shadow, it never gets left behind. And now she's taken her secrets with her. The accident was a pivot point in all our lives. Yet only two of us are left alive and neither of us remember anything about it.

Chapter Twenty-Three

Seven years ago

It's one of those hot summer evenings that stirs the blood and makes you think that anything is possible. The car windows are down and the waft of the warm summer breeze on my bare skin feels like a lover's caress. I rest my head against my arm and smell the sweet stickiness of suncream, a scent I always associate with good times. I catch my reflection in the offside rear mirror, my blond hair streaming in the breeze, big sunglasses for that Hollywood glamour and my skin golden from days of sunbathing in the garden, and feel pretty pleased with myself. I glance over at Joanna, in her white linen sundress, her designer sunglasses, her little upturned nose pink from the sun. Funny how she has grown into her looks. You could no longer say, as Mother used to, that she was the plain Jane. The Wallis sisters, despite everything, are aging well. She catches me looking at her and grins, those dimples flashing in her cheeks.

'Glad you came?' she shouts.

'No complaints,' I say, and it's true.

There's a thud in my back. James kicks the chair as he plays on his Nintendo, lost to the real world, his legs jerking like a cat dreaming of chasing birds.

'Put it down, James,' calls Joanna. 'You'll make yourself car sick.' He ignores her. It's like he's in another dimension. Still, it makes it a quiet journey for us. I think one of the reasons people are letting this technology take over is because it makes life so much more palatable for parents.

'Well, he must be keen,' I say as we pass one of those giant chicken farms, vast egg factories that blot out the sky and stink the whole town when the wind blows the wrong way. 'I mean, who would live in the Cotswolds when they could have this?'

She laughs, happier than I have seen her for years. Simon has invited us all over for a BBQ at his new place, a converted barn about ten miles out of town. It's a big move, a signal of intent. So far their relationship has been squeezed into the corners of life but now he will be fifteen minutes away and everything could change. I've been chewing it over, watching her closely, sure that any minute she's going to drop the bombshell that they're settling down together and I'm out on my ear. Would she do that to me? I don't think she would but love makes people selfish on other people's behalf. They do things as a couple they would never do on their own. If he told her to make a choice . . .

We drive through one of those perfect English villages, with the old pub, a village green, the thwack of cricket on the field by the church. We sweep onto a gravel drive and park next to his Bentley. He leads us through a large airy living room, all exposed beams and French windows and the biggest TV I've ever seen, out to a stone terrace edged by pots of lavender and trailing honeysuckle, with views over the cricket pitch towards the church and the rolling fields of wheat beyond.

He's got a silver tray ready with olives, nuts and crisps, a bottle of expensive champagne and a can of lemonade for James. I could get used to this, I think, sipping my champagne, feeling the heat radiating from the old stone, listening to the bees droning lazily on the lavender. Simon's easy company, full of little anecdotes but also taking time to listen to what you have to say, though neither I nor James are great conversationalists. And he's a good host, in his striped butcher's apron with the sleeves of his shirt rolled up. He makes sure our glasses are never empty, nothing is too much trouble, our meat cooked to order and an appetising array of salads, dips and breads, even some little chipped potatoes for James.

'I know you're a connoisseur of the potato in all its forms,' he joshes James, who looks at him blankly. I don't think he knows what connoisseur means.

We sit on the terrace, admiring the views. There's a large Georgian farmhouse just visible to the east. 'My landlord,' explains Simon, filling my glass. 'Lord of the manor. I have to doff my cap every morning.'

'You're renting?' I suppose it's a bit of a personal question to blurt out but it takes me aback. He's obviously got plenty of cash.

'Just testing the waters up here,' he says, glancing at Joanna with a smile.

Does that mean he's not sure about her, or that this is just a stop gap until they find a place together? I drain my glass, plastering a smile on my face. I look at Joanna and she's smiling, relaxed, helping him collect up the cutlery. I suppose she already knows. They must have talked about this, about their future, they already know the answers. It's just me and James who are in the dark.

I help Simon clear away plates. He's got a huge kitchen, everything's gleaming and high spec but there's something impersonal about it. There's no art, no photos, almost like he's hired the place for show and his actual home, the place with the mementoes and clutter of a life, is somewhere else. Perhaps it's because he travels so much, maybe you get used to shedding stuff so it's easy to get up and go.

'Any more trips planned?' I ask, rinsing off some glasses. 'We like your postcards from exotic places.'

'New York, Boston and Chicago coming up,' he says. 'And then in November it's South Africa and January there's a road-show to the Far East.' He reels off a list of places and mentions some sights he'd like to see. I haven't heard of a lot of them so just make appropriate 'ooh' and 'ahh' noises. 'But it's not the same on your own,' he says. 'I've asked Joanna a few times but she's tied to school holidays, of course.'

'I could look after James,' I volunteer, regretting the words almost straight away. Could I look after him? It would be all right for a while as long as I didn't have to do anything at school. He's pretty self-sufficient now.

Simon gives me a brief smile. 'Thanks, Sarah, that's good to know.'

But there's something fake about his voice and I guess Joanna has already explained my failings as a responsible adult.

I join the boy down at a rectangular fish pond, where he's poking a stick in the water. Big golden fish glide through the lily pads, coiling round one another in a graceful ballet. One of them rises to the surface, its mouth popping open, and James and I both step back, startled. I laugh at myself. 'Just when you thought it was safe to go back in the water,' I say, then sing the theme tune to *Jaws*.

James looks at me, puzzled. I suppose he doesn't get the reference. Nothing makes you feel old like the cultural lodestones of your youth becoming obsolete.

'They can't hurt you, Aunty Sarah,' he says, crouching back down to poke at the water. 'I want a fish.'

'Not much of a pet,' I say. 'You can't exactly give it a cuddle in front of the telly.'

148

He looks at me, bemused. 'Not for a pet,' he says. 'Just to have. People used to think they only have a memory of three seconds but that's not true. I am sure these fish know one another and you couldn't know one another if you didn't have a memory.'

I smile wryly to myself. I have a memory and I don't know people. Perhaps I'd be better off without a memory, maybe then I wouldn't feel this constant churning anxiety. I'm fine here because there's just one of each: one boy, one man, one other woman. Perhaps that's the key, perhaps I should just limit all social interactions to similarly dissected gatherings, using height and race and sex as landmarks by which I can navigate the world. But it doesn't work like that, does it? Life is messy, busy and confusing.

Simon calls us back over to the table. There's a magnificent pavlova and a platter of little chocolates that he's got in especially for Joanna.

'Chocolate,' she coos, her eyes wide. 'My absolute favourite.'

The cricket match has finished now, and there's the sound of children playing on the field. There's the clap of a ball hitting a bat, then shrieks and laughter as the kids scrabble for the ball in the lengthening shadows.

'Look, James,' says Joanna. 'Why don't you go down? You might know a few of them from school.'

He gives her a withering look. He is not a sporty boy. Does he even know how to play cricket?

'Here,' says Simon, 'I'll take a walk down with you. I used to be quite handy with the willow as a boy.'

Joanna makes encouraging noises and James reluctantly follows Simon down to the end of the garden, where a small gate leads out to the footpath that edges the playing field and goes around to the church. I watch, the tall man and the thin boy trailing in his wake. Simon doesn't have any kids; his wife had cancer in her twenties so it was never an option and then died in her late thirties when the disease returned. I suppose spending time with James must be bittersweet for him, a reminder of what he missed.

'Looks like they're getting on,' I say as Simon approaches the boys and asks if he can take a turn. James stands, watching.

Simon shows how to hold the bat, and bowls several wickets for the boys. James has a go at batting. I can feel Joanna holding her breath, willing him on. He misses it three times, but manages to catch an edge the fourth time, which another child ably catches to much whooping. It's painful to watch.

'I don't think cricket's his sport,' I remark dryly as James hurls down the bat.

'Not everyone can be sporty,' snaps Joanna. I think she takes it as a personal betrayal that James couldn't perform better for her boyfriend.

We watch a bit longer. Simon is embroiled in the game now, with the kids getting him to bat. He does so with gusto, belting a couple out to the boundary.

'Where's James?' says Joanna, a catch of panic in her voice as she scans the playing fields.

I'm no help. They all look the same to me, particularly at this distance and in the fading light. She heads down to the footpath, and I feel obliged to follow. I'm sure he's fine. It's not like he's a toddler any more and what harm can befall him in a lovely English village on a perfect summer's evening? But then I remind myself that that's how every Agatha Christie starts. Horror amid the wisteria.

Joanna is calling for James now, scanning the fields for him. Now that the sun is sinking low, the sky streaked bright pinks and oranges, the first star just visible, the shadows fall long across the grass. Simon comes over, his face red and shiny from the burst of exercise in the heat.

'Haven't lost the old magic,' he says, beaming. Then he notices Joanna's face. 'What's wrong?'

'Where's James?' she says. 'I can't see him anywhere.'

'He was playing a few minutes ago,' says Simon, his forehead crumpling as he looks around at the boys still scampering after the ball in the shadows. 'Did he go down to the playground by the church?'

'I'll look,' says Joanna dubiously. He's never been one for playgrounds either. Perhaps it's because he's an only child; such places aren't as much fun if there's no one to push you on the roundabout or watch you do the monkey bars.

She sends Simon to check round the church car park and the lane that leads down to the pub in case James has gone for an explore. Sometimes, I think it's like she doesn't know her son at all. I still don't think it's anything to worry about. He's old enough not to fall into ponds or go off with strangers, surely? The playground is deserted, just some older teenagers having a smoke on the swings.

'Perhaps he's back at the house?' I suggest.

We wander back, the fields alive with the chirruping and buzzing of insects. Joanna calls for James but there's no answer. When we get back to the terrace, James is there, crouched over the pond, still watching the fish.

'Where have you been?' he asks, standing up at our return. 'I was starting to get worried.'

I laugh. He sounds just like Joanna.

'We were looking for you,' she says. 'You can't just wander off like that.'

He looks mutinous. 'I didn't. I went to play cricket like you wanted, but the other boys weren't very nice. They laughed at me. So I came back and *you* weren't here.'

Joanna looks like she's chewing a wasp. She has over-reacted and she knows it and now Simon's evening is ruined. He comes back after half an hour, red faced and his eyes glassy. I don't know why it's taken him so long and can't help wondering if he's actually just been in the pub. 'So the wanderer returned, did he?' he asks, pouring himself a large glass of wine.

'Yes, so sorry, Simon. He wandered back, said some boys were laughing at him.'

Simon frowns. 'Seemed a nice bunch of kids. Good to see them out playing and not on a screen.'

Joanna prickles at once. 'Where are the parents, I'd like to know? It's ten past ten. Some of those kids look under ten.'

'In the pub, I should think,' says Simon. 'Looked packed tonight.' He sounds wistful. I wonder if he's already starting to realise how his dream life with Joanna would be complicated by James. I know it's hateful but I can't help feeling pleased. Perhaps things won't change after all.

'Well, they should be keeping an eye on them. I'd be horrified if James laughed at someone for not knowing how to play cricket.'

'I didn't hear anything,' he says. 'Just boys being boys. I'm happy to bowl a few balls for James, coach him a bit. Sport is the universal language for boys. You'll always have a pal if you can throw or kick a ball.'

Joanna chews on her lip and I look down at my wine, embarrassed. Simon has no idea what thin ice he's on. She hates any suggestion that somehow James is missing out, but she swallows her annoyance. 'I'm sure he'd like that,' she says.

'Great,' says Simon, staring down the garden to the fishpond, where James is now lying on his belly, one hand in the water. 'It'll do us both good.'

We leave shortly afterwards. I'm nicely mellow from the wine and the good food but Joanna is highly strung, her fingers twitching on the steering wheel. She revisits the cricket incident, wanting to know exactly what the boys said and whether

Simon heard. James just shrugs. 'It's no big deal,' he says.

'Didn't you hear us calling for you when you went back up to the terrace?' I ask.

'No. I went back round by the lane,' he says.

Joanna tuts. 'James, you shouldn't have done that. A car wouldn't have seen you walking in the dark.'

'But I would have seen the car and stepped out of the way, wouldn't I?' he says, reasonably.

'You must always tell us before you go wandering off,' she reminds him. 'Simon must have been frantic looking for you down the lane.'

'Didn't hear him,' he says. 'He can't have looked very hard.'

I can tell James holds the cricket incident against Simon. 'I like his place,' I say, trying to change the subject. 'How will it work for him, being further away from London and the airports?'

'Oh, he might not travel so much now. He might do more by Skype. He's even thinking of getting a dog.'

'Well, that's good news,' I say, wondering how that tallies with my conversation in the kitchen. Is he telling her one thing and me another? And what does he *do* on these trips?

Joanna doesn't say anything and puts the radio on to block out the noise of the Nintendo in the back seat.

Chapter Twenty-Four

I can't sleep. My nerves are ragged, every noise makes me jump, one bang of the plumbing and I'm back on the hall floor, my head exploding as he laughs. The psychology books don't help. Psychopaths crave attention and recognition so I know whoever did this will be circling, watching the police and waiting for my arrest as some kind of affirmation of their brilliance. The thought he could be close, watching me and trying to manipulate events, makes my skin creep. I fetch the axe from the shed and keep it close as I huddle under my blanket on the sofa, curtains drawn and the television on low for the company. But inside I'm getting angry. How dare they do this to me, to Joanna, to James? It's someone we know, someone who hates us. Someone who knows about the prosopagnosia and the anxiety. He'll be counting on those to keep me weak, and him safe. I drain a glass of shiraz and grit my teeth. I am not going to let him get away with this.

It's brave talk, and immediately a sly whisper in the corner of my brain begins to drip its poison, trying to erode my resolve. But I push it down, telling myself I have already taken the first step: when I got these books from the library I armed myself with knowledge and knowledge is power.

My jeans hang loose about my hips and I have to put on a

belt. I remember a tight little gold cocktail dress I used to own with cut outs on the waist: it would look fantastic on me now, but Joanna, somewhat gleefully I felt, sent it and all my other party frocks off to Age UK years ago. Still, if I lose much more weight I'll start to look ill so I decide on a proper breakfast. Eggs, toast and tea. I eat standing up at the sink, staring out over the garden where the blackbirds stab for worms and two fat pigeons strut along the roof of the shed.

Movement catches my eye. A man next door, doing something with bamboo canes and garden twine. It's bound to be Alan, he likes to keep an orderly garden, and even though it's barely eight o'clock I pull on my coat and head outside, pleasantly surprised to find yesterday's cold wind has gone and there's a hint of warmth in the morning sun. Alan's delighted when I call his name, striding eagerly across his vegetable patch in a pair of mud-crusted wellies, baseball cap on his head. My feet and the bottom of my jeans are sodden by the time I reach the fence. I suppose I will have to get to grips with the lawn at some point. It was Joanna who did the garden, though I think she may have paid one of the students from number 28 to cut the grass. I wonder how I would go about finding that student.

'Look at us chatting over the fence,' says Alan. 'Proper old women. Got my beans and peas going in today. Now it really feels like spring. They say it could hit twenty by next weekend.' He rabbits on in this vein for some time – where he's going to stake out his sweet peas, and how he's getting coffee grounds from the cafe in town to repel slugs – before finally realising I might have something to say.

'I've a favour to ask,' I say awkwardly. I am not very good at asking for help, and feel hot and uncomfortable forcing the words out. But Alan's face lights up like I have bestowed on him a great honour – and he doesn't even know what the favour is yet.

'I wondered if I could borrow your computer for a little while. The police took ours and—' I'm about to launch into a whole thing about how quick I'll be, feel free to say no, but he cuts me off, already the conversation is running away again, and he's gesturing for me to squeeze through the gap Joanna hated and saying he'll make me a coffee while the PC boots up.

Perhaps this is how normal people function, I realise with surprise. They ask for help, and people are happy to give it, and neither side twists themselves in knots, agonises over what words to use or how to repay a simple favour. It's just an ebb and flow of kindness. No big deal. It's a revelation to me and I can't help thinking how much harder I have made my life by shutting myself off from people.

I follow Alan across his garden and look up at our house, noticing how you can see right into James' room from here, and how clearly you can see the bottles of shampoo through the frosted glass of the bathroom window. I make a mental note to make sure I always lower the blind.

I remove my wet trainers and socks at the back door, and Alan insists on taking them and putting them on the boiler. His kitchen hasn't been updated since the houses were built. The worktops are scratched and the cabinet fronts scuffed and dated. The windows are steamed with condensation and every surface is cluttered with stuff: tomato seedlings, piles of papers, boxes of shotgun cartridges. A cat is crouched on the kitchen table, daintily eating dry food from its bowl. Joanna always refused to eat any of the food Alan brought round. *You're taking your life in your hands,* she used to say if James or I accepted his offerings of flapjacks or homemade elderflower cordial. I make a mental note to tell her the cat eats on the table, and then correct myself: there is no one to share that snippet with now, and I feel the grief rush in as fresh and raw as the first morning.

Alan doesn't notice, of course. He's finally made me a coffee

– I surreptitiously wipe a couple of cat hairs from the rim of the mug – and is chatting away, eager as a pup, as he leads me through the house. The computer is in his front bedroom, which he's turned into an office. It's cold in here, condensation in the windows, and the wallpaper – pale pink rosebuds and silvery grey stripes – is bubbled with damp. The room is bare apart from a large desk and an office chair, the type you can spin around on. I have a sudden flashback to one of my earliest temping jobs in London: straddling a hot guy from sales at the Christmas party and the two of us spinning wildly, his face buried in my cleavage, his hands on my arse, the glass of cheap white wine in my hand showering our co-workers. At the time, I thought they were cheering us on but the next morning a complaint was made and I was fired. Not the man, though. I can't even remember his name now.

I shake away the memory, which suddenly seems unsettling rather than some high-spirited high jinks, and allow Alan to settle me into the computer chair, adjusting the height and fussing with the backrest. My eyes stray over his desk, the detritus of a life: a sheaf of bank statements, a letter from the hospital with a leaflet about prostate health, faded postcards and a little stack of coupons cut from newspapers. Post-it notes dot the desk, little flags that mark out important passwords and security codes. There's a desk calendar from the local funeral directors, various dates marked in biro, and a half-completed sudoku – I can see he's put two fives in one square. I carefully avert my eyes: it's horribly intimate to be sitting here, surrounded by the medical anxieties and petty money concerns of someone else's life.

He gets Internet Explorer up and running for me, and hovers for a while over my shoulder. I grit my teeth; surely he's not going to stand there all morning and watch me?

'It's to do with my health,' I say at last, a flash of inspiration.

He claps his hands together. 'Well, I'll leave you to it. Just shout if you need anything. Any problems, I'll just be in the garden.'

I hear the door shut behind me, and let some of the tension in my shoulders subside. I search the Internet for anything to do with the crash. There are many reports of crashes in the area but the dates are wrong, or it's the wrong car, the wrong county. I google Robert's name but find just one tiny mention of his death in a local newspaper archive: an article summarising recent court proceedings includes one perfunctory sentence: *The fatal accident coroner's inquest into the death of Robert Bailey, 32, in a fatal RTA on Drovers Road in November reached a verdict of accident.*

One sentence buried in one article in one local paper twenty years ago is Rob's faint fingerprint on the digital world. He departed this world before our lives were recorded and uploaded and lived for ever. He's a ghost who grows ever fainter as those who know his name pass from this earth. Joanna has gone too so now there's just me, James, and one unknown other.

I google his best man, Gary Brown. I don't have much to go on, other than a twenty-year-old photo and a name on a marriage certificate. Perhaps he was a pilot too? Suddenly the search results start to narrow down. If he was roughly the same age as Robert then he would be in his early fifties by now. I come up with two main candidates, both in the UK, both commercial pilots and roughly the same age – and one of them is black. I look at the white guy, with his salt-and-pepper hair and those full lips. Could this be Gary Brown, Robert's best man? It looks like he works for a company called Bright Air. I look up its website and jot down the phone number; it's based overseas, registered in Cyprus. I'm not sure what to do with this information but it seems important, dangerous. Could this man have had some kind of vendetta against me and Joanna?

I log into my head trauma forum and scan the threads for names I know. One regular – MrMigraine – has had to have another scan. He's got an inoperable brain tumour, which has been managed for many years but he's now entering another phase of decline. Over the years some regulars have just disappeared. Sometimes family members come on and update us about what's happened, thanking us for all the support over the years, which then leaves us survivors wondering, who's next? I log out without posting anything. I can't bear the thought of Rawlinson reading my posts and judging me.

Next, I google Joanna's murder. It's a shock to see our house on the local BBC news page with the white tent of death and the police tape in the front garden. The report includes a close up of the shrine at the gate. You can see Simon's flowers and message card prominently, a cut above the rest of the supermarket carnations. The local paper's website runs the story in more detail and I gasp to see a colour photo of Joanna on the screen: we're not the sort of family that's used to media attention. It's an unfortunate shot, taken a few years ago when she had that awful fringe and before she went low-carb. The camera has caught her with her eyes half closed and her mouth hanging slackly, as if she's about to fork in some chips. I wonder who supplied the photo. They clearly didn't know her well: she'd have been mortified to be caught like that, she always policed photographs with a ruthless unsentimentality, binning any that she deemed unflattering. I tell myself this is something I can do for her. I'll dig out one of the good photos of her, with her highlights done and in the height of Atkins mania, and send it to the paper. It's not right they have this image of her out there – it's not representative of the woman she was.

There's a heavy tread on the stairs and Alan puts his head round the door. 'Can I get you anything, cup of tea?'

'No, I'm all done, thanks.'

He walks up behind me. 'Oh Sarah, don't be looking at that. You'll only get upset again.'

Again? I am upset all the time. 'I'm going to send in another photo. This doesn't even really look like her.'

He peers forward over my shoulder, coffee breath by my ear. 'You're right. That won't do at all. I'm hoping James will pop up today to film the appeal and we need to engage the public sympathy. She looks like a half-wit ...' He trails off. 'Sorry, love, you know I thought the world of JoJo.'

Do I know that? I think back, and realise he probably was very fond of her, of all of us really. He certainly spent enough time trying to insinuate himself into our lives.

'What time is James coming?' I'd like to see him too, see if I can talk him into moving home.

'He just said maybe later.'

Classic James, he hates to be pinned down.

'Alan, did James ever speak to you about his dad, or the accident?' We're back in his kitchen now, where I've reluctantly agreed to another cup of tea. I shift a pile of parish magazines from a kitchen chair and sit down, while he bustles about looking for clean mugs. 'I've tried looking for details online but nothing comes up.'

'Ah,' he says, setting down a mug of tea and pulling up opposite me. 'We're talking early days of the Internet. Not all papers were online then. You'd have to go to the British Library in London. Me and James used to talk about doing a road trip down there but you know how it is, life gets busy and somehow you put things off ...' He trails off.

I nod along. I have somehow put off half my life. I drink my tea, trying not to notice how sticky the table is under my fingers, and then push back my chair.

'I must be getting back. I like to stay near the phone in case there's any news.'

160

'Go around the back again,' warns Alan. 'While you were upstairs, I noticed people hanging around the front taking photos like it's a tourist spot. If they don't move on soon, I'll get my hose out.'

Chapter Twenty-Five

Five years ago

I am playing gooseberry, again. James is running on ahead with Enzo, Simon's dog. He likes this, being entrusted with the lead and getting to shout instructions. Maybe we should get a dog. I know Joanna isn't keen. She isn't a pet person. After the kitten went missing, she refused to get another one, citing mess. Now she gives Enzo the side-eye when he comes up and rests his big doggy head by her Boden skirt. They look like a Boden catalogue right now, James running on ahead, kicking up the leaves, and the affluent couple holding hands, dressed in their autumnal knits and expensive wellies. I drag behind, trying to let a discreet distance build up so they can talk in private. I am the luckless chaperone in a Jane Austen novel, the loveless spinster aunt trying not to listen as she bends over her needlepoint.

And it's such a perfect day. Golden light spills through the trees and the leaves are a furnace of colour against the bluest sky. We're doing the long route round the old Deer Park and it's good to be out walking again. We come out of the woods and a Georgian hall sprawls before us, its yellow stone glowing in the buttery sunlight.

Simon gives me his phone and asks me to take a photo of him and Joanna against the backdrop of the deer park and the mansion in the background. It's a beautiful picture, truly worthy of a catalogue.

He chortles at this. 'A second career beckons,' he laughs.

'Well, let's hope,' remarks Joanna dryly.

A shadow passes over his face at this reference to an old argument. Joanna doesn't like his job. She thinks it's immoral that he advises the super rich on how to reduce their tax bills but he has all sorts of statistics on how much tax the top ten per cent pay and how the country would go to the dogs without their contribution. Truthfully, I think she just hates all his travelling; it hasn't reduced at all, really, and he's had to get a dog walker for Enzo. She's still carrying a grudge that he can't make her work Christmas do – she wanted to show him off. I know her new boss made a jibe about her phantom boyfriend when she didn't need a plus-one, again. It was only a joke but it obviously touched a nerve. I suppose when everyone else is all coupled up it gets harder and harder to keep turning up alone. Look at me, I'm finding it uncomfortable and this is just a day trip to our local National Trust.

I decide to give them some space and offer to take James and Enzo for an ice-cream while they explore the house. They brighten at this but James insists he wants to tour the Hall too; apparently, he's doing the slave trade in history and he wants to see what they spent all that blood money on. Joanna is so thrilled that James is showing some interest in something vaguely academic that she doesn't have the heart to put him off. It suits me to hang out with Enzo, who, worn out by capering alongside James, ambles happily at heel round the gardens, although I decide I'm with Joanna on the issue of whether to get a dog; it just encourages people to come up and talk to you, spoiling an otherwise pleasant walk.

I meet the others back at the cafe terrace. Their faces are like thunder and I can tell there's been another argument. James sulks at the table with me, hunched over his phone, while Joanna and Simon hiss at one another in the queue for the coffees.

'What's happened?' I ask James.

'Simon had a go at me again and so Mum had a word,' he says, pulling out his phone.

'What did he say to you?'

James shrugs. 'He doesn't like it when things don't go his way. I suppose I was cramping their style. And he was banging on about bloody private school again.'

This has been another source of acrimony. Joanna likes to moan about James's school, how the teachers don't get him, the kids are rough, there's not enough homework or there's too much homework. And Simon, to give him his due, listens very patiently but, and I think it's part of being a bloke, he wants to come up with solutions. And he thinks going private would do it. But that gets Joanna's back up, as if he's implying she's failing her son by sending him to state school.

Now I think about it, there have been a lot of little niggles and complaints recently. She's upset that she hasn't met any of his friends. She feels he's ashamed of her because she can't match their glitzy lifestyle.

'One of his friends is on his third wife, and she's twenty-four,' she said. 'Imagine us all going out for dinner and me sitting next to her. I'm almost old enough to be her mother.' I didn't say anything but she *is* old enough to be her mother. I understand her feelings, and they may well be valid, but if she keeps finding fault she's going to push him away. As James points out, rich men like to have things their own way.

They come back now with steaming coffees and hot chocolates but the atmosphere is frigid. They're not really looking at one another and talk at me brightly, pretending like nothing's happened. Simon tells me a long story about some artefact in the Hall and I catch James rolling his eyes.

Simon stops talking and looks at James. 'James, if you don't like my conversation then maybe you'd like to tell us what you enjoyed about the Hall.'

I glance at Joanna. Her face is frozen, white with anger. 'Let's leave it there, shall we?'

My eyes flick to Simon, to Joanna, to James. Of them all, only James seems unperturbed. 'I liked the hidden door in the bookcase the best,' he says. 'Fitted by the fourth earl.'

It's such an improbable reply for someone who apparently never pays attention in class that I can't help smiling. Joanna too, I can tell she's pleased that James has redeemed himself for whatever happened inside.

Simon's face is pinched with anger but he controls it well, his voice like ice when he finally speaks. 'I liked that too,' he says sourly, and I can't help thinking it doesn't reflect well on him to be trying to score points over a boy.

I look at Joanna, at the little squeeze she gives James, the little 'told you so' look she gives to Simon, and I can tell she's thinking the same thing too. Like a restored artwork in a National Trust building, it seems the veneer on Simon is starting to crack, revealing something very different underneath.

Chapter Twenty-Six

Alan's on the phone. It is only a couple of hours since I left his place, and I can't help but feel that now I've given him an opening he'll be round all the time. I remember the pattern from before, how any encouragement led to a snowballing of contact.

'Switch on now, BBC local news,' he directs. 'I'll be round in ten to discuss. Pop the kettle on, love.'

What? But he's already put the phone down. I switch on the TV with a creeping feeling of dread. Sure enough, the news-caster is just rounding up a story about leaking water mains when the picture in the background switches to footage of our house just after the murder, with the white tent still up and people in crime scene suits trampling over our flowerbeds on their official business.

Suddenly the footage jumps to a group of people, about ten in all, standing outside an office building, a couple of whom are holding handmade signs that read *Justice for Joanna*. Now there's a close-up on one of the group: a man, with thinning salt and pepper hair and bristly jowls. His teeth look yellow. The caption reads, *Alan Warner, victim's neighbour and friend*.

'We're here to launch an appeal for witnesses,' he's telling the presenter. 'It's been over a week now and we're concerned the police are more interested in harassing members of the family than making arrests.'

I wince at his words. I don't see how attacking the police is going to help us. The camera switches now to a slight young man with floppy brown hair and prominent cheekbones. The caption reads, *James Bailey, victim's son.* I hold my breath, wondering how he will cope with the limelight.

'My mum was a lovely lady, a much-valued member of the community, and we're appealing for people to come forward with information, anything at all, that might help the police bring her killer to justice. Someone, somewhere, knows something and I beg you, please ...' His voice cracks, and the older man edges into shot and starts talking again.

'If you were anywhere in the Broom End area of Market Leyton on the night of March 28 then please get in touch with police. Whoever did this would have been covered in blood. Someone somewhere knows this person, will have seen them trying to dispose of clothing or acting strangely, please get in touch with the police.'

The man holds up a handwritten sign, with a number to call, but he aims it at the wrong camera, before quickly correcting his position.

The report then switches to a pretty dark-skinned lady, with very short dark hair. The caption tells me this is DS Noor.

'We certainly echo calls for people to get in touch if they think they know anything about this crime. Although can I please direct them to the helpline.' A different number flashes up on the screen.

I switch the TV off, just as there's a knock on the back door. I groan. He must have run. I open the door and assess the figure standing there: tall, burly, right age range, no cap but the voice gives him away.

'Sorry, forgot to put my cap on, Sarah, but it's me, Alan,' he babbles, and already he's in the kitchen.

I peer over his shoulder, hoping to see James. 'Is James with you?'

'Sorry, love, he had to get back to work, least that's what he said. Between you and me, I think he's got the heebie-jeebies about coming back here, you know.' He nods towards the floor. 'I told him it's all cleaned up, like, but he looked a bit peaky, he's just a young lad still, eh?'

I swallow my disappointment. I understand, of course, but I wish he'd come. It makes no sense him doing shifts and living in that grotty house share when I could look after him here, at home.

'Well,' says Alan, clapping his hands together. 'What did you think? How was my first television appearance?' He beams at me expectantly.

'Very good.' It's odd to be critiquing someone's appeal for your dead sister's killer but it seems churlish to rain on his parade when he's doing this to help me. 'Although I don't think DS Noor was impressed.'

'Oh, the mess up with the number. That's their fault, they didn't cooperate with me, you see, so I had to use the general switchboard number off their website. She had a word with me afterwards. Apparently, they don't want that number clogged up with calls but if you don't make an appeal you won't get any calls. Better the wrong number than no number at all, that's my thinking anyway.'

'I suppose you're right.'

He grins at me, and I spot the plaque build-up on the incisors that the TV picked up. He must be a careless brusher.

'You betcha,' he says, plonking a plastic bag on the table. 'There are two types of people in this world, Sarah. The complainers and the doers. If I see something wrong, I just have to fix it.'

He opens one of my cupboards. 'Case in point,' he says. 'I've bought you some bits because I know you're a homebody and I thought to myself I bet her cupboards are empty. Look here, these baps are fifteen pence on yellow sticker but they'll be fine toasted.'

He's also brought me baked beans, tinned sausages, more biscuits and some cheese scones he's made himself. I won't starve but I may get scurvy – unless wine has vitamin C? It does come from grapes after all. Could I ask Alan to pick me up more wine next time he's at the Co-op? I decide against it. I don't really want people to know how much I'm drinking. It creates the wrong impression.

He flicks the switch on the kettle. I can't help but notice how he's increasingly making himself at home. I want to feel annoyed but it's actually quite nice to have a bit of company. The house is so empty without Joanna. He's chatting away – something about the sugar tax, I think – sort of puffed up, like an athlete after a big game. Pumped, that's the word.

'Did you like the signs we had? Polish Bob helped me. We wanted to use a photo of Joanna too but it would have cost fifteen pounds per sign. James was brilliant, of course, he's a good-looking lad, which never hurts. Don't look at me like that, you know it's true.' He glances at me sideways. 'You'd be good too, you know, it would add more punch to have the two of you upfront in the campaign.'

'No!' I am still reading the psychopath books and I know it's typical prime suspect behaviour to insert themselves into the drama of the police investigation. The last thing I need is to draw any more attention to myself.

'OK, OK,' says Alan, holding up his hands in mock surrender. 'I just thought I'd ask one last time. Oh, you've got the latest edition of the *Gazette*, let's have a gander while you get the tea made. Kettle's boiled.'

I fish around for teabags and sniff the milk. Alan's on about the road works planned for the A5 and the cutbacks to the library. I try to block it out and keep myself focused on the steam from the kettle, the white bloom of milk into the dark tea, the tinkle of the teaspoon. Mindfulness they call it these days, the papers are full of it, every two-bit celebrity out there claims to practise it. Me and my fellow Headliners have had a chuckle about this: head trauma patients are mindful by necessity.

No need for a fancy app. I can put you 'in the moment' for free with a sledgehammer to the skull. Nothing more mindful than anterograde amnesia.

That was a quip from Redneck82, who based on the style of his postings to Headliners had had a rather colourful past before a brawl at Cheltenham – the racecourse, not the jazz festival – left him with a caved-in skull and life-long apraxia, memory issues and fatigue. I remember I'd responded with a stream of laughing emojis, and a suggestion we go into business together.

Who's bringing the sledgehammer?!! LOL

I wince at the thought of Noor trawling through my online postings and deciding my joke, admittedly bad taste, is somehow evidence of my propensity to murder.

'Hello, hello, what's he doing here? Haven't seen him around these parts for years, not since him and Jojo parted ways.'

Alan's prodding a finger at a photograph in the paper. It's a photo of my house, with the police car outside and a crowd of people on the other side of the police tape.

'Who?' I ask, leaning over his shoulder and looking as his finger jabs at the crowd of onlookers. I notice a couple of Alan's fingers are taped up, the plasters grubby and frayed at the edges and make a mental note to bin the cheese scones.

'Here,' says Alan. 'This chap behind the big copper.'

It's hard to get a clear impression. The newsprint gives the photos a grainy finish and the face is so small but I see a man, perhaps in his fifties or sixties, with a wide-set face, sandy hair brushed forwards, his face grave and frown lines between his eyes.

'Who is it?' I ask again, starting to get irritated. He knows I can't recognise people and I don't like being toyed with.

'That's Jojo's ex. That's Simon Carmichael. Here, outside your house.'

Chapter Twenty-Seven

Four years ago

Joanna has locked herself in her bedroom. She's been crying again. I don't know what's gone on between her and Simon, she's refusing to talk about it. All I know is he appears to have buggered off to the other end of the country, not even a phone call, just a text message that dropped her like she's a poisoned apple. Harsh. I admit there have been times I've been jealous, and fearful, of her relationship with Simon so I'm pleased as I scan my own reactions that there's no hint of satisfaction at this result. I just feel really bad for her. Perhaps I'm not such a bad person after all.

Joanna keeps her feelings locked up. After the first messy night when she got the text, when she got drunk and ranted wildly as she found he'd blocked her number so her increasingly hysterical calls and texts disappeared into the ether, she's kept her grief private. But I see her red eyes, the blank way she's just going through the motions, her mind elsewhere. She drove over to his place yesterday evening and found it deserted, bare: furniture gone and a To Let sign up. He's disappeared as coldly and completely as a fish sliding out into the dark waters of the ocean, no trace left behind.

'Do you think he had another life? A wife?' I asked over breakfast. She's not eating, just stirring her tea mindlessly.

She shrugged. 'What else could it be?'

'Maybe the holiday, maybe he got cold feet?' They'd been planning a week away in the Lake District for a food festival.

'It was his idea! No, it's someone else. That's why he's ended it so finally.'

I have another suspicion but I'm too much of a coward to mention it. Joanna has baggage. There's James, who's a typical moody teenager, and then there's me, and I'm just difficult with no prospect of growing out of it. Perhaps it was too much to ask of a man used to his own ways. But if Joanna hasn't thought of this I don't want to put it into her head. Our relationship can be tricky enough as it is, and I don't want her to start thinking I'm standing between her and a second chance of love. So I keep quiet, and agree that Simon's a cheating bastard, which is a likely scenario after all. I mean, who cuts and runs like that?

We're hosting book club this month. I thought she would have cancelled but no, here they are, at the door, and Joanna's still crying in her bedroom. Do they know about Simon? I dither at the top of the stairs. I wish James was here, at least he could open the door, but he's round at Alan's working on a project for school. I knock on Joanna's door.

'You decent, Jojo? Do you want me to tell them to go?'

I hear nothing, and am about to head downstairs when she opens the door. She's put on a clean top, and done her make-up. Her eyes are a little puffy but she forces a smile.

'Life goes on. And God, I need a drink and a laugh.'

There are five of them in the group, with me as an honorary member given that we're hosting this month. I have memorised these women, the little features of their hair, their voices, their build – like the tells poker players exploit – and feel reasonably confident in their company. There's Mandy, a brassy blonde with a filthy laugh who I've discovered to my surprise is a law lecturer at the university; Carmen, Joanna's friend from work with the olive skin and a flash of silver that runs in a streak through her dark hair; Carmen's sister-in-law Juno, who wears big glasses and doesn't contribute much – I'm sure, like Joanna, she hasn't always read the book – but always brings a box of macaroons, which more than makes up for it. The only one that takes the book side of it seriously is Jess, who gets a bit tetchy when the conversation veers onto parenting woes or celebrity gossip.

It doesn't help that Jess is also teetotal while the rest of them are on the prosecco. I used to think Jess was boring but now that I'm reading more I understand her frustration, especially when it's a good book, like this week's choice: *Life After Life* by Kate Atkinson. Mother would never believe it. She always thought my failure to be a reader – one of her few approved leisure activities – was a sign I was a deviant in the making. But look at me now. Reading proper grown-up books. Not even rom-coms or murder-thrillers, but proper literary books and enjoying them.

Carmen and Juno are waiting on the doorstep, armed with prosecco and macaroons. Juno hasn't even bothered to bring a copy of the book with her. Jess crunches over the gravel behind them, with her usual offering of sickly buttercream-topped cupcakes and the journal she uses to keep notes on each book.

I lead them through to the living room, listening to the hum and crackle of conversation: ailing parents enquired about, a PTA spat giggled over. I pour out the fizz, wondering if Joanna will share her news. She's so secretive I bet half of them don't even know Simon exists. But to my surprise, she downs her glass of prosecco and boldly shares the news of Simon's sudden departure. Not only do the group know of his existence but most of them have met him. I suppose I only ever see one in five book clubs when we host the night. While I'm skating the surface, just seeing the top of the iceberg of their lives, these women go much deeper, their lives entwined in ways I can't fathom. And that's just book club – there are also work dos and Zumba sessions and quiz nights for the PTA. Kate Atkinson is, for now, forgotten, and even Jess doesn't seem to mind for once. There's a lot of sympathy, more wine is poured, and Simon's name is mud. Mandy arrives a little late, so then we have to go through the whole story again. She's outraged on Joanna's behalf, and reckons, as the others do, that he's clearly had some other woman in the background all this time.

'God, I'll castrate the bastard if I ever see him again,' she says, miming a cutting motion with one hand and holding out a lipstick-smeared glass for a refill with the other. I notice her long pink talons and wonder how she gets anything done; maybe law lecturers only talk and never have to write?

'No fear of that,' says Joanna. 'He's done a professional job, gone without a trace. I'll never see him again, I know that.'

'Cold,' says Jess. 'He must have been planning this for a while, right? I mean, you can't just up and go.'

Joanna's eyes are glassy. 'I just feel like such a fool. Never saw it coming.'

My eyes search her face, wondering if that's entirely true. She's focused on something Mandy's saying – she always has to be the centre of attention – and gives me a small, distracted smile as I refill her glass. Yet I'm sure it was only a month ago she said she was a bit worried about Simon's health. He's been down ever since his dog died and then he'd asked her to come to his place because he didn't want to drive, which is unusual for him, and when she'd got there he'd been distracted and on edge. And the last time I saw him I thought he'd looked tired and drawn, like a man with a million things on his mind. Or a guilty conscience.

'What an utter twenty-four-carat shit,' says Mandy, a sentiment with which we all concur.

It's Jess that brings us back to the book, and it's interesting how timely it is. A book about reliving your life again and again until you get it right seems to strike a chord with all of us. Of course, we're not in a position to slay Hitler or stop wars but for women in our forties and fifties each of us seems to have clocked up enough *Sliding Doors* moments when our lives could have taken a different path.

Carmen says she wouldn't have eaten for two in every pregnancy. 'Ten pounds two the last one,' she says, moaning. 'Can you imagine?'

'Big bones,' says Juno. 'All the fellas in our family are big.' Her do-over would be a different job. 'No way would I go into teaching again if I knew then what I know now. Not enough money in the world.'

'Hm, what would I do differently if I had to do it all again?' asks Mandy. 'Use factor 50 in my twenties and botox in my thirties. Seriously ladies, until I've put the slap on it's like looking at my mother in the mirror.'

We all reassure her, of course, that she looks fantastic for fifty-three, which is exactly what she wanted. Jess says her regret was not emptying the joint bank account before her ex had his mid-life crisis and spent all their savings on a yacht for a round the world sailing trip with his twenty-seven-year-old co-worker.

'Of course, she left him, so now he's got no money and lives in a one-bed flat in Derby,' says Jess.

It's a story we've heard before, told with the practised jauntiness of someone who's putting on a brave face, but there's a dangerous undercurrent of hysteria just below the surface.

'Derby? You couldn't be further from the sea! Don't get me wrong, I'm glad he's gone, just wish I'd got the money instead of a half share of a fucking boat he refuses to sell!'

We all drink some more and then it's my turn. What would I do differently? The tone of the answers so far – apart from Jess's, which had been on the edge between laughter and tears – has been light-hearted so I try the same. 'I wouldn't have sent a Valentine's card to Gary Williams when I was eight,' I say, remembering the heart-festooned piece of paper declaring my undying love. I'd slipped it into the desk of my beloved only for him, red-faced, to get caught with it to the endless mirth of the rest of the class. Seriously, that stayed with me throughout primary school. Even Mother heard about it. She said later it had been an early warning sign of my lascivious nature. 'I never lived it down and to this day I have hated Valentine's Day.'

'Amen to that,' says Mandy.

'And of course, I wouldn't get in a certain car twenty years ago. That was a bit of a bummer too.'

There's a bit of nervous laughter to this. Joanna gives me a fierce look, and mutters something under her breath. I only catch the word 'fuck'. I glower back at her. I wasn't saying it to have a go at her but to acknowledge what for me has been the defining moment of my life. Of course that's what I'd change if I could, that car crash ruined my life. Or do I have to pretend that just because I'm functioning normally on the surface that everything is OK? Because it really isn't. Of course, I don't say any of this. As usual it all simmers along under the surface, while Jess steers the conversation back onto the book and the morality of killing Hitler if you had the chance.

The kitchen door slams, and there's the sound of cupboards being opened and shut in a kind of fury.

'James!' calls Joanna. 'Come in and say hello.'

We hear the rattle of plates and spoons. The fizz of a can being opened.

177

'He's like a bottomless pit at the moment,' says Joanna, a little embarrassed.

'Teenagers,' says Mandy knowingly. 'I couldn't fill mine at that age.'

'James!' calls Joanna again.

Eventually, he appears in the doorway. He's suddenly so tall, all arms and legs, a little off balance like he hasn't quite got used to his new centre of balance. There's a sprouting of acne on his chin, soft down on his upper lip, and the deepening of his voice still takes me aback. How hard this age is, half man, half boy. It all seems to have happened so quickly.

'James, there you are,' says Joanna. 'You eaten?'

He nods, keeping his body largely hidden behind the door-frame. I don't blame him, I feel like that a lot of the time and I know there are members of this group that won't let him quietly slink upstairs.

'Hello, stranger. How are you?' I knew it would be Mandy. It's as if she's on heat; she's even twirling a coil of her bottle-blonde hair round her fingers. I dread to think what she's like with her students.

'Alright.' His face flushes a deep red, and his body sort of folds into itself. I feel a rush of sympathy for the boy. I know that feeling, where even someone's gaze is like a physical pain, a flash of heat against your raw skin that you shrink back from.

'Handsome young man you've got here, Jo,' says Mandy.

'I know,' says Joanna. Her voice is so flat, and she doesn't even look at James; perhaps it's because she's busy refilling her glass with the dregs of another bottle.

James hovers, unsure. 'Night,' he offers, his voice a rasp, rattling past his newly prominent Adam's apple.

'Night, love,' says Joanna, her concentration on the cork of another bottle. I glance at her anxiously, wondering if I should rein her in and, if so, how I should go about that. I'm not used to being the responsible one. I'm so focused on Joanna, with her face flushed, her movements clumsy, that I don't notice James' flight, I just hear the thunder of his feet and the slam of a bedroom door.

'Typical teenager you've got there,' laughs Jess. 'Nothing to worry about.'

Joanna says nothing, pouring herself another and then sloshing more wine into Mandy's glass, like she needs any encouragement. I take the bottle from Joanna and top up Carmen, Juno and myself – I think it's best we have more to limit Joanna. Jess, of course, is happy with her J20 – she's on her third, so that plus the cupcakes mean her blood sugar must be through the roof.

I glance over at Joanna as I place the bottle on the floor next to me, out of her reach. Her face is dark, brooding over her glass of wine.

'I think I know the lesson I've learned from life,' she suddenly announces in a break in the conversation. Her voice is a little loud, a little slurred. 'Be careful what you wish for.'

She hiccups loudly and it's almost comical but her tone is so bleak that no one laughs.

'Be careful what you wish for, ladies, because it just might come true.'

I help Joanna to bed that night, taking her upstairs even before her friends have left. I lie her down, and then fetch a pint of water, which I leave on her bedside table. She's going to feel rough in the morning. I want to ask her what she meant, what had she wished for that had turned so sour? But she smiles up at me, slaps a drunken hand on my arm and says, 'Just you and me now, sis,' before falling into a kind of stupor. I tiptoe out, closing the door gently behind me. James' room is bathed in a blue light, which means he's still up and on his computer at half past eleven on a school night. Perhaps I should go in and tell him to turn in? But somehow I don't feel I have that privilege so I head downstairs and show everyone out.

Mandy hugs me extravagantly on the doorstep.

'You look after her,' she slurs. 'She's special that one, she doesn't deserve that shitbag treating her like that. You tell her, we're here for her.'

I reassure them all that yes, yes, I'll look after her. Yes, of course she deserves better, yes, there are plenty more fish in the sea. It's with relief I finally close the door on them. It seems to have taken so many words just to say goodbye and now my brain is done. I'm not going to tidy up. That can wait until tomorrow. I bolt the door and turn to head upstairs when I'm startled to see James standing there, watching me.

'So, he's gone then,' he says. It's more of a statement than a question. He'll have heard the conversations, all a variation on a theme, as the women left the house.

'Yes. Sorry, James. Seems like he's not been the gent he tried to make out he was.'

I'm surprised Joanna hasn't already told him. There had been a few 'male bonding sessions', as Joanna called them, where Simon took James on a tour of the Bentley factory at Crewe and they'd been to watch Stoke get thrashed by Chelsea before they were relegated. It doesn't seem right he finds out like this, second-hand, overheard in the hall while his mum sleeps it off upstairs.

'Right.' He absorbs the news. 'Is she OK?'

'Bit tired and emotional.'

'OK. Night then.'

I want to say something else. I want to reach out to him, to fold him in my arms and say, 'Don't worry, love, it's not your fault'. Because I know how kids' minds can work, twisting and turning the strange events of the world to put themselves at the centre, both for the good, and for the bad. It's such a simple set of actions and words but somehow my body can't follow through: nobody ever showed me how to do that, how to love, how to hug, how to comfort and now it feels like I'd be play-acting, copying things I've seen other people, normal people, do. So instead, I just stand there and say 'night' and watch him retreat upstairs, alone. I tell myself I'll go in to see him in the morning, and say those things then, and give him the hug he needs now that another father figure has abruptly vanished from his life. But deep down I know I'm lying to myself. I won't go in and see him in the morning and somehow the distance that has been growing between the three people in this house will continue its glacial advance.

Chapter Twenty-Eight

I'm rattled by Simon's mysterious reappearance. Had he and Joanna reignited their romance, and if so, why didn't she tell me? Yet again, I'm staring at the iceberg bobbing on the surface and wondering just how big it is below the waterline. I need to talk to someone inside the magic circle. I dig out Joanna's address book and call Carmen on her mobile. She answers, and her voice sounds fearful. I suppose the number must have flashed up on her mobile as Joanna Home. She probably thought she was getting a call from beyond the grave.

'Sorry, Carmen, it's me, Sarah. I didn't mean to upset you.'

'Oh Sarah, how are you? I just can't take it in. We're all in shock.'

'I know, I know.'

'Every time I look over at her desk ...' I hear her voice crack but she recovers control. 'I just can't believe she won't be coming back.' Carmen sniffs loudly. 'And what about you? How are you managing?'

'I'm OK. You know.'

'And James?'

'He doesn't say much.'

'The police have been here, and they've spoken to a few of us. I just can't think who would do this to her.'

182

'I know. I keep going over it again and again. Carmen, you probably know her better than me.'

'Really?' She sounds bewildered, perhaps they weren't as close as I thought. 'Well, I suppose we bonded over the infertility really. It can be such a lonely soul-destroying experience.'

'Infertility? But Joanna has James.'

'Yes, her miracle baby, that's what she said. But before then, I think she had a very hard time.'

I wrack my brains. I don't remember Joanna talking about infertility treatments. I suppose that was in the period after her marriage but before the accident, the years that remain a murky fog to me. Was James an IVF baby, then? I wonder if he knows. I suppose it doesn't make any difference how the sperm meets the egg, although it might explain Joanna's fierce mothering of her miracle child.

'People don't understand, and the treatments are so gruelling.' Carmen sniffs again. 'We live in a very child-centric world. You reach a certain age and people just assume ... Joanna was one of the few people who understood how it feels.'

Me too, I guess. I've sort of written that part of my life off. You may as well pack up my uterus and ovaries in a box for all the good they do me. I don't even have any interest in sex any more. It's like that side of me has withered and died, but I don't feel it as a great loss. It's just another loss, one of many. It's the sum that matters not the parts.

'She was a good listener,' I say, trying to keep the conversation rolling. 'I was wondering, though, was she seeing anyone, Carmen? I thought she'd sworn off the Internet dating but maybe she was seeing someone again?'

'The police asked me that. No, as far as I know she was having a break from men. That last one really put her off. He was a shit. But really her heart wasn't in it. I don't think she ever really got over Simon.'

'Yeah, I know what you mean. I still don't really know what happened there. Did she talk to you about it?'

There's a pause, and it crosses my mind she's trying to be diplomatic. Perhaps she also thinks he left because he didn't want to be saddled with me.

'I don't really know what went on. She thought he had another life, another woman, you know, all lined up somewhere else.'

'And?' I can hear there's something else.

'I don't know. I did wonder if he got back in touch. About a year ago, she said something that made me think he'd sent her a message or she'd found something out about him.'

'What did she say?'

'She just said she understood why he did what he did. She said sometimes it's better to rip the plaster off in one go than drag it out. Not very romantic. Who talks about their relationship like it's an old plaster?'

I feel like the air has knocked out of me. I am sure the old plaster is me, and she'd been wishing she'd got rid of me years ago.

A phone starts to ring insistently in the background and she says she has to go.

'Oh, one more thing, Sarah. My boss, Alex, wants to come and see you. We've got some flowers and a card from everyone. Just thought I'd better forewarn before we turn up. He's a bit of a steamroller when he gets an idea in his head.'

I groan inwardly, that's all I need. I know I'll be on high alert now, unable to settle. Alex, wasn't he the knob? Can't they just dump the flowers at the gate like everyone else? But of course, I don't say any of this. *Don't make a fuss, Sarah.* Besides, it might be interesting to meet this Alex. I mean, it's weird, isn't it, to come here? Isn't that classic killer behaviour, coming round to snoop about the crime scene, to keep an eye on me? I just can't think why. Did she find out something about him? Working in HR, she would have been privy to all sorts of information. Did she have something on him?

I call Carmen back to see if she knows anything about this Alex but her phone goes straight to voicemail. I stew over her news. *Sometimes it's better to rip the plaster off in one go than drag it out*. Was that really me, was I the old plaster she should have ripped off and binned? Tears sting my eyes. It just all seems so monstrously unfair, and I'm sad for myself, for Joanna, for Simon, for James. So many lives fucked up because I survived a car crash.

I go into the kitchen and pour myself a glass of red. I drain it in one, feeling the heat of the wine snake down to my belly. There's about a glassful left in the bottle and I neck that too. I just need to get out of my head for a while, to escape the self-loathing that makes me want to flay the skin from my hateful body. I am no stranger to self-harm, my right forearm and both my inner thighs bear the criss-cross of white scarring from earlier periods of despair but right now that particular outlet offers no relief: I can't stomach the sight or smell of any more blood.

The phone rings and I snatch it up, hoping it's Carmen so I can quiz her about Alex. But no, it's Alan, again.

'I've got something to show you.'

Chapter Twenty-Nine

Alan's waiting for me on his side of the fence, a mug of tea in each hand. 'How's that for service?' he says, thrusting a brew at me.

'Thank you.'

I can tell he's dying to tell me something but is waiting for a big reveal. I wish he wouldn't, I feel too tired and heavy for games. The conversation with Carmen weighs on me. I'm convinced now that Simon dumped Joanna because he didn't want to take on her baggage – and that Joanna had come to the same conclusion. God, she must have resented me but, to her credit, she hid it reasonably well. I'm not sure I would have done so well if the roles were reversed.

I follow Alan through his messy kitchen and up to the computer room. He's got the window open and the curtains are flapping in the spring breeze.

'Not too cold for you, is it?' he checks.

'No,' I reassure him. It's a lie but I'd rather be cold than breathe in the damp mustiness of a neglected house.

He settles me in the chair and then draws up a stool for himself, just that bit too close. For a moment our knees touch and I quickly pull away, trying to quell the flutter in my hands and hoping he can't smell the wine on my breath.

'Now then,' says Alan, operating the mouse. 'Remember how our mystery man disappeared? Poor Jojo couldn't find him anywhere, he deleted all his accounts, changed his numbers. Well, what do you think of this?'

He pulls up the professional networking site LinkedIn to show the headshot of a middle-aged man with sandy hair, blue eyes set a little too wide, giving him an almost boy-like, simple expression. He's clean shaven, in a pale blue shirt and navy tie, and looks like any other businessman. The man's name is John Carmichael, and it says he's a freelance business adviser.

'Is that him?' I ask.

'Oh yes. There's a little tool you can use, face recognition software, very handy, it finds images on the Internet and bingo, there's your man. You can change your name see, change your hair colour, but you can't change the features and dimensions of your face, not unless you go for radical surgery, of course.'

I glance at Alan sharply. I never realised he was so computer literate. It makes me think, could he have set up a fake Facebook account for me? But again, I'm left with that huge why? Why would Alan want to kill Joanna? I look at what he's showing me on the screen. This businessman, in his tie.

'John Carmichael. It's not the right name.'

'John was his middle name, wasn't it?'

I can't remember. Who would remember that? It seems the Internet would. Alan has found an old Facebook posting of a group of businessmen on a golf jolly. Simon Carmichael has been tagged in the photo as Simon J Carmichael.

'So, where is he? What's he doing?'

'He's keeping his privacy settings pretty locked down now,' says Alan frowning, leaning so close to me our elbows brush. I shrink into myself to avoid touching him again. 'There's no contact details on here, no location. We could message him via LinkedIn.'

I mull over the possibilities. 'What would we say?'

'Well, there's a perfectly innocent reason to get in touch. You could say you wanted to let him know what happened to Joanna.'

'Or thank him for the flowers,' I say. 'He sent a big bunch of her favourite roses at the gate.'

'Bit flash,' says Alan dismissively.

'I spoke to Joanna's friend, Carmen. She said Joanna had forgiven Simon. She wasn't sure if maybe they were back in touch.'

'Interesting.' Alan rubs a hand over his chin, thinking. 'Shame the police have got your computers. We could have checked her emails.' He turns and grins at me. 'Look at us, a couple of detectives. We're the original odd couple, hey? Bonnie and Clyde.'

'Weren't they murderers on the run?'

'You know what I mean.' He turns back to the computer screen, scrolling down Simon's LinkedIn profile. 'What kind of business adviser is he anyway?'

'Tax stuff. Joanna hated it. He rented a barn conversion at Little Walden but he travelled a lot. London, Malta, Dubai, Cyprus.'

'Where the rich folk hang out, eh?' says Alan. 'Be interested to know exactly what his business was, perhaps it was something shady. If you're helping the wrong people hide money, well maybe he pissed them off or knew too much and Joanna got caught in the cross fire.'

I think about this. It's certainly an interesting angle. Perhaps Joanna had discovered he was up to no good, perhaps it was Simon she'd been referring to, not her boss. Perhaps Simon, or someone he worked with, had decided to shut her up for good.

'Why now though?' muses Alan. 'They split up years ago.'

'But if they'd got back together ...' I say.

'I always felt that Bentley was all a show, you know. Proper rich folk, old money types that own half the country, they used to rock up at the boarding school where my folks worked in battered old estates and rusty Land Rovers. Never flash. Didn't need to be.'

He falls into a brooding silence, scrolling pointlessly down Simon/John Carmichael's limited profile page. 'We should message him, see if we can draw him out.'

I shake my head. 'No, I'm going to leave it, Alan. I think things like this are best left to the police.'

His face falls. I am spoiling his game. But this isn't a game. This is a man in your kitchen butchering your sister, her blood pulsing through your useless hands, his arm round your neck crushing the air from your body.

'What are you going to tell the police?'

'I'll tell them he's been hanging round. That they might have been in contact again.'

'Tell them it was very suspicious the way he left before. That shows cold blood right there, callous bastard.'

He's right. Simon might have been all bonhomie and gins in the garden when things were going his way. But when they didn't, he just severed all ties, a forensic cut, no mercy shown. I chew the skin on the side of my thumb. I should make it clear to Noor just how ruthless he could be.

'Can you check another name for me?'

'Sure. Who is it?'

'Gary Brown. He was the best man at their wedding, another pilot. Just wondered if he might have been harbouring a grudge after the accident.'

Alan frowns. 'What kind of grudge? Who could have a grudge against Jojo?' But he's already busy, looking for Gary Brown, pilot, and he manages to find him on LinkedIn. It seems everyone's on there.

189

'Based in Kenya,' says Alan. 'Nairobi. Do you want to message him?'

'Yeah.' I feel safe if he's over in Africa. 'I'll tell him about Joanna. He might want to know, he was at their wedding.'

Alan sets me up with an account and then squidges over to give me room to type.

Hello Gary, you probably won't remember me but I met you twenty years ago at Joanna and Robert Bailey's wedding. I am sorry to be the bearer of bad news but I thought I should let you know that Joanna was very sadly taken from us last week. I am sure Robert would want you to know. Best wishes, Sarah (Joanna's sister)

'Very nicely put,' approves Alan. 'Though of course he'll remember you. Who could forget you?'

I smile politely, this kind of stuff from Alan always makes me uncomfortable. 'I've got another name to search. It's Alex someone, one of the directors at Vernon Guise Associates.'

Alan types it in and a profile pops up straight away. Alex Fuller, director of business development and innovation. The photo is a striking black-and-white shot, designed to make it look like he's been caught mid-meeting, leaning across a desk, his hand pointing at something. He's handsome, young, confident, the very image of a dynamic modern businessman and clearly a big shot on LinkedIn, with a packed CV, glowing personal recommendations and lots of articles written by him on subjects I can't really fathom.

'Who is he?' asks Alan.

'Just someone she talked about now and then,' I say.

'Not surprised, bet half the women in the office were talking about him,' jokes Alan. 'I could do with another brew. You want to check your emails or have a browse while you're here?'

I smile at him. 'Thanks, Alan. I'll be down in a couple of minutes.'

'We should tell James,' he says, as he shuts the windows. 'He should know we've got a credible suspect and that you've tracked down a pal of his dad's. It would mean a lot to him. I'll give him a call later.'

He clumps off downstairs and I take a deep breath, centring myself. I log in to Headliners, to catch up on the news from the regulars. I notice with interest there's a new thread entitled *OK, so this happened* from Mrs007, a fellow prosopagnosia sufferer whose postings have changed over the years from outpourings of grief and anger when she developed the condition following a stroke aged just twenty-seven to funny little stories or uplifting observations about her new life, usually accompanied with the hashtag #blessed as she found a job and got engaged. Part of me is inspired by her positive attitude – that little lick of hope, that maybe I, too, could yet find a new life – and part of me seethes with jealously.

I click on her latest posting aware there's a hateful little worm inside my brain that hopes the 'this' in the title of her thread refers to some blot in Mrs007's happy-ever-after ending. It serves me right. The post opens up an artful black-and-white photo of a baby's tiny hand curled around a woman's perfectly manicured finger. *Meet Baby007. Love at first sight. OK, so I can't pick her out from a line-up of babies – even a mother's love can't circumvent my brain's fried wiring – but love will overcome. #blessed*

Tears blur my vision as BettyBoo72 adds her congratulations to the thread. I don't know Mrs007 but I have followed her story over the years. She's always been a gracious and considered member of the forum, with her honest posts offering wit and wisdom to those in need. She deserves her happy ending but these are not happy tears; I'm crying for me because the comparison is so bleak, I'm further away than ever from my happy ending. Mrs007 has gone out into the world and made the most of life, despite her disability, and has been rewarded for it. I have let fear shrink my world, and now I am reaping my own bitter harvest. I think about starting my own thread, sharing my growing despair and isolation. But even here, on this anonymous forum, I am too proud to ask for help.

An email alert pops up just as I'm closing the Internet browser. I can't help myself. It's right in front of me.

Subject: Johnny Brooks memorial

Alan mate, thought you should know there's a vigil planned to mark the anniversary though I'm told it's best you don't come. Sorry, mate. Know you were close to the lad but . . .

The email goes on but that's all I can read without clicking on it. The name Johnny Brooks rings a bell, something Joanna told me about a boy who had died. Anxiety flutters in my chest and I feel that familiar tightening in my throat. I need to get out of here, out of this house.

I head downstairs, through the kitchen, where the cat is licking a small puddle of milk from the table. My stomach rolls and I stumble out through the back door where I find Alan standing on his patio, doing something with compost and seed trays. Two mugs of tea steam on the lichen-crusted patio table.

'Alright, Sarah? You look a little pale.'

I swallow, pushing past the hard lump in my throat. Standing in the fresh air, watching the white clouds skip across the blue sky and breathing in the fresh smell of grass cuttings, the panic retreats.

'I'm OK.'

'Take a pew.' He gestures to a crusty wooden bench with a compost-stained hand, little black crescents of dirt under his nails. I wonder, fleetingly, how often he bathes. 'You can help if you like. I'm just planting these up though they'll be staying in the house for a bit. After the sun yesterday, there's now talk of a frost. Jojo always used to say you're never really safe until May, eh?'

I nod my agreement, that does sound familiar. I look across at our garden, thinking about how she loved to sit out on a summer evening on her fake rattan armchairs, drinking rosé, catching the last of the sun on her legs and watching the bees go crazy on her riot of rose bushes, honeysuckle and potted lavender. I wonder how I will ever keep it all going.

My eyes drift down the length of the two gardens, ours a long lawn, edged by flowers and sprawling hedges, capped by a string of leylandii so solid they almost form a wall, hiding us from the snooty neighbours at the back. Alan's is a working garden, with most of his lawn dug up for vegetable beds, and the bottom given over to a large shed, beyond which there's a scrabble of ivy-choked trees and brambles.

I sip my tea, looking at that thicket of trees. If I was a killer, I'd want to make a discreet escape under cover of trees, across empty gardens, into the night. The people at the back of our house have security lights that come on like football floodlights every time a cat crosses their lawn but Alan's garden backs onto an overgrown wilderness where an old hippy doesn't believe in cultivating nature. She once told us she liked to sunbathe nude amid the wildflowers, and James' eyes had almost popped out of his head. No wonder he spent so much time in his bedroom; it faces her wilderness.

'Can I have a look down there, Alan? Just wondering, you know, I mean if I was covered in blood and wanted to get away quickly ...'

'The police had a poke around down there but I wasn't impressed. They didn't even have dogs. You see these fingertip searches on TV but not our lot, oh no.'

We walk down the long garden past his shed – 'My workshop, where the magic happens,' he says proudly – behind which there's the boundary fence and the thicket of briars and ivy-clogged trees.

I stop in my tracks, startled to see dead rats and crows strung along the back fence. The rats' mouths are curled back in one last snarl, their little teeth glinting bone-white.

'Deters vermin,' says Alan matter-of-factly, seeing my disgust. 'These buggers would eat my patch bare if I gave them the chance.'

The dead eyes of the crows gaze out at me accusingly as I try to pull myself together. I keep my eyes fixed instead on the wilderness beyond the fence. There are footsteps down here, in the soft mud by the fence, but they could well be Alan's, as he strung up his macabre harvest. On the other side of the fence there's too much greenery to see any footsteps but it does look like the long grass has been trampled down fairly recently.

'It's empty over there right now,' says Alan, nodding towards the hippy's house. 'Cancer.'

He whispers the word, as if even to say it is to invoke some ancient curse.

'She tried to treat it with herbs and crystal therapy but then her daughter intervened and now she's in a hospice in Stoke.'

Everywhere I look I see death. It haunts us all, in the shadows. People don't talk about it but it's always there, stalking us. A wind chime jangles in one of her trees, and I like to think of her spirit still here, blowing free on the breeze, among the feathery grasses and the budding tree tops, not sedated and trapped in a hospice bed.

I peer past the dark banks of rhododendrons towards the house, where the conservatory windows are clouded with dust and mould and greenery crawls over the walls. The upper windows stare back at me, blank and unseeing, and the old gutters sag. The house looks like it's been neglected for some time now, and I feel sorry for the old hippy, her and her house fading together. Did somebody know? Did they see an opportunity to get close to us, to watch us, to plot the perfect getaway? I feel my skin prickle in the deep shade of the trees, picturing someone in there, standing back from the windows, staring out at us.

'I suppose if this killer was local he'd know the place was empty,' muses Alan. 'He could hop over here, get through her garden and then he'd be away. Really, the police should have been down here with dogs. He must have been covered in blood, those clothes would have been like a butcher's apron . . .'

My stomach lurches at the thought of all that blood. Joanna's blood. The man would have needed an escape route where no one would see him until he got washed up and changed. Did he know the hippy's house was empty? Could he have used her house to get changed? Perhaps he's even been using that place as a base to spy on us.

Noor should get a search warrant and investigate. Something strikes me then. 'Could dogs even smell anything with these dead birds and things here?' I wave in the general direction of the fence, unwillingly to look at the corpses again. I think about that email again, a vigil for Johnny Brooks. Joanna's voice, *A boy died, I told you we couldn't trust him.*

'Oh yes,' he says confidently. 'A police dog is a highly trained animal. They can be trained to seek out dead bodies, traces of blood, drugs, explosives. Do you know dogs are now being used in medicine to sniff out tumours, epileptic seizures and signs of disease like MS . . .'

I'm not sure what to make of this so I turn to move away, suddenly shivering with cold. My fingers brush against the soft feathers of a dead crow and I shriek as a cloud of flies rises from the corpse. Alan laughs but I'm angry. So what if they eat his bloody peas? I push past him and out into the sunlight again, keen to put distance between myself, the abandoned house, and Alan.

Chapter Thirty

Six years ago

Joanna comes home from Zumba, her face red and her hair lank with sweat. She keeps trying to get me to go but I can't bear the thought of being in a room with so many people. I use the excuse of my bad leg but she laughs at me. Apparently, there's a woman of eighty-one who goes. I don't see how that's supposed to make me feel better.

'I was right again,' she says, running herself a glass of water at the sink. 'I knew it.'

I brace myself, wondering what I've done wrong now. It's clear I'm in for some told-you-sos.

'So,' she says, practically bursting with self-righteousness, 'it turns out our neighbour next door has form when it comes to losing little boys.'

We haven't seen Alan for a couple of weeks. It's been in the papers, though, so we've got the gist, and the whole town is talking about it. One of the boys in his youth group, the Young Explorers, got lost while they were on a camping weekend just outside town. They'd apparently been doing something called a night walk and this lad had somehow got lost, fallen into a stream swollen by rainfall and washed ashore a few hundred

196

metres downstream. Clearly a horrible scare, with the boy taken to hospital to be treated for shock, but he was unharmed and I didn't get why there was such a fuss. His parents had been up in arms and there was going to be an investigation into safeguarding. Alan had already stepped down.

Joanna hadn't been impressed; up until a month before, James had been a member of the group but he'd pulled out. I think it was because he was worried about going camping, after all, he still sometimes wets the bed and boys can be so cruel. That time on the school residential had been horrific and frankly I wouldn't be surprised if he wasn't left with lifelong issues. The school should have done more to protect his dignity, although James doesn't help himself; Joanna had packed night-time pants but he'd been too embarrassed to wear them. That little problem has got better now but I don't blame him for not wanting to go camping.

'It happened before,' Joanna repeats, leaning close as if somehow Alan might hear from next door. 'Up in Lancashire. And the boy *died*.'

'What? Same thing exactly?'

'Almost. This one drowned.'

'Jesus Christ. How old was he?'

'Same kind of age. Twelve, thirteen, I think. I mean, once is a coincidence, right? But twice?'

She seems strangely gleeful. Perhaps it's just the relief that James got out in time, it does strange things to you to believe you could have been a hair's breadth from disaster and somehow escape.

'I knew there was something about him,' she says. 'I knew it.'

'But it was an accident, right? I mean, he didn't kill him.'

Joanna arches her eyebrow. 'Either he's incredibly lax when it comes to looking after these kids, in which case it's just lucky it hasn't been worse, or he's got some strange impulse.' There's a dramatic pause, her eyes opening wide. 'Perhaps he tried something funny with them, they panicked, he panicked, who knows. It's not good, and I don't want James going around there any more.'

'OK, OK. But you tell him, he's your son, I wouldn't know what to say.'

'I'm sure it's all over the school already,' she says. 'More will come out. It always does once people see other victims coming forward.'

I shiver, I can't quite reconcile this with the Alan I know and it seems a shame to rob James of this one friendship if it is all just bad luck. But I won't push it, I know this is already marked up as a blot in my copybook as I was the one who encouraged James to join the Young Explorers.

Joanna hands me her phone to show me a report in a local newspaper about a town mourning the death of a boy, Johnny Brooks, aged thirteen. There's a quote from his mother about how they'll never get over this, especially knowing he would have died alone and scared in the pitch black. No wonder Alan left the area, came here to start again.

Joanna pops a dried apricot in her mouth – she's heard they're good for iron – and chews thoughtfully. 'What we have to hope now is that he'll move again. People will be suspicious, bound to be. I just hope it's soon. If it goes on the market, it might be worth making a bid, you know.'

'What for?' I scoff. 'One house not big enough for you, Rockefeller?'

'One for you, one for me,' she says.

That knocks me a bit. Does she want me out of her hair? I suppose it must cramp her style a bit having her sister here. And it might be nice to have my own place, do it up how I like. I'm not such a huge fan of the shabby chic motif. Even so, I'm a bit hurt. I thought we were getting on well.

'Or even James,' she says. 'A nest egg for him, he could use it to pay for university.'

'University?' He doesn't strike me as the academic type although I hear they let almost anyone in these days.

'Yes,' she frowns. 'University, why not? He's a bright boy, he just needs to apply himself. The teachers don't seem to be able to engage him. It can be a sign, you know, of being gifted. I did think maybe Bryant House might be able to draw him out but Cat says that place is sport obsessed and I'm not paying twelve grand a year for him to learn rugby.'

Personally, I think she's deluded. Gifted? James is no slouch but he's in his own little bubble. I think she'd be better just leaving him alone, really, he'll find his own way, most kids do in the end. Joanna and I know better than most the pressure of an overbearing parent that wants to mould you to suit their own agenda rather than let you be yourself. But I don't say anything. I know from experience such conversations need to be handled with tact.

She's got more to report the next day. The school gate festers with gossip, little seeds of news quickly bloom into hideous distortions. Joanna is in her element. 'Apparently the kid, Dean Withers, a lovely little lad from that farm at Brine Hill, is all messed up in the head.' She swirls her finger next to her temple. 'Claims it was a zombie that took him away, pushed him in the stream. Can't sleep at night, wetting the bed.'

'Poor kid.'

'Yeah. Obviously, an overworked imagination, makes you wonder what the parents let him watch on TV but even so, what on earth was Alan thinking ...'

She breaks off, suddenly. James is hovering in the doorway. 'What zombies?' he asks.

'Nothing, love,' she says. 'Just some kid having bad dreams.'

'Wetting the bed?' He sounds almost hopeful, like he's realising it's not just his secret shame. I knew I was right about why he left Young Explorers.

'You shouldn't be earwigging,' chides Joanna. 'It happens sometimes. I told you, it's completely normal.'

'Are you talking about Dean Withers?' he asks. 'Everyone at school was talking about it.'

Joanna glances at me. 'Well, yes, his parents are very upset but he's going to be fine. No lasting harm. I don't want you to worry about it.'

'I'm just worried about Alan,' says James. 'I know it wasn't his fault. And he loved the Young Explorers.'

'Did he now?' says Joanna archly. 'Well, I'm afraid that's the end of the Young Explorers for him.'

'Oh.' James looks downcast but then he brightens. 'Still, maybe he'll have more time now.'

'Oh yes,' says Joanna. 'I think he's going to have a lot more time. Let's just hope he doesn't expect to spend it hanging round here.'

Chapter Thirty-One

James' television appeal has triggered something. The phone has rung and rung and there have been three reporters knocking on the door. I feel under siege and seethe with resentment that Alan has put me in this position. The phone starts ringing again and I snatch it up, ready to scream down the line at them to leave me alone but a familiar voice stops me in my tracks. Dr Lucas. I'm desperate to see her but it's bad news; she's off to a medical conference in the States for at least three or four weeks.

I bite my lip, blink back tears. I have never needed Dr Lucas more and for the first time in our relationship she's off to a medical conference. And for three or four weeks! I feel a little flash of anger. It's unreasonable, Dr Lucas has never been anything but supportive, but it seems like every person I've ever counted on is disappearing from my life. The only person to stick by my side is bloody Alan.

'Sarah, are you there? You alright?'

'Yes, sorry. I'm OK.'

'How are things going? I saw James on the news.'

'Yes, he's appealing for witnesses.'

'They said the police were harassing members of the family. Is it you, are you OK?'

'I'm OK, but as far as I know I'm the main suspect. Can you

believe it! As if I would hurt Joanna, I can't function without her.'

'Oh Sarah, I'm so, so sorry. I'm missing her too.' She sniffs loudly, and I realise they must have become good friends over the years. In fact, in a way, Joanna knew Dr Lucas longer than I did because I was not really a functioning person when I first transferred to Hillwood House. I wonder if Dr Lucas would know anything about Joanna's secret life?

'She was very fond of you,' I venture. 'I don't suppose she ever told you if she was in trouble at work? Or knew something about one of her bosses?'

'No, dear, and patient confidentiality and all.'

'Oh, I just thought as she wasn't your patient, maybe as a friend? I'm just racking my brains trying to think who would do this . . . I mean, was she seeing anyone again? I felt like she was seeing someone recently, someone she didn't tell me about.'

'I'm sure she would have told you if she wanted you to know.' There's more loud sniffing in the background and I can't help thinking it's a very cryptic response.

'I wondered if Simon was back on the scene.'

'Would he dare show his face again?' asks Dr Lucas. She sighs heavily. 'She was unlucky in love, wasn't she? Remember that awful man with all those women he was dating?'

'Yeah, the police have spoken to him.'

'Have they? Why?'

'They're following up anyone she had any contact with. They know the killer is someone she knew so they're going through a list and eliminating people. I suppose if they don't hit a match, there'll be just one name left. Mine.'

'How are they finding people?'

'They've got her computer and phone.'

There's a silence in the background. 'Darling girl, what an awful worry for you. And poor darling James. He looked

202

haunted on the telly. Anyway, I'll be in touch. It will be a while, as I said, this conference is unavoidable but I'll be in touch when I get back.'

We say our goodbyes, and I slump to the floor, feeling defeated and bereft. Why does everybody leave? I sit, watching the shadows lengthen across the living room floor, thinking of all the times I've sat in here, pouring out my heart to Dr Lucas, her presence a soothing balm to my troubled mind. There are not many people you can trust with the deepest secrets you try to hide even from yourself, but she was special. Her desertion now feels like a particularly cruel betrayal.

There's a knock on the door. My heart sinks. I can't face having to shoo another reporter away. What do they think I'm going to tell them? I pull my blanket round my shoulders, shrouded in the gloom of the curtained room, determined to sit this one out. Maybe I should call Alan and tell him to get his hose out.

There's another knock, then the sound of someone pushing open the letterbox. I prickle with anger at this gross invasion of my privacy, my fists balling in my lap.

'Sarah! Sarah, are you in? It's Carmen, and Alex, from Vernon Guise.'

Carmen and her boss. I take a deep breath and steel myself, ready to face The Knob. I run my hands through my greasy hair and sniff my armpits, wishing I'd had a shower. I feel a mess and I'm sure I look one but I don't have time to do anything about it. I open the door to find myself face to face with a giant floral display in a wicker basket.

'Sarah? Deepest condolences from everyone at Vernon Guise Associates.' The speaker is a tall, athletically built man in a dark suit, a white shirt so bright it practically gleams in the sunlight and a fatly knotted silk tie. He's got dark hair, eyes the colour of cornflowers and a strong jawline. A woman hovers behind him and I know at once, from that badger's streak of silver running through her hair, that it's Carmen.

'I'm Alex Fuller,' the man says, and I feel like he's watching me for my reaction. Does he expect me to recognise that name? I'm sure I never heard Joanna share his full name; it was always just 'that knob Alex'. 'I worked closely with your sister and she was an asset to the company. We're going to miss her terribly.'

I nod and try to take the basket off him but it's surprisingly heavy so he offers to carry it through for me. I flutter anxiously as he makes his way to the kitchen, hoping it isn't too much of a mess in there. Carmen, in a smart navy coat and high heels, follows him through, giving me an apologetic smile and mouthing 'sorry' as she passes.

Alex puts the lilies down on the kitchen table. It's the kind of arrangement better suited to a church or hotel lobby, and the smell is cloying in our small kitchen. I wonder why anyone thinks this is an appropriate gift for someone struggling to just get through the day. *Don't make a fuss, Sarah*.

'Thank you, very kind of you,' I murmur. I'm not really sure what's expected now. Why have they come here? Why not just leave the flowers at the gate like everybody else. 'Would you like a cup of tea? Or something?'

'I'm good,' says Alex, like that's the end of the conversation. I look at Carmen with a questioning glance but she just shakes her head and gives me another weak smile.

'Shall we go into the living room?' At least we'll be away from the lilies in there. I lead them through, quickly dropping my blanket and pillow down the side of the sofa, clearing away a mug and plate, a pile of unopened mail from the chair.

But Alex doesn't want to sit. He paces the room, and I feel my hairs prickle. He's like a caged animal, full of restless energy, and his presence seems to fill the room. I glance at Carmen again, perched on the edge of the sofa, eying her boss nervously. I have never seen Carmen like this before, anxious and on edge. Is it Alex, or is it being here, where it happened?

'I felt it was important to come,' says Alex. 'Joanna was a valued member of the team. We're like a family at VGA, you know, it's hit everybody hard. She'll be a difficult act to follow.'

'Yeah,' I say. I'm about to add how she loved her job but he's already talking again.

'It was a terrible shock for everyone. There's a card with the flowers so you can read our thoughts at your leisure and see how much we treasured her.'

I smile weakly. Carmen is staring at her shoes, her hair falling in a dark curtain round her face.

'I didn't want to leave it too long before we reached out,' says Alex, moving to the window and staring out through the patio doors to the overgrown lawn. I look at his back, at the breadth of his shoulders, the way he holds himself, and feel the hairs on the back of my neck stiffen. 'I needed to get this done today as I'm off tomorrow as I've got an Ironman.'

There's an expectant pause and I sense I'm expected to say something. My mind whirls. Ironman's a character from those comic books films, I've watched a few with James and actually enjoyed them. There's one where the main characters are a human, a racoon, a green-faced alien and a tree so that even I could follow the plot, but I'm struggling to see what this has to do with Alex.

Carmen senses my confusion. 'The Ironman is a triathlon,' she says.

Alex turns to face me, his blue eyes blaze with the fervour of belief. 'Not just any triathlon,' he admonishes. 'It's a two point four mile swim, 112 mile cycle and a marathon to finish. No breaks. I'm surprised Joanna didn't tell you her boss was a nutter. I must have bored her rigid with my training schedules.'

'No, she didn't say anything,' I say. 'But she's used to that kind of thing.' I catch myself, I'm talking about her in the present tense again. 'My nephew does a lot of ultra-events. Mountains. Crazy stuff.'

His brow narrows. 'Nephew? Is that Joanna's son?'

'Yes, James.'

'Is he here?'

'No, he lives in Shrewsbury.'

Alex nods, hands on hips. 'I would have liked to see him too. Will you tell him we've been to pay our condolences?'

'Yes, of course.'

He claps his hands, pleased. I can see him mentally ticking off another task on his to-do list; our grief is just another job to him. He looks round the room again, lean, powerful, used to getting his way.

'So, this is Joanna's kingdom,' he says, straightening a picture on the wall. 'I knew she'd have good taste. Feminine but not over the top.'

I share a glance with Carmen, wondering where this is going. 'She was very house proud,' I say. I think that's one of the things that upsets me the most, that her castle, her retreat, has been violated like this.

'Did she talk much about work?' he asks, picking up a framed photograph of James in his school uniform.

I hesitate. I'm not sure what the right answer is. She talked about her workplace, about the petty disputes, the office flings, her obnoxious boss, but not about the work she actually did.

'Not really,' I say. 'Confidentiality, you know.'

He raises his eyebrows and replaces the photo frame. I find I can't take my eyes off him as he prowls the room, there's an animal heat about him, a dangerous glint in his eye. He knows he's attractive and he feeds off it. Carmen's watching him too, and I wonder if there's something going on between them. A lot of women would find him attractive, there was a time when

I would have been one of them, but having a slab of muscle and sinew crush the air out of you tends to make you wary of dangerous men.

'She was always so professional,' he says, his blue eyes on me. 'I don't think there was anything that went on at Vernon Guise she didn't know about and have under control.'

Is he testing me, trying to find out what she might have told me? I feel anger flame inside me. Is this him, is this the bastard that killed her?

'That was my sister,' I say, forcing my voice to sound bigger and bolder than I feel. 'She was the most organised, most on it person I've ever met. She always did the right thing, whatever the cost.'

I study his face. Do I see something there, a flicker of disquiet? Have I got to him? He smiles and his white teeth gleam. 'That's what I mean,' he says. 'We'll never find another one like her, isn't that right, Carmen?'

'Absolutely,' she says. 'She was one in a million.' There's a little catch in her voice. She looks at me, and is it my imagination, or do I see a warning there? 'And how are you, Sarah?' she asks, her voice full of concern. 'Are you alright?'

'Just taking a day at a time,' I say.

'You know where I am,' she says. 'If there's anything you need.'

'Thank you, really, thank you.' I look at her, trying to read her. Does she know what Joanna knew?

Alex is already looking at the gleaming hardware on his wrist. 'We need to be going,' he says. 'I've got a three o'clock.'

'Good luck in your triathlon,' I say as I show them to the door.

He gives me a quick look. 'An Ironman,' he corrects. 'A triathlon is for the mad, an ironman for the criminally insane.'

I catch my breath. It's a strange choice of words and I think

207

someone like Alex doesn't say anything without calculating the impact it's going to have. Well, he doesn't intimidate me.

'Good luck with that,' I say, holding his gaze.

Carmen flutters to my side, clicking her car key so her little Audi flashes into life. She gives me a brief hug on the doorstep. She smells of jasmine and coconut shampoo.

'I'm so sorry,' she breathes into my hair.

I'm not sure whether she means about Joanna or for bringing Alex here. 'What did Joanna find out about him?' I whisper, feeling her stiffen in my embrace.

'Meet me at Caspers tonight,' she whispers. 'Eight o'clock.' When she pulls away, her face is white, her eyes scared.

I watch them get into her car and drive away. I go inside, lock the door, my whole body shaking. Joanna called Alex a knob. She was wrong. He's dangerous.

Chapter Thirty-Two

Five years ago

There has been a fierce frost. The garden crackles white, the grass brittle underfoot. Joanna's new rosebush shrinks in on itself. 'Well, that was a waste,' she says sadly, fondling a frost-limp rosebud.

I shrug, shivering in my dressing gown, my breath a geyser of steam into the cold morning. 'Hey ho,' I say, as movement catches my eye next door.

It's a man in a cap and a gangly teenager walking down next door's garden together.

'What time did James get up and go over there?' asks Joanna, frowning at the two figures as they tramp down to Alan's shed. Her voice has an accusatory tone, as if I'm expected to account for the boy's movements.

'Don't know.' You're the parent, I think mutinously, but I don't say anything. She can be very touchy when it comes to James. Even though she's relaxed her ban following that whole business with the Young Explorers, I know she doesn't like James spending too much time with Alan, though I can't help thinking he wouldn't be round there so much if she made more of an effort with the boy. Sometimes it feels as if she never says anything to him that isn't an instruction or a criticism, and I know how it feels to be on the receiving end of that kind of love.

'Oh, what now?' she exhales, pulling her cardigan tight. The two of them have pushed through a gap in the hedge, down where the leylandii have left the ground barren round the back of Alan's shed.

They make an odd couple walking up our lawn. Alan big and lumbering in his flat cap and big green wellies, James shorter and slighter in matching wellies, his cheeks ruddy with the cold under his blue beanie hat. James is holding two dead pheasants, cradling them like babies, while Alan has a dead rabbit slung over one shoulder and a plastic bag in the other.

'Oh God,' moans Joanna, quietly under her breath. 'That's just what we need.'

'Look, Mum,' calls James. 'Look what we got.' He's beaming, his eyes bright with excitement as he holds the pheasants aloft for her to admire. He points to the plastic bag Alan's holding, in which we can see two little plucked bodies, like tiny chickens, wrapped in plastic. 'They also gave us a couple of prepped pheasants as a reward so we can have some for tea.'

'He made a great beater,' says Alan, clapping a big hand, raw with the cold, onto the boy's shoulder. 'We're back early though. They were going up Gravelly Hill and I'm still getting over my little procedure.'

'That's OK, Alan,' says James. 'I don't mind.'

Joanna's face is white with fury. 'You should have checked with me,' she says. 'He can't be off traipsing through the countryside without me knowing where he is. He's got his mocks to prepare for.'

I steal a glance at her. Until she saw him in the garden with Alan, she thought James was still up in his bedroom. And I can tell Alan knows this too. For a moment I see something in his eyes, a flash of anger, but then it's gone. I have never seen Alan angry and wonder what that would look like. I guess some people don't have it in them.

'Sorry,' he says, swallowing down whatever retort he had in mind. 'We should have checked with you first. At least you know he's had a good morning of exercise and he's provided for you ladies, too.'

And he and James again hold up their catch, grinning like mad hatters.

'You shot a rabbit?' Joanna asks James, her voice dripping ice.

He shrinks under her gaze, and stares down at the birds in his arms as if seeing them for the first time.

'Oh no,' laughs Alan, who seems oblivious to the undercurrent of tension between mother and son. 'We trapped the rabbit.'

'Trapped!' Joanna is aghast.

'That's worse, isn't it?' I ask. 'Surely they suffer? At least with a gun it's quick.'

'Depends on how good a shot you are,' chortles Alan. 'This morning one of the birds was wounded and my pal Jimmy, he's the keeper on the shoot, had to put it out of its misery.'

'You won't guess how,' says James.

'Wrung its neck,' I say, refusing to be shocked. I am not the ingénue James takes me for, I have travelled in my time and certainly saw worse in the villages of Sinai when they readied the lambs for Eid. That was a great trip. I'd love to go back to Egypt.

'Well, actually, Jimmy's old school,' says Alan, looking a bit uncomfortable. I think even he has picked up on the disapproval radiating from Joanna. 'It's an old groundsman's trick. You bite through the bird's skull into the brain. It's instant.'

'Not this time though, Alan,' pipes up James.

Alan shoots him a quick look. 'No, ha ha, he had to bash its head in the end. Jimmy's clearly not got the teeth he once had.'

There's an awful silence. Joanna glares at Alan. 'Seriously?' Her voice is as icy as the hard ground and Alan's bravado withers like her rosebuds.

She points at James. 'Go in and get washed.' He moves towards the house but she stops him. '*They* stay out here,' and she gestures at the pheasants.

James drops the birds like they're on fire, and they land with a soft gelatinous thump at Joanna's feet. She takes a step back, her lip curled with disgust.

Alan starts to apologise again but Joanna silences him with a look. 'He's a boy,' she hisses. 'In what world do you think this is appropriate?'

'He's almost old enough to serve Queen and country,' he says, which I figure is a spirited response given Joanna's mood. 'I'll guarantee he'll have seen worse stuff in video games or on the Internet. And for the animal, it's a better life than a battery hen or a broiler or a pig or most of the animals you eat.'

'It's not like you're vegetarian,' I venture, trying to play the peacemaker but I only succeed in diverting her anger from him to me.

'I might have known you'd take his side,' she says, before turning back to Alan. 'Have you forgotten what we talked about last year? I thought I'd made my thoughts clear.'

She stalks off and I wonder what that was about.

'Thoughts on what?' I ask.

But he's unusually silent, looking down at their catch with a sad look. More secrets. Why does nobody tell me anything? Are these two in on secrets now? I think back to last year and coming home from picking up my prescription to find the pair of them deep in conversation in the garden, where they'd been burning leaves in one of those dustbin incinerators. Joanna was

212

staring grimly at the dark plumes of smoke billowing across the garden, one gloved hand held across her mouth and nose. I'd wandered down to join them and got the distinct feeling I was interrupting a private conversation. Both of them were shifty and uncomfortable, Joanna poking determinedly at the fire, pushing debris deeper into the flames to try and make it catch, anything not to meet my eye. Had they been talking about me? Or had something else been going on, something between the pair of them?

'You think it's cruel to shoot them?' asks Alan suddenly, breaking into my thoughts.

I look down at the animals, at the beautiful colours of the birds with those magnificent tail feathers and the soft down of the rabbit and its bright black eye, and wonder if there's something wrong with me that I don't feel upset or angry like Joanna. This is life, isn't it? Eat or be eaten, hunt or go hungry. I'm just glad I'm higher up the food chain than a pheasant.

'Not if you plan to eat them,' I say. 'Don't see how it's different from buying it from a supermarket.'

'Oh, it's different,' he smiles. 'We should be close to our food. I didn't mean any offence, you know, boys have a natural curiosity in this kind of thing.'

I suppose that's true. Better this than pulling wings off flies or whatever cruel things boys are supposed to do. And at least it's exercise and fresh air, not festering in his room on that bloody computer.

Alan collects his dead animals and touches his finger to his cap in some kind of gesture of solidarity. I nod, uncomfortable; I don't want to give him any encouragement.

'By the way, Sarah,' he says as he turns to go. 'We're going to need to talk about that old pear tree. Think it's got blight and will need to come out.'

Whatever. I trail inside, shivering, and curl under a blanket on the sofa with a book. James, watching some mindless cartoon, steadfastly ignores me. Joanna is upstairs, in a pair of smart trousers and her M&S cashmere, spritzing perfume on her wrists.

'Seeing Simon?'

'Work,' she says sharply.

'But it's the weekend.'

She sighs heavily. 'There's a bit of a crisis on. I need to go in for a few hours. Keep an eye on James, please. Make sure he does his homework. And I don't like this hunting and trapping. It's not good for him.'

'OK, no problem.' It's not a big ask, James is pretty self-sufficient these days. 'What work crisis?'

She picks up her handbag and one of her big scarves. 'Oh, just the usual.' She flashes me a quick tight smile. 'At least it's the weekend so I'll be able to have the bloody air conditioning off.'

The temperature of the office is one of her long-standing gripes. 'Go get them, sis,' I say, secretly pleased I can set my own agenda without Joanna getting at me to do things. I have big plans.

I spend most of the afternoon in bed with Joanna's book club read for this month. I didn't expect to like it because it's set in the past but I liked the title, *Wolf Hall*, though I was hoping for some actual wolves. Despite my misgivings, I found myself absorbed in this world, so alien and yet so familiar. I wished I'd known books could do this earlier, before I failed my exams and crashed out of school. At some point, I must have fallen asleep, the wintery sun on my face and the book on my chest. It's the smell that wakes me up and for a moment it feels like the smoky kitchens and gamy feasts of Tudor England have seeped into real life. I head downstairs, and push open the kitchen door.

'Oh gawd,' I say as I inhale onions and meat, herbs and brandy. The windows are fogged with steam and the table is strewn with chopping boards, herbs, vegetable peelings and spilled flour.

A man and a boy, caught mid-conversation, fall silent and eye me warily.

'Thought we'd make you a spot of tea,' says the man, who I guess at once is Alan. 'Eat what you kill and all that.'

James looks at me, his eyes pleading for me not to kick off. I feel like Henry VIII, which way will my favour fall?

'What you cooking?' I ask, looking round the steamy kitchen, where the big pan simmers on the hob.

'Pheasant hotpot,' says James proudly, his face shiny with heat.

He has a sharp vegetable knife and is bent over some twigs of rosemary. 'There's wine and brandy in it so you and Mum will love it.'

I stifle a smile. It's a fair enough observation.

'A peace offering,' says Alan. 'After this morning.'

'Just make sure this is all cleared up before she gets back,' I caution, backing out of the kitchen to get my book and wondering what she's up to. It's been more than a couple of hours.

But, like a comedy, at that very moment I hear the key in the door. I find her in the hall, taking off her coat and scarf, peeling off her high heels. 'That's better.' She wrinkles her nose. 'What have you been up to?'

I nod towards the kitchen, hoping Alan has taken these few moments to smarten up the table and worktops. 'Nothing to do with me.'

The smile fades from her face and she pushes open the door

215

to the kitchen with a grim determination. It's a little neater and Alan is slopping soapy water in the sink as he scrubs at a pan.

'What's this?' she asks.

'Peace offering,' he says. He dries his hands on one of her fancy tea towels, which has become a sodden, stained rag.

'James, have you even started on your Maths?' James looks up startled from the carrot he's been chopping. Joanna's eyes narrow. 'That knife is too sharp for him,' she admonishes Alan.

'You can do more harm with a blunt knife,' he says. 'Every lad should know his way round a sharp knife. It's safer to know what you're doing. You should be proud of him, he's a natural shot and now he's cooking what he helped catch. Puts most boys his age to shame.'

I have to say I agree with him. I don't see the harm in it. Joanna moans when he's on his computer and at least he seems happy for once amid the vegetable peelings and the steam. But Joanna will not be mollified. She leaves the room, her face sour, and retreats to watch one of her shows until Alan finally leaves.

I taste the stew; it's good, earthy, meaty and flavoursome, although perhaps a little fatty for my tastes. James glows at the praise and talks me through the day, from the gory details of the dispatched pheasant to the trapping of the rabbit to the herbs they used to flavour the stock. I don't think I have ever heard him say so much in one go.

When he goes up to his room, Joanna finally emerges and looks round her kitchen, her nose wrinkled with disgust.

'It's not bad,' I say, scraping clean my second bowlful.

'It turns my stomach,' she says, and she tips the tureen of stew down the sink.

'That's a waste,' I remark.

She turns and looks at me, her eyes flashing. 'I don't want to encourage this,' she snaps. Then she pauses, blinking back tears. 'You wouldn't understand.'

She heads up to bed and I look at the steaming stink, the plug clogged with chunks of meat and pieces of carrot. She's right, I don't understand but I wish someone would fill me in.

Chapter Thirty-Three

Caspers is a little bar just off the High Street, down Butcher's Row, one of the narrow cobbled lanes near the church. Fairy lights twinkle round the window and a chalkboard outside tells me it's gin o'clock. I have never really liked gin but it seems to be all the rage now: Joanna had a collection of fancy gins; rhubarb, plum, violet. It all tasted bitter to me.

I am twenty minutes early so I decide to take a circuit of the town to kill time but I quickly get lost amid the twist of cobbled lanes. I find myself in Salters Court, by the bakers where that journalist bought the carrot cake, and the memory ramps up my anxiety, reminding me how vulnerable I am, how easy it is for people to trick me. The street comes out onto a little row of shops, a dusty haberdasher's and 'Olde Time Barbers' that I've never seen before, and I realise I've completely lost my bearings. There are some steep steps that lead down between two grimy buildings and I scurry down, expecting to come out onto the High Street but instead find myself in a little courtyard smelling of curry. A man in chef's whites is smoking by an open doorway and watches me with tired eyes. This is wrong. I head back up the steps, my heart thundering in my chest. It is ten to eight now, and I'm keen to arrive early at Caspers to make sure I'm there first; that way I don't run the risk of trying to find her in a crowd.

Footsteps behind me echo off the high buildings. I swallow and pick up my pace, twisting my ankle on the cobbles, my breath ragged. The footsteps are closer now. Have I been followed, has someone been watching the house, biding their time to get at me? Noise suddenly fills the narrow space; it's the church striking eight. I glance back and see a man just rounding the corner. He's wearing jeans and a biker jacket, a helmet in one hand, his big boots striking against the cobbles. I gasp, and pick up my pace, almost running now. I turn another corner and I'm in Butcher's Row and relief soaks me as I see people up ahead; a woman laughing as her high heels skate over the cobbles, and the bright lights of the bar. I check my watch: eight o'clock.

A hand grabs my arm and I scream.

'Hey, Sarah, hey, it's me, Carmen.' I spin round, and look at the woman at my elbow. She's my height, in a long navy coat, jeans and a pretty blouse, a witch's streak of silver in her dark hair. She pulls me into a hug and I recognise her scent. 'I've been looking out for you, I knew meeting like this might be difficult for you.'

Footsteps come up behind us and a man appears, in biker jacket and jeans. Is it my imagination or does he give me a strange look as he passes? I look at Carmen but she doesn't notice anything. Instead she's smiling at me, guiding me into the dim bar, where people are laughing over vast goblets of gin, nodding their heads to a bluesy seventies soundtrack. We sit at a little table in the window, cocooned in the gentle glow of the fairy lights and a sputtering candle, sipping cocktails: rhubarb gin for her, a mojito for me.

'I'm so sorry about Alex,' she says, squeezing my hand. 'He's like a bulldozer. He was insistent we came in person. I tried to say you're grieving but, well, he doesn't listen.'

'Joanna hated him. I mean, I see why, but was there something else, something she knew about him?'

Carmen glances around anxiously. 'She'd been compiling a report on him. One of our apprentices came forward, accusing him of sexual misconduct. It was he said, she said and the board were reluctant to act, but Joanna wanted it on his file. Then some stuff was found on this woman's computer, social media stuff boasting about how she'd been obsessed with him, about how much she'd enjoyed it, how she was going to retire on her tribunal pay-out. She said she'd been hacked but it looked bad, like she was setting him up. The woman was sacked, and he was then the victim. People felt bad for him. I mean, he's a good-looking man, right, people could see how it could happen, that someone could get obsessed by him.'

'Bet he loved that.'

'Oh yeah. But there were other women. Sometimes we'd hear whispers, gossip, but the women didn't want to say anything on record. They just wanted to put it behind them.'

Don't make a fuss, don't rock the boat ... I recognise that impulse, I think grimly.

'Some of them got unexpected promotions. A couple just left. He can be very –' she hesitates, staring down into her drink '– very charming, very convincing. But also very physically intimidating. It's hard to describe. You don't want to cross him. One woman, I don't know if she'd confronted him, but these awful images began to circulate of her, sex stuff, her head on porn images, it was awful. Her marriage broke down. Nothing to link it to him, of course. But the women, well, I think they knew. It sent a message.'

'But Joanna?'

'She took it to the CEO but all she had were whispers,

rumours. And he's like a god there, you know. His results are phenomenal. He pulled off a deal that transformed the company. And he's married, he has the perfect Instagram family. That's what Joanna hated, the hypocrisy of it. He just seemed to keep getting away with it.'

'But you think she found something out, something to finish him?'

Carmen looks down at her drink, tears in her eyes. 'Yes.'

'What was it?'

Her voice is a whisper. 'Me. He assaulted me.'

The breath rushes out of me. 'Oh God, Carmen, I'm so sorry.'

'We were at a conference, there was a big gala dinner. I'd had too much to drink. He can be very charming, very funny when he's in the mood. It was very quick really. In the ladies toilets, he followed me. He had his hand over my mouth.' She falls silent, struggling for composure. 'He laughed and said he always wanted to know what went on in the powder room.'

'You told Joanna?'

'Eventually. I was just so ashamed, so angry with myself, thought it would ruin my marriage. And who was going to believe me? People saw us drinking in the bar. He took a selfie of us laughing together, I'm leaning forward – you can see right down my dress.' She flushes. 'He sent it to me that night, like he was warning me that no one would believe I wasn't up for it.'

'What did Joanna say?'

'She said we're going to nail his balls to the wall.'

Oh, Joanna.

'She was very good, very discreet, she got another woman to come forward. She had a file, she said, she was going to take it to the police, not give the firm any chance to cover it up again.'

'He killed her. To keep her quiet. Have you told the police?'

Carmen looks down, embarrassed. 'No. I don't want it all to come out. Brett still doesn't know.'

'But, Carmen, this is why she's dead. We have to tell them.'

She looks at me, her eyes full of tears. 'There's no point, Sarah. It wasn't him. He wasn't even in the country when Joanna ... I'm in charge of his travel arrangements, he was flying back from Portugal that weekend.'

I bite my lip with frustration. I'm sure it was him. When he was in the house, I felt it, the power and cruelty of him. He's the right build, and clearly the right temperament. I will have to tell the police, I don't care what Carmen says. I could be going to jail for this prick if we don't.

We say our goodbyes in tearful hugs. I walk home quickly, my keys gripped between my fingers like knuckledusters, jumping at shadows. I wish Joanna had shared some of this with me, I could have supported her. I wish I'd listened more when she was moaning about work. I was always so self-absorbed. I turn in to Speldhurst Road, brooding over the incriminating file. Where did she keep it? Does Alex have it now, did he get the information out of her when he attacked her?

I'm getting close to home when a man steps out of the shadows ahead of me. He stares at me under the gloom of the streetlight, his face as startled and anxious as I feel. For a moment his eyes search my face, looking for something.

'Sorry,' he mumbles. 'Thought you were somebody else.' And he carries on walking, away from our house.

I'm shaking by the time I reach our drive. Who was he? Was it a reporter lurking outside? I don't think it was Alex, the build and demeanour were wrong. Maybe it was innocent, a passer-by who mistook me for somebody else. I lock the door, pull all the drapes and then collect the axe. If Alex comes in here again, I will make good on Joanna's promise and nail his balls to the wall.

Chapter Thirty-Four

DS Noor and Rawlinson are here before breakfast. I had left increasingly urgent messages on Noor's phone and the moment they're in the house, I start to tell them about Alex Fuller and the secret dossier that Joanna compiled. Noor listens patiently, then rifles through a file, running her finger down a list.

'He was overseas, Sarah,' she says. 'That's why we haven't spoken to him.'

'He may have been booked on a flight but it doesn't mean he was on it,' I say desperately. 'I know it was him. He had a clear motive. He's the right build. He's a bully. He threatened other women, manipulated their social media.'

'These are very serious allegations,' says Noor quietly. 'Joanna should have come to us with them.'

'She was going to,' I sob. 'He got to her first.'

Noor and Rawlinson share a look. Do they believe me? It's impossible to say. They have the most amazing poker faces.

Noor writes something down. 'We'll look into it, Sarah. I promise.'

I expect them to go then but it turns out they're not just here to listen to my paranoid ramblings. Noor wants to talk about money. At once I'm confused because I left all that side of things to Joanna. I mean, she was the earner so it made sense for her to pay the mortgage and take care of the bills. I don't even know how much she earned. I have my own bank account, of course, a basic current account into which Joanna used to put money after my benefits were cut, and a savings account, where I've got my share of the proceeds from the sale of Mother's house. It's not a huge amount but I guard it carefully. It's not that I'm mean; I just have this barely articulated fear: what if something happened to Joanna and she couldn't support me any more? Or she met someone and set up house with them? I admit it was a scenario that played on my mind a lot when things seemed to be getting serious with Simon. I think about how much money I used to get through before the accident, it was like water flowing through my fingers – make-up, clothes, drinks at lunchtime, cocktails after work, taxis and take-away coffees – and can't help feeling horrified. I never thought the money would run out, that there would always be time to earn more. But who would employ me now?

But Noor doesn't want to talk about our monthly incomings and outgoings, about which I know little. She wants to talk about our investments and savings, about which I know nothing. Joanna, it seems, has been very astute with money. Rob's life insurance has been wisely invested in a series of buy-to-let properties and then she made gains on the sale of her house when she moved from Berkshire to Shropshire, plus there is the money from the sale of Mother's house. Her estate is conservatively valued at more than £1.4 million. 'Though there would be taxes and death duties, of course,' says Noor into the stunned silence that follows.

And then there's her will. James and I are her sole heirs but he can't get his until he turns twenty-one – before then it all goes to me. I suppose Joanna didn't think she'd die for years and years, that James would be a mature man with a family of his own by the time her will ever came into play.

Noor looks up from her notes. 'What do you make of that, Sarah?'

My mouth has actually fallen open. I am amazed at the sums involved and stunned that she would trust me enough to leave that kind of money to me. I am profoundly touched by this.

'I had no idea,' I manage to squeeze out.

Rawlinson, thighs splayed in the armchair across from me, rolls his piggy eyes. 'You had no idea,' he scoffs. 'Pull the other one.'

Noor shoots him a look, then turns her attention back to me. 'No idea about what, Sarah? The money, or the will?'

'Both. I didn't think she had that kind of money. And she never talked about her will.' More secrets. 'It's not the kind of thing you talk about, is it?'

Noor shrugs. 'Well, actually, a lot of people do talk about things like that. Particularly when you reach a certain age, and there are children involved, people like to put plans in place, just in case.'

Just in case. I don't think anyone foresaw this. Joanna would have expected to live for decades yet; she was a fanatic for smear tests, cholesterol-lowering yogurts and multi-vitamins. Nobody would have expected her to die before fifty. And as a result, I am sole heir to a £1.4 million fortune. To think just over two weeks ago I was wobbling about sponsoring James for a fiver in his charity walk. And then slowly it dawns on me, how terribly bad this looks. I try to keep my face neutral, despite the rising panic, aware Noor is watching me closely.

'You know what I must be thinking, right?' says Noor, like a bloody mind reader. 'I mean, you know how it looks. James turns twenty-one later this year, halving your share of the money. People kill for a lot less.'

'No, no, no.' I start shaking my head. It's like a nervous tic, I can't stop, this no is so emphatic it has to come from every pore in my body. 'I didn't even know about the money, or the will. I just wouldn't. No, no. Just no.'

'But you see how it looks.'

'Yes. But I didn't do it. I don't even like money. I never spend anything.'

'Not spending anything and not liking money aren't mutually exclusive,' drawls Rawlinson. 'Some people just like to have it.'

'Not me, not me.' I know this is a lie, but at this moment it would be best if they think I'm a monk or a communist. 'I'm not into money. I mean, look.' I gesture at myself, in my supermarket jeans and Joanna's old hoody.

'These sums of money, they do things to people,' mutters Rawlinson darkly. 'You'd be surprised what we see people do over much smaller sums.'

'But not me.' They scrutinise at me, like Victorian physiognomists looking for signs of sin and depravity. 'Does James know?'

'Yes, we've already spoken to him. He said he doesn't care about the will. He just wants us to catch the killer.'

'I'll give him his half.' I curse myself silently; I should have said this straight away. 'I would never keep it all. It's rightly his, all of it.'

Rawlinson smirks. 'That's big of you.'

'You don't know me,' I snap. 'Don't you judge me.'

He leans forward, resting his elbows on his knees, his belly squashed uncomfortably against his thighs. 'You know the golden rule of murder investigation? Look at who benefits. Nine out of ten times, you'll find yourself looking at a murderer. And the last time? It's a nut.'

I can feel my face flush. I know what he's saying: I fit both categories. But I keep my mouth shut. I can't afford to lose my temper, not in front of them.

Noor makes a note, then she looks up and lobs a swerve ball. 'Tell me about Doctor Lucas.'

'Doctor Lucas?' My mind is still trying to process the news about the will.

'You told us you continued to see her as a private patient after you moved away from Berkshire?'

'Yes. I went through a dark patch after the move here and Joanna, well, I think she was struggling to look after me. She knew how much I trusted Doctor Lucas, I mean she helped turn things around for me when I was at Hillwood House, so she looked into whether I could see her as private patient.'

My eyes well up. It was such a kind thing to do. Joanna was good like that. She saw a problem and she wanted to solve it. Just like at work, trying to nail that bastard no matter how much it cost her. And it cost her everything.

'When was this?' asks Noor, breaking into my thoughts.

I try to think back. James was still quite young, I think, when Dr Lucas first came to the house. I seem to remember there was Lego everywhere and Joanna got flustered about the mess, banishing him to the front room.

'Ten years ago at least,' I tell Noor.

'Ten years?' She raises an eyebrow and makes a note. 'She's been coming to see you for ten years?'

'Or on the phone. Sometimes just on the phone. She's very busy.'

'And when did you last see Doctor Lucas?'

'About three weeks before Joanna ... We're due another session but obviously, all this.' I make a vague gesture towards Noor and Rawlinson. 'But we've spoken on the phone a couple of times, yesterday evening in fact. She's very worried about me.' But not so worried that she can't piss off to America for three weeks, I think bitterly.

I look at Noor and Rawlinson and there can only be what I

would call a shocked silence. I shift uncomfortably in my seat, a sudden wave of adrenalin flooding my body. What have I said, have I just incriminated myself in some way? But how, what on earth has Dr Lucas got to do with all this?

Noor breaks the silence first, speaking slowly and deliberately as if I'm hard of hearing.

'So, you spoke to Doctor Lucas yesterday on the telephone. And what did you talk about?'

'How I'm coping with Joanna's death.'

'Do you feel like you're coping, Sarah?'

I eye her warily. 'What is coping in a situation like this?'

Noor puts down her pen and looks at me, her eyes are sympathetic. 'Sarah, after our last conversation we went down to see Doctor Lucas at Hillwood House.' She clears her throat, and now it's Noor who looks uneasy. 'She says she hasn't seen you or had any contact with you for almost seventeen years.'

Chapter Thirty-Five

Ten years ago

I am like a teenager on a first date. I have had a long bath and cut my toenails. Hair neatly combed, mascara applied and I am wearing a new blouse from the supermarket, which is very pretty as long as I don't stand near a naked flame. I've even painted my fingernails bright pink – there's a bit of smearing but this kind of close dexterity shows how far I've come since the days when I couldn't even do up buttons by myself. It's important to me that Dr Lucas should see how well I'm doing; I don't want her to be disappointed. Somehow, I always felt like I was her star case; she was just starting out in her career when we met at Hillwood House and she always said there were people who go their whole careers without treating someone with prosopagnosia. I don't want to let her down.

I flit nervously round the house, unable to settle. I glance into the front room, where James has been banished with his Lego. He glowers at me – earlier I accidentally broke a bit off one of his bizarre contraptions – then returns to rooting around in his vast tub of plastic bricks. At least he's out of the way, and Joanna is keeping herself busy in the kitchen. 'Don't worry, I'm not going to cramp your style,' she says, laughing at me.

When the knock does come, I'm in too much of a state to open the door. Joanna goes, chuntering to herself at my ridiculousness although she's smiling too: I can tell she's happy for me. It's a long time since I've felt this kind of excitement about anything.

Dr Lucas is fatter and older than I remember but then I chide myself: it's been ten years and we've both changed. Her hair falls in extravagant strawberry-blond curls, and her eyes are bright and inquisitive, flashing between me and Joanna, taking everything in. She embraces me in a bear hug, which takes me aback, in a good way. I was right, she is as pleased to see me as I am to see her.

'Darling, it's so good to see you and you look so amazing,' she gushes in that rather plummy voice I know so well, although I catch a hint of something, a regional accent I hadn't noticed before, just creeping in behind the posh-girl vowels. 'I've often thought about you and how you would be getting on.'

'Thank you so much for this,' says Joanna, helping Dr Lucas out of her coat. 'Can I get you anything? Tea? Coffee?'

Dr Lucas takes a tea with two sugars, which probably explains the weight gain; I'm sure she was an Earl Grey and lemon drinker before. I take her through to the living room, where she settles herself into a chair and looks around, nodding appreciatively.

'A lovely place you have here,' she says. 'It's good to know you're being so well looked after.'

'Joanna's really good to me,' I say.

'I promise I didn't bribe her to say that,' says Joanna, bustling in with the tea tray. We have the best mugs, I note, and a plate of quality biscuits, not the basics range. 'Now I'm going to leave you two ladies to crack on. Just shout if you need anything.'

We wait in silence until the door closes, then Dr Lucas turns to smile at me expectantly.

'Let's get started, shall we?'

She asks me some questions about my prosopagnosia, looks through my VIP book with interest – 'You will need to add me in now, I'll get Joanna to take a photo before I go' – and checks how I'm sleeping. I tell her about the anxiety attacks and my new anti-depressants and my battle to lose the weight I put on last year, and then I glance down guilty at the biscuit in my hand. She chuckles softly, and helps herself to a second biscuit.

'Darling, please, don't beat yourself up. Sometimes we have to be kind to ourselves and show ourselves a bit of the love we didn't get as children. I think you look beautiful.'

It's such an unexpected thing for her to say, and it strikes right to the heart of my insecurities about who I am now I'm not who I was before the accident. And suddenly we're talking about so many things, about how I'm feeling as a person not just as a patient, about Mother, about my crazy teenage years, my escape to London and how it's only in my dreams I feel like that person again. And Dr Lucas is making it all feel better, like she's lancing a boil and letting the pus seep out, cleansing my system of the poison I've been holding on to for so long. The next thing I know she has me lying on some cushions on the floor. She kneels next to me and places her hands, hot as stones warmed in the sun, on the back of my neck and the base of my spine. Rationally I know this is completely weird but I crave her touch, the comfort of her hands, the reassurance of her murmurs, her motherly bulk next to me. I weep some more into the cushion under my head and Dr Lucas soothes me, urges me to let the pain out. Shortly afterwards, wrung out and utterly at peace, I fall into a deep dreamless sleep.

There's someone in here with me, tiptoeing across the now dark room. My eyes adjust to the gloom and I see a child – James, it must be James – creep over to the sofa and rummage behind the cushions, retrieving small pieces of Lego. I watch, not yet ready to rouse myself from this deeply relaxed state. The boy finds what he's looking for, then turns to look at me, his eyes flicking the length of my body prostrate on the floor. Our eyes meet and his expression is unreadable. I hold his gaze for a moment, and then he shrugs, whatever the crazy aunt is up to now is none of his business, and he's gone.

I lie there a little longer, trying to understand what happened. How did Dr Lucas get me to open up like that? She seemed to instinctively understand how I was feeling, all that stuff about Mother and my lost self-esteem. And I can't begin to explain whatever took place on the cushions, the way the heat from her hands seemed to suffuse my whole body, releasing so much pain and tension that I actually feel physically lighter.

I shift my body position and breathe in the warm still air of the living room, hearing the distant gurgle of the water pipes and the relentless scrape of James' small hands in the Lego tub. Usually I can't bear that noise but this evening even that can't touch me.

I walk across the hall to the kitchen, where I can hear Joanna and Dr Lucas talking and laughing like old friends. It dawns on me that they must have got to know each other pretty well while I was at Hillwood House and for a moment I feel uncomfortable at the thought Joanna probably knows things about my medical history that even I don't know. It's not a new thought but this time it provokes a little stab of jealousy; nothing I have in my life, not even Dr Lucas, is ever entirely mine but must also always be shared with Joanna.

I push open the kitchen door, blinking in the bright light, and find the pair of them sitting at the table, sipping tea and finishing off the best biscuits.

'Hello, sleepyhead,' says Joanna with a smile. 'We were going to come and get you soon. Doctor Lucas has to get off.'

'A long journey ahead,' says Dr Lucas. 'How are you feeling, my lovely? You're looking five years younger, if you don't mind me saying.'

I grin. I don't mind at all. 'That was amazing,' I say. 'I feel so relaxed.'

Dr Lucas smiles happily. 'I just gave you a short blast of healing. I could tell you needed it. You were very receptive, you soaked up so much energy from the universe, like a plant that's been parched of rain. It will stay with you for a few days.'

'Wow. We never did any of that at Hillwood House.'

Joanna looks a little flustered. She has such a practical, conventional mind, she probably doesn't believe in healing energies.

'I'm a big believer in holistic healing,' explains Dr Lucas. 'You can't treat the patient just as a set of symptoms, you have to treat the whole being, body, mind and spirit. Of course, in the NHS, this is seen as a luxury even though it's proven that if you treat the whole patient we would actually prevent so many problems and save the NHS billions of pounds every year.'

'Wow,' I say again.

'It's heartbreaking really, because my private clients make so much more progress than my NHS case load. But you can't argue with bureaucracy.'

'Tell me about it,' says Joanna, even though, as far as I can tell, she is one of the high priestesses of box-ticking and form-filling at Vernon Guise.

There's a shout from the other room, and the sound of the entire box of Lego being upended. Footsteps thunder up the stairs, and a door slams. It's what Joanna and I have come to call a 'Lego meltdown'. Best ignored, I think, but Joanna usually panders to him.

'I wish you could work your magic on James,' she says,

staring ruefully into the bottom of her mug. 'We're going through another phase.'

She says it like Dr Lucas would know about James, and I wonder when the two of them resumed contact. How much time did it take for Joanna to persuade Dr Lucas to see me privately, and, more importantly, how much is this costing? Again, I feel that nasty prick of jealousy that Joanna should be so close to my Dr Lucas, but tell myself not to be ridiculous; if it wasn't for Joanna, Dr Lucas wouldn't be here.

'It's that difficult age,' says Dr Lucas. 'Hormones, my dears, they rule us. Just be glad you haven't got a daughter, then you'd know difficult.'

Joanna doesn't say anything. I know she'd love another child but time is running out.

'She already knows difficult, she's got me,' I say, trying to lighten the mood.

Dr Lucas laughs but Joanna glowers darkly. 'Lucky me,' she says.

Chapter Thirty-Six

I am in shock. Have I been making Dr Lucas up? All those healing sessions, the phone calls, the gift-wrapped tissues every Christmas, could it all be a delusion? Perhaps my brain injury is much worse than I imagined. I take myself to bed and fester there, watching vapour trails and crying piteously. They will put me in a home. Or Broadmoor. I am not sure I can be certain I didn't kill Joanna now. Perhaps my brain has conjured up this killer to explain my own actions. I know Joanna was scared of me; after all, she never took the bolts off the doors and she did call the police that time. I hate myself. It can only be a matter of time now, Noor will come back and take me away. I don't know why they haven't already. The evidence looks damning even to me.

There's a sound downstairs, a knock on the door, a rattle of the letterbox. I pull the covers over my head. I don't want to know.

'Aunty Sarah, it's me, James.'

James! He's probably the only person in the world I would get out of bed for now. My hands tremble as I pull back the chain. Please, please let it be him and not some horrible new delusion. I pull back the door and study the young man, with the sweep of dark hair and the sharp cheekbones. I am sure it's James. I would know his voice anywhere. And look at that bone structure; grief has sharpened his angles. I throw my arms around him and catch the smell of cheap aftershave and cigarettes. I didn't know he smoked but now is not the time for a public health lecture. It's just so good to have him home.

'It's so good to see you, James.'

He pulls free and hovers on the doorstep.

'It's OK,' I say, following his eyes. 'Everything's been cleaned up. Look, we can go into the living room, he didn't go in there.'

'No,' he says, shaking his head. 'I need to see where it happened. It's worse not knowing, my mind imagines the worst. I need to see.'

'Of course.' This is what Dr Lucas — the real Dr Lucas from the days of Hillwood House, not whatever phantom I've been conjuring — would call closure. I am struck by what a mature and sensible young man James has grown into. It just shows that we should never be judged by our teenage misdemeanours. Look at me: I now live my Mother's model celibate life.

I open the door to the kitchen, wincing as I picture it through James' eyes. I scurry to tidy away the unwashed mugs, the breadcrumbs and butter smears on the worktop and hide the empties by the overflowing bin. Joanna has been gone less than a fortnight and already the kitchen is a slum.

'Where?' asks James.

I point wordlessly to the tracing that marks the high tide of Joanna's blood. He stares transfixed, his face ashen.

'Was it quick?' His voice is a whisper.

'Yes. There was a lot of blood, it would have been quick.'

James bites his lip and stuffs his hands in the pockets of his hoody. He nods grimly, his eyes on the floor.

'I had to see.'

'I know.' I touch his arm lightly and he flinches. Is he scared of me or are his nerves just rattled? It's a lot for a young man to take in and he looks like he hasn't slept properly for a week.

'Would you like a drink? Tea. Coffee. Something stronger?' He shakes his head and I rack my brain to think of something to tempt at him. He never did like hot drinks and always preferred those sickly cans of Fanta and Sprite. I should have bought some when I went to the Co-op, I should have anticipated this moment and got things in he would like. It's the kind of little touch Joanna was so good at. *You're always so self-centred. You never think of anyone outside your own bubble.* That's what Mother used to say. And Joanna too on days when she was really mad with me. Is it true? I feel like I spend a lot of time thinking about other people but maybe it's only really in relation to how it impacts me. It just won't do. James must be the focus now. He's barely an adult and this is too much for him to bear on his own.

'Do you want to see her room, maybe pick out some keepsakes?' He looks at me sharply and I realise it must sound as if I'm already taking possession, offering him some crumbs while I live high on the hog. All I want is for him to find some comfort among her stuff – it has brought me comfort to wrap myself in her clothes, to touch her things, drink in her scent.

'Maybe another time,' he says. 'I'm not ready yet, it's too soon to be picking through her stuff.' It sounds like a rebuke and I wonder if he can tell I'm wearing her clothes. 'I keep expecting her to walk in.'

His voice chokes up and I want to hug him again and make everything alright. It used to be so simple when he was little: a Mr Man plaster, a kiss on the forehead and a sweetie to make the hurt go away. But there's a brittleness to James today, an icy wall he's built to protect himself, from the horror of the situation, or from me? Is he scared of me too? Does he suspect me?

'I keep talking to her,' I say, trying to find some common ground. 'I even miss her nagging me to empty the dishwasher.' James smiles dutifully. He looks so thin and I have an urge to feed him. 'What would you like to eat? We could get a take-away.'

He shakes his head. 'No, thank you. Actually, I must be going.'

My face falls. So soon. I hoped this was it, he was back for good. 'Why don't you stay, we've got so much to talk about. The funeral. Your plans. And I can look after you, help you get yourself sorted out.'

I'm gabbling, as if words might bind him to me. But he shakes his head emphatically.

'No. It's too weird for me right now. I had to see but I can't stay.' He forces a smile and looks at me. 'It will be better next time, I promise. I just had to get this out of the way.'

He's so brave, I blink back tears and manage a weak smile in return. 'You'll come back soon. Or I could come and visit you?'

He raises his eyebrows. He knows this is a big deal for me. 'I'd like that, Aunty Sarah. We could go for a walk along the river. Or maybe a drive into the hills. I feel like I can breathe up there, think, you know, about her.'

'I'd like that. Let's do that.' It could be just what we need.

'I'll call you,' he says.

I nod, not trusting myself to speak. 'Where are you going now?'

'I'll probably pop my head round, say hello to Alan. And the police want to check something with me.' He looks suddenly shifty, and I feel cold with dread.

'What?'

James looks pained. 'They want to talk about you, and Simon.'

'Simon?'

'They think, I don't know, it sounds mad saying it out loud, maybe you and Simon ...'

'What!'

'It's stuff they've seen on Facebook and some forum. I dunno. Don't worry, Aunty Sarah, I won't say anything.'

My head is spinning. Me and Simon? Those bloody fake Facebook posts. Who would do that? And what forum? Are they looking at Headliners again? But I never posed on there about Simon, or did I?

'Me and Simon. James, nothing ever, ever happened. I don't know where they're getting this stuff from.'

'Yeah,' he says, shrugging his backpack higher on his shoulder. 'That's what I'll tell them.'

He's edging towards the hall, away from me. I am losing him, their questions are seeding doubt in his mind, I can see it in his eyes. 'James, please. Family should be together at a time like this. And I'm worried about you ...'

He's in the doorway now. He hesitates, then turns and looks me in the eye. Gosh, he's a heartbreaker, with those purple circles under his eyes and those chiselled cheekbones.

'I just need some time, Aunty Sarah. I'm so confused. They keep asking all these questions ... They keep talking about you and Mum like you hated one another ...' He gives a funny little smile. 'Sisters, huh?'

I swallow. 'I loved Joanna,' I manage to croak.

He smiles sadly. 'I know, Aunty Sarah.'

I swallow, slightly reassured that maybe he doesn't think it was me.

I lock the door behind James and go upstairs to peer out of Joanna's bedroom window. I see James' head bobbing beyond the hedge as he walks down Alan's drive. He stands on the doorstep, checks his phone, then glances up at our house. He sees me and gives a cheery wave. I raise my hand tentatively

239

and shrink back from the window, feeling chilled to the bone. I know now it won't be long before there's a knock on the door and Noor comes to take me away. I am on borrowed time and need to make the most of it.

Chapter Thirty-Seven

Alan pops round. His face is grim. 'I've something to show you,' he says. 'Brace yourself.'

I follow him warily down the garden and through the gap in the hedge. There's still the bite of frost in the air but the spring sunshine is already pulling its teeth and you can tell it will be one of those days when you can smell summer coming.

Alan's got his computer fired up and it's open on LinkedIn. I have a message, from Gary, Robert's best man. The words hit me like a punch in the face.

I don't know who you think you are contacting me like this. You and that miserable witch ruined Rob's life. He was my best mate and I still miss him. Stay away from me and never contact me again or I shall get my lawyer onto you.

'Wow,' I say, sitting back in the chair.

'Yeah, pretty unpleasant,' says Alan. 'I wondered whether to show you but I thought you deserved to know. He clearly didn't like you or Jojo, we should definitely tell the police.'

'But if he's in Africa?'

'Well he's a pilot, isn't he? He can fly anywhere in the world.'

I nod, chewing on my lip. I try to picture myself telling Noor and Rawlinson about my latest suspect, a pilot from twenty years ago who lives in Nairobi, imagining their reaction. They already think I'm delusional. I don't see much point fighting this any more.

'Thanks, Alan,' I say sadly. The aggression of the message just deepens my gloom. I am fully resigned to my imminent arrest now. They will probably undertake psychiatric evaluations. I will be locked up in a nut house, no prospect of release.

I should get my affairs in order first, perhaps write a long note to James, explaining everything. I can't bear for him to think I'd intentionally hurt his mum. I head home and pick up the pile of post that's gathered over the last week. Pastel envelopes, cards with pictures of flowers or sunsets. Handwritten messages. *So very sorry. Be much missed. If there's anything we can do.* I don't recognise most of the names. There are letters from the bank, her credit card company, her gym. There's a little stack of official envelopes for me too, informing me that I'm clocking up unauthorised overdraft charges. I'll have to transfer some money across from my savings account but without my phone or computer that's going to mean a trip to the bank.

I take some deep breaths, trying to muster myself to leave the house. How did this happen? How did I go from someone who would hitchhike to Glastonbury or trek round Sinai without a care in the world to someone who can't leave the house?

The bank is empty apart from one man who's doing something with bags of change. A woman in a dark grey skirt suit walks straight up to me. According to her name badge, her name is Lucy. I am a little flustered by her approach, wondering if she knows me. But no, it seems it's just a general meet-and-greet to see if I need help using the new Smart Self Service kiosks. I look at her with pity: I love dealing with the robots but this poor fool is guiding me towards her own employment oblivion. Besides, it seems there's a glitch. The machine doesn't recognise the details of my savings account. Lucy frowns.

'Unusual,' she says. 'Would you mind coming with me, Miss Wallis?'

I follow her to a small room, where photographs of country scenes create a bland backdrop to the financial decisions that chart the highs and lows of our lives, loans, mortgages and pensions. Lucy has long squared-off nails painted a brilliant pink that attack the keyboard with a kind of violence. I wonder how much it costs to keep her nails in such a state of shiny flawlessness. She excuses herself from the room, and I allow my mind to wander, wondering what it would be like to work in a place like this. Perhaps I could manage this? With everyone wearing name badges, and all the customers having to present their names and account details, there's no reason I couldn't operate in this kind of role. But if machines are coming in to take the jobs, it doesn't seem worth the effort of retraining.

Two women come into the room. I peer at their name badges. Lucy and another woman, Janet, who I can tell is the boss. She now peers at the computer screen, and looks again at the paperwork I have brought in, then looks up at me with a worried face.

'I'm sorry, Sarah,' she says – and I can't help noting the power play, Janet gets to call me Sarah but to Lucy I am Miss Wallis – 'but I think there's been a misunderstanding.'

'What do you mean?' I lean forward in my seat to peer at the screen.

'You withdrew all the funds and closed this account a couple of days ago,' says Janet. 'Thursday.'

'What? There was about twenty-three thousand pounds in there.'

'No,' says Janet, staring at the screen. 'It was down at two thousand five hundred and you withdrew all of that.'

'No, I think there's been some mistake. I never really touch this account. These are my savings. I don't touch them. There should be twenty-three thousand pounds.'

Janet shakes her head, her lips pursed. 'This account was closed,' she repeats, speaking very slowly and clearly. 'You withdrew the final two thousand, five hundred, which is the maximum we allow as a withdrawal without prior notice, two days ago.'

She angles her screen so I can see. The two of them watch me, their heads tilted in sympathy, their faces bland.

'Well, where did the money go? Did I put it into another account?'

Janet purses her lips and shakes her head. 'We will try to track the online transfers for you but the cash withdrawal, well, we don't know what you did then.'

Could Joanna have done this, could she have been moving my money somewhere else? Perhaps she was trying to get me a better savings rate? It's the kind of thing she was good at managing. But the most recent withdrawal, well that certainly wasn't Joanna. Could it have been me? Is it another hallucination?

I look at Janet and Lucy with tears in my eyes. The shame of this. I will be a story they tell their colleagues and families, probably with shock and pity at first, later it will become funny. A joke. But there's nothing funny about this. I notice Lucy is looking very hot in the face and she's fidgeting in her seat. I don't know why she's embarrassed, I'm the one with the neurological impairment.

'I'm so sorry,' she suddenly blurts out. 'I didn't know but I think I may have served you, well, not you, the other day.'

Janet looks at her sharply. 'What's that?'

'I just remember someone coming in and withdrawing quite a large sum in cash. We even had a little joke about her having her bodyguard outside.' She flashes a look at her boss. 'She had all the right paperwork,' she adds defensively.

But Janet is tense now. She makes excuses and the two of them exit, leaving me to stew. I'm left wondering what's going on. Is it me, or it is them? I sit there, sweating and anxious, aware of that horrible tightening in my chest, the constriction in my throat. I can't breathe. I hinge over, stick my head between my knees and clamp my hands over my ears. Please let it pass, please let it pass. The blood pounds in my ears and my breath is shallow and ragged. I know it's panic but it feels so real, like I might actually pass out this time or go into cardiac arrest.

A door opens behind me and footsteps approach. A hand on my back. 'Sarah, are you all right, can you hear me? Can you take a deep breath for me?'

There's a crackling noise, the static of a radio, and a disembodied voice comes over the airways. I crack open an eyelid and there's a black boot in my eye line. The hand is still on my back. I tilt my head and squint up. There's a blonde woman in a police uniform, looking down at me with concern, a large mole on her cheek. PC Casey Crown. The panic ebbs enough for me to suck in a deep breath. I hold it then let it out, shakily, for a count of three. Almost at once I feel my racing heartbeat slow, and I do it again.

'That's a girl,' says Casey Crown, her hand still warm and solid against my back.

A fat teardrop rolls down my cheek and plops onto the cheap carpeting.

'It's all right, Sarah,' says Casey Crown. 'We'll get to the bottom of this.'

I nod, dumb, I am out of words. I am so tired, wrung out by the adrenalin surge, and feel like I could sleep for a day and a night.

'It's OK, Sarah,' says Crown. She shares a glance with the bank staff hovering in the doorway. 'We'll handle this now.'

I let my head hang forward again, the knots in my muscles slowly unwinding as the oxygen filters through my body. I don't understand what's just happened but it's very clear there is something very wrong with me.

Chapter Thirty-Eight

I am back in the peppermint cream room at the police station. I have been sitting here for ages and am onto my second cup of tea when the door opens abruptly. A police officer comes in, a woman, with blond hair and a mole on her cheek. She wants to check if I've ever signed over a power of attorney for my affairs. No, not that I can remember, although I probably should have. I have clearly not been of sound mind for some time now.

'Joanna took care of everything,' I say. 'She was organised like that.'

'Anyone else? A neighbour, or relative?'

'No.' I shake my head emphatically. Joanna would never have trusted Alan and everyone else is dead. Now I only have James. It's not much to show for five decades on the earth.

I'm left alone again. At some point, a woman brings more tea and a cheese sandwich. I don't get a glimpse of the left side of her face so don't know if it was Casey Crown or someone else. I try to keep my mind empty and not panic. It isn't difficult. I am wrung out after the panic attack. It's actually almost a relief to be here. There's nothing I can do here other than what I'm told, and I have got quite good at that over the last twenty years.

The door opens and a small woman in a dark trouser suit clicks forward purposefully on high heels. Even before she introduces herself, I am pretty sure this is DS Noor and by an educated guess I assume the big bloke trailing in her wake is DC Rawlinson.

They sit down opposite me and Rawlinson at once confirms his identity by assuming his usual slouch. Noor sits neatly, legs crossed, her neatly manicured hands splayed on top of a file. I notice she wears no rings and I suppose to be this senior so young she must be married to her job.

'Sarah, thank you for coming in,' she says as if somehow I'm here of my own free will and not because I was bundled into the back of a car after my meltdown at the bank. I wonder what she's got in that file. Is it more salacious details from Facebook, about affairs with Simon or perhaps details of where my money has gone? I don't know what I've been up to but perhaps my damaged lying brain is cleverer and more pro-active than the conscious one.

'I know this must be very distressing for you coming so soon after Joanna's death,' says Noor.

I nod. I am just waiting now, wondering if they'll cuff me, and how that will feel.

Noor opens the file and pulls out a series of photographs. They're black and white images that look like they've been lifted from CCTV. They appear to be of a woman in a shop. Noor spins the photos round and spreads them out so I can get a better look.

'Do you recognise this woman, Sarah?'

I give Noor a sharp look. Is she trying to be funny, or has she forgotten I have prosopagnosia?

'I know you have face blindness, but I also know you're a good observer and pick up on other features to identify people.' She smiles at me. 'I know you clock me from my stature, and

Rawlinson from his posture' – the oaf scowls at this, and makes a faint effort to sit a little straighter – 'so I wondered if you have any clues as to who this is.'

This is not how I was expecting this conversation to go but I play along, a little puffed up that she's noticed how I spot things other people don't. In fact, I'm not sure anyone else has ever commented on my observational skills. Everyone else just focuses on what I can't do – even me.

I pore over the images and the first thing that strikes me is that this isn't a shop – it's my bank. The person is fat, bundled in some shapeless coat and a large scarf, with long wavy hair. She's wearing a hat, a sort of jaunty beret, and carries a large bag.

'Anything?' prompts Noor.

I shake my head. It's hard to get a feel for a person from these grainy black and white images. There's not enough detail, colour or movement.

'What about this one?' asks Noor, pointing to two more photos that show the same woman outside, walking away from the bank. In one, she has her back to the camera and it's just a shot of a stout, shapeless figure heading towards a car parked outside the bank. But in the other photo, she's turned sideways to open the car door, and in that moment her hair has lifted slightly, caught on a breeze, and you can see the corkscrew of the curls in relief against the side of a passing white van.

I pull the photo closer and study it. Those curls, streaming down her back like a pre-Raphaelite heroine. I stream through my Rolodex of memories and one name stands out. But it doesn't make any sense and I'm reluctant to say who I think this is.

'Sarah?'

I look up from the photo and see her watching me with her bright earnest eyes.

'I'm not sure,' I say, hesitantly, and I catch Rawlinson rolling his eyes extravagantly. 'Why are you showing me this?'

'This is the person who withdrew the money from your bank account.'

'What?' I stare at the photograph intently, my head swimming. So it wasn't me, I haven't been secretly emptying my own accounts. The relief makes me giddy and my eyes flush with tears.

'Have you ever heard of a person called Xanthe Heard?'

I repeat the name slowly. 'Zan-fer-heard?' It sounds made up. I don't know anyone with that name, of that I'm sure. 'No. Who is she?'

I peer again at the photograph. Why would this stranger be able to steal my money? How do you even go about doing that?

'Sarah, have you ever seen this person before?' presses Noor.

I pull the photo closer and study it again.

'I don't know,' I say. It's the truth but the hair troubles me. It reminds me of someone, but I know it can't be them; that person has been the figment of a diseased mind.

'The hair,' I say at last. 'Maybe. It's silly but Doctor Lucas has hair like that.'

'Doctor Lucas? Your psychiatrist from Hillwood House in West Berkshire?'

'Yes, it's just the hair, that's all. But I know it's silly, you said she hadn't seen me for seventeen years so ...' I don't know what else to say.

'That's right,' says Noor gently. 'But this isn't Doctor Lucas. We went to see Doctor Lucas at Hillwood House and she doesn't look like this. Doctor Lucas, the *real* Doctor Lucas, has shoulder-length brown hair, and she's much taller.'

'Oh.' I let this news sink in, like water percolating its way through thirsty ground. My brain feeds on these droplets of information as the ground shifts under my feet.

'Now, Sarah, this is going to be difficult but could this

person—' and here Noor taps the black and white photograph with a delicate finger '– be your Doctor Lucas?'

'What?'

'Is this the person you've been having private sessions with at your house?'

My mind spins and my face flushes hot. I keep my eyes on the photograph, I don't want to meet their eyes: no doubt Rawlinson is smirking while Noor is full of pity and I don't know what is worse.

'You mean someone's been impersonating Doctor Lucas?' My voice is barely a whisper.

Noor nods grimly. 'Possibly.'

I shake my head. 'Impossible. Joanna arranged for Doctor Lucas to come to the house. She would have known straight away that the person was an imposter. She'd met the real Doctor Lucas.'

Noor gives me a rueful look. 'Sarah, we've already taken this person – Xanthe Heard – into custody. She says she was working for Joanna.'

'What?' I struggle to understand what Noor is telling me. I have never heard of Xanthe Heard before, how could she be working for Joanna?

'Sarah, Joanna hired this woman to pretend to be your Doctor Lucas.'

Chapter Thirty-Nine

DS Noor is being very kind. She even fleetingly held my hand when I got distressed. Her fingers are so thin and delicate they made my hands look like the hams of a prize brawler. I just can't believe Joanna would perpetrate such a deception. She was so straight and honest, and, frankly, I didn't think she had the balls to pull something like this off.

But Noor is insistent Joanna colluded with this charlatan Xanthe Heard. In fact, Heard has happily confessed to the whole thing and is proud of it, claiming that I'd improved leaps and bounds under her care compared to that of the so-called doctors.

'Mrs Heard has a strong belief in her healing powers,' says Noor dryly. 'She said she'd created a healing dome made from universal light to keep you safe at number twenty-two.' I remember that: I used to like thinking about my light dome, keeping me safe, healing me, but now I think about it, the dome became a cage, the house became my prison.

'What a wacko,' mutters Rawlinson.

It's the most sensible thing he has yet contributed, although he spoils the effect by then adding: 'They're parasites, preying on the weak-minded.'

I just don't understand why Joanna would do this to me.

So much effort, so much risk, to try and convince me I'm still seeing my old psychiatrist.

Noor watches me carefully. 'I'm sorry, Sarah, I know this must be hard to take in.'

'I just don't understand how this happened.'

Noor nods. 'It seems Joanna met Mrs Heard at a spiritualist church. I believe she was seeking comfort after the death of her husband.'

A spiritualist church. After everything Joanna and I went through growing up, how could she seek comfort in the arms of those charlatans? It starts out being about God's love but it's not long before they're rooting out demons and your kids are on their knees in the cellar praying for salvation.

'I think they struck up a friendship of sorts, with Mrs Heard acting as an advisor and counsellor to your sister. Then she was asked to pretend to be Doctor Lucas to help you recover, a deception she was happy to undertake because' – and here Noor consults her notes to quote verbatim – 'she said she "has a responsibility to use her powers to heal the afflicted whenever she can". To her credit, she does seem to have genuinely cared for you, Sarah.'

I pinch my skin to stop myself crying. She was a good actress, I'll give her that. Just enough medical jargon to make it plausible while she introduced the crystals and the light energy. And I believed her, when I felt the heat of her hands, the comfort of her touch, I truly believed she was tapping into some universal energy that was helping me get better. And the things I have told her! Was she then reporting on me to Joanna? I blush at the thought of my secrets being dissected by the pair of them, perhaps over cups of tea at the kitchen table even while I slept in bliss after a healing. How could Joanna allow this to happen?

Something else strikes me. 'What about the pills she sometimes gave me?'

Noor looks down at her notes. 'Herbal remedies, valerian and rosemary.'

No wonder my brain is messed up. No wonder I'm having panic attacks. I've been treating a serious neurological trauma with light energy and fucking valerian!

Tears fill my eyes but I wipe them away fiercely. I am angry now, there is no time for self-pity. 'Why did she take my money?'

'She claims she'd been undercharging Joanna for years and was only taking what was her due. She'd made a couple of smaller online withdrawals in the past but when she heard about Joanna's death, she realised she would never get paid unless she took matters into her own hands. The final cash withdrawal was because she was scared the police would be monitoring your online accounts. She says it was a sort of un-written agreement between them that she'd always be looked after. And she claims you said the same thing when you gave her your bank details.'

'Why would I do that?' I demand. But even as I say it, I have a hazy recollection from years ago of complaining about Joanna being too controlling about money, about needing more independence.

'She had your passport too, would you have given her that? Do you think you might have given her permission to take your money?' She asks the question very gently, treating me with kid gloves. I know they think I'm mad.

'I wouldn't have given her my money,' I insist. 'It's the only independence I have left.'

Rawlinson gives me a look. 'Well, not if you inherit your sister's estate,' he points out. 'Who knows, maybe you and Heard cooked this up between you?'

My mouth actually falls open. 'What? I didn't even know she existed until today.'

'Sarah, we're going to dig into this,' says Noor. 'The timing, given what happened to Joanna, it warrants further investigation.'

I feel the breath escape from my body. I didn't know how much tension I'd been holding on to but I feel shackles slip away. I think this means I'm off the hook, for now. Whoever this Heard is, she has bought me time. And I intend to use it.

'Is she here?'

'Who?'

'This Heard woman.'

Noor nods. 'She's still being questioned, yes.'

'Can I see her?' I just want to know why, why did Joanna do this to me. I need the closure, as this imposter herself liked to say.

'Absolutely out of the question,' says Noor. She extends her hand and I shake it. Her long fingers are cold and soft, her grasp surprisingly firm. 'We'll be in touch, Sarah, when we know more. Don't go anywhere, OK?'

She disappears down a corridor, her high heels tapping, nodding greetings to a uniformed officer walking the other way. Rawlinson, who's been charged with escorting me out of the station, sees me watching and shakes his head. He gestures for me to walk ahead of him, and I feel his lumbering presence at my shoulder as we head back towards reception.

'Thing with DS Noor,' he says, reaching over me to swipe a key card entry system. 'She ticks every diversity box and gets every promotion. It looks good. She's got her psychology degree and her masters and she thinks she's bloody Sherlock Holmes. But it's the big boss who calls the shots.' He points upwards. 'And the message coming down from on high is it's time for an arrest, particularly with all this press attention.'

He pulls open the door, which opens out to the reception area, and looks down at me, a nasty smile on his face. 'Noor's smart, but she's green. The boss isn't going to let her play detective much longer before he makes the call. He's already told her as much. If I were you, I'd drop all these stories and start thinking about how you're going to cooperate. It will play much better for you in court.'

He smirks unpleasantly and gestures for me to step through the door.

'Like she said, don't be going anywhere.' And he lets the door slam shut behind me.

I stand outside, sucking in the fresh air, feeling a light drizzle on my face. Everything has changed. My perception's off, like one of those surrealist paintings, or maybe it's only now I'm seeing things as they really are. This morning I thought it was my brain I couldn't trust. Instead, it seems it was my sister.

Chapter Forty

It takes an hour to walk home, my mind reeling from Noor's revelations. I pause at the gate and look down at the shrine. The little candles have burnt themselves out, the flowers have shrivelled and curled inside their cellophane wrappers and a teddy holding a red heart sags limply. There's a framed photo of Joanna, under which someone – I'm guessing Alan – has written *Justice for Joanna*, with the police hotline number. I stare at her face, those blue eyes, the dimples, the artful highlights to mask the grey, and realise I didn't know her at all. I thought it impossible anyone would want to murder my loving, dutiful sister but now I'm not so sure. I sweep up an armful of flowers and dump them into the wheelie bin. I make three trips until the pavement is clear. I pause for a moment and look at Simon's yellow flowers, the card with the simple message. *I will never forget you.* Did he know the real Joanna? Did anyone?

The house is in darkness, and it somehow seems changed since I left this morning on my trip to the bank. Now it feels a sombre, menacing place, where the person I lived with was conspiring against me, laughing at me, using my disability against me. I go inside and shut the door, listening to the sounds of the house. It is so quiet. A car drives past, its tyres hissing on the damp road. Something inside me stirs, something subtle, and I sense a memory, long buried, like a creature hiding in the silt of a murky pond, shift in the darkness. I stay still, trying to see, but the memory is deeply buried; all I can catch is a trace of it, a bubble that rises to the surface – a man in an empty hallway, kissing me in the gloom, lit only by the light of the streetlamp outside, then the sound of a car. It's gone. I cannot get it back, though I linger in the hall like a phantom in my own home. It doesn't feel like a home any more. It feels like a place where bad things happened, where secrets were whispered and lies were told and everyone pretended everything was perfectly normal.

Something needs to change. I wrinkle my nose in disgust at how I've been living, sleeping on the sofa, living off biscuits and wine, my clothes piling up in a crumpled soiled mess. I grab an armful of clothes and throw them into the washing machine, then head upstairs for a bath. I hear someone knock on the kitchen door and know it will be Alan; he'll have seen the bathroom light on and like a moth he's back. I wonder if he knew about the Xanthe Heard con. Probably not, I doubt Joanna would have shared a secret like that with him. She never liked him and barely gave him the time of day.

I scrub my greasy hair with Joanna's best shampoo and then soak until my fingers turn white and wrinkly, and the boiler runs out of hot water, the pipes chuntering and spluttering. I pull the plug, disgusted at how dirty the water looks, long strands of my hairs drifting like seaweed. I wrap myself in towels and then head for Joanna's room to get some clean clothes.

'Bitch,' I say out loud as I pull open her wardrobe. 'You secretive bitch.'

My heart is cold as I rifle through her clothes, selecting a black jersey maxi dress from Hobbs I've long coveted and a Joules sweatshirt over the top. Even though it's all too big, it still looks better on me, I think vindictively, but my heart isn't really in it. I want to hate her but standing here, in her room, looking at the photos on her dressing table, the framed paint-splodged handprint of a four-year-old James and her artsy wicker heart, all I feel is a profound sense of loss. This was my sister, and I didn't really know her at all. She tried her best to look after me. Perhaps it all got too much. Perhaps she couldn't do it any more. God knows, the stuff I can remember is bad enough, the incandescent rages, the confusion and tears, that time I smashed the car into the wall. Perhaps Xanthe Heard was where you turn when there's nowhere else. And it helped. It may have been a fairground gimmick, shadows and mirrors and lies, but it seems I was desperate enough, ill enough, that that was all it took. It helped.

I fall to my knees, crying. I wish more than anything I could have one last conversation with Joanna. The conversation we never had when she was alive. Just to understand her, why she did this, and how she really felt, about me, about Rob, about Simon, about our childhood. I drag one of her Prosopagnosia Collection cardigans out of her wardrobe – this one's green with a waterfall hem that she stopped wearing because the moths attacked one sleeve – and drape myself in it.

She was always so organised. Her shoe boxes stacked neatly in the bottom of her wardrobe, a basket where she kept her scarves and belts, and a big hatbox at the back. I don't remember Joanna ever wearing a hat – she always said they were aging – so I pull the box out and wipe the dust off the top. But inside there isn't a hat, there's just some letters and cards, a homemade Mother's Day card and a gruesome find of an old matchbox rattling with James' milk teeth.

I flick through the letters and cards. A postcard showing bright fishing boats bobbing in a sun-streaked harbour. *Malta's lovely, but not half as lovely as you, Chuckles. Miss you so much.*

259

Sxxx There are cards from Dubai, Sydney, Hong Kong, New York, Las Vegas, which again leaves me wondering exactly what Simon's job entailed. Was he into something dodgy? Do finance jobs really involve so much travel these days?

I turn over a card. A large Valentine's Day card, with a picture of two squirrels kissing before a full moon, their tails entwined in a heart shape. For a rich man, he had very pedestrian tastes. Chuckles, urgh. I open up the card idly. But this one isn't from S.

> Darling Joanna,
> you are the sunshine in my day,
> the bright moon in my nights.
> I love you more every time I see you,
> you're always in my sights.
> Love from someone closer than you think

The card isn't signed but I realise, with a sickening lurch, I recognise the handwriting. I've seen it recently, on Post-it notes, letters and calendar reminders. It's Alan's handwriting, I'm sure. *Someone closer than you think*. Oh God, did she know it was from him? Why has she kept it all these years? Was something going on between them? Surely he wasn't the mystery man of recent months. I look at the card, certain it isn't recent. He sent this some time ago, and she's kept it. Was it just vanity, or did something happen between the two of them? Is that why she hated him so much? I realise, staring at the poem, that I'm holding a motive right here in my hands. *You're always in my sights*. It has a sinister ring. Was it jealousy, a spurned lover's revenge?

I will have to show Noor. I rifle through the hatbox looking for more letters from Alan but it appears to be a one off. There are a couple of Valentine cards from Simon, some saucy love letters from Rob that make me blush, and some of James' daub-ings from nursery. There's a thick envelope tucked down the side and I pull it out and find it contains a wad of cash, mainly twenties, perhaps £600. I let out a long shaky sigh, at least I have some cash now.

At the bottom of the box, I find a photo album I don't remem-ber seeing before. I open it, not expecting much: photographs don't mean a lot to me unless they're labelled, but of course Joanna's neat hand has inscribed the names, the place and dates of photos stretching back to the 1970s. I pore over faded snaps of two little girls in cords and T-shirts, solemn faces under bowl cuts, or sitting primly in party dresses, Mother hovering like a grim governess in her Sunday best, her beady eyes always on us and not the camera.

Here we are in school uniform, our faces frozen with back-to-school nerves and our lace-up shoes shined to a polish. Joanna has a prefect badge in one photo, and later, as a teenager, she's deputy head girl and house captain. Of course. There's a photo of her on the stage at school, receiving a certificate. *Joanna, award for best history essay 1986.* Her hair is mousy brown and pulled back from her face in tight braids, a smattering of acne across her chin, her school shirt too tight across her chest.

I suppose I was already the black sheep by then. I turn the page, expecting to find my high school photos and recoil in horror. My photo has been mutilated. The girl with the blond hair has had her eyes scored out and a biro has been used to turn my front teeth black. In the next one my eyes are again scratched out, and the biro tears through my face in crazy jagged spikes. My name has been scrubbed out and replaced with the word BITCH. Page after page, as we travel into adult-hood, our school uniforms swapped for leggings or bootcut jeans, in every photo my face has been mutilated. Eyes gouged out, teeth blackened, or sometimes I'm just decapitated from the photograph altogether. There's one of me, Joanna, Rob and Mother and I'm ripped out, just my feet and knees visible. It feels like an actual assault, the hate that has driven this sustained and methodical destruction radiating from the pages.

I shut the album, sick to my stomach. Did Joanna hate me that much? Not only has she mutilated virtually every image of me but she kept this album, hidden in this hatbox with other keepsakes and treasures. This wasn't a one-off rage. This was an anger that lived and breathed for decades. Has she been conspiring against me all this time? Did her jealousy warp her into someone I don't know? I think about the plain Jane with her braids and sensible shoes getting her history essay award and how somehow that person morphed into a well-off, well-dressed corporate high-flyer with her Hobbs dresses and her LK Bennett heels and her highlights. She went on dates, attended parties and joined book clubs while I stayed at home, with my books and my pills, locked in a prison of my own mind, slobbing around in my jeans and sweatshirts and supermarket trainers. At some point the trajectory of our lives crossed over, and she went up and I went down. Did she somehow make this happen? Did she cause the car crash? Did she separate me from my psychiatrist to stop my recovery? Did she arrange that Heard woman to keep me dulled and compliant? These are dark thoughts but they do something to me. It's like when I used to cut myself, the way the pain brought relief and clarity. Now the pain runs deep through my being, a scalpel-sharp wound beneath the skin, releasing not blood but anger, which seeps into my veins with a clear cold purpose. When I leave Joanna's room, the hateful album kicked across the room, I am not crying or anxious, I am angry.

Chapter Forty-One

I wake with a sense of purpose, tidying, cleaning and putting on a wash. I am determined to live my best life, and not let Joanna's legacy of jealousy and hatred ruin my remaining years. I've put the Valentine's card in a food storage bag – the closest thing I have to an evidence bag – and leave a message for DS Noor to call me back urgently. I can't settle; I'm so desperate to share this news and have the card in the proper hands. I bang the hoover around and scour the worktops in a kind of mania but it all evaporates the moment I hear the front door. Could it be DS Noor already? The shape through the glass is petite. I dither but whoever it is has already seen me.

'Hi there,' calls a woman's voice I can't place.

Reluctantly, I open the door a crack and peer at her. She's early twenties, and has a high swishy ponytail and a bright eager smile with unnaturally white teeth. I have noticed that about young people these days, they all have amazing smiles.

'Hello, Sarah,' she says as she steps forward and holds out her hand. Instinctively I take it, and we shake hands. By now she has stepped through the door, both feet on the mat and I can't help but admire the sheer moxie of the move. I wonder if the Jehovah's Witnesses have upped their game and at once I have a flashback to the few times Joanna and I had to trail about proselytising with Mother, handing out leaflets and hot with embarrassment whenever we saw someone we knew. We were so miserable that Mother stopped taking us: she said our surly faces were putting people off. We both had extra sessions with Pastor Louis after that to find out why the Holy Spirit wasn't filling us with joy.

'Sarah,' says the woman on the doormat, still clasping my hand. 'My name's Charlene Winnington and I'm with the *Leyton Advertiser*.'

'Oh no,' I say, snatching back my hand.

'I just want to hear your side of the story,' she says. 'It's been more than a week now. Obviously, the local community are campaigning for action and your nephew has made a heartfelt appeal for witnesses but we haven't heard from you yet. Are you happy with the way the police investigation is progressing?'

I swallow. 'I'm sorry, I don't want to comment.'

'It must be a terrible time for you,' she coos, looking up at me through black-framed glasses. She has very blue eyes, and a sprinkle of freckles over her nose. She is exactly how a Hollywood director would cast an earnest young reporter, I think.

'It might help to talk about it. And if we put your story out there, along with James' appeal, it might jog some memories, you know, and put pressure on the police.'

I think about Noor, and the pressures she's already under. Constantly battling the impression she's only there because of her sex and her colour, under pressure from her boss and undermined by a boorish junior. It doesn't seem fair to pile on more pressure but then I remind myself that Noor isn't my friend.

'I've a lot of experience covering these cases,' says the reporter – something I write off as a blatant lie given her unlined face and the fact she writes for a paper that gets its knickers in a twist over uncollected bins – 'and sometimes we do find it helps to keep the case in the public eye. You never know what might break a case, especially if the police are following a narrow line of enquiries.'

She seems to put significant weight on this last phrase and I grow uncomfortable. Does she mean they're just focused on me? I wonder how much contact the reporter has with the police. I wouldn't put it past Rawlinson to be running his mouth off down the pub. Suddenly I can't bear it any more, the feeling that everyone thinks it was me, that I could have stabbed Joanna. Everyone seems to have forgotten I'm a victim too.

'I think they have a few suspects,' I blurt out suddenly. My eyes instinctively drift over to the right, over the fence, into Alan's front garden. *You're always in my sights ... someone closer than you think ...*

The reporter is quick, I'll give her that.

'Someone close to home?' she asks, following my gaze.

I blush red. I didn't mean her to laser in on Alan like that, or did I? Isn't that deep down exactly what I want to happen, for Noor to investigate Alan and leave me alone? That card must surely mean he's a person of interest. That's what they say on TV, isn't it?

And it's almost like a voodoo curse, just to think of him conjures him up. He walks past the bottom of my drive, clutching the paper and a Co-op bag. I hold my breath, aware he's hovering at the bottom of the drive, clearly noting that I've removed the shrine. He won't be able to pass that up without comment but he sees me talking to the reporter and heads up his own drive. He waves at me, the paper held up like a salute.

'Your flowers have gone?' he shouts.

I nod but don't say anything. I can tell he's dying to find out more and to ask about my visitor but I don't want to give him an opening. The thought of him spying on Joanna all these years makes my stomach turn.

'Pop round later,' he shouts, fumbling in his pocket for his keys. 'Got some bits for you.'

I clear my throat, as both I and the reporter watch Alan open his door and move inside.

'Person of interest,' I mutter, and the reporter's attention snaps back to me.

'What's his name?' she asks. She has a notebook and pen out of her pocket quicker than a gunslinger on a fast draw.

'Alan Warner.' I say. She's poised to ask more questions but I get cold feet. I don't want anything in writing linking me to this. After all, I may be living next to a cold-blooded killer.

'Sorry,' I say, as I get the door and begin to press it firmly closed, forcing her to step back. 'I can't talk now.'

I lock and bolt the door, wait for my racing heart to settle. I am pleased with this. Noor might ignore my concerns as further ramblings of a mad woman but she won't be able to ignore the press when the little reporter starts nosing around.

The phone rings. It's PC Casey Crown, calling to let me know that Joanna's body is now ready for release. Her voice is soft, and I like to think she believes me even if none of her colleagues do.

'I thought you should know.'

Body. There is something about that word that is so final. That is all she is now, a sack of organic material already decomposing, stripped of whatever life force, whatever spark, made her a person. The grief rushes in like a wave and I breathe deeply, steadying myself. *Remember how much she hated you*, says a small voice in my mind, and I know then that I can get through this.

'What do I have to do?' I ask. Surely they can't expect me to collect her in a taxi?

'Nothing at this stage,' says Crown. 'I believe arrangements have already been made. Mrs Rose Wallis, your mum, she's already making arrangements for the funeral.'

The world stops spinning. Everything slows. The phone drops from my hands. I can hear Crown saying something, asking if I'm all right, and then the line goes dead. I must have misheard. I crouch down to pick up the phone but have to put my head between my knees, fighting for breath. I focus on breathing, on the weave of the carpet, on the dust under the sideboard. I focus on the little things my senses tell me are real, right here, right now.

Because this is impossible. Mother has been dead for twelve years.

When I can breathe again, I call back, convinced there has been a mistake. Casey Crown is insistent, however, and goes over the contact details for whoever is claiming to be Rose Wallis: Hinstock Hall, a residential home outside Aylesbury, just twenty miles from where we used to live. I can tell by her voice she thinks I'm losing it again. She says she'll pop round to see me later and she's going to get DS Noor to give me a call.

Mrs Rose Wallis, still alive, still in Berkshire.

I do not know what to think. Is this confabulation? Has my brain decided that because I don't see Mother she must be dead? But I am sure I remember the funeral: just me, Joanna and a couple of workers from the care home. I was surprised Aunty Karen hadn't come or anyone from Mother's church but Joanna had explained that dementia is a cruel disease and Mother had slipped from their lives many years before. There were some dreary hymns, a reading from Corinthians and a wander round the crem, our high heels sinking into soft turf, before a cup of tea and a slice of fruit cake in a farm shop cafe where I had a little cry. Joanna was remarkably dry-eyed, which she brushed off.

'I've done my grieving,' she explained. 'The dementia took her from us years ago, Sarah. This is really a blessing. I'm glad for her.'

Now, of course, I look back and realise she didn't cry because Mother wasn't dead – so who's funeral was that? Some random old person from the care home? Those spa weekends, was she really visiting Mother? But why would Joanna lie about this? Did she want to hog Mother all to herself? She always was the golden child, always desperate for her approval.

I pace the house, realising I didn't know my sister at all. She has lied and manipulated me for years. I'm even wondering now if she's really dead. They haven't let me see the body after all. Could this be some grotesque trick? Is that why James isn't around, is he in on it, have they actually moved away together and are living it up on some beach? Has it all been some elaborate ploy to ditch me?

These dark paranoid thoughts take me to a dark place. I tell myself to calm down. Joanna is dead. I saw the blood and Noor and Rawlinson have seen the body and they couldn't possibly be in on it. Or could they? I am not sure I can trust anybody now. I think about calling Hinstock Hall and asking to speak to this Mrs Rose Wallis, but it could all be another trick. It's easy enough to fake an old woman's voice. No, I shall have to go and see for myself. After all, these years I finally need to know the truth.

Chapter Forty-Two

This is it. I am going back to where it all began. I am physically shaking as I pull on my denim jacket, one of Joanna's big scarves and some sunglasses. There may be tears. There's a beep outside and I peer out at the taxi, then double-check everything: the envelope of cash, a photo of Mother, my keys.

I'm just locking the door, trying to still the violent tremor in my hands, when a tall man looms over me. I desperately search for tells – his height, his build, that receding hair – but it's only when he speaks I realise it's Alan.

'Sarah, what the heck have you been saying to the press?' I have never seen or heard Alan angry before. This man is visibly shaking, his fists clenched into white balls of contained rage and instinctively I shrink back, afraid.

'I've had some journalist round at mine, asking if I'm a person of interest to the police, if I was in a relationship with Jojo and asking all sorts of questions about that poor lad in Yorkshire. Did you say something to them?'

'I don't know what you're talking about,' I say primly, edging past him towards the car.

'I thought we were going to stick together on this. But I see what's happening, you're trying to save your own neck by pinning it on me.'

He points a finger, wrapped in a dirty plaster, and jabs it at the air near my face.

'Everything all right?' The taxi driver has got out of the car and is watching us. The intervention seems to bring Alan to his senses. He lowers his hand, the fight suddenly gone out of him.

'I thought we were friends, Sarah,' he says, bitterly. 'I thought you were better than the rest.'

He steps away, and disappears down the garden, his shoulders hunched. My anxiety soars through the roof and I think about aborting the trip. But the pull of Mother is strong: there are so many questions and they won't get answered hiding away in the house.

As the car pulls out into the road, I look over my shoulder through the back window and see a face at Alan's upstairs window, staring down at me. I hurriedly turn around, and will the driver to pick up speed, the hackles on the back of my neck rising as I feel that cold gaze boring into me.

We arrive at Stafford train station and I rub my sweaty palms on my black jersey dress. I have been dreading buying the train tickets, which for some reason my anxiety has built up into a massive hurdle. I don't know how any of this works any more. The ticket hall is busy, with students hauling vast rucksacks and business people huffing at the queues, and I rush to the toilets, sure my airways are closing up. I study my face in the mirror, but while my eyes are wide with panic and there's a vein pulsing in my forehead, there's no sign of my lips turning blue. I talk myself down, reminding myself about the scene in the bank: I thought I was dying there too and I didn't. I just have to ride it out. I focus on my breathing and force myself back out into the ticket hall, and in the end, other than the eye-watering cost of the ticket, the transaction is painless. The man is polite, helpful, and hands me a wad of orange tickets. I find my way to the right platform, and stand there in a state of hyper-alertness, obsessively checking the time, my tickets, my money, my keys. God, how do people do this every day?

When the train arrives, I get on, and search for a seat. There's one at the back, near the toilets, and I sink down, damp with sweat but relieved to have got this far and to know that for the next two hours I am unreachable: no pop ins from Alan, no unexpected calls from Noor and Rawlinson, no reporters posing as neighbours. I am just another stranger taking a train journey. Nothing to see here, folks.

But as the train rattles south, my mind turns to Hinstock Hall, and Mother. I chew on my nails. I wonder how ill she is? Well enough to arrange a funeral for Joanna, or did a member of staff do that on her behalf? I can't help picturing a reunion, Mother's face streaming with tears, me sobbing in her arms. We will sit and hold hands, we'll make plans for the future, she'll rub my back and make everything all right. I won't be alone any more. I'll have a mother again. I well up, just picturing these scenes, even though my adult brain recognises how unlikely this is. Mother was never the hugging kind even when I was a little kid. And why has she not made any effort to get in touch with me all these years? Or did Joanna tell her I was dead too? Was my sister really that cruel?

At Reading, I take another taxi, anxiously watching the meter tick, and realise how easy it is to burn through money once you're out in the world. It is a good job Joanna has made me a rich woman.

Hinstock Hall squats behind tall hedges on the edge of a small picture-postcard village. No doubt it was once a beautiful Georgian vicarage but now the green lawns have been torn up to make space for a car park, its elegant windows are marred by functional slatted blinds and an ugly red brick annexe stretches away at the back, more than doubling the footprint

271

of the original building. I get out of the taxi and can already smell the disinfectant.

The cool reception area, in shades of beige and coffee, reminds me of an upmarket Premier Inn. There's a huge vase of lilies by the reception desk and my stomach churns at the scent; they will forever remind me of Alex Fuller, invading our house with his false condolences, fishing for news about what Joanna knew, poor Carmen quivering in his wake. I still think Alex is the most likely suspect but Noor seems determinedly uninterested. He probably has powerful friends. I know I will never smell lilies again without feeling this impotent anger.

A woman in a neat blouse greets me from behind the desk.

'Is Mrs Wallis expecting you?' she asks, with a strong East European accent.

'I'm her daughter,' I croak. I wipe my wet palms on my dress again.

'Joanna, isn't it?' she says, typing on her keyboard.

I swallow. 'Yes, it's Joanna.' Clearly the news hasn't travelled.

'You know where to go? I think they're in the day room.'

I nod. I can do this. I am Joanna Bailey and I have been here many times to visit my mother. I hesitate. 'Can I use the bathroom first?'

She points it out and reminds me to use the hand sanitiser. 'Infection control.' She smiles at me. 'Very important.'

I promise to use it and make for the bathroom. It gives me time to gather myself and take out the photo of Mother. I don't want to accost the wrong old lady or let them try and foist some imposter on me. Trust no one, I tell myself. You're on your own until you know what's been happening.

I leave the sanctuary of the bathroom and walk purposefully down a corridor. There are helpful signs, showing where to find the dining room, the day room, the gardens and the bedrooms.

I pass a small room with a sink and mirror where a hairdresser is busy blow-drying an old lady's hair. Others wait patiently for her services, some staring vacantly at the walls or nodding in their wheelchairs.

I pop my head in and speak to the cheery hairdresser. 'I'm looking for Mrs Rose Wallis in the day room?'

'Straight ahead, love. She was one of my first today, all pretty for you.'

I nod my thanks and continue down the corridor. So, Mother's sentient enough to get her hair done. She's not dribbling in a bed or at death's door. My anxiety starts to spike again. Am I really about to meet Mother after all these years?

I can see the day room ahead, a long airy room painted yellow, with windows that run its length, providing restful views of the gardens beyond. At one end of the room, chairs are arranged in a semi-circle round the TV and at the other end the chairs are clustered into small groups round little tables, where people can play cards or dominos. Those that can. Those that can't are stranded in wheelchairs, their chins nodding on their chests. The smell of disinfectant is stronger here, and there's another undertone too, of cooking, and too many people inside for too long. It doesn't help that the heating is on high. It brings back memories of Hillwood House; the heat, the astringent scent of hand sanitiser and the bustle of care workers in sensible shoes. The intimacy of it all.

One of the old men sees me and shuffles over. His fly is undone and there's a food stain on his chin. 'Is it dinner time?' he asks.

'Sorry. I don't know.'

'Eh? Is it dinner time?'

'I don't know, sorry.'

He turns away, then turns back. 'It's always a roast on a Wednesday. Fish on a Friday. Roast on a Wednesday.'

'OK.' Today is Thursday.

'Fish on a Friday,' he says. 'I think it's time. They said it was time. I'm going to check. Fish on a Friday. Fish on a Friday.'

He keeps repeating it, like his mind has got stuck in a groove and can't get out. I'm flustered, not by his behaviour, perseveration was common at Hillwood House and I saw a lot worse there, but his flapping is drawing attention to me.

Another resident approaches, leaning on a walker. She's so withered and bent, like one of those bare wind-blasted trees you see near the coast, I'm amazed she can manoeuvre the metal frame. Her shoulder blades stick out like stunted wings under her M&S jumper and the legs that emerge from her tweed skirt are as thin as sticks.

'Chicken today, Stan,' she barks. 'Go and sit down. You're making a fuss.'

'I'm going to sit down,' he says, his mind grasping on to the new information, and he shuffles slowly away.

I smile gratefully at the woman, thankful for her intervention. She narrows her eyes at me, watching me carefully.

'So, you're awake then,' she rasps. 'Joanna said you were in a coma.'

The world spins dizzily around me and I float out of my body, weightless, breathless. I can't speak, I can't move.

'You been struck dumb?' she asks. 'I heard you weren't all there.'

The rudeness of it is like a slap across the face and I snap back into my body. I take a deep breath and fumble for the photograph, comparing it feature by feature to this shrunken harridan before me. The same beady eyes, that downturned mouth, like life is a perpetual round of disappointment, and that ferocious tilt of the jaw like a soldier roused for battle. Oh yes, this is my mother, and she hasn't changed a bit. The irises

274

may be slightly clouded now and the whites yellowed, but her eyes still flash with challenge.

'I think you'd better come with me, don't you?' she says.

Chapter Forty-Three

I find myself once more cast back into the role of child. I am a grown woman of forty-six yet this shrivelled woman with her walker and stick-thin legs wields a power over me. I trail behind her, my guts twisting with anxiety. There will not be a joyful reunion and I was a fool to ever hope for such a thing. My mother withheld her affection when I was a child; what a fool to think it would be given now. But not everything is the same; this time I can feel a difference inside me, a little spark of anger that just needs the right tinder to catch: why did you never love me, you heartless bitch?

She leads me to a room at the far end of the red brick annex. It's pretty sparse for a life; a neatly made up hospital bed, a cheap pine wardrobe and a bedside table where the essentials of her life are distilled to a box of tissues, a large print Bible and a bottle of Robinsons lemon barley water. Against the wall there are two pleather-covered high-backed armchairs, the kind you find in doctor's waiting rooms, and a table with a half-completed jigsaw. Above the bed there's a print on the wall I remember from home: mountains, a lake and a couple of Highland cattle in the foreground. I don't remember us ever going to Scotland yet somehow this print has accompanied my mother through the decades, whereas so much else has been shed.

'You'd better sit down,' she says, gesturing to one of the chairs.

I perch uncomfortably, aware of her eyes burning into me. She doesn't seem surprised to see me. Most people would show some emotion at the news their long-lost daughter has finally awoken from a coma but Mother appears to be chewing on a wasp at my sudden appearance.

'I thought you,' I begin, but before I can continue she starts talking over me. It's something I remember from childhood; she was always so certain of herself that she had to speak when she wanted, regardless of what other conversations were already underway.

'I always thought it was divine retribution what happened to you, yet here you are, up and about, not a scratch on you.' She glares at me, and I am taken aback by her anger. I wonder if it's a symptom of her dementia, I know it can cause mood swings, aggression and personality changes. Although this isn't so much a change in personality, as a personality distilled over time to its purest, most potent essence. Her words drip with the concentrated poison of the righteous.

'Joanna told me you were dead.'

'Hah!' She spits the sound. 'Bet you liked that, didn't you? Sorry to disappoint you but I'm still here and now I'm going to be burying one of my own children. The wrong one at that.'

I recoil from her bitterness. Why does she hate me so much?

She moves towards the bed and lowers herself down awkwardly. She is so light she doesn't make a dent in the tightly made bed. But her soul is heavy, dripping poison. I am left reeling with her vitriol. Of all the ways I pictured this scene, I never imagined this.

'Why are you in here?' I blurt out. She's frail but I don't see anything wrong with her apart from her black heart.

She looks at me with a low cunning glance. 'It costs a lot to stay here, you know. Joanna pays, but then she did get the proceeds from the house so it's only fair. The money's in a trust though so don't get your hopes up. The accountant came the other week to make sure.'

I dig my fingernails into my palms. The woman is hateful and I'm sick of it. I came here for answers not her bile. 'Why did Joanna lie to me? Why did she say you were dead?'

'Why did she say you were still in a coma?' She says it like it's a rhetorical question, like I should already know the answer, but there's something shifty about her, something searching in her query, and I suddenly realise she doesn't know the answer either. Joanna has played us both for fools.

She peers at me, those beady eyes flashing with something like enjoyment at my discomfort. 'Not a scratch on you,' she repeats. 'Typical. You ruin Joanna's life and then you get to waltz off into the sunset, no memory, no guilt.'

I clear my throat, unnerved by her unremitting hostility. 'I was hoping we might, that finding you, we might, after all these years ...' The words stick in my throat. I can't choke out what I was hoping for. The hope shrivelled and died before we even reached this bleak room.

'I told you then and I'll tell you now. I'll never forgive you. Joanna always was too soft.'

I can't bear it any longer. 'What are you talking about? Forgive me for what?'

'The moment you met Robert you were throwing yourself at him like some cheap tart. You couldn't bear for your sister to have someone you couldn't have. You lured him in, foolish idiot that he was. Even on the wedding day you were making eyes at him.' She spits the words.

I can't believe it. Me and Robert. I recoil from the thought but I feel the chime of truth in her words. Somehow, deep down, I have always known this. This is the man at the party, the kiss in the hall, the secret lurking in the silt of my memories.

'You broke her heart. All of our hearts. Though can't say I was surprised. I should have broken you as a child.' I shiver at her words; our childhoods were bleak enough. 'We disowned you. We all did. Not that it stopped you. Like animals you were. You flaunted that bastard child in Joanna's face even though you knew she was barren.'

Barren. Bastard. The horrible biblical judgements. 'I thought you were a Christian. These things you're saying ... I don't believe you.'

'Nothing would prevail upon you to get rid of it. But God took care of it. He always does in the end.'

Does she mean I had a miscarriage? She smiles nastily, she is pleased her god took my baby.

'I don't believe you. Joanna never said anything. And we've lived together for the past twenty years while she's kept you stuck in here.'

That shocks her into silence for a moment. She's not used to people talking back to her. Like all bullies, she can give it out but isn't so keen on taking it.

She stands up, and nods her head over her shoulder, gesturing for me to follow her. 'I've got something to show you.' She shuffles over to the wardrobe and pulls it open awkwardly. 'Down there. The black file.'

It's a large box file, dusty and smelling faintly of mothballs. I lift it up and place it on the table, scuffing jigsaw pieces out of the way. I can see she's jemmied together some bits of blue sky, but I'm not going to fix it. I am only just containing myself from flinging the lot on the floor and setting fire to the place.

She sits on the bed and sorts through the box file, her hands bent with arthritis, keeping the lid angled so I can't see the contents. It would be so easy for me to grab the box and see whatever I wanted but I wouldn't give her the satisfaction. She pulls out a brown envelope and hands it to me. Inside there are yellowing cuttings from the paper; this was the news that just missed the Internet, the truth that has been hidden, buried in dust and silence for twenty years.

'Most families have certificates, birth announcements, job promotions. That's what you brought us.'

I take the envelope and know at once that this is the murk, the silt, the sludge of my life. Everything I've been hiding from myself will be revealed when I read the contents. I should be afraid, but I'm not, I'm hungry, feasting on the details, gorging on the horror until I can take no more.

Horror crash driver was drunk.

Police are appealing for witnesses to Saturday's horror crash on Drover's Lane that killed a man and left a woman fighting for her life. Cops believe the driver, twenty-six-year-old single mother Sarah Wallis, had been drinking before getting into the car with her one-year-old son and another man, believed to be a family member. The infant was taken to hospital with minor injuries while the driver was airlifted to the John Radcliffe Infirmary in Oxford, where she is reported to be in a coma. The man was pronounced dead at the scene. His name has yet to be released.

Hero lorry driver Gary Marchant, who swerved off the road, avoiding a head-on collision with the car, said the Escort had been going too fast and on the wrong side of the road at the time of the crash. 'That woman and baby are lucky to be alive,' he said.

The dread seeps over me like paralysis. This is the accident Joanna never talked of, these are the answers she never gave me, and now I have them I don't want them. I feel sick. I killed Robert and brought my injuries on myself. *But the baby lived.*

I look up from the cutting, my words are wild. 'What happened to the child? Where's my child?'

280

My mother looks at me with disgust. 'Justice was done. You took Joanna's husband and killed him. But Joanna got your son.'

My mouth falls open, the cuttings falls to the floor. I can hear my Mother saying something, getting at me to pick them up, but it's just distant words. I have a son. James is my son.

I walk to the window and press my head against the cool glass, trying to process what I've just read. I have a son. I must go back, I have to tell him. I take a long deep shuddering breath. This changes everything.

Then I see it. The reason she's in here. Everything is blank. It's like something has switched off inside her. She's sitting up and her eyes are open but there's nothing there. Her right arm hangs slackly and there's a patch of something spreading across her skirt. Oh fuck.

'Mum, are you OK?'

Her mouth moves but no sound comes out and spittle spools off her chin. Oh fuck. There's an emergency pull cord by the bed and I yank it hard and then run out in the corridor, calling for help. A woman in a carer's green uniform bustles up. 'What is it, love?'

'My mother, there's something wrong.'

'Oh dear, Rosie, come on, love,' says the woman. She's suddenly joined by a couple more staff and they take over, lifting my mother's painfully thin legs onto the bed, checking her pulse. 'Get her pills,' says someone.

I am helpless. I know nothing of my mother's medical condition, or the pills she takes. She is almost a stranger to me and it feels wrong to be here, watching her in this vulnerable state. I wring my hands in anguish. I can't believe this is happening here, today, now.

One of the care workers comes up to me and puts a hand on my shoulder. 'Don't worry, dear, I know it looks scary but we're used to it.'

'She's done this before?'

'More seizures now. It's difficult to get the dosage of epilepsy meds right in older patients because they're typically on so many other meds.'

'She has epilepsy?' The irony of it. My anxiety med, pregabalin, is used to treat epilepsy.

The woman gives me a strange look. I suppose as the daughter I would be expected to know my mother's medical history.

'It's very common in her age group, I'm afraid.' She gives a funny little laugh. 'It sucks getting older, right?'

I don't know why she's including me in this. I don't consider myself old. In some ways, so much of my life has been on hold that I still feel I'm in my twenties, stuck in suspended animation.

'Will she be OK?' I nod towards the bed, where my mother lies prone and a nurse is busy unrolling her wet tights.

'Yes, dear, but we'll get her to hospital to get her checked out. It could be quite a wait. I'm afraid ambulances don't rush here.' She smiles ruefully. 'Why don't you take a turn in the garden? It's a nice day.' She nods towards the sliding patio door, a brisk smile on her face.

I get the sense they just want me out of there, and I'm glad to go. I don't feel any obligation to be here for Mother. She has always hated me and it frees me from any pretence. She can rot in here, bullying the other residents, having her seizures and slowly losing more and more of her capacities. Her god can look after her now.

I step outside and lift my face to the sun but the big expanse of sky makes me feel dizzy. Or is it just my brain? So many thoughts collide. My mother is alive, still a bitch. My sister lied to me for years. I was a bitch. I had an affair with my sister's husband. I killed him in a car crash. I had a child. And Joanna took him.

Chapter Forty-Four

I get the receptionist to order me a taxi. She thinks it's because I want to accompany Mother to the hospital and is surprised when I say I need to get to the train station.

'You're sure?' she asks.

'I have to get back,' I say primly. 'For my son.'

How delicious it is to say the word. I am filled with a fierce longing for him. Now that I know the truth I can't believe I didn't see it before. Of course he is my boy, look at those bones, the straight hair, his slim build. No wonder Joanna never liked any interaction with the authorities, she was probably always terrified they would work out he wasn't her son. Is that why we moved away from Berkshire, to be far away from anyone who would know the truth? Is that why she tore me away from Dr Lucas, to make sure I never unearthed any troubling memories? How could she do this? I can't blame her for hating me but to take my child and raise him as her own? That's cold.

James must have been so little at the time of the accident and I was in a coma for so long that he would have quickly forgotten me. Tears roll down my face as I think of myself lying prone in a hospital bed while my boy is taught to call another woman 'mummy'. You read about infertility driving women mad, how they have urges to steal babies from prams or maternity wards.

James, with his cheating dad dead and his mother in a coma, must have seemed like a gift from heaven. Perhaps she even told herself it was her reward, that after so much heartbreak and humiliation, she was to be gifted the child she'd always craved. Even so, it takes some balls to step forward and present yourself to the world as the mother. So many lies, each one building on the other, like layers of sedimentary rock laid down over the years, the weight of it all distorting and compressing the truth until nobody can tell what's buried underneath. Perhaps she even believed she was his mother in the end. After all, Mother, the only other person who knew the truth, was consigned to a home and written off as dead. It's so callous, so at odds with everything I thought I knew about my sister, and yet, as I'm finding out, there was so much she kept hidden.

The train is busier heading north but I manage to squeeze into a seat next to a businesswoman who doesn't even look up from her laptop. I am in a daze, staring out blankly as fields and farms race by, knowing I will never come this way again. Whether Mother lives or dies, I will have no part of it and I won't let her burden James either. At least Joanna's lies spared him from the drip drip dip of Mother's poison.

It's hard to sit on the train, surrounded by people living normal lives when my body can barely contain the turmoil inside. The businesswoman gets off at Rugby but no one takes her place and I wonder if I carry a taint, is there some evolutionary gene that tells people to steer clear of those marked by so much tragedy?

I sigh heavily, louder than I expected, and it catches the attention of a woman sitting across the aisle, gainfully trying to keep a toddler quiet with an assortment of snacks and toys.

She smiles at me. 'Know just how you feel. Long day, huh?'

I would bet Joanna's fortune she doesn't know how I feel

but I appreciate the sentiment, so I simply agree it has indeed been a long day.

'Almost there,' she says, and offers me one of her kids' sweets. 'They're surprisingly addictive,' she grins.

Her attention is immediately pulled away by the child, a little thing with ginger curls and snot crusted round his nose. He has big dark eyes and his sticky little fingers have that adorable Michelin Man chubbiness. I can't believe I once grew one of these inside me. How strange not to have any memory of this miraculous event. I must have been fat, my belly stretched taut, my breasts magnificent. Did I breastfeed? Instinctively I put a hand to my breast, trying to imagine what it would have felt like to have a baby clamped there. I like to think I would have breastfed, that I would have been a glorious earth mama in a boho dress and a baby on my hip as I strolled barefoot along a beach. But for some reason I was stuck in some fateful triangle with Joanna and Rob, living down the road from a mother that disowned me, driving my kid around country lanes while pissed. I was not a good mother. I don't deserve to have someone like James in my life.

I pop the kid's sweet in my mouth, and at once feel the lifting surge of a sugar hit. I watch the mother and child play together, tears welling in my eyes as I'm hit with the grief of what I've missed all these years. I turn away and wipe my eyes surreptitiously but I can still see the mother and child in the reflection of the glass. She's a good mother, I can tell, talking quietly to him, playing silly games though she must be so bored of them right now. I wonder what kind of mother I was that first year, but however hard I try, I can't imagine myself playing silly games or singing little counting rhymes. The truth is I was a cheating lying stone-cold bitch who had an affair with her sister's husband. I need to be honest with myself; I have never been mother material and maybe it's better it was Joanna who raised him. Joanna even looked like a mum, always has, ever since she hit puberty. I know that sounds cruel but I'm just being honest. She only really came into her own later, when she was free of Mother I suppose.

Those mutilated photos make sense now. God, Joanna must have hated me. So why did she have me come and live with her after the accident? She could have stuck me in a home some-where, like she did Mother, and lived her life as a single mum. She'd have snared Simon then, without me lumbering around like a giant angry gooseberry. Why did she stick by me after what I did to her? I can't understand it. I threw a grenade into her life but got to walk away unscathed by knowledge or guilt. Even when we argued, when I was raving and she was seething with resentment, when she had to put locks on the doors and deal with my endless fuck-ups and mood swings, she never slipped up once, never once brought up the affair, or the drink driving, or the child I'd had with her husband. What was it Mother said? I'd flaunted James, the baby she craved.

I cringe from myself. I am a wretched specimen of a human being. I have been reckless with other people's lives, and they have paid for it. I thought I wanted to know the truth but now I think it was better to stumble on in ignorance. It hits me that my behaviour – the recklessness, the drink driving, the callous disregard for other's people's feelings – would score me highly on Hare's psychopathy chart. Two tears roll slowly down my cheeks and I close my eyes. Mother was right all along, she saw the taint of sin on me and knew it would lead to our ruin.

'Are you all right?' It's the mother from across the aisle. She has slipped into the seat next to me bearing tissues, her toddler watching us warily from across the way.

I force a smile that must be more of a grimace, and try to look normal. 'Just a bad day,' I say, sniffing into the tissue. 'Thank you.'

'If you want to talk?'

She has a very soft voice, and a lovely calm way about her. I'm sure she must work in some kind of caring profession, perhaps a nurse or therapist, but I am done with talking. I put my trust in Dr Lucas and that was so cruelly betrayed.

'I'm fine,' I say. It's all I can manage without bawling.

Her toddler has climbed down from his seat and wobbled over to her, pawing at her to be picked up. That instinct, to be held, to be close, how deep it runs. Tears run down my cheeks. I had a son, and he was lost to me.

The woman gets off at Stafford too. I hover, feeling useless as she collects up the snacks and drinks and plastic treasures, and does complicated things to a pushchair. I offer to help but she waves me off with a smile.

'I have a system. It doesn't look like it, but I do.'

She's so cheerful and unflappable. I am in awe. I think back to the few times I was in charge of James when he was small, and how hellish I found it, unable to keep him amused for more than five minutes, struggling to handle toilet mishaps, my fingers fumbling on his tiny buttons and my mental state utterly defeated by his tears. Perhaps it was right that Joanna took over. At least she could organise nappies and school runs and make chit chat at the school gate. At least she could recognise her own child in a school play.

The train stops and I help the mother manoeuvre her pushchair off the platform. We say our goodbyes, the little boy agitating in his pushchair. I can't believe I had one of these once.

The clouds are gathering, the first drops of rain coming down as I wait in the queue for a taxi, trying not to think about how much today has cost. Still, Joanna was a rich woman. The estate can afford it. I must find James. The words keep repeating through my mind like ticker tape. Find James, find your son. It's like a homing beacon, long dormant, has suddenly been switched on and is calling me to him. I have to find him and try to explain everything, tell him that I love him and I'm sorry, sorry for everything. How will he take it? He's always searched for the truth about his dad, how will he feel knowing I killed Rob? He might hate me, and rightly so. I deserve it. And he deserves to know the truth.

I lean forward and speak to the driver. 'Actually, change of plan. Can you take me to Shrewsbury, please? Sorry, I've just remembered there's something I need to do there.'

'Shrewsbury.' He sucks his teeth. 'You're the boss. Whereabouts?'

I try to remember the name of James' street. 'It's in the Frankwell area.' I can picture the little terrace where he rents a room. 'Just drop me near the Welsh Bridge.'

He nods, and I see him tap something into his sat nav. Forty-eight minutes. I settle back in my seat and close my eyes, rehearsing what I'm going to say.

Chapter Forty-Five

The cab driver tunes the radio to mawkish love songs that match my mood. I close my eyes and let my mind drift in a kind of dream state, images form and then dissolve. A hand on my waist, a stolen kiss in a darkened hallway, the crunch of a tyre on the driveway.

And then another image. Me, sitting in a hospital gown, my belly swollen and my fat white feet stuffed into flip flops. Blood trickles down my thigh and my heart is as closed and cold as a stone. It's a fleeting glimpse, the image comes and goes as quick as a wild animal taking flight among the trees, and I can't bring it back. But I know then that I gave birth and I did it alone, I know this deep in my soul. Rob wasn't with me. No sister, no mother, no friend. I can't remember what comes next. I can't remember the birth or the baby. I'd love to remember that first year with James before the crash stole our future. Perhaps it will all start to come back to me now. A crack has been opened, and maybe more memories will seep free.

We're into Shrewsbury's twisting lanes now, crawling through traffic under the railway bridge. Revellers are singing by the Quantum Leap sculpture, a great spine twisted from concrete, and beyond the river runs dark and silent.

'Whereabouts?' asks the driver, moving slowly through traffic lights over the Welsh Bridge.

I scour the streets, trying to remember the route we took when we dropped off James' boxes. 'By the theatre, please.'

We stop in a pool of yellow light from a street lamp and I peel off more notes to pay the driver. It's quiet here, although I can see people in local pubs and bars, laughing over glasses of wine, their faces lit up by friendship and candlelight. I wonder if James is one of them. Perhaps not, he's never been one for big groups.

I take a couple of wrong turns, until I recognise a pub on the corner of a terrace. This is it. I remember joking with James that he won't have far to stagger home but he'd just looked at me sourly. 'We're not all alcoholics, you know.' He could be very puritanical.

His house is in the middle of a terrace of workers' cottages, with big sash windows and neat front doors that open straight onto the street. When he moved in, I remembered thinking it's the kind of little house I would like: neat and full of character. Most of the houses have colourful front doors and window boxes planted with geraniums or herbs but number eight is clearly the student property: its red front door is scuffed and its white window sills are flaking paint like dandruff. Over-stuffed wheelie bins emit an unpleasant odour.

I knock, wringing my hands anxiously. James is still reeling from Joanna's death, am I really going to land him with all this? Perhaps I should think it through first. I risk ruining our relationship for ever. He might refuse to ever see me again. But doesn't he deserve to know the truth? He was always searching for answers and I have some experience of what that's like; the feeling everyone else is in on the joke and you're on the outside, your insides churning with a nameless anxiety about secrets you don't understand and your past a black hole that breathes down your neck every day. James needs to know. Besides, it's bound to come out in the end. Dirty secrets always do and I'd rather he heard it from me than Mother. But, oh God, what shall I say?

I'm still dithering when the door is wrenched open by a muscular young woman with blue hair, who glares out at me. This, I guess, must be Blue. She's wearing tiny shorts and a T-shirt that reads *Mickey Mouse must die*, which seems harsh. There's a highly detailed tattoo sleeving one arm and further artwork inked down her leg. I wonder if the two connect, spiralling round her washboard abs.

'Hi, I'm here to see James.'

'Who are you?'

'I'm his, er, aunt.' I am too chicken to say mum. I don't know how he would react.

'You know what happened, yeah? Fucked up, right?'

I nod. It certainly is. 'Is he in?'

She shakes her head. 'Think he went to sort stuff out at home. Cleared out with a bag days ago. Didn't know he had other family, made out like he was the last in the line. Dad died when he was little, right?'

I nod, thinking how sad that I didn't even warrant a mention. I was a none person to my own son, not even a footnote in the story of his life.

'If he does come back tonight, can you get him to call me? It's important.'

'Sure. And if you see him first, tell him he owes us for the rent. I know it sounds cold at this time but life goes on and we all got bills to pay.'

'I'll tell him.'

I'm left then, on the street, in the middle of Shrewsbury. It's late now, people are tumbling out of pubs in cheerful gaggles, music and light spilling onto the streets. There's a sudden burst of sirens close behind me and I almost jump out of my skin. An ambulance races by, its blue lights strafing the town.

I wonder if the police are looking for me, if I'm a wanted person. Noor had warned me not to leave town but it's not like I've done a runner. I've done nothing but cooperate. But I know I'm on borrowed time. Like Rawlinson said, Noor will cave under pressure from her boss, it's the smart thing to do for an ambitious woman like her.

I cross the river again and head up the hills towards the big public schools. I'm pleased with how much my fitness has held up given I'm largely housebound. I think of all the miles I trudged with Alan, across the hills, striding out amid the purple heather and scrambling up narrow tracks. It's funny, the more time I spent with Alan the less strange he seemed. Perhaps Joanna worked that out too, perhaps they did get into a relationship at some point. It doesn't mean he killed her. I wonder why he never sent me a Valentine's card. He seemed sweet on me at one point and there was even talk of us going for a twenty-five-mile-walk, using his bothy as base camp. It would be good to have somewhere like that to go to now. I need some space to think, to digest everything that's happened, not just Joanna's death but all the revelations about my affair with Rob, the car crash, the baby, Mother, Dr Lucas. I need to work out where the truth ends and the lies begin. So many lies. Back in the hills, nothing but me and the wind and the sky, maybe there I could find the space to unpick them all and start to work out who I really am and what I did to my family.

Chapter Forty-Six

Twenty-four years ago

Nothing has worked out how I expected. Not that I expected anything. But you hope. You hope people will behave better, although I know that's a bit rich coming from me. I never intended any of this to happen. It's important people understand that. I'd hate people to think I planned for this. You can't plan love. If that's what this is. Or was.

I noticed him straight away, of course. The first time Joanna brought him home I knew he wasn't really her type. They were mismatched from the start. He was an eight, maybe a nine, she was, realistically, a six. Not saying it to be cruel but you can't ignore these things. Events back me up there. It wasn't just that he was a looker, though he was, especially in that uniform, it's that he had that twinkle in his eye. A little bit dangerous, you know? Confident. Someone who ran at life and ate it up. I was surprised he was with Joanna, really, because she's always been cautious. The good girl. Mother even seemed to warm to him which is testament to the wattage of his charm offensive, although she had her doubts, even then. At their engagement do in a fairy lights and chalkboard gastro-pub, Mother leaned across the summer pavlova to mutter darkly in my ear, 'She'll need to keep him on a tight leash,' thought I doubt even she foresaw what was coming. After all, at that time I was still in London, living my best life, while they were planning to set up home in a neat little newbuild outside Newbury.

It was at their wedding, however, that I can mark the first milestone. I was, I admit, feverish with envy, stewing unhealthily in my own resentments and disappointments. I was between jobs and couldn't make my rent in London so I'd moved home to get back on my feet and found myself in the midst of Joanna's wedding preparations. Suddenly her life was on the up, a house, a car, a husband, a career. When he wasn't flying, Rob was always by her side, an arm casually resting across her shoulders, a finger stroking the bare skin of her arm, a hand lingering on her waist as he cleared the plates from the table. I couldn't take my eyes off them. Why couldn't I find someone like that? The jealousy curdled in my blood all summer and by the time of the wedding I was rotten with it. A better person would have been happy for her but I was bitter with my own disappointments, swilling back the cava as we got our make-up done, making chippy comments about the weather. Still, I did find it in me, when she turned around, in her big dress, the veil cascading down her back, her dimples on full beam, to say how beautiful she looked. We embraced, tears in our eyes, until Mother, who'd refused any make-up, said we'd waste that fancy mascara muck if we didn't get a grip.

By the time of the reception, I was running wild, my updo uncurling like the fronds of a fern, my uncomfortable satin shoes discarded as I danced with my arms in the air, hips sway-ing. I could feel eyes drawn to me and I was drunk on the sheer giddy pleasure of it all. A hand snaked round my waist, a voice in my ear, whisky breath on my bare shoulder.

'Time for a dance with your brother-in-law?'

I'd felt his eyes on me ever since I hit the dance floor,

predatory, devouring me. He held me a little too tight, a little too close. We made a very beautiful couple and I knew even then, from this one dance, what could happen if I let it. That power, it's intoxicating. I tried to resist but as I found out, Robert always gets what he wants in the end.

And so it began. The first time was in his car, parked down one of those country lanes that doesn't really go anywhere and just peters out in an overgrown copse. I suppose I should have asked how he knew about this hidden lover's lane, it didn't occur to me that I wasn't the first woman he'd toyed with behind Joanna's back. I was sure we had a unique connection, that it was a trick of fate he'd married her, some wonky wiring in the universe's grand plan. I knew if he'd met me first we would have been married and Joanna would have been my bridesmaid, and all would have been right with the world. Somehow, I felt that justified what I was doing.

But the truth is I didn't even think about Joanna that much. I was so wrapped up in the affair. We had assignations in his car, in the properties I was supposed to be showing to prospective tenants, in a lockup where he kept an old car he was meant to be renovating. He was away a lot, of course, and I'd quiz him viciously about his activities on his long-haul trips to Florida or Hong Kong. He would just tease me.

'You cat,' he would say, 'I love it that you get so jealous. It's how I know you really love me.'

Yet just moments later he would be complaining about Joanna, about her moods, her jealously, her tears. They were having IVF treatment and the hormones were sending her mad. He said they barely had sex any more.

'She has my sample. I'm redundant now. We're more like brother and sister,' he would say.

Joanna would tell me her side, how he's cold and disinter-ested, doesn't seem to care about the rollercoaster emotions, and how she's put on almost a stone. I make the right sounds but inside there's a horrible little malignant smile of triumph: she doesn't know, she doesn't know.

The affair binds me to them. Like a moth to a flame, I am drawn to them and London's bright light dims. I rent a poky flat and manage to hold down my temp job at the letting agency, even getting a small pay rise. And I am pulled into Mother's dark orbit again, re-igniting a long dormant hunger for her approval and attention even as I bridle against her bitter observations and morbid prophecies. *IVF is unnatural meddling that will result in an abomination. There will be a reckoning for these doctors playing God. Joanna should focus on her husband and God will find a way.*

'You're too fat, Joanna,' she pronounces one afternoon. 'You always were a greedy child. Be careful or that handsome husband will develop a roving eye.'

I'd felt bad for Joanna then. I could tell the hormones were playing havoc with her system and she was often on the verge of tears. But I was too craven to rebuke Mother and too selfish to give up Rob.

If anything, we got more reckless. Back off a red-eye from Hong Kong, he was meant to be sleeping but bleary-eyed and bristling with stubble, it was me he wanted, not sleep. He pulled me inside before the neighbours could see, pressing me up against the wall with a fevered urgency; we hadn't seen one another for two weeks. The skies were already darkening, one of those winter afternoons when night crashes into day and steals the light by half past three, and we didn't hear the car until the headlights strobed the hall. Joanna, home early, put her key in the lock and we sprang apart as if zapped by cattle prods, hastily re-arranging clothing and trying to straighten mussed up hair. You'd have to be wilfully blind not to know what we'd been up to but somehow Rob won her over, smooth as butter, sliding over the awkwardness with a practised charm, even raising a smile from his suspicious wife. I was quickly dispatched and my blood boiled at the thought of the two of them upstairs together, Joanna enjoying her conjugal rights. Was it a chore for him? I burnt with jealousy, sitting down the road in my car, my knuckles white on the steering wheel, watching the upstairs lights with a fierce intensity. I knew it wasn't right, that this couldn't continue, that those fevered moments of ecstasy in the hall weren't worth these endless hours of writhing pain. Something had to change.

Chapter Forty-Seven

I walk to the retail park on the edge of town, glad to find a McDonalds where I can collapse into a bench seat with a hot chocolate, burger and chips. My legs are trembling with the burst of activity but it's a good feeling; I should never have stopped walking. I head next for a twenty-four-hour super-market, one of those giant warehouses that sells everything, from beans to televisions. I buy a new mobile phone and wonder why I didn't think of this before. It makes a dent in my pile of cash but it's worth it to feel connected to the world again. I also upgrade my outfit, buying jeans, a gym T-shirt and some surprisingly comfy trainers, shedding the now stained and crumpled maxi dress in the supermarket toilets. I keep my denim jacket and the Joules sweatshirt though, it was one of Joanna's favourites.

I go back to the McDonalds for another hot chocolate and to charge my new phone. I like it here. It's anonymous, functional and everyone's heads are down on their screens. I finally get the phone up and working, and check my emails and Headliners. No one from the forum has noticed my absence. I scroll through my historic posts, wondering which of them have been seen as incriminating by Noor and Rawlinson. Is it like the Facebook account, will there be fake messages in which I discuss hating my sister and wanting her money? I log out quickly. Perhaps they're even registering when I log in to the site, perhaps that in itself would look bad for me.

I look again at Alex Fuller's profile on LinkedIn. It seems to me he had the most obvious motive and is a ruthless, ambitious man with the physical strength to overpower the two of us. Yet the police seem convinced he was out of the country at the time. I brood over his picture and mull sending him a message, telling him I know what he's done. It would shake him, perhaps he would make a mistake and reveal himself. But the memory of that arm round my neck, casually pressing down, squeezing the life from me ... I am too scared to provoke Alex Fuller. Joanna was far braver than me.

I google Alan's name and find the report of the incident in Lancashire. Johnny Brooks, that was the boy that died. It comes back to me now, how it was all dredged up when a local lad, from a farm at Brine Hill, had a similar accident. Once is unlucky, twice is what, deliberate? I can't believe it, I mean, why would Alan want to hurt those boys? People said nasty things at the time, I remember that he got very down for a while. I look at the photo of Johnny Brooks' grieving parents standing by a shrine of flowers and teddy bears and feel deeply unsettled. There's no way the deaths of this boy and Joanna could be connected, or is there? I look round the brightly lit diner and think Alan could be here now, watching me, and I wouldn't know. *Always in my sights.*

I shiver and go outside to call a taxi, the creeping paranoia making me suddenly wary of the other people in the diner. Outside, in the dark and the drizzle, I can watch them. I wait impatiently in a puddle of yellow light from a street light. The homing urge is upon me again, a yearning to find James and explain all that has happened. He's probably looking for me and getting worried. I am never out late. My cab pulls up, its windows fogged and smelling of air freshener. I slip into the back seat, relieved to notice that my fellow diners don't even look up from the screens.

The taxi travels quickly through the empty streets and soon we're in Market Leyton, watching the familiar landmarks go by. The farm supplies shop, the library, the church, the Co-op. There's no one around. This is not a party town.

We turn into Speldhurst Road and I can see at once there are two police cars outside the house. My heart sinks. Is this it then, have they been waiting for me? Noor's boss has finally given the order and my arrest will close the case. Back slaps all round, another promotion for Noor and the real killer rubbing his hands while James is left on his own to try and pick up the pieces from the train wreck of his life. I swallow, forcing down a hard ball of panic that has lodged in my throat. I'm not ready, not yet. I just need a bit more time, time with James, time to make peace with Joanna, before they take me away.

'How far down is it, love?' asks the driver.

'To the bottom, please,' I say, slinking lower in my seat as we pass number 22.

The driver pulls up at the junction with Clive Grove, a little road that ends in a cul-de-sac. 'Here alright, love?'

'Just give me a minute,' I say. My mind is whirling, trying to work out what to do. I should just turn myself in but what if they don't let me see James to explain? I just need some more time.

The engine ticks over, and I wonder how long my money would last if I asked the driver to just circle the ring road while I work out what to do.

There's a sudden thump on the window next to my face and I scream, scrabbling back from the window.

'What the fuck?' shouts the taxi driver, twisting round in his seat to see what's going on. There's a face at my window, a man, his face pale under the streetlights, a black hoody covering his head.

'Aunty Sarah, it's me.' The voice, I know him. 'James. Sorry I scared you.'

'It's OK,' I say to the driver, holding my hand over my chest where my heart is thundering like it would break free from my rib cage. 'I know him. You can let him in.'

'You sure?' asks the driver. 'You know him?'

'Yes, it's my nephew.' Again I duck out of using the word son. This is not the time or place for a conversation like that.

The door lock clicks and James pulls open the door and climbs in next to me, filling the car with the smell of rain and night. His shoves his backpack into the footwell and turns to face me, raindrops clinging to those long lashes, a lock of damp hair stuck to his forehead. We embrace, lightly, and he's damp and cold to the touch.

'What are you doing out here?' I ask. 'You're soaked.'

He smiles, sadly. 'Well, I thought I was going to be moving home to live with my lovely aunt but when I get here there's no sign of her, no red carpet, no fatted calf and I'm locked out! It's like she didn't even mean it about me coming home.' He looks at me. 'Sorry, that was meant to be a joke. I'm teasing, of course. I don't expect you to sit in and wait around in case I drop by.'

I clear my throat. 'You're moving back?' My voice is so small, the question is so big, it is more than I dared hope for.

'Well, if you'll have me. It won't be for ever, I just . . .'

I grab his hand, it's ice cold to the touch, and kiss the fingers. 'James, stay as long as you like. It's really your house, your home. I know this is the right thing to do.'

There's a discreet cough from the front seat. 'You want to get out here?' asks the driver.

James twists in his seat and peers through the back window

down the road. The police cars are still outside the house. 'I can't face dealing with them now, Aunty Sarah,' he says. 'They're relentless. I feel like they're trying to poison me against you.'

I knew it! I bite my lip and shake my head. Whatever happens, I'm going to make a complaint about their harassment.

'Can we head out of town?' I ask the driver, who's tapping his fingers impatiently on the steering wheel. 'We'll give you directions in a minute.'

His eyes meet mine in the rear-view mirror and he gives me a strange look.

'I've got money,' I add, hurriedly. 'Don't worry. We'll pay you.'

He nods and turns the car into Clive Grove, heading for the turning point at the top end, near the little wooded copse. We used to take James there when he was little, stamping in muddy puddles and collecting conkers.

'When did you get here?' I ask, thinking how strange that all this time I've been lurking in Shrewsbury he was waiting for me here.

'This evening after my shift. But you weren't in. I was going to pop round to see Alan but the police arrived and went to his house first.'

'Alan's house?' I chew on my lip. 'Why, is he a suspect? He used to fancy your mum, you know?'

'Ha,' snorts James. 'Why am I not surprised. He was a lonely man.' He glances at me, shyly. 'He liked you too for a while.'

'Yeah, but I'm not really girlfriend material. So those cars,' I say, as we turn back into Speldhurst Road. 'They're for Alan, not me.'

James shrugs. 'They've been knocking on our door too.' He grins ruefully. 'Don't judge me. When it started raining, I thought I might have been able to force the window on the utility room. But when I saw the coppers, I just hid in the back garden and then nipped over into Alan's and out through that abandoned house to cut back along Laurel Grove. Not exactly dignified behaviour. Couldn't believe it when I saw you roll up. Sorry if I gave you a scare.'

We're approaching our house again. We both shrink into our seats and James pulls his hoody up. I keep my head turned the other way and see a man standing across the other side of the street, half hidden in the shadows of Mary's laburnum. His hands are deep in his pockets and the look on his face is intense and searching. His gaze settles on the taxi and, as he locks eyes with me, I instinctively sink deeper into my seat, like a hunted animal.

I hold my breath until we're out of the road and heading into town. I turn to tell James about the man but he's got his phone out, busy typing away.

'Alan wants to know where we are,' he says, frowning at his screen.

'Where is he?'

'That's what I'm asking him,' says James, his thumbs moving like lightning. He looks up and stares out into the night, chewing on his lip, troubled.

'Do you trust Alan?' I ask him. They used to be so close. I suppose Alan was as close as he got to a father growing up.

He looks at me sharply, then stares out of the window again. We're on the ring road, heading south. Perhaps the driver is just going to keep circling until we run out of petrol or money.

'Yes,' he says, finally. 'I do. Maybe he did have a crush on Mum. It sounds like a lot of men did. But I really don't think he'd ever hurt her. He's a soppy old git really.'

I nod in agreement. That's my assessment too. It's good to think me and my son think alike on some things. God, my son. I am sitting inches from my son. And he doesn't know. I swallow, my mouth as dry as salt.

303

'There's something I need to talk to you about,' I venture. 'Perhaps we could go to your place?'

He shakes his head, fiercely. 'I've checked out of there, Aunty Sarah. I need to be home, with you. Besides, they were trying to stiff me on the council tax.'

I think about telling him what the blue-haired woman said about the rent but decide to leave it. I'll settle that later for him. It's the kind of thing mums do.

'I know,' I say, an idea springing to mind as I see the sky brightening to the east, a pink stain spreading over the horizon. 'What about a walk in the hills? I've been dying for some space and air. I was actually thinking we could ask Alan if we could use his bothy, maybe camp up there for a night or two. I just need to get away. I feel trapped here. And we could talk then, properly talk and walk. The fresh air and exercise would do us both good.'

He looks at me and smiles. 'You sound just like Mum.' He nods to himself, thinking it over. 'Yeah, why don't we do that. We can take my car.' He leans forward and talks to the driver, directing him to the Aldi on the edge of town. 'I left it parked there. Thought it best to arrive on foot if I'm going to turn up on your doorstep homeless, harder for you to turn me away.'

I punch him playfully on the arm. 'Don't be silly. It's your doorstep, and I'd never turn you away. I can't tell you how happy it's made me.'

I stop talking, aware I'm dangerously close to tears. He takes my hand and gives it a squeeze. 'Yeah, I think it's for the best. Mum would be pleased too.'

'She was a hero, you know?'

'What?'

'She found out some stuff about her boss, you know the one she hated. She had a secret file on him and was going to give it to the police.'

304

He looks at me. 'What, you think it's her boss now? Have you told the police?'

'Yeah, they're not interested. They say he was abroad at the time but I think he's clever enough to fake that.'

He makes a little impatient noise. 'Everything's taking so long,' he says. 'It's hard to live, not knowing.'

His phone pings, a new message.

'Is it Alan? Ask him if we can use his bothy. Get the directions.'

'I know the way,' he says, thumbs moving over his phone. 'Alan took me up there loads.'

'Did your mum know?' I'm sure she would never have approved.

James rolls his eyes. 'You know I'm almost twenty-one, right? I haven't had to ask my mum for approval for a long time.'

'Yes, of course. You're still a little boy to me,' I say. 'And always will be, even when you've got your own kids.'

He makes a groaning noise. It's hard somehow to imagine James as a grown-up, with a wife and kids. He seems caught in suspended animation, unworldly, innocent. I wonder momentarily if he's gay. I've never been aware of any girls on the scene, or boys for that matter. I suppose that will all change in the next few years, particularly now he's a rich man. If I'm not in prison, I will have to be vigilant, make sure people don't take advantage of him. Perhaps it's something we can talk about while we're walking, or over a campfire under the stars.

We pay our patient taxi driver and climb into James' battered car. It's filthy, even by my standards, the dashboard dusty, crumbs strewn over the seats, crisp packets and empty Coke cans in the footwells. It smells of cigarettes and something I can't identify and there are strange stains on the upholstery that I try not to think about. James dumps his backpack on the back seat amid what looks like the remnants of a tree, bits of bark and leaf and soil.

'I was helping a friend move some logs,' he says, when he sees me looking. 'I'm the only one with a car.' He's clearly very proud of this so I make sure I don't say anything negative about the state of it. Thank God Joanna never saw it like this. He would never have heard the end of it, especially if she saw those fag butts in the empty Costa cup.

But at least it goes. It makes a horrible noise when he turns the key but once it gets going it sounds reliable enough. And I'm pleased to see he's a careful driver, indicating at every roundabout and never topping the speed limit. He keeps his phone on his lap, though, his eyes flicking down when it lights up from time to time with messages or notifications.

'Want me to check those for you?' I ask.

'Er, Aunty Sarah, mobile etiquette. That's a no.'

I laugh, and wonder if it's a girl who's so busy messaging him. If so, I hope it's not that woman with the blue hair and the Mickey Mouse T-shirt.

'I got myself a phone today,' I say, pulling out my shiny new phone. 'Can I text you my number? You'll have to give me yours though. All my contacts are on my old phone.'

He reads it out to me and I dutifully type it in. 'The police still got your old phone? What's that about?'

I shrug. 'I don't know. I never did anything with it really. But –' I take a deep breath '– I know they think I killed your mum. I didn't of course,' I add hastily, just in case he has any doubts, 'but they don't have any other leads as far as I can tell. When I saw them tonight at the house, well, I think they were coming for me.'

He gives me a sharp look. 'Really? You think they're going to arrest you? But that's crazy.'

'I'm glad you think so, James. It is mad. But apparently the chief inspector or whatever just wants the case closed and I was there, covered in your mum's blood. But it's important to me that you know, you really know, I didn't hurt your mum. I loved her. And I think she was the only person who truly loved me.'

Tears burn my eyes. It's true. I betrayed Joanna in the most heinous way and she stood by me and cared for me every day, even when it compromised her own hopes for happiness. She could have put me in a home and left me to rot. Instead I led a good life, and even if I wasn't a mother, I was an aunty, and a sister, and a part of the human race. That's love.

'So, let me get this right,' says James, as we turn off an A-road onto a little B-road, the hills suddenly looming like dark bruises against the milky dawn sky. 'What you're actually saying to me, is that right now you're on the run? Is that what this is?'

I catch the playful lilt in his voice, and grin back at him. 'I am officially on the run. Just for the weekend, mind.'

'Whoo Aunty Sarah,' he cries, holding up his left hand. We high five and the little car barrels down the twisty, turny lanes, deeper into the valleys, further into the hills. Despite the grief and the fear and the worry, for the first time in days, in weeks, in months, I find myself laughing out loud. We are off the grid and we are finally free.

Chapter Forty-Eight

Twenty-one years ago

I wonder how it would have ended if it hadn't been for the baby. Would it have petered out, come to a natural end with no one hurt and just some secret memories that prompt sly smiles over Christmas dinner? Instead we created something, and destroyed everything. I had not paid much attention to contraception. After all, Joanna had filled me in at length about the low mobility of his sperm. But my cycle was as regular as clockwork and I knew within days that something was wrong. I hugged the knowledge to me, like cupping a match between my hands; this was something small and precious, something that could change everything. I had won. My wonderful body had come up trumps for me again. And he was delighted. He punched the air and leapt around the damp room of the attic flat I was supposed to be showing to some poor unsuspecting tenant.

'I knew my boys could do it, I knew they had it in them!'

Strange, how it was all about him.

It did not take long, however, for the euphoria to leach away, like a reservoir over a hot summer. Drop by drop you don't notice, then one day there's nothing left but barren, cracked earth and your lover is telling you to abort the miracle baby you just created. I was surprisingly calm. He said we had to think about Joanna but it wasn't her we talked about. Instead he said the cost of the IVF was breaking him, how he was under unbelievable stress, how he has thought about ending it all.

'I'm not sure I can do this, babes, I'm not sure I can cause this much pain,' he sobbed, pouring out his misery like a pipeline spewing oil, polluting my happiness.

I surprised myself by how calm I was in the face of his distress. I felt a cold hard core settle inside me, solidifying like cooling metal. Perhaps this is what it is to be a mother; you don't indulge the weakness of others. He might not have the strength but I do. I went to the scan alone. I bought a photo and studied it, trying to discern from the amorphous grey shape what was growing inside me: a champion, a loser, a lover, a bully. There were no clues but I knew this: if I couldn't cleave him to me with a child then I would never hold him. And I had risked too much to give up so easily. Suddenly his trips were longer, he was more jetlagged and needed more rest. I didn't say anything. It was shock, I thought charitably, he just needed some time to lay the groundwork to tell Joanna. But time was running out for me.

Joanna worked it out first. I suppose the hormones made her hyper-sensitive to such things. Mother was disgusted. When I wouldn't name the father, she assumed it was because I didn't know.

'I can't bear to look at you,' she spat. 'Get rid of it or we're done.'

I laughed in her face, which sounds defiant but actually I was terrified. When was Rob going to step up and acknowledge me? But he was running scared, I could see it on his face.

Joanna came to me in tears. Mother had forbidden her to see me and I think this was the only time in her life she had ever disobeyed. She must have been desperate, and she was; she suspected, at last, that Rob was seeing someone else. I tensed, my stomach knitted with a perverse anticipation: now it would be out in the open. 'I followed him,' she sniffed. 'He spent all afternoon in a Premier Inn in Leek. Why? It's not near an airport! I know he was with someone.'

My world imploded. He'd told me he was on a long haul from Shanghai. He was seeing someone else. I ran from the room and vomited, Joanna by my side, holding my hair back, checking I was OK. Sometimes she liked to sit next to me and feel the baby kick. She knew more about pregnancy hormones and foetal development than me. By now I was fat, there was no escaping it, my ankles were swollen, my breasts vast. I never wanted to be a single mother. I wanted what Joanna had and the baby was my passport to that life, but he wouldn't leave her.

I decided to take matters into my own hands. I rocked up uninvited to Mother's birthday tea and was granted ten minutes access, though she wouldn't look at me, the card was unopened, the hand-tied bouquet dumped in the sink. She grumbled about the cake – *Why did you waste your money on this, I'm happy with a piece of Battenberg* – and something just snapped in me.

'Joanna, you need to know something.'

Rob's head whipped round, his face white with horror, gesturing for me to stop. But I couldn't stop, the words spewed out of me, defiling the room with their stink. 'This is Rob's baby. We're in love and I'm having his baby.'

My words were bold but I was trembling all over. I waited for him to confirm it, to stand by my side, put his arm round me, but he didn't move. Everyone was frozen, like my words had cast a spell. A curse. Joanna was white-faced, moaning softly, like an animal in pain. Mother recovered first. She looked grimly satisfied, almost as if I'd given her the best birthday gift ever, as she marched me out.

'Don't bother next year,' she hissed, shutting the door on me. Rob got to stay, though.

I had the baby alone. My midwife had been pressing me to draw up a birth plan, to find a birthing partner, but there was no one. My London friends had gone. I deserted everyone to chase forbidden fruit and so I ate my bitter harvest alone. I had no ambition but to get this baby out with minimal damage to my vagina – I need that to be in working order to find myself another man. Does that count as maternal instinct: don't die, don't be deformed, don't rip my perineum to shreds?

It hurt, of course, but I took every drug going and only needed two tiny stitches. The midwives said I did a brilliant job and we all cried. They handed me a little mottled chicken with strands of dark hair and eyes screwed shut against the world. I never knew baby fingers were so small. The baby slept in a plastic tub next to my hospital bed while I assessed the state of my body: why was I still so fat? I thought I would snap back into my skinny jeans like all the magazines say. Blood trickled down my leg. I didn't expect the bleeding either, or the leaking breasts. I waited for Rob to come and visit. Perhaps it's just as well he didn't. I travelled back to my flat in a taxi, still wearing my maternity jeans.

I'm never alone now, James is always with me. But I am so utterly alone. A nurse comes to visit and is sad I've given up breastfeeding already, but I don't really remember getting going. Nothing seemed to come out even though my nightshirt's soaked with leaking milk every morning. She's worried about my state of mind but I fake my way through her questionnaire. Of course, I'm a bit blue. I've just had my sister's husband's child and my family has disowned me.

Rob finally shows his face, bearing a bottle of duty-free gin and a huge teddy bear. He's surprisingly tender with the baby and even changes a nappy better than I can. But I see through him now, like he's made of baking paper, slick with grease.

He leaves me with a wad of twenties and says he'll set up a direct debit for monthly instalments. 'The IVF is extortionate, Sarah. It's killing me, but it would break her heart to stop, especially now.'

He says it like it's all my fault, my fault Joanna can't have children, my fault the IVF must go on, my fault he can't leave her. I barely listen, wrapped in a hormonal cloud, watching the baby sleep in his dad's arms, just how it should be. I fall asleep within minutes.

Joanna comes to visit two days later. I can't imagine what it costs her to come, to see her sister, and her husband's child. She personifies grace and strength and I think I have never hated myself more. I cry a lot, quietly in the corner of the room, while my sister cuddles James, changes his nappy and gives him a bottle. She's a natural; when she looks at James lying cradled in her arm I know what love is. She cries as she leaves. An apology wouldn't even come close to stitching the gaping wound between us and there's nothing else to say so I just shut the door in silence.

Chapter Forty-Nine

I must fall asleep for a while because when I wake up the road signs are unintelligible. We are in Wales, the land empty of people but full of sheep. Streams plummet in white streaks down precarious hills and the road twists daringly close to the side of a foaming river. I crane my neck to see the tops of the hills but mists shroud the uppermost reaches, creating an impression of limitless size. This is the land of the giants. If this was Joanna's box set, a dragon would come flying through the mist any minute.

'Morning, sleepyhead,' says James with a grin.

'Sorry,' I say, stretching in my chair. 'It was a long day yesterday.'

'Almost there now,' he says, peering through the windscreen. 'Look.' We bank sharply down a narrow lane to a place where a wide stream crosses the road. He stops in the middle, water all around us, a devilish look on his face. 'You'll have to get out and push, Aunty Sarah.'

I nudge him with my elbow. 'Do I look like I was born yesterday?'

He laughs, and presses the gas, the little car shooting forward out of the ford. He seems happier out here, more relaxed, more at ease. Perhaps it's being away from Speldhurst Road, the pressure of Joanna trying to be the perfect mum and the warping weight of all those secrets, all those lies. Or maybe it's simply that he has always been an outdoors person. I bet he could name every flower in these hedgerows.

The road narrows again, ferns touching the sides of the car, and the trees close above us until the light is thick and green, coils of mist picked out by the headlights. We have been swallowed by nature and just as I start to panic, the road suddenly levels out. I spot a wide muddy layby and a cock-eyed signpost, almost lost amid the bracken, that points to a steep track up the hillside.

There's one other car here, a neat little Audi with a National Trust sticker in the back window.

James frowns. 'Don't see many other people walking out here,' he says. 'Oh well, we'll soon lose them. Not many walk as far as we're going.' He turns to look at me, his face concerned. 'You sure you're strong enough to do this? It's a solid hike up to the bothy.'

'Yeah, I'm good.' In truth, I am worried about my fitness, but there's no way I want to miss out on this. We need this time and space together, to grieve and heal and come to terms with everything that's happened.

He hands me a waterproof and I'm glad of the extra layer. It's cold just standing here, in the damp valley. He stuffs bottles of water, snacks and other essentials in his backpack, then hauls it up onto his back.

'A proper boy scout,' I smile.

But he doesn't smile back. 'They were from the charity trek. I didn't use them all, you know, after they told me . . .'

Of course. He was pulled out before the final checkpoint to be told his mother had been killed. Poor kid. He needs this hike more than me.

'Alan's bothy is pretty well equipped but it's good to be prepared.'

'Now you sound like your mum,' I say.

A butterfly suddenly dances out of the mist, circles my head and is gone. It feels like an omen. If I was minded, I would even say it was a message from Joanna, a blessing on us. I glance at James to see if he saw it too.

'Argynnis adippe,' he says. 'High brown fritillary.' And with that, he leads the way over the stile and up into the hills.

The first part of the walk is steep and I worry, as my breath ing becomes ragged and my thighs burn, that I won't be able to keep pace but after a mile or two the ground evens off a bit. James is very patient, waits for me and pushes me to have water and snacks.

'You're doing great, Aunty Sarah,' he says, beaming at me. 'Pace yourself. We've got all day.'

'That's what worries me!' I laugh, taking off my waterproof. But I'm determined to keep going. We don't talk much. I've decided not to broach the big subject until we've arrived. I am too out of breath to do it justice. The ground gets steeper and the landscape is barren, no trees, just heather and the oc-casional gorse bush. The track becomes a rutted narrow path, sometimes broken by loose scree, or edging slippery rocks.

As the mist thickens, I realise how easy it would be to lose your bearings with no signposts or landmarks visible. I hear the cry of a bird of prey circling somewhere nearby, a long melancholy call and that momentary distraction is enough for me to lose my footing. I stumble and bash my knee on a rock. No damage, just another bruise to add to my collection. James is striding on ahead and I scurry to close the distance before he's lost to the mist. We plod on for what feels like hours, me sometimes stumbling over a hidden root or jumping when sheep suddenly emerge from banks of heather, unimpressed by my laboured ascent of their territory.

I hear the waterfall before I see it. We turn a corner and my face is wet from the spray of the foamy torrent, which crashes down into a rocky fern-edged bowl. We stop and admire the view, and I take the opportunity to guzzle down a chocolate bar and a can of coke, hoping for a sugar lift. I can feel the fatigue settling on me, my legs trembling slightly with the exertion. James, however, looks like he could keep this pace up all day.

'Isn't it great?' he shouts over the roar of the water.

I nod, and take a photo with my phone, but it fails to capture the power, the noise. I wish it was sunny, I bet you get rainbows here, and decide I'll come back another time.

We veer off in the other direction now, a steep scramble up a trail slick with spray from the waterfall. The narrow track twists away from the waterfall and we climb up through some trees before emerging onto another open expanse of moorland. Suddenly the mists part and the sun bursts through. I stop, raising my head to drink in the light and warmth like a swimmer bursting through the surface of a lake. A plane steams overhead and I think of my bed at home and the days lost to watching the vapour trails. How much better to be out here. I have a renewed taste for life up here, a life with James, my son. I will not waste any more time locked away.

We trek on and the mists come down again. I am not sure I can go much further but James says we're almost there, pointing to a small copse that has sprung up in a narrow gorge buttressed by two hills. It's a steep descent into the gorge, which James manages elegantly but I lose my nerve and slide most of the way on my bum. Briars catch at my legs and I'm glad of the thick jeans. I follow James closely, for some reason unnerved by this dense little thicket of woodland and bracken after the open moorlands. Twisted trunks and gnarly branches loom up out of the whiteness, which seems to press in on us like a shroud. Even the birds are still now.

I feel eyes watching me, and stifle a scream when a jay screeches past. We emerge into a small clearing, with a ring of blackened grass in its centre, where there's clearly been a campfire at some point.

James grins at me. 'Welcome to Alan's home from home,' he says, his arms out wide, his head thrown back to look up at the canopy of green.

'Are we there?' I ask, looking around.

James jerks his chin and then I notice it, a wooden shed with a corrugated iron roof, the grooves mossy green and clogged with acorns. The shed is stacked on cinder bricks and there's an old milk crate set in the ground as a step. It looks rundown and damp, and suddenly I'm not so sure this is a good idea. This isn't the charming shepherds' hut I'd pictured and I real-ise James and I possibly have very different conceptions of what roughing it means.

But at least we're here. No more walking today. I crouch down by the campfire and try to picture me and James sitting here tonight, maybe sharing a beer, crying and laughing as I tell him what I've found out. I touch the burnt embers, notice there's something amid the charred bits of wood. I flick it over with my fingertips and then recoil as if the fire is still lit. There, partially burnt, is a piece of fleece, black fleece with strange markings in white and green, markings that make part of a wider pattern, a pattern of teeth and jawbone. It's the facemask the killer wore.

I scrabble back from the fire, the images of that night spool-ing before me like a horror film. James is busy getting things out of his kit bag but he suddenly straightens up, his attention caught by movement. But it's not me he's looking at, it's some-thing else. The door of the bothy swings open and a man stands in the doorway. And he's got a gun.

Chapter Fifty

Twenty years ago

After that first visit, Joanna comes regularly. We don't talk much. I never ask about Rob. They've separated and he's been staying with his mate Gary, but he's working on her. He's told her it was a brief fling, that I seduced him when he was depressed about the IVF, that it meant nothing. She tests his lies on me and I don't have the heart to correct her, how really he wanted us to move away, start again in Dubai or Singapore.

Mother is piling on the pressure for them to get back together and have a baby of their own to erase the taint of my disgrace. At least they know his sperm works now. I can't believe Joanna listens to this nonsense but she has always been desperate for Mother's approval. I suppose the two of them will wear her down eventually and Rob will be back, all sins forgiven. Joanna is already assuming the guilt for his adultery; she thinks it's her fault, that she put too much pressure on him, she became moody and fat and stopped making an effort. She is the only innocent one in all of this but again I don't correct his lies. I have lost the right to an opinion. I don't trust myself not to make things worse. My heart breaks for her. I've done this to her. I try to tell myself if not me, then it would be one of his other women but I know my betrayal is the deepest, darkest cut of all.

I start to look forward to her visits. I had never anticipated how hard this would be. I am tired to the marrow of my bones and I crave adult company. I have become one of those people who gabbles at shop assistants and health visitors. And it's not just their company; it's the reassurance of having another adult in our orbit so that, if only for a few moments, the responsibility is not all mine, crushingly all mine. James is so small and vulnerable and I am all he's got. I have a lifetime of bad decisions in my wake so how can it be right that I'm now trusted to make the right decisions for him? I feel him watching me, and worry even he knows I'm a loser, hanging on by the skin of my teeth. And we have no money. I can't work because there's no one to look after James, and the money from Rob is sporadic and never seems to go far enough. Joanna helps. She always brings an envelope of cash and discreetly leaves it under one of James' bottles on the kitchen counter; it's a clear message that the money is for him, not me.

She's good with James. She has a knack for nappies and clothes and bottles and knows all the latest weaning guidelines. He's crawling now and she brings round plastic plug covers, drawer locks and a stair gate to keep him out of the kitchen. I feel like a zombie; when he was newborn he spent hours asleep in his basket but now I can't take my eyes off him. He barely seems to nap in the day and the flat is a steamy tip of plastic debris and drying clothes, our constant companion the inane babble of children's television. Joanna encourages me to take him to the park, to the library and baby groups, but I can't. My shame follows me like a foul smell and I sometimes catch the stink; the side-eye of the woman in the Post Office, the murmurs of the two Boden mums in the library; Aunty Karen cornering me at the tills in the Tesco Express.

'You dirty skank,' she harangued me. 'I don't know how you dare show your face.'

A stream of invective rang in my ears as the security guard accompanied her out, telling her she was barred.

'I don't care,' she screamed. 'I wouldn't be seen dead in any shop that dirty bitch uses.'

My face burnt red as the eyes of the other shoppers bored into me. People tried to look away and talk about something else, but I knew they couldn't help themselves.

Rob is a stranger. In ten months, he has seen his son just six times. He blames his work schedule and the difficulties he faces now he's over at Gary's but I'm sure he's still shagging around, despite Joanna watching him like a hawk. He claims to love 'his little man' but he's not very hands on: he takes James for long walks round the park in his pushchair, once round a local petting zoo and once to a soft play barn. Every time nappies go unchanged and James returns hungry or fractious. I resent Rob's ability to just hand the baby back, and fly off into the sunset, literally, while I'm stuck here, rotting away.

But he's as suave and charming as ever, and while I know it's just a cheap veneer I still feel the old pull of lust and convince myself we could still make it work if only Joanna was out of the picture once and for all. They have been going to marriage counselling and she's been taking him to Mother's church. There is talk of him moving back home for Christmas, a new start, wiping the slate clean. 'He's a new man,' she says, trying to convince herself. 'I think we rushed trying for a baby. He just needed more time. It was his way of acting out.' She speaks like this now, since she's been seeing the counsellor. It seems to me everyone is rushing to make excuses for him.

I realise I am running out of time. If I am to claw him back and make a real family for James then I need to act before he moves back in with Joanna. I start to make more of an effort with how I look, wondering if he still feels the same. I've lost all the baby weight now and despite the dark circles round my eyes I know I look good, certainly better than Joanna. I show him what he's missing, always witty and relaxed, making everything about him, giving him a glimpse of my cleavage or a flash of the black lace knickers he used to love when I kneel on the floor to do James' nappy. I know Joanna won't wear the kind of underwear a man like Rob expects.

It's Joanna who gives me the idea of the shopping trip. It's James' first birthday next month and she wants to take him out and splash some cash. But this is a difficult anniversary for me. I can't believe almost twelve months have gone by and I'm still on my own with the baby. It's time for Rob to face up to his responsibilities and do the decent thing. I need to nip this moving back to Joanna in the bud. If I could just spend some time with him on my own. She wants to take James on her own for an aunty-nephew bonding session to a Christmas market. She is beside herself, she loves the thought that people will think he's her son. I'm careful to arrange it for a day when I know Rob's around and then get my nails and hair done and buy a new bra. You would never think I pushed a seven-pound baby out of my body less than a year ago and I shiver with anticipation.

But Joanna ruins it all. She's got a raging bladder infection and can't get out of bed. 'We'll rearrange,' I promise, slumping my head against the wall, sick with disappointment. I know I have lost him. But Joanna serves him up to me. She decides Rob should go in her stead. 'No need for James to miss out because of me,' she says. 'Rob will come and collect him.'

I look at James and smile slyly. I will not miss this chance.

Of course, nothing ever goes according to plan. He's already in a mood and even more so when I tell him I'm tagging along.

He sees through me, of course, but I know how weak he is; if I flatter him enough, flirt enough, I know I'll have him crawling back. It sounds heartless but really this time it would be a clean break, better for us all: James would grow up in a proper family unit and Joanna would soon find someone else, someone who actually loves her and treats her with respect.

We go in my car because he can't be arsed to swap the car seat round into his. He seems to fill the space in my little Ford and every time I change gear I'm aware how close my hand is to his thigh; it's so tempting just to reach out and squeeze the hardened muscle under his jeans or to lean over and plant a kiss on the arm so casually draped round the back of my headrest. Does he notice that I've had my hair done and have finally lost the baby weight? I laugh too loudly at something he says and he grins; god, he's so pleased with himself.

We go to the Christmas market, which I always thought was a bad idea with a baby. I tell myself it might be romantic, perhaps we might even find some mistletoe to get us started, but the enforced jollity and the endless hawking of goods is depressing. Rob buys us both a mulled wine; it's overly sweet but I down mine in a couple of gulps and hold out my empty glass for another one. 'Oi oi,' he grins, 'someone's thirsty.'

We lock eyes, and for a moment I see it, that predatory instinct in him, the flash of the old Rob. I raise my eyebrows suggestively, I need him to want me again. I can't do this on my own. But he suddenly gathers himself, pulls the shutters down, he can see the danger up ahead.

It's a relief really when the rain drives us from the Christmas market into the shopping centre. I'm feeling scratchy and resentful by now. I used to love shopping but now I'm constantly broke. I can't remember the last time I treated myself. The anger uncoils within me but I force myself to laugh and simper; I must be everything Joanna is not. We go into Mothercare and Rob is wary; I'm tempted to go mad and really hammer his credit card but that's the kind of passive aggressive measure Joanna goes in for. Instead, we delight in James clubbing at some bright plastic tat and just buy some very sensible new sleepsuits and a couple of books. Rob looks relieved and I wonder if the IVF is still clobbering him.

We need to eat but everywhere is so crowded now the rain has driven people inside. We queue up for a table at one of those chain Italian eateries, which seems to be full of families and squawking brats. It's not quite the day of seduction I'd got planned but I'm determined to make the most of these precious hours together. I don't think I can bear another year just me and James.

We're shown to a table but James' nappy is heavy with wee and of course Rob expects me to change it. I don't say anything, just toddle off happily with James on my hip, because it's important he sees what a great mother I am, how easy life would be if it were just the three of us. And despite the rain and the long morning, I still look hot, much better than any of the other mums in here. I waltz back out, baby on hip, a smile on my face, aware that I'm attracting admiring glances from the other dads. But Rob's glued to his phone, his thumbs flittering over the keyboard. I bet he's texting another woman, and, with a sudden lurching coldness, I realise this is how Joanna must have felt all those hours and hours when he and I were texting back and forth like teenagers. Once he flew a plane to China having been up all night sexting with me; it made me feel hot to know I had that power over him. He couldn't resist me then but now he's oblivious, hooked on another woman's sexy one-liners.

'Who is she?' I ask. I try to sound flippant, off hand, but even I can hear the bitter edge to my voice.

He looks up sharply, and I see a mean glint in his eye that I don't really remember from before. 'It's work,' he snaps.

Yeah right. I grab a passing waitress and order a large glass of Chablis. If I'm going to have to sit here while he sexts another woman I'm not going to do it dry. Rob shoots me a warning look.

'Don't kick off,' he says, nodding at James.

'I'm not the one texting my latest shag while I'm out with my son,' I hiss.

'And my old shag,' he smirks.

I don't like that. I wonder how old his new one is. Still, I suck it up, determined to play it cool and show him what he's missing.

'Look at us now, talking like two normal humans,' I say, looking up at him through my eyelashes. 'People would never guess what we've done.'

He looks at me sharply. 'Let's not play games, Sarah.'

I gulp down my wine, fuming silently.

We settle James in his highchair but he's soon grizzling, sucking on breadsticks and fussing for juice. It's one of those places that provide pots of crayons and paper place settings for children to colour in but he keeps trying to suck the stubby crayons and then bawls when we remove them. We feed him more breadsticks, which dissolve in a horrible biscuit mulch down his chin, and then, when his lunch finally arrives, he doesn't eat. I try not to fuss but this is just so miserable, and Rob's back on his fucking phone.

The bill is hefty, particularly as me and Rob have only picked at our food and James has mainly scattered his over the floor. Rob throws down a wad of cash.

'May as well just burn it,' he says.

'You sound like a grumbling old dad,' I joke.

He glares; he, too, doesn't like being called old. 'Like you'd know,' he says, which is a low blow.

We walk back through the Christmas market. James mithers to buy a helium balloon in the shape of a reindeer. 'Clip clop clip clop,' he cries.

Rob rolls his eyes when I get him to buy it. God, I'd forgotten how sulky he can be. Perhaps it's the wine on an empty stomach, or just the horror of the situation, but I grab the pushchair and run with it, James squealing with excitement, his balloon like a kite in the air.

'Clip clop clip clop.'

'For Christ sakes,' says Rob as we approach the car park. 'Can we just have five minutes of peace. My head is pounding.'

'Diddums.' I am not in the mood to tolerate his precious need for quiet. How does he think I cope? I have it 24/7.

'Give it a rest. How much have you had to drink anyway?'

This question gets lost as it's suddenly discovered that James needs an urgent nappy change and we've lost the parking ticket, which is the only way out of the multi-storey. Rob swears loudly and kicks the wall. It costs twenty-five pounds for a new ticket.

We get into the car, the windows fogged up from our hot bodies. I get the blowers roaring and we head out, through rain slick streets. I take a roundabout too fast so that James wakes up and starts bawling.

'For fuck's sake,' shouts Rob. 'Are you drunk?'

I swear back at him but it's shaken me up and I slow down, concentrating hard on the roads. We're out of the town now and the road is black. I put my high beams on and then keep forgetting to lower them when cars pass on the other side.

His phone keeps vibrating and lighting up in his hand. Whoever she is, it's the early days of the relationship, those fevered text marathons, the way every little thing they send makes you smile inside. And the audacity, to keep at it with me next to him and his poorly wife at home. The jealousy is like a drug, it pumps through my veins and overpowers my system. I can't believe this is my life. Tears flood my eyes and I wipe them away angrily. I'm not going to cry. I just need to make him pay for what he's done. He has to understand what a wrecking ball he has been through all of our lives. I play out the scene in my head, what I'll say, how he'll cower and apologise and realise the error of his ways. The scene is so vivid and I hone my lines until they zing. I don't even notice the speed creeping up, don't appreciate the full extent of the bend until suddenly we're into it and I'm going too fast to stay in my lane.

'For fu—' yells Rob.

A lorry ploughs round the bend towards us, its lights like a spotlight that briefly illuminates the interior of the car as bright as day. And then everything goes black.

Chapter Fifty-One

James stands, warily. He holds out a hand towards me, gesturing for me to stay still. He does not have to worry; I am paralysed, frozen with fear.

The man takes a step forward, standing on the upturned milk crate, the gun hanging down by his side. Is it Alan? Or Alex? It has to be Alan, this is his bothy. I can't believe Alan would come into our house in that horrible skull mask and kill Joanna. Why? Because she didn't respond to his advances, or because she did?

'What are you doing here, Sarah?' It's Alan. I know that voice. I open my mouth, but no sound comes out. I can't believe it's him. How could he do this to us? My mind churns through the events of the last week. How could he come and bring me shopping, help me look for clues on the Internet, launch that appeal for witnesses knowing what he'd done? It's all classic psychopath stuff but he was so convincing. I have been such a fool. Joanna always said not to trust him.

'She's with me,' says James, calmly. He's so still, not frozen like me but more like an animal-handler dealing with a cornered beast. 'Come on, big guy, put the gun away, you're scaring her.'

He takes a step forward and I want to scream at him to stay

still. I know at that distance the shotgun won't kill but if he moves much closer it could do a lot of damage.

'Why is she here, James?' repeats Alan. There's something demented about him, a wildness I've never seen before. I can see his hands trembling on the gun and wonder how much strain he's been under trying to keep this side of himself hidden.

'Why are you here?' asks James, taking another step closer. 'What are you doing here, what's that gun for, eh?'

Alan's watching him, his eyes narrowed.

'It doesn't have to be like this,' says James, taking another small step forward.

He's close now, too close, and Alan trains the gun on him.

'Alan, please,' I cry, suddenly finding my voice and scrabbling to my feet.

James waves a warning hand at me, gesturing at me to stay back. He's determined to handle this but he doesn't know what he's facing. He wasn't there, he didn't see Alan in that horrible skull mask, that pink knife slicing so quickly, so expertly through the air.

'Alan, put the gun down,' I plead.

'What is she doing here?' Alan repeats, his eyes fixed on James.

James waves another hand at me. 'Sarah, please,' he hisses. 'Let me handle this.'

I feel a little flame of anger at being dismissed like this. He's just a kid, I'm the grown-up here, I should be the one handling this. But I swallow down my anger, after all, I'm not sure what to do either and the barrel of that gun is hypnotic, like the two black eyes of a snake drawing us in.

'Come on, Alan, put the gun down.' James is like a cat. He's so still, yet slowly but surely he's inching closer.

'I don't understand how it came to this,' says Alan, and

there's a catch in his voice. 'How on earth did this happen? The police have been camped outside the house, you know.'

James casts an anxious look at me. I know he wants me to keep quiet. I don't know what he thinks I'll say. All I want is for Alan to put that bloody gun down.

'I know, Alan,' says James. 'We saw them.'

'You've seen the police?' There's a strange look on Alan's face. He looks confused, lost, as if he's suddenly wondering what we're all doing here, why he's pointing this gun at us. I wonder if he's all there. Perhaps he's in the grip of a mental health crisis, or maybe this is dementia-related hallucinations and paranoia? Does Alan even know what he's done?

'Yes,' says James softly. 'We've seen the police. No arrests. Everything's all right.'

'Everything's all right?' he echoes. 'How can it be?' He gives a funny strangled kind of laugh and in that moment James quickly covers the final distance between them, twists the gun from Alan's hands and then jabs the gunstock down hard, striking Alan on the forehead and nose. There's a horrible crunching noise, and Alan falls backwards, hitting the ground with a thud that knocks the air out of him. James stands over him, panting hard. I race over, my hands over my mouth. Alan's forehead is split open and blood gushes down his face, getting into his eyes, his mouth. I think his nose may also be broken, it's at a strange angle and there's a funny rattle when he breathes.

James kneels down and presses his fingers to Alan's neck.

'Oh my god,' I say, tears springing to my eyes at the sight of so much blood, that awful rattling noise. 'Is he all right?'

James is silent, his face whiter than bone, the sinews in his neck taut and tense. I am worried he is in shock, he is so pale.

He touches Alan's pulse again. 'What were you thinking, old man?' he murmurs, his eyes fixed on Alan's face. Is he crying?

I'm not sure and I tentatively put my hand on his shoulder.

'It's OK,' I tell him. 'It's OK.'

I feel him stiffen at my touch. He turns his head, and looks up at me, his face contorted with anger. 'Look what you made me do!' he snarls.

I flinch. His anger is so unexpected. He must be in shock. He turns, his attention back on Alan. My eyes slide from James to Alan, whose face is now a bloody mess, one eye closing as the skin around it swells with fluids. He tries to say something but the words are indistinguishable. He's definitely got a broken nose. His one good eye locks on mine but I have to look away; he killed Joanna. I hope it hurts, hope it really fucking hurts.

It's as if James somehow hears my thoughts. He turns to me, his face cold and drawn.

'You think he killed Mum?'

I point towards the burnt embers. 'He's burnt the clothes. I can see a piece of the mask he wore.'

James nods grimly. 'You hear that, Alan? She knows.'

Alan shakes his head, his one good eye looks wild with fear. I suppose he thinks we're going to take our own kind of revenge now. I glance away again. I can't bear to look at him. I pull out my phone and examine the screen. There are two tiny bars of signal.

James looks at me sharply. 'What are you doing?'

'I'm going to call the police. It's over to them now.' I suddenly feel limp, defeated. I should be relieved that we know the truth, that I won't be going to prison, but I am so shaken that it was Alan, the man who insinuated himself into our lives over so many years. Perhaps we'll be able to move forward now, to grieve and give Joanna a proper burial. I glance at James. 'Don't worry, you won't be in any trouble.'

Alan makes a strangled noise on the floor again, his words contorted by his mangled airways and the blood frothing from his forehead and nose, almost as if he's gargling in his own blood. I suppose we should turn him onto his side, into the recovery position, but I can't bear to touch him.

'Put the phone away,' says James. 'We're not calling the police. Not yet.'

'James, it's over. Let the police take over now.'

He reaches up and snatches my phone from my hand, then hurls it across the clearing. My mouth falls open with shock. What the fuck is wrong with him?

'James,' I say. My voice comes out a little high, a little note of fear creeping in. What does he want to do to Alan? I want justice for Joanna, but this isn't it. 'James,' I try again, focusing on my breathing, trying to keep my voice low and steady, the same way he spoke to Alan a few moments ago. 'James, this isn't right.'

He stands up wearily, like he's an old man, his weight leaning on the gun. 'Help me get him inside,' he says.

I shake my head. We should just call the police and get on with our lives. Hurting Alan isn't going to bring Joanna back.

James scowls and hands me the gun. I uncock it; I am so jittery I don't trust myself not to accidentally shoot one of us in the foot. James bends down behind Alan, puts his arms under Alan's and then sort of heaves him upright. Alan gives a terrible moan, and sways on his feet, one hand touching his broken face, wincing with the pain. I look away, nauseous.

James takes the gun off me. 'Go inside,' he says, although it's not clear if he's talking to me or Alan. 'We need to talk.'

Alan takes a lumbering step forward, towards the hut. I hang back. I don't like the look of the place, with its horrible metal door, the damp windowless walls, the smell of rot that seems to seep from it.

'Let's go in. We all need to talk,' says James, putting an arm round my shoulder. 'I need to work out what to do.'

331

'What to do? James, there's nothing to do. We just need to call the police. Please.' There's a pleading note in my voice. I don't want to be party to whatever he's got planned. It isn't right. 'This isn't going to bring her back, nothing will.'

'You just worked that out?' If it's meant to be a joke, it comes out wrong.

Alan's on the step leading into the bothy. He says something and now he's standing up his airways are clearer. It sounds like 'not her'. James lets go of my shoulder and pushes Alan into the hut.

I watch, panic rising in my chest, the hairs on the back of my neck standing up. I don't want to go in there, it's so dark, and there's an awful smell.

'No, I'm feeling a bit panicky. I'll sit here, on the step.'

James puts his arm round my shoulder again, gives me a reassuring squeeze. 'We need to sort this out,' he says. 'All of us are in this together now.'

He stands back to let me pass but my legs are frozen. I know, I just know, that bad things are going to happen in there. I have to keep him and Alan apart somehow and I've got more chance if we're not all in a little dark hut together.

'James, come on. There's more space out here.'

He looks at me and shakes his head, his eyes are cold and determined. It reminds me of when he does his training for his charity treks; he sets himself a target and sticks to it with that same grim doggedness, whatever it takes.

I open my mouth to try and persuade him, try and get him to back down from whatever course of action he's planning, but he gets in first.

'Please, Aunty Sarah. Let's not make this any harder than it has to be.'

I step into the hut. The smell hits me like a wall, and I know then that I was right. Bad things are going to happen.

Chapter Fifty-Two

The metal door clangs shut behind me and I whirl round. I have to get out of here, the smell, oh my god the smell, but James is already in behind me, drawing a bolt across the door. I gag, the smell filling my mouth, my eyes, but nothing comes up. I pull the neck of my T-shirt up over my nose, and look at him, my eyes watering. How is he not affected by the smell? I try to push past him to get to the door but he puts two hands on my shoulders and gently but firmly pushes down onto a mildewed cot bed that runs down the left side of the hut. Alan sits next to me, his shoulders slumped, and he's holding a filthy rag to his face, trying to mop up the blood. He doesn't look at me.

I take in our surroundings with a fascinated horror. It's a large hut, lit by a couple of bare light bulbs that appear to be connected up to what looks like a larger version of a car battery. I see now that the hut is actually built over the entrance to a cave, with the back wall made of uneven rock that stretches into a low narrow tunnel, almost like an old mine shaft running into the bowels of the hill. A dirty coat hangs on a peg along with a canvas bag filled with cartridges, and propped against the wall by the door is a big shovel, an axe and the shotgun. Down the right side of the bothy there's a cluttered trestle table. Some items are readily identifiable, a tea-splattered kettle, a cheap camping stove and spare gas canisters, a box of Tesco value teabags.

But that's where normal ends. The table is littered with animal body parts: a bird's wing, a couple of decapitated rabbits, unidentifiable guts strung out and writhing with maggots, and most disturbingly, a long dead tabby cat with its eyes gouged out and its front legs nailed to blocks of wood like some monstrous mock crucifixion. I clamp my hand tightly over my mouth, determined not to scream. I look away, down at the rotted, filthy floor and notice a stack of well-thumbed porn magazines by the foot of the bed. But this isn't the usual top shelf material, its deeply sadistic, possibly illegal. I feel sick to think Alan was planning to bring me here. What did he think would happen, did he want to seduce me on this stinking cot bed, force me to enact some of the stuff in these snuff magazines? Chillingly, I remember him telling me I was lucky to be alive and I realise what a close call I've had. This is where he planned and rehearsed his crime. Is that what all these mutilated animals are, test runs on how to stab and kill and maim with maximum effect? Is that why he killed all those crows and rats? Was he thinking of Joanna when he killed them and strung them up along the back fence? Maybe I should let James get to work on the sicko. As if he can read my thoughts, Alan turns a baleful eye on me, watching me wearily. I shuffle away from him, he makes me sick.

James pulls out a little stool from under the workbench and perches on it. He's so tall his legs are bent almost comically, like a grasshopper, but nobody smiles. He sits and runs his long fingers through his hair, a gesture I know so well. I want to reach out and touch him, reassure him we can still pull back from this, go back to safer ground before we go deeper, out of our depth.

'James, what are we doing?' I ask softly.

He looks up at me and runs his hands over his face. He looks so tired, shell shocked almost, like he just woke up and is wondering why he's sitting in this filthy hut with me and Alan.

'It's alright,' I say, feeling a little flicker of hope that maybe now I can get through to him. 'Let's get out of here. We don't need to be here. The police can piece this together by themselves.'

'Let her go, lad. She doesn't need to be here.' Alan's voice is thick, like he's got the head cold from hell. The gash on his forehead has stopped bleeding but it looks raw and angry, while the swelling round his nose and eye reminds me of a bloated dead fish.

James sighs heavily. 'Ever the gallant, eh?' he says. 'Much good it did you.'

Alan turns his one good eye to me. 'You weren't supposed to know. I've made a terrible mistake.'

James rolls his eyes. 'Just shut up.'

I hold my breath. It feels like the three of us are balanced precariously on a cliff edge; the slightest move now could tip us all off. Perhaps Alan senses it too because for once in his life he stays quiet, his one good eye just roving over the workbench. Maybe he's thinking about all the good times he's had there, torturing those animals. My breath catches in my throat. I can't believe we never picked up on the signs. Maybe Joanna did. She once told me, 'We can't trust him with James'. Even then, she had the mother's instinct. I didn't. I never did. And, oh God, James spent so much time with him, we thought it was better for him to be round at Alan's than sitting upstairs on his computer. James has been up to this cabin before, has he seen this stuff before? Why didn't he tell us? He should have said. But he was a kid. Perhaps he thought this was normal. After all, he had no other father figure in his life, thanks to me. Oh God, it's all so deeply messed up and it's led us to here. I hug

335

my arms around myself and shiver. I can feel the cold radiating from the cave at the back of the hut. Somewhere I can hear the distant plink plink plink as water drops onto rock. This place is so different from the delightful rural retreat I'd conjured in my mind. How could James have thought this was a suitable place for us to hide out? Is it because he's still a kid really, he just doesn't see what I see?

My eyes wander back to him and I'm unnerved to find him watching me.

'What are you thinking?' he asks.

I swallow, my mind racing, desperately trying to find the right words that won't send the three of us off the precipice.

'I'm thinking we need to get out of here,' I say slowly. 'This is a job for the police, not us. It won't let him off, you know. Look at this place. The police will piece this together. They'll know what he's done, that burnt face mask alone links him to Joanna and then this, the rehearsal, the practised sadism against animals, the porn —' it feels like I'm reading directly from the psychopath-tick list '— and they'll piece it together. DS Noor is a psychology buff, she'll probably link him to other crimes. I don't think they go straight from cats —' I feel the word catch in my throat as I glance at the desiccated animal parts on the workbench '— to people. There'll have been other people, other victims.'

James is listening intently. 'A psychology buff,' murmurs James. He looks round the hut, his eyes coming back to rest on Alan, who's moaning softly in the corner. I inch further away from him, my flesh creeping to be in his proximity. Those big calloused hands, with the dirty plasters and the broken nails, what horrors have they committed.

'She's thorough, that policewoman. He won't get away with this, James, I promise you.'

'Justice,' says James. 'It's so important.'

336

'Yes,' I say. 'Justice.'

James nods. It feels like we've got a pact. We're going to walk away and DS Noor is going to nail Alan for Joanna's death, and anything else he's done.

James tosses his phone on the cot bed between me and Alan and starts rifling under the workbench, looking for something. He pulls out a green plastic container, the kind you use to get petrol for your lawn mower. He shakes it and there's a slosh of liquid.

I look at Alan, at his staved-in face, the blood crusting black round his nostrils. He has a dazed look, and his skin, where it's not caked in blood, is a horrible grey. I wonder how much blood he's lost. I shiver again and suspect we're all in shock.

Alan's one good eye catches mine. 'Jojo,' he says and I think, oh God, he's confused, he thinks I'm Joanna, when James suddenly lunges forward and hits him hard, a backhanded slap across the side of the face. Alan's head whips round, and some bloody matter flies free from his nose and lands on me. I shriek, desperately trying to flick it off, images of Joanna's blood, the endless hot pulsing tide that soaked my hands, suddenly filling my senses again.

James has his face close up to Alan, jabbing his broken nose with his finger. 'Don't you say her name,' he hisses, viciously. 'Don't you dare say her name!' He pulls back from Alan and sits down on his stool, breathing hard. I watch him, scared. I really think he means to kill Alan and he's going to make me watch. He looks up suddenly, catches my eye.

'You've ruined everything,' he says bitterly. 'Like you always do.'

Chapter Fifty-Three

James stamps out of the hut, and I can hear him rummaging around outside. I want Alan to explain what's going on but I'm scared of the answer. Are they in this together, did Alan groom James to become a partner in crime?

There's a buzz next to me, and James' phone lights up with another message. I glance down.

James, come on, let's talk. Just tell us where you are and we'll come to you.

The name of the message sender has been inputted in his phone as DS Whore. There's a string of texts from her.

James, let us talk to Sarah. We need to know she's OK.

James, we know you're with Sarah. Let's talk about this. We can help you.

What do these messages mean? Ice water floods my veins, a creeping dread filtering through my being. I reach for the phone, I'm going to call her.

Alan, slumped in the corner with a filthy rag pressed to his face, sees what I'm doing and shakes his head. The door to the hut is suddenly flung open again and James fills the doorway. Does he know I've seen the phone, that I have slid it across the damp blanket until it rests just next to my leg? I work very hard on keeping my face neutral while my fingers seek out the home button, wondering how to press the emergency call button without him noticing.

'I can tell you've got something to say,' says James, studying me. He's sat back down and has the green container on his lap; the faint smell of petrol reaches me. 'You could never be a poker player, Aunty Sarah.'

'I don't know what we're doing here.' I look around the hovel, noting again the position of the gun, the axe, the shovel, then taking in the door, with that heavy bolt.

'We're putting things right. You have a knack for fucking things up, Aunty Sarah.' He pauses, runs his hands through his hair again. 'Or should I say Mum?'

It's like a blade of ice has sliced me from top to bottom. The ice water in my veins reaches my heart, chilling it.

James laughs, delighted. 'I know everything,' he says. 'You have no idea how much I know.'

'When?' I croak. 'How? Did Joanna tell you?'

He laughs. 'She was a closed book that woman. So repressed. Tight as a clam. No, her accounts told me. Granny's care doesn't come cheap, you know. Once I'd cracked Mum's passwords, it didn't take long to track the payments. There I was wondering why Mum's sending all this money to this nursing home when she won't help me out so I went down to pay a visit. Said I was Mrs Bailey's accountant, just wanted to check on her invoices. They were very accommodating, even took me down to meet Mrs Bailey's mother. You can imagine my surprise. And then we got chatting and oh, the things she had to say. She wasn't very complimentary about you. Granny's a peach, isn't she?'

I shake my head, my mouth dry as a desert. There's thunder in my ears and my heart hammers like a steam piston. James knows. I glance at Alan, does he know? I can't tell, he looks very grey and has sort of retreated into himself.

'Did you tell Mother who you are . . .?'

'No. She's not my cup of tea. And, I have found, it's useful to be the one who knows the secrets. So don't come to me with your faith in psychology buffs, I know more than any of you. A psychology buff! This dead cat knows more about psychology than DS Whore.'

I hate that, that little play on her name. It's so crude. Not like the James I know. He's always been prudish, hates it when Joanna makes a comment about Poldark or that weatherman she likes.

I chew on my lip, knotted with anxiety. *He knows*. Tears flood my eyes. 'James, you have to know, I was a different person back then. I had no idea. I can't remember.'

He waves a hand. 'Yeah, yeah, we've heard it all before. Save it. I know what you did. You shagged your sister's husband, had a baby and then killed him in a car crash. I don't think we can blame any of that on anxiety, can we?' He punctuates 'anxiety' with a silly voice, making quotes marks in the air with his fingers.

'James, please. I'm so so sorry but I didn't know. But your mum, she forgave me. She looked after me.'

'Yeah, yeah, saint Joanna. We all know that one too. Except neither of you fooled me. I saw through you both. She lied to me my whole life. There's not a day of my life that bitch wasn't lying to me.'

'James!'

'And you, you're a murderer. You killed Dad with your drinking. But you never got arrested. You never faced justice. You go into a coma and everyone's sorry for you and they all forgot about Dad. But I didn't. I didn't. I never forgot.'

He nods towards Alan. 'He's the closest thing I had to a father but you and Mum always ran him down, despised him, used him. Pair of parasites, both of you. And you were getting away with it. All your lives, getting away with it. Killing, shagging, lying, stealing.'

His eyes are black with hate. He looks at me, a fleck of spittle in the corner of his mouth. 'I am your justice. The bitch is dead for all her lies. She never really loved me, you know. Once I wasn't the cute little baby, she tired of me. I saw it. She was on heat for another man and couldn't be bothered with me any more. And you, you fucking murderer, you were meant to go to prison, serve the time you should have served when you killed my dad with extra added on. Like interest on a loan. It was perfect. Little crumbs of evidence laid out for months. That police whore just had to follow the clues and you would have been arrested by now. It was so easy but you both fucked it all up with your meddling. This is all on you, you're making me do this!'

He's shouting by now, working himself into a state, and then suddenly he's down again, his voice calm, cold. And somehow it's more scary. He tips the container, the liquid sloshing inside. 'And now I'm going to have to clear up your mess.'

He unscrews the lid, throwing the contents over the workbench, the bed, the floor by the door. He notices his phone and snatches it up, out of my hand. He glances at it and smirks. 'Nice try, Aunty Sarah, but you didn't manage to make the call.'

I lunge for the axe. It's heavier than I thought and it's hard to get any swing because there's not enough room. James laughs, and easily wrenches it from my hands with the same speed and fluidity of movement as the killer. How did I not see it before? The petrol smell fills my mouth and I think I might wet myself. It's clear what he plans to do.

'They'll get you,' I say. 'You won't get away with this.'

He smiles. 'As you pointed out, all the evidence is here, in Alan's hut. And it's all going to burn, along with you both. A tragic accident, when you tried to confront him. And poor me. No family left. I suppose the money will be a comfort.'

He produces a lighter and sets fire to a rolled-up twist of paper that he touches to the petrol on the workbench, blue flames quickly licking the debris. He unbolts the door and stands on the threshold, satisfied.

'This is your justice, Aunty Sarah. Capital punishment. I should have done this from the start instead of relying on our justice system.'

He drops the paper twist on the floor, where it quickly coils into a yellow flame, black smoke snaking upwards and then devours the spilt petrol, like a monster coming to life. The door opens, a flash of green and drizzle, and then James is gone, taking the axe and shotgun with him. I lunge for the door but he's too quick, too strong. It slams shut behind him, and even when I launch my body weight against it, ramming my shoulder against the metal, it doesn't budge and I hear the padlock click finally, fatally, into place. Already the flames are licking at my shoes, curling round the doorframe. I launch a frenzied attack with the shovel, targeting it at the hinges, but the heat of the flames against my feet is unbearable and I have to step back.

'Don't waste your time.' Alan grabs my arm, pulling me deeper into the hut just as a flame catches on the old coat hanging by the door. Acrid smoke fills my mouth and I know we're going to die. The workbench has caught quickly, the mutilated remains lost to a cremation, as flames dance, yellow and blue, and plumes of grey smoke swell and bloom.

Alan pulls me on until we reach the rocky back wall of the shack, cold and damp to the touch, the wood attached to some kind of metal frame that is bolted into the rock. I probe the seam with my fingers but it seems solid, although the wood splinters when I slam the shovel into it. Given time, I'm sure

I could break through but we are out of time. I look round wildly, my eyes streaming and blind; Alan has gone. I panic, he's left me to die alone, it's all been a trick but then I feel a tug on my sweatshirt, pulling me down to the floor. I crouch down, where the air is a little cleaner, and find him with my fingertips, crouched down where the rocky back wall gives way to a low narrow cave, the air here still wet and cold.

'Hands and knees,' orders Alan. 'Keep going. It gets narrow but you mustn't turn back. Keep going. It will widen out further on.'

'What?'

He pushes me roughly forward and I graze my head against the rock roof. 'Crawl,' he orders. 'And don't turn round. I'll follow.'

I move forward gingerly. I have no choice. Behind, there is only death. The air is poison. I crawl on my hands and knees, feeling mud under my hands, which then turns to rough rock, the pitted pockets wet to the touch. I lift wet fingers and run them over my sore eyes, my lips. Alan bangs into me.

'Keep going,' he growls. 'Don't stop.'

I can hear the flames now, like a roar, and there's a sudden pop and crash, and then the traces of light wink out. The light bulbs in the bothy have blown, eliminating our only source of light. I have never seen darkness like it, it's like a living thing, a force all its own. I cannot even see my own hands as they inch me forwards. Panic bubbles inside me. Where are we? How long is this tunnel? What if we run out of air? Behind me I can hear Alan, his breath laboured, his body scraping the sides of the rock. He's bigger than me, he fills the tunnel behind me, like a cork, and the tunnel is narrowing. The roof pushes down, the walls press in. If I get stuck, how will I get out? Alan is a plug, blocking my escape.

A whimper escapes me. My breathing is too fast and the air

isn't feeding my body. Is it panic, or poisonous gases from the fire? It is so dark. I could be blacking out, how would I know? I swallow the urge to scream.

'Sarah. Keep going. You will have to wriggle but you must keep going.' Alan is behind me, his hand reaches out and squeezes my ankle. 'You can do this. It gets wider. I promise you.'

I don't know what to say. I don't know if his promises are worth anything. But I can't think about any of that now. Everything is focused on just moving forwards. I'm down on my elbows now, the rock just brushing my hair. I squirm and wriggle, my breathing laboured. I am so tired, this unnatural belly crawling is exhausting. I come to what feels like a dead end, just a narrow gap ahead.

'I don't think I get can through.' I can hear the hysteria in my voice.

'You can. It's like a u-bend. You have to wriggle. I've done it before,' says Alan. 'If I could do it, you can too. Come on, Sarah, you can do it. Use your hands, feel your way.'

I reach out, patting out the shape of my world. It is narrow, hard and damp, twisting tightly to the left and the roof pressing in.

'I can't.'

'You can.'

I turn onto my side and start to worm my way round. I can't imagine Alan getting through here, even as a young man. What if we're stuck here? The air seems to be getting fouler, there's a taint of smoke choking its way through the darkness. Perhaps it would have been better to go fast in the flames than slow here, trapped in the dark, our oxygen depleting.

'Move,' says Alan. 'We don't have time.'

Why don't we have time, has he noticed the air too? But it's enough to make me fight on, feeling my way, my fingertips scrabbling at the rock, inching myself forward like a worm. I keep focused, telling myself it's not my problem if Alan gets stuck but deep down I know it's not true. If he gets stuck, I'm dead. How would I ever find my way out without him? Focus, I tell myself, focus and move. It's exhausting and slow, my body twisting onto its side, my elbows scraping on the rock. Suddenly I'm through the worst of it, the roof is higher, there's more air around me.

'I'm through, I'm through!'

'Good, good,' wheezes Alan. 'Keep going. Its straight down now. A little steep in places but there are no more tight spots like that. Keep going until you come—'

'I'm waiting for you.'

'No!' he barks. 'You have to keep going. Get out of here. You can get to the police.'

'I'm waiting for you.'

'Sarah,' his voice is soft. 'I'm six feet. I have a belly. I'm not a fit man. I am going to be some time.'

I sob, on the edge of despair. I can't go on my own. I could take a wrong turn, get lost, trapped here in the dark like a rat.

'Let's rest a bit,' I say, fighting to control my fear. 'Get your strength and try again.' I hear more scrabbling and rustling, more panting. 'Did you know what he is?'

'Joanna tried to warn me,' he says, his breath heavy. 'I wouldn't listen. I always thought she was hard on the boy but she saw things, noticed things. Then she came to believe he was involved in that incident with Dean Withers, one of my Young Explorers who got swept away in the river. She found clothes James had hidden away, a black costume, a zombie mask, a diary with these horrible thoughts ... She confronted him and he said it was a prank that went wrong, that Dean had been bullying him. I knew that wasn't true. Dean was a sweet lad. But I think James was jealous, because he knew Dean was a favourite of mine. She came to me, she was upset because she'd been hard on me about the incident, do you remember? But we decided to keep it quiet. It was already becoming old news. We burnt the costume, gave James a telling off. I thought it was just a phase. But I think Jojo never really relaxed round him after that. She didn't like him mixing with people, worried how he manipulated them, hurt them.'

I let this sink in. Joanna knew. Is that why she kept him clear of psychologists and health visitors, she knew they'd recognise it, perhaps take him away? She'd kept him hidden, her stolen baby, watching with horror as over the years his unsettling behaviours became more menacing. So when she said we can't trust him with Alan, it was the boy she was scared of, of what he might do.

'The bothy?'

'I haven't been up here for years, you know, the problems I had after my procedure. A bothy's no place for a catheter bag.' Oh, that kind of problem, I hadn't realised. 'But that police-woman came round. Kept asking about James. They'd found a problem with his alibi, you know. Wanted to know if I knew where he'd go if he was in trouble. I knew straight away it would be this place but I didn't tell them. Thought I could talk him round myself. Stupid, stupid.'

'Did you know about me, that I was him mum?'

'Jojo never let on,' said Alan. 'I think some secrets are best left buried.'

The word buried unsettles me. I feel the panic build again, the thought of all that rock above us. What if we never get out? They would never find us.

'Don't. Wait. For me,' says Alan, panting again. 'James knows about this tunnel. We don't have the luxury of time. I'm almost through. You, go. Straight ahead, the tunnel splits. Make sure you take the left branch, it will lead you to the waterfall. You'll hear it. Go left.'

'Left,' I whisper. 'What's right?'

'It connects up to the old mine workings but they flood this time of year. They lead out further down the hillside but it's not worth the risk. Head for the waterfall. I'll join you.'

I nod, I'm shivering violently now, the ends of my fingers numb with cold. I can't afford to stay still, I need to keep moving. I reach ahead, feeling my way. The darkness is so intense it is like a living thing, breathing, palpating, embracing me. My mind wanders and questions flare like little fires as I suddenly re-examine our lives through the prism of this new knowledge, so many little episodes suddenly make sense: the artwork that worried his teachers, the constant fights at school that we always put down to school bullies, that fire on the school residential, the boy, Alan's favourite, led off to drown in a stream, and, oh God, what really happened to our kitten?

I remember his mood swings as a teenager; we thought it was hormones, never guessed it was the empty charade of a psychopath learning to mimic emotional responses.

I shuffle slowly onwards. The ground suddenly starts to slope away from me. I'm crawling downhill, water running beneath my knees and hands, seeking earth. I dip my head and lap greedily. The water is ice cold and tastes sulphuric, gritty, delicious. I drink and drink, feeling my strength build. I follow the tunnel, sometimes wriggling on my belly again, but more and more on hands and knees, the air clean and moist. There's a roaring in my head, like my skull is full of blood, but it gets louder and louder and I realise it's not me, it's the waterfall. Somewhere ahead there's a mountain's worth of water tumbling and frothing, finding its way down.

'I can hear the waterfall,' I shout over my shoulder. There's no answer and I wonder if Alan is still or stuck or if he just can't hear me. 'Alan! The waterfall.'

There's still no answer. I inch ahead with my fingers, scared of missing the turning and finding myself in the flooded mine shafts. In the end, it's easy to find because light filters in, showing me contours and shapes, including the tunnel that branches down to the mines. I wait here, where I can crouch, panting and sore, drinking in the wonder of the thinning darkness. If I ever get out of here, I will never sleep the day away again, the light, the light alone, is too precious. I look back anxiously, wondering where Alan is.

I can feel cold settling deep in my bones. I shout back for Alan but there's no answer. I wonder how long I should wait? Should I crawl back up to find him? But I can't bear to give up the light. Alan had told me to go on, not to wait. Surely it's better for one of us to get out and raise the alarm.

I'm about to move, when I hear something, something close. And it's coming from the dark of the mine shafts to my right. I freeze and the hairs on my arms and neck stand on end, my breath catches in my throat. Is it an animal? Something moves, dislodges some loose stone, splashes in a puddle. And then a light, a bobbing beam, strobing the darkness, searching. It's the worst kind of animal: a psychopath.

I inch myself down the tunnel, towards the light, towards the roar of the water. James must have run round to the old mine shafts and come up that way, checking to make sure Alan and I haven't escaped. Perhaps he watched the bothy burn down, and then checked the smoking remains for our bodies. Or maybe he's just being thorough. God, if he'd spent as much time on his school work or his CV as he has butchering and killing . . .

The ground has levelled out now and I can see a tight bend ahead. If I get round that corner then I'll be out of sight for a while. I just hope Alan doesn't suddenly crawl out from the darkness, he'd be a sitting duck. I round the corner and my senses are assaulted by light and noise. The tunnel opens out into a chamber fringed with ferns and moss behind the water-fall. A curtain of water streams past, rainbows suspended in the spray. I catch my breath. How on earth am I supposed to get down from here? I walk to the edge, tentatively, and spot a narrow ledge to the left, running from the cave to a rocky outcrop from where I could probably, possibly, scrabble up to the tree-topped hillside. But everything is so slick with water, and the drop below is dizzying. The sound of the water reverberates round my head. It's hard to think clearly. My legs tremble with fatigue, and I wonder whether I'm in any fit state to attempt a climb that would be a challenge even on a good day.

'I don't fancy your chances, Aunty Sarah.'

My heart leaps into my mouth. I should have gone while I had the chance. I turn and see he's just five or six steps away, a heavy torch in one hand, the axe in his other. I never even heard him approach over the roar of the water.

'James, what have you done?' I ask. 'Please, we can still stop this. I'll say I killed Joanna. You can have the money and go.'

He laughs hollowly. 'That's big of you. That's my money anyway, but I'm not doing this for money. This is about justice. Justice for my dad, Robert Bailey, a man you all conveniently forgot about after you killed him. And justice means a life. I'm not the bad guy here, you're the one making me do this.'

He takes another step forwards and I instinctively step back, one foot landing in the water that pools by the cave edge.

'What about Dean Withers?' I ask, stalling for time, desperately trying to think of a way out. 'Nobody made you do that.'

He scowls. I can tell he doesn't like to think he's a bad guy. 'He was annoying,' he says coldly. 'Always hanging round

Alan, taking up all his time. Pathetic. And he told his parents I was bullying him. He needed to be taught a lesson.'

'He was a kid, James. He almost died.'

He smirks. 'That was kind of the point.'

There's a movement behind him. I daren't look, daren't give the game away, but I glimpse a hand, a shoulder, a head, rounding the corner. Alan! But I won't look. I glance over my shoulder; the edge is so close, one step and the water would dash me down like a spider caught in a drainpipe. Could I jump through the water, somehow come out the other side into calmer water, like a plunge into a swimming pool? Oh God, I've never liked swimming. James watches my frantic calculations with a curious smile on his face.

Alan inches forward. His face is a mess of red and black, and he's stooped, limping painfully. I have to keep James talking, have to give Alan a chance to stop him.

'Did you hurt our kitten?' Alan is almost in touching distance. I keep my eyes fixed on James' face, desperate not to betray the limping figure coming up behind.

James smiles unpleasantly. 'It may have had a little accident. You know, Mum caught me with it. I had to pretend to be upset then. She thought it was a fox that hurt it.'

No, she bloody didn't, I think to myself. She never let us have another pet because she *knew*. She bloody knew he couldn't be trusted with animals. And that went for me too. I was offended when I once overheard her telling Simon that she could never leave me and James alone together. Did she think, like she did with Alan, that he might manipulate me, hurt me? I feel a rush of love and grief. She was always trying to protect me, even when I'd hurt her so much.

Alan lunges, an ugly lumbering rugby charge, his bulk taking James by surprise. The two topple heavily to the ground, and I quickly step aside before they knock me over the edge. They grapple, Alan breathing hard, barely moving. James is strong, swinging his torch to land a blow on Alan's head. Now James is on top and he punches Alan hard, then pulls a knife from a sheaf on his belt, pressing the blade against Alan's good eye.

'You fucking idiot,' he says. 'I didn't want to hurt you too. Why did you have to get involved? This is family business.'

'Leave him alone then, James,' I say. 'Get off him. Let him go. You can do what you want to me.'

My voice is trembling. I want to sound brave but I'm terrified. 'Let him go and you can do what you want to me. Hurt me. Like you did that cat. I bet you've always wanted to do that to a real person, haven't you?'

He looks at me. I can tell I've piqued his interest, there's a flicker of something in his eyes, some hunger that's wakened.

'Interesting,' he says. 'Go on.'

'Do what you want. Then leave me in those tunnels. No one would ever find me, not until it was too late. You'd be away, long gone. Rich, free. And you'd have served justice, you know, for your dad. For Robert.'

'A cruel and unusual punishment,' he says. 'Aren't you scared, Aunty Sarah? You've never been brave.'

'I'm terrified,' I say, truthfully. 'But you have to let Alan go. He won't tell anyone. Please.'

James gets off Alan and stands back. I rush to Alan and give him my hand, haul him into a sitting position. I'm not sure he can stand. He looks in a bad way. James smiles and rubs his hands on his thighs with something like delight, like a glutton remembering a good meal. There's something almost sexual in his anticipation.

'I'm going to take you up on your offer, because you've touched on something I've always ... But the big guy, well.' He rubs his thighs again, his eyes black with longing. 'He knows what's got to happen. You're not really in any position to make deals. You don't really have any leverage here.'

'I'll fight you every step of the way. But if you let Alan go, I'll cooperate. You can do what you like to me.' My voice quivers, my breath rasping in my throat. I can barely speak, terror is shutting down my body.

James smiles a funny little smile. 'I don't think you understand me yet. I don't want you passive. I want you fighting for life. I need to see everything.'

'No,' moans Alan. 'You're not doing this, Sarah. It's madness.' He's on one knee now, trying to brace himself to get to his feet. He doesn't have a hope in hell of getting out of here on his own. He needs urgent medical attention.

And then I look at James. He's standing a couple of steps beyond Alan, his back to the waterfall. I see him, like a silhouette, my son, a tall broad man, his floppy hair wet with the spray from the waterfall, his beautiful face marred with the cruelty of his eyes. He sneers at me, clearly satisfied at his own superiority, thinking he's got us, and it's that look, that cock-of-the-walk glint, that suddenly makes him his father's son.

Was Rob a psychopath? He was certainly reckless, callous and imbued with superficial charm that ticks so many boxes on the Hare checklist. Is that where James gets it from? Maybe it's nothing to do with me and Joanna and our house of secrets. And then I realise it doesn't matter. It doesn't matter why James is doing this. He's an evil man, who will never feel anything, both the bad feelings of guilt and shame and fear but also the good feelings, of love and joy and compassion. And that's a horrible way to live. It's like being born with essential organs missing, a half-life, a Gollum. I look at my son, and then I do the only thing a mother could do; I rush him, with all my weight, barrelling my shoulder into his midriff so I hear the air rush out of his lungs as we crash into a wall of water. Then gravity opens its pitiless maw, mother and son lock together, and are gone.

Epilogue

Six months later

We emerge blinking from the gloom of the church into one of those glorious autumn afternoons, when the light is buttery and soft and the trees blaze in a riot of flames against cloudless blue skies. Horse chestnut shells litter the soft grass and brown leaves crunch underfoot. It feels like a gift, this last burst of heat on bare skin before winter creeps in and steals the precious light.

Despite the late October warmth, I've brought a thick cardigan with me; I move so slowly now that I often feel the cold. I lean heavily on my stick, which sinks into the damp grass. I move carefully, ignoring the pain that shoots up my hip as I have to side step a decorative urn full of bright pink carnations.

'Shall we rest?' Samira looks at me with concerned eyes.

I shake my head. It's better if I keep going while I have the momentum.

She slips her delicate hand under my arm and I smile down at her. I seem to have shrunk since the accident but I still tower over her.

We have become friends of a sort, after she won my grudging respect for not only spotting the truth about James but also holding off her boss when he was determined to make an early arrest. She says she was only doing her job but I know it takes a certain strength of character to do the right thing when everyone is telling you to do something else. If she hadn't doggedly worked the case, I would be in prison now and James would be free to kill again.

And it's becoming increasingly clear he would have. While much of the evidence of his crimes was destroyed in the fire, Samira says they're busy piecing together his movements over the past five years. There's already an investigation into the fire at a residential centre on the Welsh coast, where he once stayed as a teenager, and a former school friend has been found dead in suspicious circumstances. 'He enjoyed it,' she says. 'He would only have got bolder as time went by.'

I have told her I don't want to know any more. I need all my strength so I can cope with the present and start to build for the future. I have a lot of lost years to make up for. My days and nights are painful. I broke my pelvis, most of my ribs, punctured a lung and my left leg has been rebuilt. I take a lot of painkillers and face years of operations and physio to regain mobility but I am lucky to be alive. I have James to thank for that. His body cushioned me from the worst of the impact. He died instantly, the doctors say. I do not grieve him.

His downfall, says Samira, was his arrogance. 'That alibi,' she said one day as we sat chatting over barely palatable hospital tea. 'It was just too good.'

Much to her boss's irritation, she'd decided to relook at everyone's alibi after the forensic scene analysis backed up my story of lying unconscious in the hall while Joanna's body was untied and laid on the floor. Flight manifests backed Fuller's alibi, Simon was captured on CCTV at some services on the M25 and Alan had no alibi; he was at home. James' alibi looked watertight, every movement logged on a smartphone app. 'He was very keen for me to check his statistics,' she said. 'That cocky confidence, almost like he was dying to tell me how clever he'd been, it just got my spider senses tingling.' Working in her own time, she downloaded all the data points of James' expedition in Snowdonia, mapped them against all the other competitors, and then tracked down those competitors who, according to their own checkpoint timings, should have had eyes on James at key points to verify his Strava alibi. She discovered there was a gaping hole where nobody saw him – the very time when the killer was in our house. The fellow competitors put it down to his phenomenal fitness and his inside knowledge of the hills, allowing him to streak miles ahead while they made camp for the night. And then one competitor, a Spanish girl who had flown back to Madrid the day after the competition, told Noor she'd mistakenly carried some of James' stuff for that key part of the route.

'I found it at checkpoint nineteen,' she said. 'We had the same bag, you see, and he must have picked up mine and me his by mistake. He was so sweet about it. I couldn't believe it when I heard his mum had died while he was on the walk.'

How easy to get someone else to carry your phone and log your miles, and all the while you're sixty miles away committing what you think is the perfect murder. Once Samira had a crack in his alibi, it didn't take long to begin to chip away at the veneer of the perfect son. There were disturbing reports from teachers. A loner, with no friends and a fascination with violence. The string of employers who had to let him go for poor attitude and on at least one occasion a questionable assault on another employee. She found one of Joanna's former boyfriends, the Brummie named Paul, who claimed James had vandalised his car; soon after Paul had dumped Joanna, claiming he was getting back with his ex. There was a neighbour who alleged James had killed her cat. Then Simon Carmichael finally emerged, saying James had tried to kill him twice. It was he who alerted the police to find us. He'd seen me and James in the taxi together and knew something was wrong, that I could be in danger.

I've seen Simon a couple of times in recent months. He had been back in contact with Joanna after he worked out that James had left home. They'd worked together on the Alex Fuller case, keeping all the evidence on Simon's laptop. Simon had been straight to the police with the file, convinced Alex had murdered her, but when it became clear Fuller had been overseas at the time, he realised with horror that it must have been James. He'd long known James was trouble: he thought the boy had scratched his Bentley that first visit to his house in revenge for his humiliation on the cricket field, then there'd been an incident where all his fish died, and then his dog ... He'd argued repeatedly with Joanna about James' 'ways' but, whatever her private fears, she couldn't accept how bad it was, not then. But things escalated until they were life threatening. He discovered his brakes had been tampered with and he came home one evening to find his kitchen smoked out, so Simon just left, hoping that without him around James might calm down. 'I loved her so much. I left a note, explaining everything but I guess James intercepted it. He was so clever. What he could have achieved if ...'

He went straight to the police with his concerns and was relieved to find that DS Noor was already digging into James' alibi. He took to hanging outside the house, worried about me. 'I bumped into you once but you didn't recognise me. And then when I saw you in the taxi with him, I just knew.' He'd called Noor straight away and the police had started looking for us, triangulating his position from his mobile phone.

I make all the sympathetic noises but I still feel bitter. Perhaps if Simon had been more vocal in his concerns about James, or if he'd stuck around, then maybe, maybe Joanna might still be here. Dr Lucas, the real one, says I need to forgive, after all he brought so much happiness into Joanna's life during those last months when they rekindled their romance, keeping it secret for safety reasons. 'Don't hold on to all these "what ifs",' she counselled on a hospital visit. 'They will only torment you.'

It was good to see my Dr Lucas after so many years. She brought a posy of sweet peas, some nice toiletries and a bottle of prune juice (hospital food is terrible for your bowels, she said, which made me cry because it's exactly the kind of practical and thoughtful gesture Joanna would have made). After I calmed down, she filed and painted my fingernails, a touchingly intimate gesture and one that did make me feel more like me. We talked a lot about Joanna.

'You won't remember how hard it was in the early days,' said Dr Lucas gently. 'You were very disturbed. For a while you had anterograde amnesia, which means you couldn't make new memories, and then you'd clearly blocked out the trauma of the years leading up to the accident. Every day you would wake up and not know who James was. Every day you rejected ever having a son. Didn't know who he was. You were angry, of course, and frustrated. And remember, from James' point of view, you've been in hospital so long he can't remember who you are. You're a stranger who he's told to call mummy but Mummy says she doesn't know who he is. I can see how it happened. How one day Joanna just put an end to this constant cycle of rejection and upset and told James to call her mummy now. After all, whenever they were seen out and about, people just assumed she was the mum anyway. And so they sort of fell into it, and while your short-term memory came back, your other memories remained buried and Joanna was very careful never to trigger them, never to give you any cause to doubt her version of the truth.'

357

Dr Lucas shrugged. 'Perhaps that was wrong. But she didn't do it to spite you. She was just trying to make the best of a terrible situation.'

It made sense. I understand why Joanna did what she did, and why we all had to move away. Once you have told a big lie you have to double down. You have to mould the world to fit the shape of the lie. And that means new people, new town, new job. And no more Dr Lucas. That's what I find so hard, I said, the deception of hiring Xanthe Heard to pretend to be Dr Lucas seemed so calculated and cruel.

'I can only assume she was desperate,' said Dr Lucas. 'It was a way to manage you. And I suppose there was a comfort for you to talk to this familiar person.'

I still cringe inside to think I fell for such an audacious deception but Dr Lucas thinks I'm being too hard on myself. 'Recovery from a head injury is tough, Sarah,' she said. 'After you moved away, you were doing it all by yourself. You were having crystal treatments when you should have been seeing a professional. But you will now, won't you? Promise me you'll engage with proper therapists, get the counselling you're going to need. I think you'll find CBT very helpful for managing your anxiety. You have a second chance of life right now and you must grasp it, Sarah.'

I know she's right, of course, but it's very hard to believe I deserve that chance. I destroyed Joanna's life. I stole her husband. I killed him. I made her life difficult and hard and I never told her how much I appreciated her love and support. On good days, I wake up dreaming of her. On bad days, I daren't fall asleep.

Samira Noor has been a huge help to me. She has told me not to blame myself for James. 'Psychopaths come from all sorts of families, Sarah. I've seen it, loving, normal parents and a monster grows in their midst.'

She's now working on the Alex Fuller case. He's been questioned under caution for sexual assault but no charges have been brought – yet. Joanna's dossier has been a big help but women are still wary of reporting him; there's that lingering shame, the fear of exposure, of not being believed, of Alex exacting some awful revenge. He's lost his job, though, so at least Carmen can walk into the office every day without feeling sick. 'I'll get there,' said Samira. 'A man like that will think he's immune, which means there will be so many victims in his wake. And I just need one of them.'

I was discharged from hospital six weeks ago, and rent a ground floor flat nearby while I continue my physiotherapy. The Speldhurst Road house is up for auction. It has a certain notoriety so will go for a knockdown price. I don't care. I am going to move to a small town in the Shropshire hills and start again, away from the people who will always whisper behind my back. With Samira's encouragement I have signed up for a part-time degree programme in psychology. I can study by distance learning so I don't have to worry about meeting people, although there's a study week in the summer semester, which I'm already anxious about. Samira says she'll drive me there herself if necessary.

'You jumped at a known killer and pushed him off a waterfall. You can do a week's campus study,' she smiled.

People think I'm doing the course to learn more about psychopaths but actually that's not what interests me. I'm interested in how we can help our brains handle stress and anxiety. It was Alan's suggestion, actually.

'Don't look back, Sarah,' he said, when I was chewing over my studies, wondering which modules to pick. 'Look forward, and try to help other people. It's the only way to find peace with your past.'

He's moved on too. He sold his house a couple of months ago

and has a little two bed in Shrewsbury, where he's already on the neighbourhood watch and a volunteer librarian two days a week. He refuses to talk about James. I know he blames himself for not going to the police straight away. He shuts down when the subject of James comes up and remains relentlessly upbeat, though he seems to have aged about ten years in the last six months. We see each other regularly, nothing romantic, but now I have two friends, which is two more than I had six months ago. But I have lost a sister and the loss only deepens the more I understand.

Alan's waiting for me and Samira at the grave, with the shovel and a large David Austen rose bush, its glorious yellow flowers attracting the last of the bees. He's in a suit and there's no cap on his head but I recognise him because he has a wide scar running down his face and he's wearing a polka-dot bowtie. It's incongruous and silly, but it makes him easy to recognise. It was his idea. He doesn't much care what he looks like. Like Joanna and those hideous cardigans, he's generous like that.

'All right, ladies,' he says. 'All set for you to plant her.'

He lifts the bush and settles it into the hole he's dug. Samira and I take it in turns to shovel in the soil and the effort leaves me sweating. We step back and admire our work. Yellow roses, Joanna's favourite.

'Should we say a prayer?' asks Alan.

I shake my head. I am done with prayer. Mother still lives on in her home. I pay the bills but I will never see her again and there will be no rose bush for her grave.

'Joanna, I love you, sis.'

Samira squeezes my hand and we stand and admire the roses, and the neat gravestone with its simple inscription.

Joanna Bailey. Beloved Daughter, Sister, Mother.

Acknowledgements

Remember Me is the brainchild of publishing mastermind Francesca Pathak, a human dynamo who Gets Things Done. I'm in constant awe of her boundless energy, creativity and professionalism.

Huge thanks to my agent Hannah Sheppard of DHH Literary Agency for making dreams come true and for her steady presence and thoughtful counsel in a crazy world.

To all the team at Orion Crime for their energy, enthusiasm and attention to detail. And many thanks, too, to Rebecca Bradley for her invaluable help on police procedure.

To everyone who has given me so much support along the way: my parents, Paula and James, sister Shirley and in-laws Janet and Jeff. The fantastic support, affection and gin provided by The Circle of Mucklestone Mums, you know who you are. To Jane Johnson, for the ski-lift therapy and laugh-out-loud texts. To Amanda Turner, for the trampoline-and-hide-and-seek marathon that let me complete the copyedits.

Above all, to my wonderful husband and fellow author Adam for his endless support, wise advice and all the laughs – thank you for everything. To Maya, Elliot and Thomas, for putting up with two parents who write and for all the joy you bring.